The Storm Within

"Well, Dinah, is it sorry you are?" The deep, resonant voice with its rolled *r*'s made her turn. As she did, she loosed her grip on the stays she had been holding. A sudden yawning of the ship sent her tumbling off balance into the man's arms.

"Excuse me!" she said quickly, trying to free herself, but the man's arms held her more tightly, making her heart beat faster.

"Dinah," Alexander said softly, feeling her body beneath the heavy cloak. He bent his head until his mouth found hers.

Their lips met, gently at first. Then his arms tightened, his mouth pressing against her lips until she could feel his teeth as his tongue forced its way inside. Dinah could no more resist him than she could the hot blood pounding in her veins or the thrill of sudden desire. . . .

SHE WOULD FOLLOW HER PASSION
AND HER PAST TO THE ENDS OF
THE EARTH AND BEYOND. . . .

Also published by POCKET BOOKS/RICHARD GALLEN

This Golden Rapture
by Paula Moore

The Fire Bride
by Julia Wherlock

Nicole Norman

HEATHER SONG

PUBLISHED BY POCKET BOOKS NEW YORK

A POCKET BOOKS/RICHARD GALLEN *Original* publication

POCKET BOOKS, a Simon & Schuster division of
GULF & WESTERN CORPORATION
1230 Avenue of the Americas, New York, N.Y. 10020

ISBN: 0-671-41463-1

First Pocket Books printing November, 1980

10 9 8 7 6 5 4 3 2 1

POCKET and colophon are trademarks of Simon & Schuster.

Printed in the U.S.A.

PART I

New York to
Edinburgh—1895

Chapter 1

🌹 🌹 🌹

THE TALL SLENDER young woman drew aside the curtain to look out at the gathering dusk. A light mist was falling, and the gaslights in Washington Square were ringed with shimmering halos. Here and there, lamps glowed behind the curtained windows of the small rooms in the second-story apartments above the stables and carriage houses in the mews.

The summer of 1895 had been warm, although far from the heat wave which the city had suffered the year before. September, however, had been ushered in by cool rain. Heavy clouds hung over New York, alternating gusts of rain with drizzle that was too heavy for fog and too light for genuine rain.

To the young woman in the simple black dress, the whole city seemed to be mourning with her. The wet cobblestones below had an ebony sheen, and the traffic a hundred yards away on Fifth Avenue was muffled by the drizzle. Even the piercing shrillness of a police whistle was muted, and the clanging bells of the horse cars were dulled. Only the sounds of a horse's shoes, sparking metal on stone, rang clear and sharp as a cab turned off Fifth Avenue.

The horse, its wet bay coat burnished to bronze under the gaslight, must have known its work was over; its master at home after a day on Wall Street. It snorted eagerly, picking up its hooves smartly, and trotted toward a white-washed brick carriagehouse farther along the alley from where the young woman was standing.

Dinah Murray sighed. The very sight of the eager horse depressed her.

Although Dinah had been christened Diana, no one had ever called her anything except Dinah since her own baby tongue had lisped Dinah out of Diana. When she was fourteen, only two years ago, she had insisted on being called Diana after she had read the story of the huntress goddess in Bullfinch's "Age of Fable." Her mother had, with good-humor, tried, but even Dinah had finally admitted that her awkward, still immature body, her unusual height and coltish legs, made Dinah more fitting. She was even taller now and still too thin, regardless of the curve of her breasts. Months of sitting by her mother's bedside and tending her had left their mark. Mrs. Murray's long, lingering illness and death had sapped her daughter as well as herself.

Her future seemed as dim as the once cozy sitting room, now clothed in the dark shadows of dusk haunted with memories that her mother's death a week ago made painful.

The girl shivered, hurrying to pick up the brass oil lamp with tiny rosebuds painted on its milk-glass chimney, and light it to warm the room with its brightness. She had filled it only that morning, not because it needed filling, but for something to do, and in her preoccupation she had overfilled it. The wick smoked but did not light until she had let three matches burn almost to her fingers. Finally, the flame shot up in a flash of orange-tipped yellow that hollowed out her thin cheeks under the high cheekbones, making her appear gaunt and older than her years. She replaced the chimney, lowering the flame. She tried not to look at the rosebuds because they reminded her of her mother.

How painstakingly her mother had used fine brushes to teach painting to Lucy Bradley, whose governess she had been. It had been one of the arts that Mrs. Murray felt every young lady of the late 19th century should know.

Dinah turned quickly from the lamp, but wherever she looked, memories arose. Tears came to her amber eyes, darkening them to brown, at the sight of a piece of half-finished needlework, another talent her mother thought every young lady should know, wrapped in a napkin on the mantle over the brick fireplace where coal waited in the grate. The needlepoint kept Dinah from going to the fireplace to light the fire despite the chill room.

Mrs. Murray had started it the day she had come home from the doctor's after learning she had cancer and there was nothing he could do. She had carefully traced the rampant unicorns, giving infinite detail to their horns and to the border of thistles. The weaker she became, the more important the work became. Although she had set herself a daily goal, more often than not Dinah had had to take the work carefully from her fingers when the drugs finally overcame her mother with sleep. Mrs. Murray had managed to finish only one unicorn and the top border of thistles before weakness had numbed her fingers and she had reluctantly begun to work the royal blue background.

Perhaps, Dinah reflected, it was just as well that she would soon have to leave these rooms over the carriage house that had been her and her mother's home for as long as she could remember. She had been only a few months old when her mother had been hired by the Bradleys. The coachman, whose bailiwick these rooms normally would have been, was a bachelor, and Mrs. Bradley had given them to Mrs. Murray and Dinah. Once the Bradley children had grown, Mrs. Bradley, now widowed, had invited Mrs. Murray to remain as her secretary and companion.

No one could have been kinder than Mrs. Bradley. She had let Dinah have the run of the main house across the garden on the Square and had permitted her mother to teach Dinah along with the children of the household, despite Dinah's being much younger. The result was that Dinah had grown up with a sense of belonging in the gracious house. If she slept in the tiny, low-ceilinged rooms with their white-washed plaster walls that faced the alley, she had lived and daydreamed in the elegant Greek revival house.

She ate with the servants in the large, warm basement kitchen, talking to them when they were not busy, but her dreams were reserved for the formal rooms above. One day, she might be a lady entertaining in the living room with its marble mantel supported by Ionic Greek columns. Another day, she might be the Greek Diana worshiped in a temple formed by the rectangular arch of the Greek columns and carvel lintel dividing the living room from the dining room. Still another day, she might be an archaeologist searching for mystical symbols in the figured carpet or the plaster ceiling rosettes. Then, there were the books she read in the back library and the pretended climbing of the Alps up the narrow back stairs and down the gracefully curved front stairs.

In so many ways she had been treated more as a well-loved child of the house than the child of a servant. But then, her mother had been treated as more than a servant, too. During Mrs. Murray's illness, Mrs. Bradley had insisted on having the best physicians and had paid the bills. She had even offered to move Mrs. Murray into a spare bedroom in the main house where she could have more comforts. Mrs. Murray had refused, preferring to stay in her own room. Now, Mrs. Bradley had invited Dinah to remain in her employ as her secretary, although Dinah would have to move into a tiny room on the top floor in the servants' quarters.

Dinah had hesitated. She would have to work, she knew, because her mother had left her little money. Still, she was not sure that she wanted to stay in this house with its memories and where there were no other young people except for Mrs. Bradley's maid. She would like to marry one day and have children, and how could she meet a prospective husband here? Yet, what else could she do?

Thinking of her future reminded her that Molly Carew, a maid in the Bradley house, had given her the morning edition of *The New York Times* that Mrs. Bradley always received with her breakfast tray. Dinah picked up the paper, settling herself in her mother's rocking chair in its usual place by the table with the lamp.

September 5th, 1895—soon, fall would be here. The leaves on the trees in Washington Square would change color, then drop, dry and crackling, with the approach of winter. Had it been only eight months since her mother had received the fatal news?

Tears again came to Dinah's eyes, and she turned quickly to the headlines to distract herself. Cuba was in revolt against the Spanish, led by the Cuban poet, Jose Martí. In Armenia, Sultan Abdul Hamid was slaughtering Armenians. The Japanese were defeating the Chinese in Korea. Dinah's full lips tightened. She did not want to read about death.

Her slender hands and long fingers trembled, tearing the pages as she turned to the want ads. There were plenty of jobs for maids, even a few for companions and secretaries and governesses. If she were a companion, however, she was just as well off—perhaps better off—staying with Mrs. Bradley whom she knew than working for a stranger. Besides, she owed so much to Mrs. Bradley.

Dinah combed her fingers in resignation through her naturally curly red hair, barely noticing her fingers' catching in the curl snarls. The long days and nights of tending her mother, even the knowledge that there was no hope, had not prepared her for this feeling of desolation and emptiness. She knew she had to get a grip on herself; she had to stop staring at night at the ceiling of the tiny bedroom where she still slept on the cot, unable to move into the double bed where her mother had died. And she had to stop the days of sleep-walking, of putting on the same black dress after she had wiped a wet cloth over her face and given her hair a token brushing.

Every morning when she arose, she said to herself that that morning she would wash and brush the snarls out of her hair, fix herself up, and present herself to Mrs. Bradley, ready to go to work. Each morning, however, she put it off, saying, "Tomorrow."

She could not go on this way, she now told herself

firmly. Her mother would be ashamed of her. Tomorrow, she would definitely go to work and try to forget the past. She would begin by asking Mrs. Bradley how to sell the few pieces of furniture that had been her mother's.

There were really so few things to get rid of. She would like to keep the rocker in which she was sitting, and the two stiff-backed chairs with Biblical scenes of Adam and Eve in the Garden of Eden worked in needlepoint by her mother. Other than those, there were only a worn rug, the couch by the fireplace, and the beds as well as a few bureaus. How strange it was that the two rooms which had seemed so cozy and comfortable with her mother alive, were actually cold and sparsely furnished. Their main comfort had been the warmth of her mother's personality.

Her mother did not accumulate belongings and knickknacks any more than she looked back at the past. Mrs. Murray had immigrated to America from Scotland after the death of her husband, yet before Dinah was born. She had wanted her child to be raised in America, which she saw as a land of opportunity and promise, and she had brought nothing with her except a few worn clothes. And her determination to raise her daughter by herself.

No. That was not quite true. There was a pin, a heavy silver brooch that she never wore, and a plaid shawl or blanket in which she had often wrapped the baby Dinah in winter and that still lay folded in the bottom of the drawer. Those two things Mrs. Murray had clung to, taking them out sometimes late at night when she thought Dinah was sleeping, to hold them in her hands for a few minutes before putting them carefully back as if they had some secret meaning. Dinah had asked about them a few times, and about Scotland. Her mother had rarely answered, only pressed her lips together, a faraway look in her eyes.

If there were any relatives in Scotland, moreover, she had never told Dinah about them. In fact, it was not until the last few weeks before she died that Mrs. Murray had brought up the past herself.

Dinah frowned, remembering how her mother in her delirium had seemed to see ghosts and talk to them. The person to whom she most often called was "Rabbie," leading Dinah to guess that Rabbie must have been her father. More puzzling was the strange phrase that Mrs. Murray had uttered several times. All Dinah could make of it were the words "lock" and something that sounded like "eleven"—eleven o'clock, maybe?

Dinah left the rocker for the window. Moving to the main house was a good idea. Molly Carew was there, and Molly was her friend.

A rapping on the door roused her from her dark mood, and she went to answer it, eager now to see someone if only for a few moments. Molly was standing, wide-eyed, on the threshold, a shawl over her head to protect her from the chill mist on her dash across the garden.

"What is it, Molly?" Dinah asked, taken aback at the excitement on the other girl's face.

"Dinah, you're to come right away! Mrs. Bradley wants you—there's a gentleman asking to see you!" Molly burst out.

"A . . . gentleman? For me?" Dinah stared at her friend, sure that Molly must be mistaken. The only men she knew were the butler and coachman who were not gentlemen and who would not ask Mrs. Bradley to see her. The only other man she knew was Mrs. Bradley's son, who was a gentleman, but Molly never knew him.

"Yes! A gentleman for you," Molly insisted. "I let him in. He's foreign. That is, he has an accent like your mother's," the girl chattered, ignoring Dinah's confusion.

Dinah picked up a shawl to protect herself from the weather. Had there been a relative, after all, whom her mother had written and not told her about? Her heart skipped a beat, pounding so loudly that she was sure Molly could hear it.

"What's he like, Molly?" Dinah asked, as the two

girls darted across the wet garden into the warmth and light of the kitchen. "Is he old?"

"Oh, no! He's young and handsome. . . ." Molly stopped, giggling. "Here, let me fix your hair." She smoothed and patted the other girl's hair, using hairpins of her own to fasten it back neatly. "Pinch your cheeks," she ordered, "so you won't look so pale."

Dinah laughed at the other girl's excitement. Her own sense of anticipation rose, but she would not admit it. "What difference does it make? It's probably a mistake. . . ."

Still, she paused in the hall to look in the gold-framed mirror at herself. Her spirits faded. She looked terrible. The curly red hair she had inherited from her mother was too bright, making her thin face with its pale ivory complexion even paler. With her straight but silently acquiline nose above a firmly rounded chin—stubborn her mother had called it—and her full mouth, she looked all nose, eyes, and mouth; and decidedly plain in contrast to Molly with her rosy cheeks and pert, turned-up nose. Not to mention too tall.

The man would just have to take her as she was, she thought, walking down the hall to the sitting room, curiosity and excitement rising once more. As she rapped lightly on the door, she raised her head proudly.

Mrs. Bradley was standing by the fireplace. Although she was older than Dinah's mother had been, Mrs. Bradley in her fashionable gown with her beautifully coifed hair appeared much younger. And right now, Mrs. Bradley's elegance, her self-assured manner, and her worldly intelligence pricked Dinah with a twinge of jealousy as she glanced about the room for the man Molly had told her about. He was standing in the shadows beyond the glow of the fireplace, in back of one of the pair of blue satin love seats.

"Mrs. Bradley," Dinah murmured politely, "you wanted to see me?"

"Yes, Dinah." The gray-haired woman left her pose at the fireplace to walk gracefully toward Dinah and take her hand. "Someone wishes to meet you. He's just arrived from Scotland. I told him about your mother," she added kindly, turning toward the man in the shadows. "Mr. Douglas, this is Dinah Murray."

The man stepped into the light. He was tall, conservatively dressed in a brown tweed suit, with black hair and deep-set eyes that studied her closely. Dinah flushed, aware of the high-necked black dress that did little for her and of her unruly hair. Nervously, she tried to tuck a few disorderly curls back into the knot which Molly had fixed.

Mrs. Bradley squeezed her hand. Dinah turned to her, surprised at the uncertainty she now saw in the woman's face. It was the first time she had ever seen even the slightest trace of confusion in Mrs. Bradley's manner.

"Dinah," Mrs. Bradley said slowly, "I know you're surprised. I am myself," she laughed nervously. "I'd like to explain. . . ."

"I think the explanations are up to me, Ma'am," the man interrupted politely in a deep, resonant voice, rolling his "r's" like Dinah's mother, as Molly had said.

"I know. You said . . . It's just that Dinah's been through a great deal. I feel responsible for her." Mrs. Bradley's voice was firmer. She looked from Dinah to the handsome man who was standing squarely on slightly spread legs, more like a working man than a gentleman.

"Of course, Ma'am, I understand that," he replied in a softer voice, although no less firm. "Still, Miss Murray is not a child, is she?"

"No." Mrs. Bradley wanted to remind him that the girl was only 16, but she thought better of it. Realizing that she was still holding Dinah's hand, she dropped it. Her usual composure was now completely shattered. If only the man had given some warning, sent a note to the house first, so she could have had at least an hour in which to prepare Dinah, she thought.

10

Dinah watched Mrs. Bradley and the man, Mr. Douglas. As he said she was not a child any more. Yet they were talking as if she were not even in the room. It made her want to prove that she could take care of herself. "It's all right. Mrs. Bradley" she set her chin firmly. "if Mr. Douglas has something to say to me then he should say it."

Mrs. Bradley looked at Dinah. As a child, the girl had seemed so independent, content to play by herself or spend hours reading, but the months of nursing her mother had changed her. After her mother's death, Dinah seemed to withdraw. Mrs. Bradley had worried, but her promise to Dinah's mother, a promise she now wished she had not made, held her back. The woman sighed. "Very well, Dinah. Mr. Douglas?"

Alexander Douglas, having made his point, was at a loss as to how to begin with the girl's eyes studying him so frankly. Despite his earlier remark to Mrs. Bradley that Dinah was not a child, he knew 16 was hardly an adult. The slenderness of the body in the black dress was that of a girl, with the promise of maturity still unfulfilled. She should have looked at him demurely, with lowered eyes, the way the women he knew did. Instead, the amber eyes seemed to appraise him in a way that disturbed him, hinting at depths within her that he could only guess. No woman had ever looked at him that way before, and he felt his heart beat faster with the unexpected stirring of arousal.

Meanwhile, Mrs. Bradley was watching them, her presence now adding to his discomfort. Speaking to her before Dinah's arrival, everything had seemed so simple. He would state his business, say what he had to say, direct and to the point. After all, what was the girl to him? Now, that had changed, and he began to wish that he had not stopped Mrs. Bradley's explanation.

"Yes, Sir?" Dinah's voice, meek enough, belied the steady amber eyes.

"I . . ." He turned to Mrs. Bradley who had seated herself on a love seat. She, too, was watching and

11

waiting. He cleared his throat, deciding one woman was enough to contend with at a time. "Perhaps, Mrs. Bradley," he suggested smoothly, "it would be best if I spoke to Miss Murray alone?"

The older woman hesitated. "Dinah?" she asked.

Dinah smiled nervously, the nervousness only partly due to the fact that she seemed to be the single person in the room who did not know what was going on. Yet the presence of the handsome man excited her in a way she did not understand. Never had such a fine gentleman spoken to her before, much less wanted to speak to her alone. The challenge thrilled her. She smiled, trying the wings of a sudden maturity and desire. "Since what Mr. Douglas has to say concerns me, perhaps it would be best."

Mrs. Bradley nodded and went to the door. Regardless of her friendship for Mrs. Murray, she could do no more than she had done. The girl must learn to make her own decisions sooner or later. "Very well, if you want me, I'll be in the library." She glanced at the two once more, seeing only a sixteen-year-old girl and an older man obviously in a hurry to get his business completed. She left the room, hesitating before shutting the door behind her.

The man smiled at Dinah, white teeth flashing in his tanned face, and said, "Come here, Dinah, and let me look at you."

"Sir?" Dinah stayed where she was, startled at his sudden use of her first name. Now she was alone with him, the earlier excitement rose, making a vein in her neck throb.

"Sir? Oh, yes." A sparkle came into his eyes, as he approached Dinah, taking her hand to lead her to the love seat.

At his touch, Dinah's body grew hot. Hastily she tried to withdraw her hand, relenting as the man's grasp held firm—and liking the feeling of her hand enclasped in his.

The man's voice was soft in apology as he said, "Forgive me for calling you Dinah so soon, but as your cousin . . ."

"My cousin!" Dinah sat down in the love seat abruptly, her legs too weak to stand.

"You really don't know," the man wondered, more to himself than Dinah. He hadn't meant to surprise her, but he was still suffering from his own shock at the fine house after expecting to find the girl living in a squalid room in poverty. Now the sight of her pale face, gone marblewhite, her eyes enormous, frightened him and he glanced around the room, noticing a decanter of sherry and some glasses on a sideboard. He hurried to pour a glass and brought it to the girl, making her sip it.

As soon as some color had risen in her cheeks, he sat down beside her. "Now, Dinah, I'll try to explain. After your mother became ill, she wrote my father who is a distant cousin of sorts, about you. Even though they have not been in touch for years, since she left Scotland, in fact, she was sure that under the circumstances he would help. She had a great fear that you might be forced into becoming a maid —or worse."

"I . . . I know." Dinah's eyes filled with tears, not for herself but for her mother. She knew what "worse" meant, from what she had heard in the servants' quarters, about women left with no money and no resources and being forced to sell all they had, their bodies. The idea appalled her. Hadn't her mother always told her that her body was a precious vessel to be treasured and saved for her wedding night?

"Then you know about the letter?" the man asked, surprised at her answer and the trembling of her body. "In her letter, she said that she hadn't told you anything because she didn't want to raise any false hope. It had been so many years. . . ."

"Oh, no!" Dinah turned wide eyes on the man. The room was spinning and she sipped the sherry before she went on. "I meant, I knew she was afraid of what would become of me." The man's handsome face and broad shoulders reassured her, in part. What she could not account for was the wild beating of her heart that he also evoked.

"I see. My father couldn't come because of business. He wanted to, as he had been looking for an opportunity to come to New York to study prospects for business here. Since this seemed an appropriate time, he sent me." Alexander Douglas smiled, dark eyes dancing above broad cheekbones. "And I am very glad he did."

His words sent a new surge of weakness through Dinah, making her heart pound so wildly that she was afraid she might faint. She was not at all sure yet exactly what the man wanted, but she knew she had to say something and her mother's training came to her help. "Thank you, Mr. Douglas," she managed to say, trying to sound composed.

"Dinah," Alexander said gently, the girl's youth and inexperience making him want to protect her, "if I can call you Dinah, surely you can start calling me Alexander—especially as we are going to be together for quite a while."

"What?" Dinah sprang to her feet. Was there to be no end to the surprises that this day held? Together—what did that mean? In what way did he mean her to be "together. . . ."

"Of course! Why do you think my father sent me here except to bring you back to Scotland with me?" Alexander laughed, pulling her gently back to the love seat and sitting himself next to her.

"But . . . but Mrs. B-Bradley," Dinah stuttered. Confusion enveloped her. The idea that she was to go to Scotland could not sink into her consciousness. In fact, all she was conscious of was the man next to her, so close she could feel his thigh pressing against her through the fabric of her mourning dress. The sensation was a new one to her, as new as the scent of the musky tweeds and the faint odor of tobacco that clung to him, filling her with an emotion she had never known before. Her senses seemed sharpened with a longing that both frightened and aroused this man, but she stayed where she was, trying to think of Mrs. Bradley. "Mrs. Bradley?" she finally repeated.

14

"She knows, and I'm sure she thinks it's a fine idea," Alexander said smoothly, adding, "since there's little here for you, Dinah.'" Actually, Mrs. Bradley had been too surprised to say anything. Still, the lie was harmless, Alexander decided, going on to explain his plans for her until he realized she was barely listening.

After so many years of having only her mother she could not grasp the meaning of having a family, much less of going to Scotland as Alexander was saying.

Alexander frowned, not understanding the reason for her silence and mistaking it for disapproval of his plans. "Dinah, you *are* going to Scotland with me, aren't you? It's what your mother wanted, and my father wants it, too. As do I," he added significantly.

Dinah's eyes were large in her white face, making her hair seem even redder than usual. "I c-can't think . . . It's all so s-sudden," she stuttered, looking terribly young in her confusion.

"Of course!" Alexander laughed in relief. "I tell you what, we won't talk about it more now. I arrived only a few hours ago. I must get settled and make some appointments. If it suits you—and Mrs. Bradley —I'll call here tomorrow about tea time. In the meantime, think over what I've said and talk to Mrs. Bradley. She seems genuinely fond of you."

Dinah nodded, not sure what to say. The man accepted her silence for assent and rose to get his hat and gloves.

"Dinah," Alexander stopped in front of her, "I don't know the reason your mother came to America. I do know from the letter that things didn't work out as she hoped. In Scotland, you'll have everything you could want. If you don't like it, you can always return to New York."

"Thank you, Mr. Douglas." Dinah rose to see him to the door. Her mind was reeling with emotions, and her confusion increased at the door where he hesitated a few seconds before leaning down to kiss her

15

forehead. "It's Alexander—and welcome to the family."

Dinah's face flamed in embarrassment. She watched him walk to a waiting hansom cab and get in with a wave and a smile for her. Then she shut the door and leaned against it.

"Dinah!" Mrs. Bradley emerged excitedly from the library, hurrying to embrace the girl. During the half hour that she had been alone, the momentary shock at Alexander Douglas's sudden appearance and brusque statement that he had come to take Dinah, to Scotland, had receded. The girl's prospects were brighter than anyone had dreamed. Still, she blamed herself for not telling Dinah about the letter after her mother's death.

To be honest, she had not known what to do. Dinah's mother had been so ill that she had not even been sure whether the woman was not living out some fantasy. She had finally decided that there was no hurry because any answer might take weeks—if it ever came—during which time she could pick the right moment to talk to Dinah.

She looked at the young girl's flushed face, her eyes so widened by shock, and felt sorry for her. She understood that Dinah still had not really grasped the portent of the visit. "Dinah, my dear," she said, putting an arm around her and leading the numbed girl back into the living room. She rang for tea, frowning to see Dinah standing where she had left her. "Come, sit down. We'll have tea."

Dinah's shock was fading behind a vortex of spinning thoughts. "You knew?" she managed to say in bewilderment, sitting on the edge of the couch and folding her hands like a little girl.

"Only a little, and that not until your mother was sure . . . she didn't have much time left." The older woman sat down beside Dinah, suddenly aware of how innocent the girl was, even more so than she had thought.

"Mrs. Bradley . . ." Dinah began.

"Shhh, my dear. Let me tell you the little I do

know. If you have any other questions, you will have to ask them of Mr. Douglas." She paused at the light knock on the door. Molly entered eagerly, but Mrs. Bradley waited for her to leave before saying anything more.

After she had poured tea for them both, Mrs. Bradley said slowly, "Your mother and I, well, were more than mistress and servant after I was widowed and the children were gone. I often asked her about Scotland and where she was from, since it was obvious she had been well-educated and had been brought up as a lady. All she ever told me was that she was an orphan and that she had been raised in Edinburgh in the household of a distant cousin who was rich and didn't approve of her marriage. As a result, she and your father moved to Glasgow. He was killed in an accident, and she came here, feeling she had nothing left in Scotland."

"But why would she never tell me?" Dinah wanted to know.

"She said," Mrs. Bradley stared into her tea cup as if searching for a better answer in the tea leaves, "she said—and I felt she was wrong—that you might be better off not knowing, not expecting anything."

"Yet, she did write. Mr. Douglas said so," Dinah commented.

"No," Mrs. Bradley corrected, sure of her ground now. "I wrote. A few months before she died, when she finally accepted the fact there was no hope of recovery, she talked to me and told me what I've told you. We discussed the matter, and I suggested she had nothing to lose by writing the cousin who had raised her. If he were dead, no one else might remember or care. Yet, there was more to gain than lose. Since she was far too weak to write, she asked me—on condition that I said nothing to you. She felt if there were an answer, there would be time to tell you. If there were none," Mrs. Bradley shrugged, "I promised I would look after you, Dinah."

Dinah looked up in surprise. "Mrs. Bradley . . ."

"You're a lovely girl, Dinah. Now, of course, things

17

have changed. A new life has opened up for you. If you prefer to stay with me, however . . ."

Dinah sighed. The decision she was suddenly being forced to make seemed too big for her years. On one hand, adventure beckoned. On the other hand, there was Mrs. Bradley's offer—but Mrs. Bradley had already done more than she could be expected to do. She shook her head. Once more, her thoughts were spinning. She picked up the cup, the tea now cold, with a shaking hand.

Mrs. Bradley guessed what was going through the girl's mind. "You don't have to make any decisions right now. Sleep on it."

"I will," Dinah whispered, remembering to tell Mrs. Bradley about the man's calling at tea time the next day. She stood up. "Thank you for everything, Mrs. Bradley. I'd like to be alone now, to think. . . ."

"Of course." Mrs. Bradley stood up. "There's no hurry to make up your mind. Remember that I'm here, if you want to discuss anything." Mrs. Bradley hesitated, studying the youthful face. "Dinah, you want to be sure, very sure. You are very young, and you are being offered a future that would be any young girl's dream." She smiled. "I am not so old that I have forgotten what it is to be your age."

Dinah smiled, trying to imagine Mrs. Bradley her age. "Of course," she said politely.

The older woman sighed. "Dear Dinah, what I am trying to say is that this is a big decision. Once it is made, once you are in Scotland, it will not be easy for you to change your mind, to come back. You must consider that, too."

Dinah nodded, only half hearing what was being said. Regardless of what Mrs. Bradley was trying to tell her, she felt she had little choice. Surely whatever the future held was preferable to the present. Yet, she could not say that to the woman who was being so kind. Instead, she thanked her again and returned to the rooms over the carriage house, noticing again how small and shabby they were. She went directly to the tiny bedroom where a small jewelry box sat on a dresser. Inside the box was the silver brooch. She remembered suddenly that her mother had once called the smoky crystal stone a cairngorn, saying it was named after Mount Cairngorn in Scotland where the stones were found. She stared at it as her mother had, as if the stone were a crystal ball.

Any answer the stone might have given was thwarted by the arrival of Molly. The girl's round face was flushed pink with excitement and eagerness to hear about the foreigner. She listened to Dinah's story, her blue eyes growing larger and larger.

The putting of the story into words sorted out some of Dinah's confusion, making the story real. It also decided her mind. She knew she had to go to Scotland to learn about her past. There might never be another chance, in which case she would regret all her life refusing the generous invitation. Besides, the invitation contained all the stuff of dreams—romance and adventure. Her heart throbbed excitedly. Not the least of her dreams was the prospect of sailing to Europe, accompanied by a dark, handsome man like Alexander. She shivered, recalling the feeling roused in her by the touch of his thigh.

Molly let her finish before saying in a subdued voice, "You're going? I would, in your place!"

"Yes!" Dinah's excitement shone in her amber eyes. "Just think—I'll be a-a lady, a real lady! Oh, Molly," she started to cry, feeling sad, too, "what will it be like to have servants . . . ?" She stopped, noticing the expression on Molly's face. "Molly," she burst out impetuously, "I wish I could take you with me!"

Chapter 2

By morning, Mrs. Bradley had had time to think, and her excitement over Dinah's future had begun to wane. Since Alexander had said he would call about tea time, by three she decided apprehensively that she could no longer wait to talk to Dinah.

Although Mrs. Bradley had been a widow for ten years, this was one of the times she missed her husband the most. He had been the friend and business associate of such financial wizards as August Belmont and Leonard Jerome and would have known exactly what to ask Alexander Douglas, who had left so much unsaid about his family and the business. She could only hope that what she asked was right and that she could tell if the man were lying. The woman sighed, and summoned Dinah.

Dinah, wearing the plain black dress, listened quietly to what Mrs. Bradley said about her doubts. The girl's hands were clasped in her lap, her fingers tightening until they were white-knuckled. Mrs. Bradley explained that even if she had not made the promise to Dinah's mother to look after her, she would still feel some obligation to make sure Dinah was doing what was best. What, after all, Mrs. Bradley asked, did they know about this stranger? Nothing, except he said he was a distant cousin.

"And so, Dinah," the older woman concluded, "I would like to know more about him and the business he claims brought him here."

Dinah nodded agreement. She, too, had had second thoughts that she did not want to admit to Mrs. Bradley. After she had gone to bed, she had lain awake, thinking of her mother. If her mother, a widow and pregnant, had been afraid to return to the uncle who had raised her, should her daughter not have reason to worry about her welcome if Alexander's father were that uncle? Was he the "family" whom Alexander had mentioned? The answers might not make any difference—Dinah was almost sure she had to go, regardless of Mrs. Bradley's offer—but she wanted to know, if only to prepare herself for what might be ahead.

Mrs. Bradley, who had been waiting for Dinah to speak, noticed the slight frown between Dinah's eyes and the tightly clasped hands. "Well, Dinah?" she asked gently.

Dinah smiled hesitantly. "I was wondering about my . . ." she took a deep breath, "my family, too."

"Then you must ask Mr. Douglas this afternoon," Mrs. Bradley, stated relieved. "You must be sure, if you're going so far away, to a strange land where you'll have no friends.'"

The statement frightened Dinah with its truth, and Alexander's arrival a few minutes later did not lessen her fear. He was so much more imposing than she remembered. It was not his height or the broadness of his shoulders, but the way he walked, with determined, slightly rolling strides, and the way he stood. His spread-legged stance was not a gentleman's. Nor were his hands, she noticed when he took her hand in his. They were large and square, the palms calloused and the fingers strong in their grip of hers.

Yesterday, shock and excitement had tightened her chest. Today, it was fear, fear that the man was not what he said he was. His bluntness yesterday, for example. No gentleman, she was certain despite her limited experience, would have been so . . . so rude! The girl took a deep breath and withdrew her hand.

Alexander studied her face, where the slight frown of worry had reappeared. He glanced from her to Mrs. Bradley, sitting straight-backed and firm-lipped on the love seat opposite the one where Dinah was sitting.

21

Smiling at them both, he thought quickly as he moved toward the fireplace that was cold today. The unseasonable chill of the day before had yielded to a warm, summer-like sun.

He took a long, thin cigar out of the breast pocket of his vest, rolling it between his fingers as he began to speak. His first words were words of apology. "Mrs. Bradley," he bowed courteously to the older woman, " 'tis sorry I am about my abruptness yesterday. The voyage from Scotland had been a long one. We had docked early in the morning, but I was concerned with arranging for the cargo. By the time I was finished, it was later than I thought and I was so eager to meet my . . . my cousin, that I came right here. It was thoughtless of me to drop in without a word or note of warning."

Mrs. Bradley smiled, partly won over by his charm. "I can well understand that, Mr. Douglas." She bowed her head in return. "Your apology is accepted."

He nodded, still rolling the cigar between his fingers. "And to you, too, Dinah, I apologize. I didn't mean to be so brusque. Somehow, although I had read your mother's letter to my father, I assumed that you knew more about your family than you did. Or," he added, "than you do. Now, I am sure that, *both* of you," he emphasized, "have questions. I'll try to answer them."

His apologies disarmed Dinah. She looked to Mrs. Bradley for help in what to say.

Mrs. Bradley played nervously with a gold bracelet. "Mr. Douglas, you did rather surprise us. I know Dinah has questions, personal ones, but I would like to know . . . You keep mentioning business?"

"Aye, Ma'am." The Scotsman, more disarming than ever, lapsed into his native dialect. "The Douglas clan is a prominent one in Scotland, but the Scots hae nae the wealth of the English. Ours is a poor land," he elaborated, "and my family has looked to the sea for wealth."

"That sounds very poetic," Mrs. Bradley mused, raising her eyebrows.

"Less poetic actually than practical. The British

Empire and Queen Victoria have need of ships and sailors. So do merchants. We provide them to both."

"You're in shipping, then?" Mrs. Bradley pressed, seeking more definite information.

"Aye." Alexander held up the cigar. "Do you mind?"

"No. My husband used to smoke." She smiled, the scent of the fine cigar reassuring her more about the man than his words.

Alexander having lit the cigar, smiled in return. "Dinah will be well taken care of. My father—and I," he added, "own twenty ships, and we're building another at Firth that will be one of the largest under the British flag, especially for the Africa trade. Our ships carry freight and passengers to almost every port in the world. That's one reason, the second one," he bowed slightly to Dinah in deference, "I'm here; to inquire into what more business we might be able to do in New York."

Dinah stared. His mention, so casually, of "the world" filled her with excitement, and her cheeks grew pink, enhancing the effect of the black dress. "You go to China, India," the names of the romantic places of which she had read rose to her tongue, "to . . . to Paris."

Points of light danced in Alexander's dark eyes. "Not to Paris. It isn't a seaport, although our ships do visit French ports." He smiled, seeing the disappointment in Dinah's face. "As I told you, we do go to Africa. The reason my father couldn't come here himself is that he was needed to draw up contracts to carry men and supplies to the Ivory Coast for building the East African railroad and to South Africa for shipment to Cecil Rhodes' new colony in south central Africa."

Dinah's previous disappointment vanished. She glanced at Mrs. Bradley who was also impressed. If Mrs. Bradley knew little of business, she had heard of Cecil Rhodes whose discoveries of gold and diamonds in southern Africa had made him one of the world's richest, most powerful men.

Alexander did not miss the look that passed between the two women, and especially not the expression on Mrs. Bradley's face. He intuitively pressed his advantage, saying to Mrs. Bradley, "Is there anything else you would like to know?"

"Just one thing." The woman smiled graciously. "While I find it very interesting where your ships go, where do you live?"

Alexander burst into a roar of laughter that startled the two women. "It does sound rather as if I didn't live anywhere. But we have a house in Edinburgh, where we live most of the year for business reasons, and we have a country place in the Highlands, the ancestral home of the clan, you might say. We also rent a house in London as business requires us to go there often." He nodded to Dinah. "And now, Dinah, what questions do you have?"

Dinah's fears about Alexander's gentility had vanished, but his saying "we" reminded her that he had said nothing of any family other than his father. Curiosity overcame her not wanting to be impolite. "Well, you said that you came here for your father. . . ." she blushed, saying hastily, "Is there anyone else?"

Alexander stared at the ash on his cigar. He knocked it into a crystal dish that Mrs. Bradley had offered, before saying, "I have a sister, Margaret, who is a few years older than you."

Laying the cigar in the dish, he went to Dinah to take her hands in his. "If it's your welcome you're thinking of, don't worry. My father is very anxious to have you as part of the family. He told me that he and your mother grew up together and were as close as brother and sister. Any hard feelings that may have been directed at your mother were not his—those died with my grandfather, your mother's uncle. And now." his grip on Dinah's hands tightened, "what do you say. Will you return to Scotland when the ship sails?"

"Yes!" Dinah's flushed cheeks flushed even pinker, not only from excitement but also from the nearness of Alexander. It was difficult for her to think of him as a cousin, and she had to remind herself he was.

"You have no more questions?" Alexander pressed. "Nothing more you want to know?"

Dinah glanced a last time at Mrs. Bradley, who shook her head almost imperceptibly. The girl felt light-headed, as if she had broken all the bonds to her former life. "No," she said, adding with an impetuosity that surprised her, "not now. Maybe later."

"So be it! Then," Alexander sat down on the love seat next to Dinah, "we must make plans. The ship, the *Star of Scotland,* sails in three weeks, which isn't much time to get ready."

"Three weeks!" To Dinah it seemed a very long time. Now that her mind was made up, she wanted to leave the next day.

"Don't worry," the man laughed, "the time will go all too quickly."

Dinah smiled, pushing back into the shadows of her mind the other questions that she had not known how to ask, about who Rabbie was and what "lock" and "eleven" might mean. But then, she could hardly expect Alexander to be able to answer those questions, which probably concerned only her mother and perhaps his father.

Mrs. Bradley ordered tea. Molly brought the tray, setting it demurely in front of her mistress. As she curtsied, her round blue eyes darted a sharp look at the Scotsman and Dinah. Dinah's flushed cheeks and sparkling eyes and the man's attentive gaze on Dinah's face told Molly what she wanted to know.

Although the young maid was happy for her friend, she was sad, too. Only yesterday the girls had been equals, but now a gap was widening between them, and not only because Dinah was going across the Atlantic. Even if Dinah were not to go to Scotland, Alexander's arrival had changed Dinah, inside as well as outside. She was no longer sitting perched on the edge of the seat, her hands clasped in her lap. She was sitting back a little, one hand resting on the arm of the love seat, with almost the poise of Mrs. Bradley.

As Molly, her eyes moist, left the room, she heard Alexander say, "Now, Mrs. Bradley, to business."

"Yes, Mr. Douglas?" Mrs. Bradley replied.

"Dinah will need clothes for the journey. I assume you will help her? Money," he added, "is no object. I have letters of credit—and instructions from my father," he added quickly, "that she is to have everything she needs."

Mrs. Bradley smiled. "I understand."

"Good." Alexander took the tea cup that Mrs. Bradley held out. Although it appeared even more fragile in his hand, he held it with a grace that showed his background. "Let's see, you'll need a heavy coat or cape, to begin with. Nights at sea can be cold. You'll also need some warm dresess, since a sailing ship doesn't have amenities like fireplaces."

Dinah laughed. "I shouldn't imagine so!" She hoped that Mrs. Bradley wouldn't insist that everything be black because of her being in mourning. Surely brown or rust or dark blue would be suitable, too.

"Perhaps," Mrs Bradley put in, "you might give me a list of the necessities and I can add to it. It was such a long time ago that I sailed to Europe, and it seems very social now."

Alexander's eyes twinkled. "The *Star of Scotland* is a freighter. Dinah will be the only passenger."

"The only passenger?" Mrs. Bradley frowned. She had expected that there would be at least a few other passengers and women.

Alexander ignored her question. He was too busy talking about what Dinah would need and his plans for the following weeks.

Those weeks were tumultous ones. Although Mrs. Bradley invited Dinah to move into the main house, Dinah preferred to stay in the rooms above the carriage house that had been home to her for so long. Mrs. Bradley understood and agreed.

Dinah's days were spent shopping. If Dinah enjoyed visiting the stores, Mrs. Bradley did, too. The time reminded her of her youth and of the happy days she had spent with Lucy, shopping for a trousseau before her marriage and departure for Baltimore where she now lived. In recent years, though, both her shopping and her pleasure in clothes had ebbed except for rare occasions when New York's social life demanded a special effort. The previous year, for example, she had looked forward to the impending visit of Leonard Jerome's daughter, Jennie, to New York with her husband, Sir Randolph Churchill, the Duke of Marlborough's son. Since Leonard Jerome and Mr. Bradley were business associates, she had eagerly awaited the expected invitations, but there had been none because of the heat and Sir Randolph's illness that sent the couple to the seashore at Newport.

Now, Mrs. Bradley supplemented Alexander's suggestions with her own. She did insist on one black dress. Other than that, she let Dinah have her choice of colors since the girl was young and she wouldn't be in mourning forever.

Almost daily, the two women explored the "Ladies Mile," the fashionable shopping district that ran from 8th Street to 23rd along Broadway and Sixth Avenue. How splendid the stores were with their magnificent facades shimmering white under the September sun, Dinah thought as she walked under the colorful awnings. She had been past the elegant emporiums with her mother, but never inside. Her mother's meager budget permitted only window shopping. For purchases, she had taken Dinah to 23rd Street, the main east-west artery that was lined with shops of all types catering to the businessmen who came to Manhattan from New Jersey on the 23rd Street ferry. The stores, with the exception of B. Altman's, were less expensive and far less elegant.

Dinah preferred Broadway to Sixth Avenue with its elevated trains. The wooden cars spitting fire overhead were noisy, spewing ashes on the street and onto the parasols women raised to protect their gowns. Her mother had called walking under the tracks as a train rattled and roared overhead a walk though the jaws of Cerberus, the hound with its fiery breath who guarded the gates of the Underworld in Greek myth.

Mr. Bradley favored Broadway, too, but because of

the stores where she was a good customer, known by name. At Broadway and 10th Street, they went to A.T. Stewarts's Department Store, the first department store to be built on the Ladies Mile, at the height of the Civil War in 1862. While Dinah reveled in the central rotunda with its double staircase and organ music, Mrs. Bradley examined the quality of the merchandise. Then they walked a block north to Mr. Creety's, with its cast-iron columns topped by Corinthia capitals and cornice decorations, all painted white. The next stop was 20th street, at Lord & Taylor's, its palatial architecture matched by what was to Dinah, clothing fit for royalty.

A favorite part of the shopping ritual was a stop for tea in the Vienna Model Bakery on Broadway, while the women checked their shopping list. The young girl enjoyed watching the fashionable ladies, who frequently met there, and she studied their manners closely.

Although Mrs. Bradley kept Dinah busy, Alexander did not forget her. During the days, he was often seeing merchants and visiting shipping offices, but in the evenings he escorted Dinah and Mrs. Bradley to dinner or the theater. He compared Luchow's on 14th Street and Delmonico's on Madison Square quite favorably to London and Continental restaurants. He also took them to the opera at the Grand Opera House on Madison Square, despite preferring the theater himself. Still, the opera was an important part of Dinah's new education.

With the dinners and the evenings at the theater, Dinah had little opportunity to talk to her new found cousin without Mrs. Bradley's presence until shortly before she was to sail. Alexander had invited the two women to have tea in the Fifth Avenue Hotel, near Madison Square, where he was staying. Since Mrs. Bradley had a luncheon and charity meeting at the August Belmont Mansion nearby, she suggested that they meet her at the hotel.

Alexander called for Dinah in a open cab. Although the day was warm, an early frost had tinged the oaks and maples in the park on Washington Square with bright scarlet and deep orange. Would it be a cold winter, Dinah wondered, as Alexander helped her into the cab. As a child, she had looked forward to the first snow and to playing in the Square where the fresh-fallen snow crackled underfoot while overhead the trees were frozen into crystal candelabras.

Memories of her childhood overwhelmed her, and she had to close her eyes. That was worse. She saw the Square as it had been then. There had been no Arch. That had been designed only a few years ago by Stanford White, the famous Society architect who had also designed Madison Square Garden, a sports arena on Madison Square, and had been finished in 1891 to commemorate the 100th anniversary of the inauguration of George Washington. The square had been an open expanse. Behind her eyelids flashed pictures of the red sled with wooden runners on which her mother had pulled her around the Square. She saw, too, the large Christmas tree, its green branches lacy with snow, and the carolers with their red noses serenading the brownstone mansions. How she would miss all that!

She turned to Alexander impulsively. "Does it snow in Scotland?" she burst out. "Do they sing carols there, too?"

The man stared at her, his jaw dropping in surprise at the irrelevance of her questions. He recovered quickly, taking her hands in his and leaning forward toward her to say with a smile, "Of course, but it's nowhere near winter—or Christmas yet."

"I know." Dinah blushed, her youth and inexperience making her feel ill at ease, regardless of her recent introduction to Society. Being with Alexander and Mrs. Bradley was one thing. Being with Alexander alone was another.

The girl looked down at her hands, held so warmly in Alexander's. What would Mrs. Bradley think, she wondered, the thought making her try to withdraw her hands. To her horror, Alexander must have misunderstood her gesture. He had been leaning forward from his position opposite her in the carriage, and at her movement he slid closer to the edge of his seat. As he did, he uncrossed his legs, managing despite the fullness of her skirt to hold her legs between his. Her right knee pressed against him. The fire spread from to her own body, to the most intimate, innermost part of her. Ashamed at the pleasure she felt, she raised her eyes to his face.

Alexander was gazing at her, breathing hard, his mouth slightly parted. "Dinah," he murmured, taking her hands and placing them on his thigh where it joined his body.

How hot he was! Beneath her gloved hands she could feel his pulse, and it filled her with indescribable desire. Her own mouth parted slightly as she took a deep breath. The air filling her lungs brought her to her senses, stiffening her body. What should she do? If she pulled away, her cousin might think she did not like him. The trouble was that she did like him, maybe too much. Her upbringing, to be polite and not to hurt another's feelings, had not prepared her for this. The heat left her, her body and limbs seeming heavy and cold.

Alexander suddenly shivered, as if in response to her. He let her hands go and leaned back in the seat opposite her, casually crossing his legs again, trying to conceal what had happened, to remember she was still a child, despite the increasing sophistication he had seen in her the past few weeks. She seemed to be changing in front of his eyes. Only a week ago, her body had had a colt-like immaturity. Now, it had a delightful softness, the slender neck showing off the curve of her breasts. Or had the curve been there all the time, only now revealed by the putting off of the modest, plain school girl's dress for fashionable gowns? Whatever had brought about the change, all he knew was that the change was both upsetting and alluring.

Dinah, released from the strange embrace, withdrew as far as she could in a corner of the carriage and clasped her hands tightly in her lap, trying to stop the throbbing between her own thighs. Again, she thought

30

of Mrs. Bradley, hot shame filled her as she realized what her friend would have thought had she seen them. Desperately she asked, "What time are we to meet Mrs. Bradley?"

"At four. We have plenty of time," Alexander told her. Again, he had a sudden urge to kiss her—she looked so lovely in the green coat with a fox collar and matching hat that she was wearing.

He forced his eyes away from her to the other carriages and horses. Too many of the horses here, like the ones in London, were poor, ill-fed beasts. The society he had heard of, the one to prevent cruelty to animals, could not be very successful. The horses' ribs protruded through coarse, dull and unbrushed coats, and their heads hung in dejected ellipses to their hollow chests.

"Poor beasties," the man murmured, thinking of the sturdy Highland ponies in Scotland, with their shaggy manes and thick brushed coats that pulled carts and carried riders with equal equanimity.

Dinah blushed. She was a poor beastie! Well, maybe she was. The memory of what had happened moments before made her shyer than ever. She listened to the rattle of the cab's wheels over the cobblestones and the creak of the cab swaying to the regular beat of the horse's hooves. The sounds increased her nervousness.

Surely there must be something she could think of to say, she thought desperately, looking around her. "Can we ride around the Square for a last time?" she finally asked, noticing they were approaching Madison Square.

"Of course." The man was ashamed of himself. He should have made some kind of conversation to put her at ease, instead of sitting there with his mind on everything except her to quiet his conflicting emotions about her.

"It's very fashionable," Dinah chattered, her eyes brightening and her face becoming more animated as she gained his attention.

"Oh?" Alexander smiled at her and told the driver

to circle the Square. "Tell me," he encouraged, relieved at not having to apologize.

"Well," Dinah said, "you know Delmonico's and the Grand Opera House. Over there," she started to point where she meant but suddenly dropped her hand in her lap, recalling her mother's admonition that it was not polite to point. "There, on the corner of 26th Street is the Jerome House. It's a club now. Leonard Jerome built it before the Civil War for his family, when it was really country here . . ." She stopped, thinking the name might mean nothing to him. She explained, "Mrs. Jerome, his daughter, Jennie, married an English lord."

"Aye," Alexander agreed, "Randolph Churchill."

"He died last winter, didn't he?" Dinah asked, sorry almost immediately for mentioning him because of the memories. The sadness and loneliness that she had not felt for weeks came back. How well she remembered the date Sir Randolph had died, or at least that the news had arrived in New York, Mrs. Bradley had told her, while they had waited for Mrs. Murray to come home from the physician only to learn that Mrs. Murray herself was dying. Dinah swallowed hard, trying to stop tears from rising.

Alexander was puzzled at the sudden change in Dinah. He knew something was wrong, but he did not know what to say except, "I've met Lady Randolph. She's a lovely woman."

"Is she? Tell me about her," Dinah urged, leaning forward.

"That's all I know. I only met her once. Tell *me* about the house," the man suggested, to keep her talking.

Dinah stared thoughtfully at the six-story brick house with its mansardic roof, tall windows, and elegant ironwork. "I've never been in it," she apologized, "but Mrs. Bradley used to go to balls there. She said the Ballroom is all white and gold and can hold 900 people, and the Breakfast Room is so big," Dinah's eyes grew large, "that seventy people could eat there!'

"If you like large houses, wait until you come to Scotland . . ." Alexander smiled.

"Your house is that big?" Dinah's apprehension returned.

"Not quite," Alexander said hurriedly, wanting to put her at her ease. "What's that building? I've noticed it before." He pointed, obviously uninhibited by convention.

"Madison Square Garden. It was built just a few years ago, for boxing matches, sports, things like that." She looked at it and at the grand houses and the more sedate brownstones standing side by side.

"It's hard to believe, but less that fifty years ago none of these buildings were here. This used to be country, Mrs. Bradley says. There was a cemetary for paupers somewhere. Circuses were held here, and baseball games." She looked lingeringly, wondering if it were for the last time, at the Square.

"Fifty years ago!" Alexander mocked playfully. "My dear Dinah, in Scotland, fifty years is yesterday. When, when we go to the Highlands, you'll see a room where Queen Mary of Scotland slept more than 300 years ago. And in Edinburgh . . ."

"Oh, Alexander," Dinah bit her lip in dismay, "whatever will I do there?"

"You'll do fine," the man encouraged. "Wait and see. You'll be a lady as grand . . . as grand," he tried to think of someone whom Dinah would recognize, "as Lady Randolph, your Jennie Jerome. You wait and see. Now, we better get to the hotel, if we're not to keep Mrs. Bradley waiting."

The couple arrived at the same time as Mrs. Bradley, to Dinah's relief. At tea, the two realized why Alexander had insisted on tea at the hotel. As a surprise, he had arranged to have hot buttered scones served. Mrs. Bradley, who had had scones in London on her trip abroad, was amused at Dinah's delight and the girl's unabashed licking of the rich crumbs from her fingers. She had started to stop her and then had decided not to. Still, the girl's childish pleasure and gesture worried her less than the expression on Alexander's face. It was tender, so tender it softened the harsh windburn lines around his eyes. She thought of Dinah's being the only passenger on the ship, and an idea formed in her mind.

After he had escorted the two women to the house on Washington Square, Mrs. Bradley insisted he come in and made an excuse to send Dinah away for a short time. Offering him a glass of sherry, she invited him to sit down.

"Dinah's very young," Mrs. Bradley began slowly. "She's only sixteen. That's too young to be going on a several week's voyage alone."

Alexander laughed. "It's a little late to think of that. Besides, she'll hardly be alone. I'll be with her."

"That's just what I mean," Mrs. Bradley admitted pointedly. "She's so young. Moreover, it isn't proper for a girl her age to be alone with a strange man . . ."

Alexander sobered, raising his black eyebrows questioningly. "Even if he's her cousin?"

"Very distant cousin," the older woman asserted, biting the words off distinctly.

"I see. You're not suggesting, at this late date . . ." The man waited, sure that Mrs. Bradley did not intend to try to keep Dinah.

"Of course, I cannot refuse to let Dinah go," the woman went on smoothly. "Still, her mother did leave her in my charge. I'd feel better . . ."

The Scotsman studied Mrs. Bradley, with set jaw and narrowed eyes. A muscle rippled warningly in one cheek. For the first time, Mrs. Bradley began to regret that she had encouraged Dinah's decision to go to Scotland. The heretofore charmingly agreeable man evidently had a stubborn, headstrong streak. She had a feeling that he could be cruel, too, if he wanted, and she was a little afraid.

"Perhaps you're right, Mrs. Bradley, he said slowly. "However, we sail in a day. Anyway, Dinah is a little old for a governess. I doubt she'd take kindly to a-a duenna or chaperone."

"I agree." Mrs. Bradley went to the fireplace to poke the fire.

"Then, I'm afraid I don't understand." The man was perplexed.

"I was thinking," Mrs. Bradley turned slowly around, "that you seem to want to make a real lady of Dinah. If that's the case . . ."

"It is," Alexander interrupted impatiently.

"Then, wouldn't it be proper for her to bring a maid? You say the voyage will take about five weeks, and during that time . . ." Mrs. Bradley raised her hands expressively.

"And you have a suggestion as to whom she should bring?" Despite the calm tone in his voice, there was a note of sarcasm.

"Mrs. Bradley nodded. "She and my maid, Molly Carew, are friends. Molly is an excellent maid, who can help Dinah with her hair and teach her other little things that a lady should know as well."

"You've discussed this with Dinah and this Molly?" Alexander's voice was now heavily and undisguisedly sarcastic. He knew she had not or she would have brought it up sooner.

"No, Mr. Douglas, I have not," Mrs. Bradley replied firmly, ignoring the tone in his voice. "I realize that you think me a foolish old lady. But Dinah is very young, naive, if you will. Until you arrived, she had never been to the theater or to a fine restaurant."

The man relaxed, not wanting to antagonize Mrs. Bradley. "Perhaps you are right. Talk to Dinah. If she's willing, and this Molly is, too, fine. They must be ready tomorrow night, however," he warned. "I'll not hold up the sailing."

Mrs. Bradley agreed that both would be ready. She saw him out, and then called Dinah.

Dinah was surprised and pleased at the suggestion. Unlike Alexander, it did not occur to her that a day was not much time for Molly to get ready. She wanted to talk to Molly immediately. Instead, Mrs. Bradley insisted that she talk to Molly alone first and sent Dinah to her rooms over the carriagehouse for the last time.

Mrs. Bradley sighed, as she pulled the bell rope to

35

summon Molly hoping the young maid would be willing. When she entered, to Molly's surprise, Mrs. Bradley asked her to sit down.

"Molly," Mrs. Bradley began, "you're an excellent maid, and I know you're Dinah's friend." As Molly's eyes grew rounder, she explained how she'd hate to lose her, yet how she felt Dinah needed her more.

Molly was overwhelmed at the prospect. "Oh, Mrs. Bradley!" she exclaimed, "do you mean it? I can go with Dinah?"

"Miss Dinah now," Mrs. Bradley corrected with a smile. "Yes, but only if you wish to go. You have only tomorrow," she worried, suddenly aware of how little time there was for the girl to get what she would need. "We can buy the essentials and I'll give you money to get whatever else you may need in Scotland."

"Oh, I don't care about that!" Molly burst out.

Mrs. Bradley smiled. "I'll miss you, Molly."

"I can't believe it," Molly stuttered, still amazed.

"Well, there *is* one condition," Mrs. Bradley began. "Molly," she took the maid's hands in hers, "you must look after Dinah. I know you're not much older, but you've seen more of the world. You've worked for other families, and you know that there's much unhappiness. . . ."

"Yes, Ma'am," Molly agreed soberly, wondering at the serious tone in Mrs. Bradley's voice.

"She should have a friend. . . ." Mrs. Bradley went on, more to herself.

Molly studied her mistress. She had worked for her long enough to tell that the line deepening between the woman's eyes meant she was worried. "You don't have to worry. I'll look after her."

"I know. I'm sure of that." Mrs. Bradley sighed.

"Is anything wrong, Ma'am?" Molly asked, suddenly afraid.

"I don't know." The woman walked to the fire place, poking the fire again. "There are times when Mr. Douglas . . . frightens me. I have a feeling that he can be very headstrong. And he is obviously a man of the world."

"Mrs. Bradley, he's such a gentleman. Dinah . . . Miss Dinah," she corrected herself, "says so."

"I know." The older woman smiled. "Just remember being born a gentleman doesn't necessarily make one a gentle man. I'm probably being silly—and getting old, but I promised Dinah's mother I'd look after her. I'd hate . . ." She shook her head, trying to banish such thoughts.

"Miss Dinah'll be fine," Molly said firmly. "I'll see to that!"

"Good, Molly. Just remember," Mrs. Bradley said earnestly, "that you and Dinah are always welcome in my home. If Scotland doesn't work out, promise me you'll let me know. I'll send you the money to come back."

"Yes, Ma'am," the maid promised, just as earnestly. Although she did not understand what could possibly be wrong with such a future as Dinah had been offered, she could see no harm in appeasing Mrs. Bradley.

Mrs. Bradley dismissed Molly, who ran across the garden to the carriagehouse where Dinah was waiting. Molly's acceptance of the offer made Dinah as happy as Molly.

"Oh, Molly, I'm so glad. And you're sure to want to come with me?"

"Of course! What's here for me? I'd be a maid for the rest of my life. Maybe I'll be a maid there, too, but at least I'll get to see the world," Molly explained.

Once Molly returned to her own room, she gave herself no time to think. There was one errand she must tend to. Taking her cloak, she went to the kitchen to tell the cook that she had an errand to do. The cook, whom Mrs. Bradley had summoned immediately after talking to Molly, let her go without question after congratulating her.

Molly picked her way carefully down the mews to a stable a few doors down from the Bradley house. The doors were open, revealing a young man rubbing down a horse. "Jim," Molly called softly.

The man turned, surprised to see Molly at that

hour. "What's up, girl? Shouldn't you be helping the cook?"

"I have to talk to you." Molly glanced around as a carriage clattered over the cobblestones, the coachman looking curiously at the two of them. "Alone," she added mysteriously.

Jim, a brawny young man with a shock of black hair, stared at her. "At this hour?"

"Oh, Jim!" Molly blushed, knowing what was on his mind. "It's important."

"Can't wait till later, eh?" Jim hit the horse on the rump, making room for Molly to enter the stable. As she did, he put an arm around her and drew her close, his mouth crushing hers.

Molly relaxed, her mouth eager in response to the kiss, almost forgetting what she had come to say. "Oh, Jim," the words burst out of her, "I am going to miss you!"

The young man let her go. "Miss me? Whatever are you talking about, girl?" He looked at her serious face and pushed her toward the rear of the stable. "I'll give him his feed."

At the back of the stable was a tack room. At one side were sacks of oats. Molly seated herself on them, squinting her round blue eyes in thought. As soon as Jim entered, she spilled out her story, the words tripping over each other. "So, I'm going away, Jim," she concluded. "I can't say no, can I? Not after how good Mrs. Bradley has been to me. And think of it, me on a ship, seeing the world!"

Jim, his hands dangling at his side, was speechless for a moment, before he gave way to anger, anger at Mrs. Bradley first of all, then Dinah, and finally Molly herself. "You can't do it, girl! Go away like that, at the drop of the old dame's handkerchief. What does she take you for? You got family here— and me besides."

Molly looked at him, seeing him in a new light. Standing there, in his shirtsleeves, with the sleeves rolled up, he was all muscle, and dirty muscle at that. What's more, he could barely read. She tossed her head, trying to soften her words with a soft voice. "Ah, Jim, that's just it—that's all I do have here, my family and you. This opportunity . . ."

"Opportunity?" Jim snorted. "You'll still be a maid, Moll, nothing but a maid, a nursemaid, too," he sneered, referring to Dinah's youth.

"What do you know about it? Dinah and I are friends."

Jim smiled slyly. "Fer now, you little fool. It all sounds like a trick to me. Why should such a fine gentleman—as you call him—be so anxious to take Dinah, and now you, away? He ain't up to no good. Of that you can be sure. Why, he'll prob'ly have all sorts of fun on the ship and then pack the two of you off to a bawdy house or the streets."

"Jim!" Molly stared at him. "He will not." She stamped her foot. "You're jealous, that's what."

"So what? Tell 'em you're not going. That's it." He hooked his thumbs in his trousers, his jaw jutting ominously.

"You've no claim on me! I'm going and that's all there is to it." Molly stood up and gathered her cloak around her. "Goodbye."

Jim barred her way. The two stared at one another, and Molly began to cry. Jim picked her up, kissing her roughly before lying her down on the feed sacks. One hand fumbled with the buttons of her dress as the other undid his trousers.

"Oh, Moll, give a feel of that," he took her hand, rubbing it against his male member that was already erect. "Ain't we had good times together, you and me?"

Molly's hand tightened automatically, her fingers massaging him. Meanwhile, his clumsy hands had given up trying to undo her dress. Instead, he raised her skirts, roughly pulling down her bloomers. Within seconds, he was astride her, driving deep into her. Gone were his former attempts at tenderness, his clumsy efforts to arouse her. Molly, nevertheless, felt a quick stab of pleasure as she always did when he penetrated her. She tried to thrust upward to meet him, but their clothes were in the way. Unable to move, she lay here, her pleasure spoiled by the quick strikes whose only goal were to satisfy the man on top of her. Her passivity excited Jim, and he satisfied himself quickly, and just as Molly, in spite of the hindrance of her clothing, freed herself enough to enjoy Jim's thrusts, seeking out the innermost parts of her, he withdrew. Molly glared at him.

Jim didn't notice. He was glowing with pride at his accomplishment. "Now, sweets," he cooed, "you ain't gonna give that up for a trip on the old Briny, are you?"

Molly, her hands busy straightening her clothes, looked up at him. "Just what makes you think you're so good?" she demanded. "You don't have anything other men don't have." She was frustrated by her own unfulfilled desire. "Besides, you don't care about me, only yourself!"

Jim's face suffused with anger. "That ain't true. Besides, you always liked the way I did it before, couldn't get enough of it, you little slut!"

"So, that's what you think of me. Well, then it's just as well I found out now. Find yourself another . . . another . . ." She couldn't bring herself to say the word.

"Aw, Moll," Jim was suddenly ashamed, "I never meant that. You know how I feel about you." He patted her shoulder clumsily.

"I know now." Molly's heart softened, but she steeled herself against weakening. "I have to go, Jim."

"Moll," he said weakly, watching her walk to the door. "Hey, Molly, sweet—" he had started to follow her, but stopped as he realized his trousers were still undone.

Molly had reached the door. She hesitated, looking around. Seeing him, his face red and sweaty from his exertions, his hands fumbling with his trousers was all she needed. If she stayed, the only future she would have would be with Jim or someone like him. Oh, she knew the future might hold even worse a fate, but Molly was not a person to look at the black side of life. Her heart rose, as she thought of the gentlemen—real gentlemen, not the Jims of the world—whom she might meet.

"Goodbye, Jim," she said softly, hurrying to the street. What a lot she had to do, starting with going over her clothes. Her eyes sparkled once more as they had when she had told Dinah that she, too, was going to Scotland.

Chapter 3

🌹 🌹 🌹

THE *Star of Scotland* was berthed at a pier off South Street in lower Manhattan. Although steam was becoming popular among new ships, the Douglases had built the *Star of Scotland* to carry sail. Because their ships were cargo ships first and carried few, if any, passengers, sail was far more practical as far as they were concerned. For one thing, speed was less important than cost, and the wind was free while coal was expensive. For another, sail meant the ships could travel farther without having to put into port for fuel and could put into any port, regardless of coaling facilities—and many of their cargoes were destined for small ports with primitive services. As a result, barkentines like the *Star of Scotland* were the maritime work horses of their day.

Since the ship was to sail before dawn with the early morning tide, Dinah and Molly's first night aboard the ship was to be spent at the pier. Alexander had suggested Dinah, and now Molly, come to the pier after dinner. There was too much to do to prepare the ship for sailing to have time for amenities that evening.

Mrs. Bradley had been glad to agree. She was relieved now, especially with Molly's shopping done. Thanks to her earlier expeditions with Dinah, she knew exactly where to go. Molly grew dizzy as she watched the waiting carriage fill up with packages. Never had she seen so many new clothes in her life. Mrs. Bradley seemed determined that Molly should have the best of everything to make up for the last-minute change in plans. Finally, the two were finished except for buying a trunk.

Mrs. Bradley sighed. "Well, Molly we've filled the carriage. If you don't mind, there's the steamer trunk of mine in the attic. You can have that."

"That . . . that's fine, Mrs. Bradley. I mean, if you're sure you won't need it." Molly was tongue-tied at her employer's generosity.

"Hardly. I don't think I'll need it again." Mrs. Bradley smiled sadly. "I wish I were going with Dinah myself, but I'm getting old. Well," she straightened her back, "let's go home now. You have to pack." She called to her coachman and the carriage weaved swiftly among the other carriages and the open-sided horse cars and drays to Fifth Avenue, avoiding Sixth Avenue where the elevated railroad always frightened the horses.

Molly had plenty of help in packing, from the cook, the butler, and even the coachman. Jim had come by, but Molly had told the cook to tell him she was busy. That was over forever. Finally, the packing was finished and she had a last dinner in the kitchen while Dinah ate with Mrs. Bradley. Then, it was time to go to the ship.

Mrs. Bradley insisted on accompanying them. While they were eating, she had sent the coachman to the ship with the trunks, afraid that otherwise there would not be room for the two young women. As a result, there was plenty of room for her, too.

The three women were silent on the drive. Mrs. Bradley was wondering whether she would ever see the girls again, while they looked out at the dark streets for a last sight of the city that had been their home. Although both girls knew they should say something to Mrs. Bradley to express their gratitude for all she had done, they were too overwhelmed by excitement to put their feelings into words. At the pier, however, they turned to her with tears in their eyes.

"Mrs. Bradley," Dinah began.

"Hush, my dear," Mrs. Bradley interrupted gruffly to hide her own emotions. "Let's have no sad good-byes." She tried to smile but had to take a handkerchief out of her pocket to dab at her eyes. "I shall miss you both." She leaned forward to kiss them, and Alexander appeared at the side of the carriage to escort the young women to the ship.

"Mrs. Bradley," he murmured, "thank you for your help."

"It was little enough, Mr. Douglas. If you want to thank me," she straightened her back, ignoring his tone and saying sternly, "thank me by taking good care of my girls."

"I will that," the man promised, his eyes on Dinah.

Molly climbed out of the carriage first. As she did, Mrs. Bradley kissed Dinah's cheek again. "Remember, my dear, you and Molly both, you're always welcome with me."

"I know. Oh, Mrs. Bradley!" Dinah threw her arms around the woman and hugged her. "Thank you, thank you," she whispered before Alexander reached up a strong hand to help her down.

Alexander hurried the girls along the pier. Lanterns flickered, illuminating the longshoremen loading the cargo and casting strangely eerie, hunchbacked shadows on the planks of the pier and on the bales of cargo still waiting to be loaded. Dinah shivered.

At the gangplank, Dinah dropped behind for one last look. Beyond the threatening shadows, Mrs. Bradley was waiting in her carriage at the end of the pier, her handkerchief a white, fluttering signal. As Dinah waved to her, the cab drove off, and Dinah

43

turned to Alexander who was smiling at her, his face unfamiliar and sinister in the lantern light.

He ushered the young women to the quarters reserved for the master, which he had given up for them. There were two cabins, both small, the larger forming a combined dining and sitting room, the smaller containing a bunk bed for Dinah and a cot for Molly. Alexander made sure they had everything they needed before leaving to help supervise the last-minute loading of cargo.

The two girls spent the rest of the evening unpacking the trunks that were waiting for them. By the time they had finished, they looked at one another. Both were exhausted. It had been a long day, and all they wanted was to sleep.

Dinah, however was unable to sleep once she was curled up in the bunk under a heavy patchwork quilt. Aside from being too excited to relax, the ship was filled with strange noises. Voices called to one another abovedecks as the cargo was loaded and stowed, thumping, banging, and scraping against the hull. The watch changed. Even when the decks and hold were silent, the ship itself called out. Planks groaned and shuddered as the tide and current changed and the ship strained at the thick hemp hawsers that ran like giant umbilical cords between the ship and the pier.

Shortly before dawn, feet pounded on the deck to the accompaniment of harsh voices calling orders. The crew was preparing to raise sails and get under way.

Dinah could not stay in bed any longer. She rose and tiptoed to the open door leading into the sitting room, one eye on Molly curled up, sound asleep, beneath her blankets, a hand under her cheek. Dinah smiled, shutting the door softly. She dressed quickly, donning the thick cloak that Alexander had insisted she would need on shipboard, and left the cabin for the companionway leading onto the deck. The ship, with only its staysails and the fore and aft jibs set, was easing into the harbor. To her right was Ellis Island with its long, low profile of buildings that were the first home of so many immigrants.

Dinah thought sadly of her mother who, only sixteen years ago, had been one of the immigrants pouring through those crowded shelters in hope of a better life. What would her mother have thought then had she known that one day her daughter would be going in the opposite direction for the same reason? Yet, it had been her mother's dying wish that she make this trip, Dinah reminded herself.

She moved out of the cool breeze into the protection of the after deck. Above her, the helmsman stood at the wheel next to a man who had to be the captain from the gold braid on his blue uniform and his cap and from the constant stream of orders he issued. In the rigging, sailors waited to unfurl the mainsails and topgallants from the yardarms.

The slowly moving ship began to move more quickly as the sheets filled with wind and the vessel caught the tide running out. Dinah leaned against the rail. They were passing through the Narrows where the rising sun was casting dark shadows over the green hills of Brooklyn. She closed her eyes, trying to engrave the picture on her mind. It might be the last she would ever see of New York and her native land. No matter what Mrs. Bradley had said, returning would not be easy. Her breath caught, partly from excitement at what lay ahead and partly from sadness at what she was leaving behind.

"Well, Dinah, is it sorry you are?" The deep, resonant voice with its rolled "r's" made her turn. As she did, she loosed her grip on the stays she had been holding. A sudden yawing of the ship sent her tumbling off balance into Alexander's arms.

"Excuse me!" she said quickly, trying to free herself, but the man's arms held her more tightly, making her heart beat faster.

"Dinah," Alexander said softly, feeling her body beneath the heavy cloak. He bent his head until his mouth found hers.

Their lips met, gently at first. Then, his arms tightened, his mouth pressing against her lips until she could feel his teeth as his tongue forced its way inside. Dinah could no more resist him than she could the hot blood pounding in her veins or the sudden desire in her loins, the desire that had suffused her body in a warm glow that afternoon in the carriage. As she remembered, too, his pulsating strength under her hands, and she fought to release herself from his embrace, ashamed of the longing that she was sure no nice young woman should ever feel.

Alexander let her go reluctantly. "I-I'm sorry," he said, although his flashing eyes and the flush along his high cheekbones belied his words.

"You should be!" Dinah blazed, trying to sound haughty and angry.

"Well, we're cousins," the man conceded in a hoarse voice, "distant cousins."

Any further apology he might have made was stopped by the captain's calling him. Alexander led her above, up a narrow ladder to the afterdeck, to introduce her to the captain.

Captain Ian MacKie was the same age as Alexander, about thirty, which seemed young to Dinah to be the captain of a ship like this. Though listening to his discussion of the best compass heading to follow after they left Sandy Hook, the easternmost point of the United States they would pass, for the open sea, Dinah gathered that he was more than competent.

The similarity in their ages seemed to be all they had in common. Where Alexander Douglas was tall, broad-shouldered, and slender, with dark hair and a complexion readily tanned by the sun, Ian MacKie was only a few inches taller than Dinah, with heavy, powerful shoulders and a broad, deep chest. Thickly muscled arms rippled beneath his blue jacket. His hair was sandy in color and as curly as her own, while his eyes were a bright, true blue in his bronze face. Lines creased the corners of his eyes with white from long hours and days of squinting into the sun.

As soon as the two men had finished their discussion, Captain MacKie turned to Dinah, who had been standing in a corner by the binnacle housing the compass. "Miss Murray," he said in a deep voice with the ring of authority to it, "excuse our talking business. Would you like some tea? I'm having the cabin boy bring us some, and you're invited to join us."

"Thank you," Dinah replied primly. "Tea would taste good."

"Aye," the captain agreed formally, "the breezes are chill at this hour."

The two men and the young woman went to the chart house on the afterdeck to have their tea. The men were respectful to one another, but Dinah thought she detected an odd undercurrent between them, perhaps because they seemed too overly polite to each other. The captain's eyes, moreover, observed her so frankly that she wondered whether he had seen Alexander's kiss from his vantage point on the afterdeck and had mistaken her position.

"Mr. Douglas has told me that you're his cousin and you're joining your family in Scotland," he said in his deep, precise tones, relieving her mind. "I hope you'll enjoy the voyage as much as I know you will enjoy Scotland."

Dinah smiled shyly. "You're Scottish, too?"

"Aye. From Edinburgh, as well. It's a fine city, finer than London to my mind, but then," he smiled, showing a dry sense of humor, "I'm prejudiced, you might say."

"I'm looking forward to seeing it," Dinah replied politely.

The captain set down his cup. "I must be getting back to the wheel now. Perhaps later, as soon as we're farther out to sea, you'd like to see the ship. It would be my pleasure to show it to you."

"Thank you," Dinah smiled. "Both my maid and I would be delighted."

She left quickly, refusing Alexander's offer to see her to her cabin. At that moment, she was afraid to be alone with him as much out of fear that the kiss would be repeated as that it would not be. At the back of her mind, too, was Mrs. Bradley's warning about her youth and innocence. Perhaps she had misunderstood the kiss for that reason.

She found Molly up and preparing to look for her. "I was so worried to find you gone," Molly exclaimed. "The cabin boy came about breakfast. I didn't know what to tell him."

Dinah laughed. She had forgotten the kiss for the moment. The salt air, the motion of the ship, and the realization she was at sea suddenly combined to make her feel as free as she had as a child, while Molly's concern made her feel older and protective. "Oh, Molly," she cried, "there isn't much of anywhere to go on the ship."

Molly grinned sheepishly. "You're right, I guess."

Over breakfast, Dinah told Molly about the invitation to see the ship later. She did not mention the kiss, although Molly, who had sometimes told her about the romantic adventures of the servants downstairs, was surely qualified to advise her, not that Molly ever had told them as first-hand knowledge. On the other hand, she did not want the trip to start under a shadow. She would wait and see what happened—and be more careful about being alone with her cousin, her distant cousin as he kept pointing out. She was more glad than ever that Molly was with her.

Molly, nevertheless, proved to be little company. As soon as the ship passed the lighthouse at Sandy Hook and reached the Atlantic, it began to roll and strain through the waves. Molly spent a half hour leaning over the rail before retreating to her cabin to lie down. The roll of the ship, as far as Dinah was concerned, exhilarated her. She felt better than she had ever felt in her life.

"You're a born sailor," the captain laughed, finding her sitting in a chair on the foredeck in the afternoon.

Dinah smiled at him, glad for the company. At the last minute, as she had looked around the rooms at Mrs. Bradley's, she had noticed her mother's piece of unfinished needlepoint and had taken it with her to finish on the ship. Working on it, however, had recalled her mother with a poignancy she had almost forgotten in her excitement,

"We'll find out when it gets really rough," Dinah said anxiously. "Our cabin boy said that this was almost a flat calm."

Captain MacKie leaned against the railing and took a pipe out of his pocket. "I'm afraid the lad's given to exaggeration. It's his first voyage. We've favorable winds and the seas are running with us. It's no storm— but it's no flat calm." he apologized, "although I hope the weather stays this clear."

"I'll take your forecast, and ask you next time about the weather," Dinah promised.

"Do that. I'd be pleased to answer your questions any time. And now," he knocked the dead pipe against the rail, "if you would like to see my ship, I have time."

As he showed her the ship and explained the various sails to her, Dinah found herself liking and trusting the captain, young as he seemed. After he had toured with ship with her, he invited her to his cabin where the charts were spread out on a large table, weighed down by a sextant. The invitation to her to have a sherry was accepted, Dinah already more at ease with him than with Alexander.

"Aren't you young to be a captain?" she asked, sipping the sherry.

"A little," he admitted, "but I shipped out to sea as a cabin boy when I was eight. So, I have more than twenty years' experience."

"At eight?" Dinah was amazed.

"Aye. I come from a large family, although I'm the only one left. The others have all gone to Canada, America, or Australia. Still, I had a choice of being apprenticed to a harrier or going to sea. Horses are fine, but the sea seemed to offer more opportunity," he stated matter-of-factly.

To Dinah, the idea of going to work at such a young age was a strange one. She knew about the sweat shops in New York and had seen young children trudging to work with lunch pails, although she

49

had never spoken to one of those children. As far as Molly was concerned, Molly came from a large family, too. Yet, Molly's mother had insisted that she go to school through eighth grade to better herself. So, Molly had not started working until she was fourteen.

"Wasn't it lonely to be so young and so far from home?" Dinah asked.

"Aye." The captain's blue eyes deepened, reflecting inward and seeing the frightened boy who had cried into his blanket in his hammock long after the men in the crew's quarters were sleeping. "I got used to it. A boy becomes a man quickly at sea, especially when it's months before he sees home again."

Dinah nodded. "And now you're captain of your own ship?"

"This is my first voyage as captain. The Douglasses are good masters, and I made many voyages for the Auld Mon as second mate, and then as first mate. When this ship was built, he offered it to me. I'm glad," the captain smiled, deflecting any questions about the "Auld Mon" who had to be Alexander's father. He added, "Otherwise I'd be on the *Star of the East* on my way to China, and I would never have met you."

Dinah flushed, the compliment pleasing her. She felt as if she, too, were growing up quickly at sea. Already in one day, she felt she had had more experiences than in her previous sixteen years. She knew the compliment required an answer, though, and she did not know how to turn it away with a casual remark. Instead, she set the glass down, standing up. "Thank you for the sherry, Captain MacKie," she said politely, "and for showing me the ship."

"Going so soon," The man rose to his feet.

"I must see how Molly, my . . . Molly is," Dinah explained swiftly.

"Then, I'll let you go. By the way, you and Mr. Douglas are to dine with me this evening. I'll see you then—and ask Molly to join us, if she's well enough," he called as Dinah fled down the campanionway.

What was wrong with her, she wondered, that her emotions could be so easily aroused. First, it had been Alexander, and now Captain MacKie had brought out similar emotions.

She reached the cabin and leaned against the door with relief. How glad she was that Mrs. Bradley had suggested Molly come with her. Yet, why did Molly have to get seasick when she needed her so badly? Dinah sighed, hurrying to the adjoining cabin.

Molly was awake and sitting on the edge of the cot. "Feeling better?" Dinah asked, noticing the girl had lost the green tinge of earlier in the day, pale as she still was.

"A little." Molly grinned sheepishly. "I'm sorry. Here, *I'm* the one who is supposed to look after you, and *you're* the one who has to look after me!"

Dinah laughed. "Maybe I just got my sea legs earlier than you. At least, we both didn't get sick at the same time!"

"True," Molly admitted gratefully, wondering who would take care of them if that happened, with no other woman aboard.

As soon as Molly had dressed, the two young women went on deck where the fresh air and the steadying breeze completed Molly's recuperation. They watched the sailors manning the sails and busying themselves with lines, while others coiled line and scrubbed the decks. The sailors were using a soft stone on the decks, the stone being called a holystone and the process holystoning, a passing sailor informed them.

Later, they returned to their quarters to dress for dinner. Dinah dressed slowly, relieved that Molly's recovery meant that she would be at dinner. Molly's presence, she hoped, would make it easier for her to face Alexander and Captain MacKie, both of whom had succeeded in making her feel she was at sea psychologically as well as physically.

Johnny, the cabin boy who had gloated over the "calm" weather, arrived promptly at seven to escort them. The child, barely nine years old, Dinah guessed, reminded her of Captain MacKie's having gone to sea at much the same age.

"Do you like the sea?" Dinah asked curiously, as she draped her cape over her shoulders.

"Aye, Ma'am, especially this ship. Cap'n MacKie is a good captain. He's fair, not like some that work ye till ye drop," the lad told her wise beyond his years.

"He was a cabin boy once, too," Dinah pointed out.

"Aye, and he says that if I work hard some day I could be a captain, too!" Johnny glowed at the prospect. "Here's his quarters, my ladies."

He had stopped outside the door. When Dinah hung back, he rapped on the door to announce their arrival.

Captain MacKie and Alexander were studying the charts, a ruler and a pair of dividers at hand. Opposite them was another man, also in the blue uniform of an officer. He was about the same age as, or a little younger than, the other two men, with hair even redder than Dinah's, and freckles peppering his face.

"Good evening, Ladies." Alexander stepped forward. As master of the ship, he was host, despite the cabin's belonging to the captain. "I'm pleased you could join us, and that you're feeling better, Molly."

"Thank you, Sir," Molly murmured with a blush. She was beginning to wish, however, she had feigned illness. The sight of the fine gentlemen, whom she considered above her, and the thought of dining as an equal with them frightened her.

Alexander served the young women sherry. The others, to a man, preferred Scotch whisky, which Alexander laughingly told Dinah and Molly was "mother's milk to a Scot."

The dinner, simple and substantial, was accompanied by a French wine. The unaccustomed alcohol relaxed Dinah and diminished her fears. Molly, too, began to feel at ease, talking animatedly to the red-haired man who was the first mate, second in command to Captain MacKie. He had been introduced as Mr. Campbell, although as the meal progressed and the formality lessened, Captain MacKie began calling him Geordie, a Scottish nickname for George.

After Captain MacKie left them, following dinner, to take star sights with the sextant and lay out the course for the night, Alexander leaned back in his chair. He was as at ease at sea as he had been in Mrs. Bradley's living room or at Delmonico's. He smiled at his companions, saying to Dinah, "You've brought the Douglas Clan luck, Dinah."

"I?" Dinah looked at him in surprise.

"Yes, you!" The man laughed. "Thanks to my going to New York, we may add Bermuda to our regular calling ports. We're on our way there now with a cargo —and with more luck, perhaps we can pick up another cargo in Bermuda for Scotland."

Dinah was childishly pleased at the compliment. "Is it far?"

"A few days voyage south-east," Alexander explained. "It's a little out of our way, but it will give you an opportunity to get used to the sea. Besides, we'll soon pick up the Gulf Stream and some tropic breezes. When we leave Bermuda, we'll follow it part way to the coast of England."

"Aye," Geordie agreed, " 'twill make the voyage more pleasant."

"You've been there, Mr. Campbell?" Dinah asked. "What is it like?"

The young first mate flushed in embarrassment, wishing he had kept his wanting to show off to Molly Carew to himself. "I've nae been there, Ma'am, but I've heard it's a lovely isle."

Molly smiled to herself. Geordie's embarrassment made her feel better. He, too, must be ill at ease, she decided.

Alexander's sharp eyes noticed Molly's slight smile. He had well understood that Mrs. Bradley's insistence on Molly's accompanying Dinah was more due to him than to any overbearing desire for Molly to teach Dinah the art of being a lady. Molly's presence on the ship might not be so bad, though, as long as she was as interested in Geordie as she seemed to be. He wished he were not so tired. The dinner two nights before had lasted late and he had slept little the past night, what with checking the cargo and having to be up early to sign the sailing papers. Still, there would be many more nights at sea. For tonight, a few minutes alone with Dinah would do.

"Mr. Campbell," he suggested formally, "perhaps the ladies would like a turn on deck. The fresh air might help us all sleep well."

"Aye." The first mate scrambled to his feet to help Molly with her cape.

Alexander turned to Dinah, getting up and pulling out her chair. "May I?" he asked, holding her cape for her.

Dinah looked at him, remembering that morning and drawing back. "Thank you," she said quickly, hurrying to join Molly and the mate.

A full moon illuminated the starlit night, casting its beams on the rigging and the sails trimmed to catch the light air. The wind had dropped with nightfall, and the ship was moving slowly. Tiny sea creatures glowed phosphorescently in the spray as the bow cleaved the water.

Dinah was amazed at how noisy the ship itself was. The past night, the crew had been busy preparing for sea, but even at sea there were sounds. Where last night the tide and current had tugged at the ship, making the planks groan against the hawsers holding it to the pier, tonight the planks creaked and the sails flapped.

"About this morning, Dinah," Alexander said quietly, drawing Dinah to one side, "I'm sorry. I didn't mean to frighten you. The sight of you with the sun turning your hair to gold," he smiled, "overpowered me."

"I sincerely hope that it won't happen again," Dinah told him primly, not really hoping any such thing.

"I can't promise such a thing—that the sun won't shine or I won't be overpowered by your beauty. I give you my word, though," he added hastily at the expression of shock on her face, "that I'll try to keep my feelings to myself."

"I hope so," Dinah replied, adding pointedly, "for your father's sake."

Alexander raised an eyebrow. "Now that I have apologized, shall we join Milly and Geordie?"

The other couple were on the afterdeck where Geordie was explaining the compass in the binnacle, which the helmsman used to steer by. He was saying that the vagaries of the currents as well as the winds often made it difficult to keep the correct heading unless the helmsman were experienced. Molly was listening eagerly, her eyes shining every time she looked at the first mate.

"I think," Alexander whispered, "Geordie has made a conquest—or is it the other way?"

Dinah had to giggle in spite of her resolve to maintain her dignity. "They do seem engrossed with one another," she agreed.

All Geordie had time for was another turn of the deck before he had to stand watch. He left Molly reluctantly, hesitating before kissing her hand, the gesture turning Molly's face as red as the man's hair. Alexander escorted the two young women to their cabin, where he followed Geordie's example and kissed Dinah's hand, his lips lingering a little too long to suit Dinah, who pulled her hand free.

The minute the two were alone, Molly turned to Dinah, excitement vying with embarrassment in her face. "Oh, Miss Dinah," she exclaimed, "it's not right for them to treat me like a lady. I'm only a maid."

"Forget it, Molly," Dinah soothed. "We're the only women aboard since the ship usually doesn't carry passengers, and we're a novelty."

"I know. And they're being polite, I suppose," Molly admitted. "Still, it's not right for me to . . . to . . ."

"Molly, dear," Dinah chided, "remember it's not so long since I was a servant, too. For now, I think it's best we forget all that. After all, we're friends, too." Dinah was thinking that it would be better for her to avoid being alone with Alexander and, to that end, she needed Molly as a friend, not a maid.

Molly nodded, still not happy over the situation. At the same time, she had found Geordie Campbell very attractive, and he had been as ill at ease under the eyes of his captain and the ship's master as she had been. "If you think so, Miss Dinah," she agreed.

"I know so," Dinah stated emphatically. "Until we get to Scotland, we must be friends first. Then, we'll have to see what happens."

"*Did* something happen?" Dinah's uneasiness had finally penetrated Molly's preoccupation with herself.

"No. Not really. It's just, well, everything is so strange at times. I mean, here a few weeks ago, as far a I knew the only relative I had in the world was my mother, and the best I could do was being a governess. Now, I have relatives and God only knows . . ." Her voice trailed off uncertainly.

"Mr. Alexander is so nice and so handsome, too," Molly pointed out, not knowing what else to say to reassure Dinah.

"I know." Dinah sighed. "And yet, Molly, sometimes I'm frightened."

"Oh, Dinah!" Molly went to the other girl and put her arms around her, feeling much older and wiser at the moment. "Everything's going to be perfect," she assured. "You just wait and see."

Chapter 4

THE FEW DAYS' sail to Bermuda gave Dinah and Molly a chance to get used to shipboard life and routine. At night, they were no longer awakened by the creaking of the ship or the whistling of the wind through the sails or the heavy tread of feet over their heads as the watch changed. Thanks, too, to the fresh air and the rocking of the ship as it sped through the waves, they slept deeply.

The first few days at sea were also a sample of how monotonous life at sea can be. Johnny brought their breakfast to their cabin promptly at eight in the morning. Afterwards, they walked around the deck, watching the sailors at their seemingly eternal holystoning of the decks and their mending of lines and sails, before sitting in chairs in the lee of the foredeck where they were protected from the wind. Dinah alternated between reading and working on her mother's needlepoint, while Molly made minor alterations in their clothing. Sometimes, Geordie Campbell would join them when he was not on watch, making excuses to draw Molly aside to point out some facet or other of shipboard life.

Alexander and Captain MacKie also visited them. To Dinah's relief, however, she was rarely alone with either man. No sooner would one appear than the other would be close behind.

The two young women had dinner at noon in their cabin, after which they would take another walk around the deck before lying down in their cabin for an hour. When they awakened, Molly polished her skills as a lady's maid, dressing Dinah's hair different ways. The two young women, in fact, spent hours fussing with the stubborn, curly hair, trying to find styles in which it would stay and that flattered Dinah. Then it was time to dress for supper, which was the social high point of their day, taken in the captain's cabin with the captain, Alexander, and Geordie Campbell.

Alexander dominated the conversation. If Geordie Campbell and Captain MacKie were more used to male companions, having spent most of their lives at sea, Dinah and Molly were too young and inexperienced to have a supply of small talk. Alexander, on the other hand, had grown up in society. That, and his broad education, gave him a wide range of subject matter. He was like an actor in center stage, loving every minute. Although he was obviously trying to impress Dinah, the attention of the others was added encouragement.

The evening before they were due to arrive at Bermuda, he was at his best. He was looking forward to doing business there and to the challenge of exploring new markets, and the sight of Dinah with her hair in curls on top of her head except for a ringlet beside each cheek, her rust dress heightening the amber of her eyes, excited him. His eyes glinted, and his mouth curved in a smile, as he led her to the seat under the sternlight.

"Sherry, Dinah?" he offered.

"Thank you." Dinah smiled, her eyes lowered. She was beginning to enjoy the pre-supper sherry and pleasantries. As she gradually lost the inhibitions that had kept her silent and anxious the first few evenings, she began to wonder whether she had misjudged Alexander out of her youth and inexperience.

Molly was more at ease, too. Thanks to the presence of Geordie Campbell, who relieved her awe of Alexander, she began to join in the conversation.

That evening, while the two women sipped their sherry and the men enjoyed their Scotch, Alexander glanced at Ian MacKie. The man, solemn and stolid as always, was gazing at Dinah with his blue eyes alight. Dinah raised her eyes to smile at him. A faint twinge of jealousy sent a muscle flickering along Alexander's cheek as he noticed that Dinah's eyes met the captain's without dropping as they did when she smiled at him. He resolved to get her attention and hold it.

"Well, Dinah," Alexander said, stepping forward and standing with his legs spread apart in the manner that Dinah had come to recognize as being not so much ungentlemanly as necessary at sea to accommodate the roll of the ship, "are you looking forward to Bermuda?"

"Oh, yes!" the girl said eagerly, her eyes turning to her cousin's face. "Shall we be able to see anything of the island?"

"I," Alexander asserted firmly, throwing a quick

look at the captain, "I shall see to that. I have business in Hamilton, and you shall go with me, if you like."

"Well, you'd best get ballast to make up for the flour and sugar we'll be unloading," MacKie pointed out.

"Don't worry, Ian, if we don't get anything else, we'll get Bermudan cedar to use in the shipyards in Scotland," Alexander affirmed.

"Aye." The captain sounded dubious. "It's your first trip, Alexander, and it may not be so easy to run interference with the other ships that make regular stops."

"I did well enough in New York, didn't I?" Alexander turned his self-assurance into an excuse for gallantry. "Besides," he gave his attention to Dinah, "my cousin brought us luck in New York, and she must see a little of the island."

"Oh, I want to," Dinah agreed enthusiastically. "What is it like?"

"Hard to find, for one thing," the captain answered shortly. "It's only about twenty miles long and a few miles wide, and the highest point is but 250 feet high. *And* it's surrounded by shoals. We'll not go into the harbor or great sound, but stay at the Dockyard on the northwestern end, what they call Somerset."

"Ian," Alexander remarked pointedly, unwilling to give up his audience, "you'll frighten the ladies with your talk of shoals, even if they are one reason the island wasn't settled until after your Virginia colony, Dinah." He began to warm to his subject, as all eyes once more turned to him, and he was glad for the information he had picked up in talking to merchants and ship chandlers in New York.

"It was discovered in the early 1500's by a Spanish explorer, Juan de Bermudez, from whom it gets its name." Alexander said. "It was too far out of the main ship lanes to be settled, though, until a couple of ships from England on their way with men and supplies to Virginia ran aground there in a hurricane in 1609. Their own ships were sunk, so they had to build two others to take them the rest of the way. After that, what with the colonies, not to mention Spanish ships on the prowl, the British settled the island and fortified it."

"The ships, the ones they built, reached Virginia?" Dinah asked, shuddering at the thought of a shipwreck.

"Of course. One of those shipwrecked was Captain John Smith, and if he hadn't reached Virginia," he teased, wanting to make Dinah laugh, "how could he have rescued Pocahontas, or she, him, whichever it was."

Dinah laughed and impulsively took Alexander's hand. "What else do you know about Bermuda?"

Alexander raised the young woman to her feet, his dark eyes holding her amber ones. "Some of the gunpowder that started your revolution came from Bermuda, I was told," he murmured, caring less about Bermuda than Dinah.

The touch of the man's hand, the closeness of his body, and most of all the dark eyes seeming so soft as they gazed on her face made Dinah glow. She could feel the warmth rising in her cheeks, and she dropped her eyes in embarrassment at her eagerness to taste his lips again. The man let her go gently, noting the blush and not wanting to frighten her once more. He knew he had time. There was Bermuda and another month at sea.

Captain MacKie watched helplessly, the sight of the color in Dinah's cheeks rousing his own feelings for her. To his relief, he heard Johnny's knock on the door announcing the arrival of dinner. "It's dinner time," he anounced, taking Dinah's arm to lead her to the table and seat next to him.

Alexander was amused at the captain's brusque capture of Dinah. He seated himself nonchalantly opposite the young woman again, picking up the threads of conversation. "There's a good hotel in Hamilton, the Princess, named after Princess Louise, one of Queen Victoria's daughters, whose husband was Governor General of Canada. She went there for her health about ten years ago and made it quite fashionable."

"That's right." Captain MacKie tried to join the

conversation. "I was in Bermuda when she was there." He turned to Alexander, losing his advantage. "I was on the *Highland Star*. She had to put in for repairs—" he stopped abruptly.

"What was she like?" Dinah aked curiously.

"A tub," the captain responded, not noticing the look of amazement on the others' faces, "too broad in the beam to sail well. Rolled with each and every sea."

Alexander started to laugh, laughing so hard that he had to use his napkin to wipe his eyes. Finally, he managed to say, "Ian, I doubt our lady meant the *Highland Star*. I think she meant Princess Louise— although she might be broad in the beam, too.'"

MacKie's face flamed. "I never saw the Princess," he mumbled. "I had duty on the ship."

"She's quite pretty, very charming," Alexander explained, his self-control getting the better of his sudden burst of laughter. "You might meet her one day at Marlborough House, when we're in London."

"Marlborough House!" Dinah forgot Captain Mac-Kie, for whom she had been feeling sorry a moment before. She thought of Jennie Jerome and her husband, the younger son of the Duke of Marlborough. "Is that where Jennie Jerome lives?"

"No." Alexander smiled, softening his explanation so it did not imply criticism of her ignorance. "The Duke of Marlborough lives at Blenheim Palace. Marlborough House is where the Prince of Wales lives. It may not make sense, but that's British royalty for you." He added for Dinah's sake, "Jennie is a friend of his, though, a very good friend," he emphasized, to Dinah's confusion. "That's where I met her, and maybe you will meet her there, too."

Dinah was more impressed than she wanted to admit. She said the first thing that came to her mind. "I have nothing to wear!"

Alexander smiled once more. If he could burst out in ungentlemanly laughter at the expense of Captain MacKie, he had better control than to laugh at Dinah. "You will," he promised. "I shall see to it."

Captain MacKie, unable to compete in promises,

was silent the rest of the meal. As soon as the dessert of pudding and fruit had been served, he excused himself, saying it was time for him to take the evening star sights and lay the course for the night.

Shortly after he left, Geordie glanced at Molly who had been silent all evening, listening and taking in the conversation. Her earlier, unqualified approval of Alexander as a gentleman was beginning to be tempered. She was not sure such talk as taking Dinah to meet the Prince of Wales was sincere or bragging. Geordie, too, had been quiet, for reasons of his own. He had made a blunder with Molly the first night at sea when Bermuda was mentioned, and he did not want to repeat it.

"Miss Carew," Geordie took a deep breath. Unlike the others, he never called her Molly, "Miss Carew, would you like a turn about the deck? It was a filling supper. . . ."

"Thank you." Molly rose to her feet, belatedly glancing at Dinah who nodded permission.

Geordie helped her with her cloak, noticing not for the first time the soft curves and warmth of the body under the simple wool gown. He waited until they were alone on deck to say, "I wish I could show you Bermuda, but I'll have to see to the unloading. . . ."

"I understand, Geordie," Molly replied, tucking her hand in the first officer's.

"Perhaps you can go to Hamilton with Miss Dinah and Mr. Douglas," he suggested.

"Maybe I won't be asked, at least by Mr. Douglas." Molly tossed her head. "What's he like, Geordie, really like? He seems such a gentleman, yet . . ."

Geordie shrugged. "All I know is that he seems a good seaman, as far as his ships and his business go. If there's a cargo for Scotland in Bermuda, he'll find it."

"That's not what I meant." Molly sighed. "It's Dinah I'm worried about—the way he looks at her sometimes. She never had a father, and she hasn't been around men at all."

Geordie looked down at Molly. They had paused in

the lee of the sterndeck, and he glanced up to be sure the helmsman could not see them. "And you have?"

"Why, Mr. Campbell," Molly noted, her eyes taking measure of the man under fluttering eyelashes. "I am only a maid, you know, and I have worked since I was fourteen."

For the first time since leaving New York, she thought of Jim who could not hold a candle to the young mate. Yes, she had made the right decision to go with Dinah, and yet . . . Jim had not always treated her as roughly and inconsiderately as he had that last time in the stable. Their stolen hours together in the same stable had often had a sweetness to them.

There had ben only one man before Jim, and she recalled him with a shudder. Her first position had been as a housemaid at a fine house on Fifth Avenue. What a wide-eyed innocent she had been and only fourteen. The master of the house was a well-known financier with a reputation for sympathy for the working classes. His wife was from Boston, very stiff and cold and distant to Molly's mind. She had pitied the man who always seemed to be dining at his club or alone because of his wife's constant migraine headaches. At first, his invitations to Molly to join him for a glass of sherry had seemed the craving of a lonesome, childless man for company. Her awakening had been rude.

Her employer had come home early one evening and summoned her to his private sitting room. What had happened afterwards, she did not care to remember, his order to her to lock the door and then to remove her clothes. When she hesitated, he had struck her and Molly, too frightened to disobey any longer, had obeyed. When she was naked, he had ordered her to pour him a drink and remove his boots. The rest was a blur, until weeping, her body a mass of bruises, she had finally been allowed to put her clothes on and go to her room. That had not been the only time. Worst of all, all the servants knew what was going on. They pitied her, but could do nothing until the cook, who was a friend of Mrs. Bradley's cook, heard Mrs.

Bradley was looking for a maid. Whether Mrs. Bradley knew about what Molly was being forced to endure or not, Molly never learned. All that mattered was that she had been hired, that her humiliation was over.

At first, after she met Jim, she had ignored him. He had won her over gradually with little compliments, a few sweets, a little nosegay of flowers. When she finally gave in, he had been very gentle and tender, seeming to think of her and her wishes. More recently, he had come to take her for granted, more concerned with his appetite than hers, which had made it suddenly seem wiser to accept the offer to accompany Dinah.

The memories flashed quickly thrrough her mind as she studied Geordie Campbell, now red to the roots of his hair. She might have no claim to virginity, but then he was a sailor and probably could have no such claim either. Besides, Molly had grown used to the loving caresses of a man and her body missed them, not that she could go to Geordie under any false pretenses.

Molly's hesitation had settled any doubts in Geordie's mind, as he had taken it for embarrassment. Thus, he was relieved as she finally spoke, saying softly, "I don't know what to say."

"Oh, Molly," he exclaimed, using her given name for the first time, "you're beautiful!"

Molly had not thought he could blush a deeper red until he did. She could not resist the temptation to tease him a little, as a result. With an air of what she hoped passed for sophistication, she gazed past his head at the stars, twinkling candle-bright in the black sky, and the moon. If she was determined that he not know everything about her, she was equally determined that he did not think he was the first man who had ever looked at her with desire. She raised a finger to her cheek, tapping it lightly. "Let's see, there have been butlers, footmen, a coachman . . ."

Geordie saw only a girl not quite out of her teens, and he reacted exactly as Molly had hoped. "Tell me more, Molly."

"And you," she smiled, "you are a sailor. You must have much to tell me.'" She looked at Geordie accusingly. "I've heard all about sailors, seen them, too, just off the docks and already drunk, accosting women!"

Geordie reddened still more. He was beet-red now. "I don't know about that. I don't get off the ship much as first mate," he added in his own defense, although he felt that what he did as a man was not the same as for a woman, for Molly.

"Hush!" Molly had seen Dinah and Alexander come on deck. They were standing mid-ships by the rail, the man with his arm around the young woman's waist to steady her against the roll of the ship. "What do you think they're talking about?" Molly asked.

Geordie half-turned, helpless against Molly's protectiveness for her mistress. The couple was illuminated in the star shine, with Alexander leaning over Dinah, his lips close to her forehead. Geordie was envious of the man's sophistication and aplomb. Although he only knew the master from the ship, he had seen him in Edinburgh escorting the Lady Mary Angus to parties, both in full dress kilt with plaid and sporran, and in a dinner suit. He never seemed at a loss with women.

"He's so handsome, isn't he?" Molly admired. "With that black hair and those dark eyes . . ."

"Aye," Geordie admitted, giving up for the moment in his pursuit of Molly. "So, you like him, after all, do you?"

Molly flushed, her attention back on Geordie too late. "Geordie . . ."

"I'll see you to your cabin," the first mate said gruffly. "Captain MacKie may have need of me."

Molly sighed, leaving the deck reluctantly. At least Dinah and Alexander were by the rail and not hidden in some corner, she thought, as Geordie left her with a brusque goodnight at her door. She had no choice except to go in the cabin and wait for Dinah.

She did not have long to wait. Dinah, her cheeks rosy from the wind on deck, entered the cabin after a murmured goodnight to Alexander who held the door for her. He kissed Dinah's forehead lightly and nodded to Molly, telling them to sleep well.

"Molly," Dinah exploded breathlessly, "what happend? I saw you and Geordie. . . ."

Molly giggled. "I was just going to ask you that." She sobered quickly, ashamed of her own foolishness, not only in worrying over Dinah but also in the way she had treated Geordie. Even so, after Dinah was in bed and Molly had extinguished the lantern overhead and gone to bed herself, she began to wonder whether her fears were groundless.

Dinah lay quietly in her bunk, but even the roll of the ship, like a cradle being rocked, did not help her sleep. "Molly," she called softly, "are you awake?"

"Yes. Is anything wrong?" Molly raised herself on her elbow, trying to see across the dark cabin.

"I . . . I don't think so." Dinah took a deep breath, not knowing how to begin.

"Is it Alexander?" Molly sat up, reaching for her robe. "Has he done anything?"

"Oh, no!" Dinah was startled. She resisted the impulse to tell Molly about what had happened in the carriage, saying, "I mean, he makes me feel, well, like a lady. It isn't that. Is it all right—proper—for me to go to Hamilton with him?"

Molly lay back, thinking. If the tables were turned, if it were Geordie and she alone, she would have said "yes" and not had a second thought about it. She was sure she could handle the first mate. Dinah was different. Yet, if it had been Captain MacKie accompanying her again Molly would have said "yes" without a second thought.

"Molly?" Dinah called.

"I'm thinking. What you said." The girl was perplexed. "Dinah, I honestly don't know. I wish Mrs. Bradley were here!" she wailed.

"Well, she isn't. It's up to me, I guess." Dinah crossed her arms under her head, staring at the faint lines of the beams overhead. "I think I'll go. I mean, it would be rather silly not to take the opportunity to see the island. I might never have another chance."

"That's right," Molly agreed dubiously.

Dinah went on, talking more to herself than to Molly. "My mother had courage. She left Scotland by herself, with no family to go to. Nothing. When she was alive, she took care of me. Now I have to take care of myself."

"Dinah . . ." Molly sat up again, suddenly worried.

"It's all right, Molly." Dinah's voice was calm. "All I meant was that now I have to make my own decisions. I'm going to Hamilton with Alexander, if he asks again."

"I could go with you," Molly offered.

"No, Molly, I'm not a child." Dinah turned over, cradling the pillow in her arms. "Let's go to sleep now."

If Dinah's breathing quickly regulated in sleep, Molly's did not. Her friend was changing, and she did not know what to make of the change. She would have to watch over her carefully, as Mrs. Bradley had said. Finally, however, she too slept.

Chapter 5

WHEN DINAH AWAKENED, she knew it had to be before dawn from the faint light coming through the portholes. She lay, still drowsy, wondering what had roused her, until she realized it was the silence. During the days at sea, she had become used to the sounds of the ship and the crew as it changed watch, set sails, and started the daily routine of holystoning the decks. Now, there was only the sound of the sea trickling in whispers against the keel and the faint groaning of the masts.

Dinah sat up, worried something had happened, her mind going to the shipwreck Alexander had mentioned. Were they becalmed or had the ship run aground on one of those shoals during the night?

She looked at Molly, curled up on the cot, her usually vivacious face peaceful. Perhaps she should awaken her, she thought, getting out of bed. No, first, she would go on deck. After all, if they had gone aground, if something were wrong, there would surely be more noise. As it was, the ship was too quiet. She picked up some clothing and went into the sitting room, shutting the connecting door.

On deck, she looked around. In the east, a faint pink light suffused the sky, heralding the sun's rising, while overhead, a few stars still shone in the pearl-gray sky. Most of the sails were furled, with only the jib set to provide steerageway for the ship. A few sailors lolled on a hatch, smoking pipes and sipping mugs of steaming tea.

Dinah had never seen, much less heard, the ship so quiet. She moved out of the shadow of the cabin, wondering where Captain MacKie and Alexander were. As she did, the captain who was standing by the wheel saw her and called to her.

Dinah joined him, asking in a hushed voice inspired by the silence of the ship, "Is anything the matter?"

"Nothing, Lass," the captain assured her with a smile. "It's the shoals. I don't want to hit one in the dark, so we're waiting for sunrise when we can see to take soundings."

"We've reached Bermuda?" Dinah looked eagerly around, seeing only the grayness of the sea and a slightly darker line ahead.

"Aye. Come here." The captain led her to the wheel where she could see straight ahead without her view being obscured by masts or spars. A light, seemingly suspended in air, blinked regularly. "That's

Gibbs Hill Lighthouse, near where we'll be docking. It can be seen forty miles at sea."

"We still have that long a way to go?" Dinah was disappointed.

"Nay, Lass. Half that, I'd say, or less. We'll be docked and unloading by noon. So, you're eager to be on land again, eh?"

"A little. I've never been anywhere." She smiled shyly. "You've been so many places . . ."

"And you will, too, Lass," the captain promised. "Now, how about a cup of tea in the chart house. It's chill standing here on deck, although the day will be warm enough.'"

Dinah nodded. She was beginning to get cold, and the warmth of the chart house, where a lantern cast a golden glow over the large charts, was attractive. Taking the cup of strong, hot tea she was offered, she moved to the chart table. "Where are we, captain?"

The captain smiled again. Here he was in his element. He pointed to one chart that showed the expanse of the Atlantic. At the left edge was the coast of the United States, at the other, the coast of Europe. A pencil line was drawn from New York to a tiny dot that seemed lost in the vast space off North Carolina.

"There," the captain explained, his finger on the dot, before taking another chart, somewhat smaller, that showed the dot in detail as actually being three islands in a rough fish-hook shape, surrounding a large bay spotted with small islands. He pointed to the western end of the fish hook. "That's the Dockyard, where we'll be putting in. Here," he moved his finger to cover a cross-hatched spot on the eastern side of the bay, "that's Hamilton, where Mr. Douglas must go tomorrow to arrange for a cargo—if he can."

"It looks so small—and so big," Dinah mused, staring at the different scale of the charts and missing the sarcasm in the captain's voice.

MacKie chuckled. "Well, Bermuda's about the size of your Manhattan."

Dinah laughed at her ignorance. "That seems large to me, too."

The captain joined in her laughter, patting her shoulder with an awkward gesture, his eyes on her face, still fresh and childlike from sleep. "Miss Murray," he began before a shout from the deck sent him outside.

The sun had risen, and the flat seas spread in a flashing silver carpet to the south where the dark shadow now had a green tinge. While Dinah watched, the captain gave orders for the sails to be unfurled and stationed a sailor forward with a sounding lead. As the sun rose higher, the seas changed color, here and there daubs of green staining the bright blue water. The green, she realized, must be the shoals that they had to avoid.

When she looked again at the wheel, Alexander had joined MacKie. His hands were thrust in his pockets, and his head was thrown back, his whole posture one of excitement that infected Dinah. She went toward them and the sailor standing at the wheel, his eyes on the compass binnacle as his powerful arms moved the wheel a fraction.

The scene fascinated Dinah. The sailor forward swung a line, knotted at various distances to mark the fathom depth, over his head and threw the lead ahead of the ship. When the line was perpendicular to the ship, he pulled it up again, calling out the fathoms, before heaving the line again. The action had the motion of a dance.

According to what the sailor called out, the captain gave orders to the helmsman, telling him to keep steady on the course or to change course two or three points east or west. Ahead of them, the line of green grew steadily larger. The wind was softer, warmer, even flower scented now.

Almost before Dinah knew it, they had reached the Dockyard, where sailors were standing by the railing ready to heave the heavy hawsers ashore to the men waiting on deck. Sails were furled and the wooden hull of the ship lurched against the pier with the grinding of wood against wood.

Alexander, who had been standing by Dinah, explaining now and then what was happening, smiled at her. "Well, we're here! Why don't you go below, have your breakfast, and later we'll go ashore."

Dinah nodded. It must be well past eight, and Molly would be worried about where she was. She hurried to the cabin to find Molly just stirring after lying awake so long the night before in her concern about Dinah.

"Get up, Lazybones," Dinah called. "We're docked. Don't you want to see Bermuda?"

Molly leaped out of bed, wrapping a robe around her as Johnny knocked at their door. The boy's shy smile as he set the tray on the table betrayed his excitement. He nodded quickly, before scurrying out toward the deck.

The two young women ate speedily and went on deck. To their surprise, the air now had a tropic warmth that must be due to the Gulf Stream that Alexander had mentioned. They looked around, and Dinah noticed that the dockyard was far more than just that. Nearby, too near for comfort, was a high wall of massive stone blocks, on top of which were embrasures bristling with the gleaming black muzzles of cannon. It was one of several forts that gave Bermuda the title of the Gibralter of the West.

Alexander was on the dock, talking to a middle-aged Englishman and Captain MacKie. Finally the three men shook hands, and the master and captain of the *Star of Scotland* returned aboard. Alexander saw the two girls and came toward them.

"We'll be unloading shortly, and you'll be in the way on deck." He smiled at their consternation. "Don't worry, I've made arrangements for Geordie to escort you ashore to see the fort, if you'd like."

"Oh, yes," the two chorused in one voice.

"I thought you might like to get off the ship for a while," Alexander laughed. "Take your time. By the way, Dinah," he laid a hand on her arm, "you and I have been invited to the Commissioner's for dinner this evening. I'd like you to dress."

Dinah looked uncertainly from Alexander to Molly.

71

Molly gave a quick nod of approval, telling Dinah not to worry.

"Wear your hair up," Alexander went on, as much for Molly's benefit as for Dinah's. He hailed Geordie, who was going toward the chart house. Geordie readily agreed to accompany the two women. He donned his uniform jacket and hat and joined them at the gangplank where a soldier was lounging under the now hot sun, waiting to act as their guide. The soldier's face was red and shiny above the high neck of his blue wool, tightly-fitted jacket with its row of brass buttons, and he mopped it with a sweaty cloth. When he saw them, however, he placed his cockaded black patent hat on his head and snapped off a sharp salute. Geordie returned the salute, although less smartly, while the two young women, taken by surprise, managed polite nods.

The soldier led them along a path beside a wide moat to a drawbridge, which they had to walk across to reach the outer gate set in the fort's formidable walls. Passing between the solid, iron-barred doors, Dinah and Molly were awed, and even Geordie, who had grown up in Edinburgh, was impressed.

The gate led to the Keep Yard, a large quadrangle rimmed by a gravel road, that also served as a parade ground. At one end, a squad of soldiers, rifles on their shoulders, were marching to the brisk accompaniment of orders called out hoarsely and yet so expressionlessly they had the sound of a familiar ritual. They wore the same uniform as the guide, the blue stained dark under their arms from the heat.

"Royal Engineers honor guard," the guide commented. "Easy duty, if yer like to march. They practice every day."

Dinah assumed the guide liked neither marching nor the hot sun that poured into the Keep Yard. If the high walls of the fort were supposed to keep enemies out, they also succeeded in keeping out any cool sea breeze. The soldier, as a result, clung to a narrow ribbon of shade cast by a solid, two-story building of large stone blocks. He paused at the edge of the shadow, near an iron-studded door, looking back at the building where only a few windows high under the eaves broke the solid stone walls.

"That's a magazine. Holds eleven tons of gunpowder," the soldier said ominously. "And that," he pointed just beyond to a similar, smaller building, "holds more ammunition."

Ahead of them, at the end of the Yard, was a third similar building, except that this one, with windows set in military precision in its walls, was in the process of being completed. Dinah watched the workmen carrying large, flat flagstones for the floor.

The soldier followed her gaze and chuckled. "Yer'd think it were new, wouldn't yer? Well, it ain't. It was started in the early 1850's, but the yellow fever killed off the convicts from England and Scotland that were building it, and us soldiers had to go to fight in the Crimea. That's the Army fer yer."

Dinah shivered, despite the heat surrounding her in a moist cloak. All the soldier could talk about, it seemed, was the Army and fighting.

She was glad to leave the Keep Yard for the lower yard, which had formed the original fort. It was small enough to have fit in one end of the Keep Yard, but its size made it even more impressive. In front of them was a pastoral lagoon, though where it flowed through an arch in the massive wall she could see the spiked iron fringe of a grilled portcullis, raised now, but poised for lowering at the first sign of any menace from the seas beyond.

"In case we're ever besieged, which ain't likely," the soldier began pompously, "you can see we're well protected by that there Water Gate against anyone sneaking in. What's more, ships can anchor under the walls, our ships, that is, and under the guns, and we can supply 'em with gunpowder and water by barge while we protect 'em by firing over their heads."

Geordie nodded. He had found the military information interesting, if the young women had not, but worthy as he found the idea of the Water Gate, he preferred to think of ships as protecting the island.   ,

The heat in the lower yard was as oppressive to Dinah and Molly as the explanations of military requirements. The two girls fanned themselves with their handkerchiefs, looking at the bright blue, cloudless sky high above the fort's walls. Near the lagoon, a broad incline, wide enough for gun carriages, led to the ramparts. To their dismay, their soldier guide now started for it.

Once on the ramparts, he pointed out the barracks at the other end of the fort, where another incline led upwards to permit soldiers to man the guns directly without having to lose time by crossing the Keep Yard. The soldier leaned against the ramparts wall in the shade of a gun to enjoy a pipe, telling the three visitors to take their time walking along the ramparts.

Despite the sun, the walk was cool, the wall so high that it caught a refreshing sea breeze that fanned their faces, offering relief from the closed-in heat of the Keep Yard. Dinah paused at one gun placement, waving Geordie and Molly on. She rested her cheek against the cool stone, staring out at the *Star of Scotland*. Thinking about Alexander and Captain MacKie, she let her mind drift and wished she were a little older so she could understand the conflicting emotions that the two men roused in her. She recognized all too well that she knew little about men. In fact, what men had she even had any acquaintance with before Alexander?

Mr. Bradley had been a distant figure, rarely at home when she was in the house and even then seldom visiting the nursery or the school room. The son, ten years older than she, had ignored both Dinah and his sister with the superiority of all growing boys. Then, there were the servants, but because of her mother's position in the house she had spent little time in their quarters. As far as relationships between men and women were concerned, she was almost totally ignorant. Granted, when she had her first period, her mother had been forced to talk to her about being a woman and having babies, giving her a vague idea of the difference between male and female anatomy. She had learned a little more from Molly who came from a large family and who was sometimes free with downstairs gossip. Yet, nothing had prepared her for the way her heart pounded when she was near Alexander, for the desire and the pleasurable sensation she had felt that day she had felt him pulsating and hot against her.

Geordie and Molly had found a niche of their own. Squeezed between the embrasure and the gun carriage, they too looked at the sea. Geordie pointed out the shoals, the patches of green on the shifting blue waters, and the islands, all of which Molly had missed by staying in her bed. Drawing her even closer, he explained that the green trees in the distance were the end of the island, which was shaped like a fish hook.

His closeness excited Molly. "You don't say," she murmured, twisting her body to see better—and so that her full breasts under the light madras dress she was wearing brushed Geordie's chest. His jacket was open, due to the heat, and she could feel the sudden pounding of his heart.

"Molly," Geordie looked at her face, the round blue eyes and the full mouth open and panting a little.

"Yes?" They were so close that her breath brushed his cheek, as her hands slipped under his jacket in invitation. His kiss was sweet on her lips, not bruising or rough as Jim's had been, and she arched with pleasure as his hands stroked her back.

Yet, this was not the time or the place. Any second Dinah or the soldier might come looking for them. Reluctantly, they drew apart. "Tonight," Molly whispered, "Dinah's coming ashore for dinner. It might be nice to have company."

Geordie grinned. "I've never known a woman like you, Molly. The girls at home, they're either on to you like flies or so frosty . . ."

Molly's hand patted his cheek. "You're different, too, Geordie, not like the men in New York."

"Then maybe you won't want to go back," Geordie suggested.

Molly smiled, "I think I know what you mean—and maybe I won't." She glanced around. "Dinah will think we're lost."

Molly left the gun port first, just in time to see Dinah walking toward her. The two girls and the man rejoined the soldier, who straightened up and knocked the bowl of his pipe against the wall. Before they left the rampart, he pointed out the grandiose house above the Keep Yard where a cliff formed a natural part of the fortifications. It was the commissioner's house, where Dinah would be dining that evening, and he claimed it was so large that the stable held eleven horses.

Dinah thought apprehensively of the evening ahead, as the soldier saw them to the outer gate, the only means of access to the fort from the land, and saluted them in farewell. The three walked toward the ship, where one line of men were still climbing the gangway, passing other men who descended with barrels on their shoulders.

"The land feels so strange," Dinah giggled. "I feel like I'm still on the deck of a ship."

Geordie laughed, moving closer to Molly. "That's because you have your sea legs. Just wait until we get to Scotland. It will take you a few days instead of a few hours to get over the feeling of still being on a ship."

Scotland! It still seeemed a dream to Dinah. In fact, Bermuda was a dream, too, even though she was here. She had the feeling that she would awaken and find herself in the carriage house at the back of Washington Square. But no, she told herself, that life was over forever. A new one lay ahead, one which teased her imagination. She would no longer be a quiet-as-a-mouse governess's child. She would be a lady, free to do what she wanted, and the dinner with the Commissioner would be a hint of what that life would be like.

Molly dressed Dinah's hair high, with the two side curls, as Alexander had suggested. The two young women, their eyes thoughtful, discussed Dinah's wardrobe, discarding dress after dress until deciding on one that left Dinah's shoulders bare. It had a matching shawl that Dinah could wear if the evening were cooler than the day, as it surely would be.

"Oh, Dinah," Molly gasped, "just look at yourself!"

Dinah stared at herself in the mirror. Almost overnight she had filled out. Her cheeks were fuller, with only a trace of hollows under the cheekbones to enhance the amber, almond-shaped eyes. The nose that she had always considered too long was still aquiline, but now it had an aristocratic hauteur, and the sun had imparted a rosy flush to her pale ivory skin. Nothing, of course, could change the redness of her hair, which took second place to the loveliness of her face.

It was not only her face that had filled out. Also gone were the hollows under her collar bones, and the tight bodice of the dress revealed full breasts, whose roundness the off-the-shoulder neckline emphasized. "If only," Dinah sighed, "I weren't so tall!"

Molly laughed. "I wouldn't worry about that. Alexander is much taller than you—and so is Captain MacKie. And just wait until they see you!"

Molly watched Dinah take the shawl and pick up her gloves. Her friend had always had a natural grace, and Mrs. Murray had insisted on good posture. The result was a fluid beauty, the head held high on the slender neck while the body seemed to float over the ground.

The young maid opened the door at Alexander's knock, eager to see what he would say when he saw Dinah. There was no need for words. He looked at Dinah and was speechless and immobile for a moment, his eyes hungrily fastened on the loveliness before him.

Dinah took his silence for disapproval. "Do I look all right?" she asked anxiously.

Alexander's mouth curved in a smile. He stepped forward and took her hands in his, bestowing a kiss on her cheek. "You are a true Diana, and I am proud to be your escort."

Alexander's warm approval gave Dinah a new confidence. By the time they were in the salon at the commissioner's house, the new hair style and gown and the glow of Alexander's approval had changed her. Mrs. Bradley would have had a difficult time recognizing the shy, retiring girl she had seen off a few days before.

The salon was hardly what Dinah had expected in a fort so bristling with military might. It was elegantly furnished with fragile, highly-polished mahogany furniture and lit by crystal chandeliers. Delicate floral wallpaper covered the walls, and fine Brussels carpets were thick underfoot.

The commssioner was a heavy-set man, his face reddened by the sun that had turned his gray hair yellow. He kissed Dinah's hand with the flare of a courtier and introduced her to his wife, Lady Anne, a slender woman in her late 30's whose lavender silk dress, lavished with lace, seemed formal for this isolated spot.

Lady Anne greeted Dinah eagerly, with the hunger of an exile for news of the world—even if that world were New York and not her native London. Dinah groped in her memory for tidbits about society she had heard from Mrs. Bradley, while the commissioner and Alexander talked business. Dinah caught the names of people whom the commissioner was evidently suggesting Alexander should see.

Dinah was relieved when dinner was announced by a black man, a descendant of slaves imported in the early days of the colony who had been freed in early 1800's, long before the Civil War. She studied the butler curiously, as he served dinner, fascinated by the kneebreeches and silk coat that she imagined worn by Queen Victoria's footmen. Her original doubts returned. How would she fit into Edinburgh if this were a sample of life there? Then, she saw Alexander's eyes watching her and their approval, and she relaxed. If Alexander were not worrying, she would not worry either, she decided, turning her attention to the conversation.

Alexander was talking about the fort, which had impressed him with its strength as much as it had Geordie. The utility of the Water Gate had particularly fascinated him.

"But you don't use it for prisoners." Alexander commented, thinking of the Tower of London.

The commissioner, a Londoner like his wife, caught his implication and chuckled. Noticing Dinah's puzzlement, he explained, "The Tower of London is an old fortification dating from long before Queen Elizabeth. Actually, it includes many buildings, but the original tower was used as a prison. Although it could be entered from London proper, it had a water gate on the Thames River, which was used to avoid the prisoners' having to be taken through the streets of London where they might attract unwelcome attention. The only prisoner who entered the Tower through the Water Gate and left alive was Princess Elizabeth, before she was queen, of course."

Dinah nodded, her eyes wide. She was learning so much that it was hard for her to absorb everything. "Do you miss London?" she asked, thinking more of herself going as far from her home as the commissioner and his wife were from theirs.

"No," the commissioner replied. "The island and its beautiful weather more than make up for London with its fog. It's a paradise, really."

Lady Anne, sitting at the opposite end of the table, said shortly, "Like the Garden of Eden."

The commissioner frowned slightly at her. "It used to be isolated, it's true, although ever since Princess Louise came here for her health, it's become quite popular. Packet boats from New York now arrive every fortnight."

"I see." Dinah was becoming more curious about the rest of the island. If it were a resort, then what she had seen so far of what seemed a fortress island was incorrect.

"You'll see for yourself tomorrow," the commissioner promised. A sudden idea came to him. "I say, Mr. Douglas, why don't I lend you a carriage and horses to drive into Hamilton? It's longer than going by boat across the sound, but it will give you a chance to see Bermuda. After all, if you're going to be doing business here . . ." He paused, turning to his wife whose comment about the Garden of Eden had made him aware of how isolated she was. "My dear, didn't you want to go to Hamilton soon to shop?"

"Why, yes," Lady Anne answered, surprised and pleased.

"Good. We could drive in with you," he offered. "Then, you can hire a boat to return, whenever your business is finished. It's a much shorter distance by water than land."

Alexander thanked the commissioner. He could hardly turn down the generous offer from an official on whose good graces he might have to depend. He was also a little relieved. Not knowing anything about the island, he had assumed the Dockyard was near Hamilton, but he had found out that the land route led along a sweeping curve, making the trip a long one. Aside from the practical reason, there was a personal one. He enjoyed riding, and the idea of riding a horse appealed to him right now.

He thought of his half-formed plans of spending the day with Dinah and regretted that it would not be what he had hoped. He almost wished now that he had not invited her, since—thanks to the commissioner and his introduction—he would be busy investigating the prospects for future trade. Thank goodness he could leave Dinah with Lady Anne.

He dismissed Dinah from his mind, however, over brandy and cigars with the commissioner after dinner, his thoughts being given over to the commissioner's suggestions as to whom he should see first. His mind was still on business as he and Dinah made their farewells and followed the soldier whom the commissioner had summoned to light their way with a torch across the Keep Yard and back to the ship.

Alexander was so silent that Dinah was confused. He had seemed so lighthearted earlier that she was sure she had done or said something to hurt or disappoint him.

They reached the ship to find several sailors relaxing on deck. The rest of the crew had been given leave to go ashore, and the sailors left aboard would have their turn the next night. They gave a polite salute to the ship's master and nodded to Dinah.

Alexander frowned at their presence. Despite his preoccupation, he had looked forward to having a few minutes alone with Dinah to say goodnight. The sight of her in the torchlight in the low dress that exposed her ivory shoulders and the rise of her breasts had aroused the same feelings he had felt on the first morning. Now, he had no choice except to escort her to her cabin where Molly was waiting and where he forced himself to say a quick goodnight.

Dinah, puzzled at Alexander's brusqueness and even more afraid she had said or done something out of ignorance, entered the cabin. A startled Geordie, sitting with his arms around Molly, stumbled to his feet. Molly, her hair loose, blushed.

"Miss Dinah!" Molly sprang to her feet. "I didn't expect you back so early." Her hands fumbled with her hair.

Dinah was too lost in her thoughts to notice the two and their embarrassment. She told them goodnight and went to the sleeping cabin to undress and get into bed before Molly joined her.

Molly and Geordie stared at one another. They had had supper and a bottle of wine, talking lightly of their separate lives. After Johnny had removed the dishes, they had sat on the small settee, Molly's head dropping against his shoulder, her cheek brushing his. Their kiss had been long and passionate, and Geordie had loosened her hair. Any inhibitions Molly might have had, dissolved in the wine she had drunk rather freely. Geordie, too, was different here, alone with

Molly and away from the ever-present eyes of captain and crew. His hands found their way to her breasts, rubbing them gently until the nipples were hard when he finally undid her buttons.

When Molly did not stop him, his hands found their way to the soft curly hair between her legs. Only then did Molly reach out to touch him, making sure his shaft was firm and hard. In Molly's experience, women were taken. Any pleasure men gave to women was in the act itself. Not that Molly did not enjoy sex. She did—more than she would admit. Granted, her sexual awakening had been far from pleasant, but with Jim she had learned to enjoy it. It had always been he, however, who instigated the act, quickly and even furtively. They had never lain naked together. At the most, Jim had removed his trousers and she, her pantaloons. And so, now, with Geordie, she had expected no more and no less.

Her body quivered under the young man's hands, as her hips rose under his hands. Quickly, he removed his trousers, one hand guiding his swollen organ into the warm depths of the eager Molly. She was panting, her breath hot against his cheek, her hands pressing his naked buttocks until he was as far into her as he could go. She squirmed against him, waiting for his ejaculation, anticipating it with the wet warmth of her climax. Geordie groaned in the swiftness of his ejaculation.

"Molly, Molly," he whispered, holding her close, "I love you, Lass."

"Oh, Geordie!" The girl kissed his cheek, one hand brushing back the shock of red hair. Tears rose in her eyes. No one had ever told her before that he loved her.

Overhead, footsteps rang on the deck, and they parted hurriedly to put on the few garments they had removed. As the steps disappeared, they grinned sheepishly at one another. Molly took her place on the settee and patted the spot next to her. "Come sit by me, Geordie. Tell me again. . . ."

Geordie sat down next to her and took her in his

arms. Neither heard Dinah's light step outside the door, which made it no wonder they were startled by her sudden appearance. Alone again, they did not know what to say. The moment for tenderness had passed.

Molly studied Geordie, his red hair, the freckles, in a new light. In all her dreams, she had never dared to dream she would find a better life than to be married to a footman who might become a butler. Now, here was Geordie, a first mate on a large ship and one day perhaps even captain of his own ship. She could be a captain's wife, no longer a lady's maid, if she played her cards right, and she began to regret her behavior.

"You must go now, Geordie," Molly whispered, her hands urging him toward the door. Against her will, she could feel her body trembling at the nearness of him.

Geordie smiled at her, saying earnestly, "I meant it, Molly. I-I love you. You . . . you're beautiful."

Tears rose again in the girl's eyes. "About tonight . . ."

"Hush. I may not be the first, but," his cheeks went red, "you have a lot to learn, my love."

"Geordie, Geordie!" Molly threw herself in his arms, forgetting Dinah for the moment. He kissed her again, more tenderly than before, leaving reluctantly but of his own free will.

Molly went into the adjoining cabin. Seeing Dinah lying on her side embracing the pillow, she undressed quickly and slipped into bed. Molly thought she would never be able to sleep, but like Dinah before her, she fell asleep almost immediately, her dreams of Geordie disturbed all too soon by Alexander's knocking on the outer cabin door to awaken Dinah at dawn.

Dinah dressed while eating a quick breakfast of tea and bread and butter. She went on deck to meet Alexander, just as a carriage and two saddle horses arrived at the gangplank. Dinah would ride in the carriage with Lady Anne, while Alexander and the commissioner rode ahead on horseback.

Lady Anne pointed out the sights along the road that followed the cliffs on the Atlantic side of the island to Dinah. Marvelous bays rimmed with pink sand nestled at the foot of enormous cliffs. Their names were a recitation of the island's lineage and history. There were West Whale Bay and East Whale Bay, Church Bay, Boat Bay, Horseshoe Bay, Chaplin Bay and Jobson Cove, Coral Bay and Grape Bay. Along the way grew tropic vegetation such as Dinah had never seen. Red and white hibiscis were just opening for the day, their blooms vivid against the dense green foliage. Purple bougainvillea wove their vines into a carpet for royalty. Here and there, passion flowers, their purple circles surrounded by yellow and red, seemed vivid brooches set with precious stones. Behind the lush flowers could be glimpsed the sparkling white fronts of large plantation houses.

As they approached Hamilton, the scattered houses grew closer together. Lady Anne turned to Dinah impulsively. "Won't you miss New York?"

Dinah smiled, explaining about her mother, and the woman nodded thoughtfully. "Still, you're going so far away. But you're young . . ."

Dinah looked at Lady Anne curiously. "You miss London?"

"Oh, yes!" The older woman sighed. "My husband doesn't—he has his work. But I often dream I'm in London, going to Court or just riding through Piccadilly, Hyde Park. . . ." She laughed. "I shall always miss it, the parties, the balls in season, the shops, and, of course, my family and my friends."

Dinah thought of the house on Washington Square. It was hard to believe that she would ever miss it with that same sense of lingering loss—her future was so full of promise.

They had reached Hamilton, the village nestling against a hill and facing the clear blue harbor and the green hills of the opposite shore, dotted by white houses. To Dinah, whose experience included only

New York and its rapid growth uptown, Hamilton was like a dolls' town, with some buildings a gleaming white, others painted in pastels. Along Front Street, the main street that bordered the harbor, were stores, most with veranda-like projections protruding over the raised sidewalk to shield pedestrians from the hot sun. They drove directly to the Princess Hotel, where the men freshened up and went on their way, eager to get business done, while the women took their time, lingering over breakfast.

As Lady Anne poured second cups of tea, she told Dinah about the shops, saying that, although they were nowhere as grand as London's and probably not like New York's, they offered a good selection. The influx of tourists the past few years, for one thing, had increased their choice of luxury goods. She suggested that before they shop, they walk along Front Street and stretch their legs after the carriage ride.

Dinah agreed. She admired the shops, noticing the women in their pastel summer dresses of fine linen, some trimmed with lace, with matching parasols to protect their English complexions from the sun. The scene was so different from the New York Dinah had left, and not only because of the women. The men, mostly with tanned faces under their broad-brimmed hats, rode saddle horses and bowed to the ladies in their open carriages, as if just about everyone knew each other.

Lady Anne nodded to a few of the women. Although she and the commissioner were invited to the plantations and big houses, living where they did, she was not familiar with as many of the island's inhabitants as the women who lived in Hamilton and St. George, the original settlement at the opposite end of the island from Somerset.

As they walked back toward the hotel, Lady Anne suggested that they go to Trimingham's first. It was one of the oldest shops on the island and had a good selection of china. She wanted to replace a breakfast set that she had brought from England but that was missing a few pieces. While Lady Anne investigated the china, Dinah wandered around the shop, gazing at the lengths of English woolens and linens.

At Smith's, a relatively new shop, she was drawn to a selection of Scottish tartans. The plaid patterns reminded her of the shawl which her mother had kept long after it was worn from being used to wrap Dinah against the cold of winter. A clerk explained that the tartans were clan symbols, each clan having its own design.

Dinah nodded and described the two-tone dark plaid with its bright red stripes that her mother had had. The clerk did not recognize it, although she brought out several to show Dinah, including a Hunting Stewart in dark green with wide black stripes and narrow ones of yellow and red.

"If your mother was Scottish," the clerk said thoughtfully, "if I knew her name, maybe we have it."

"It's Murray," Dinah told her.

The clerk shook her head. "No, we don't have it, but there is a Murray plaid."

Dinah smiled her thanks. She would have to wait until she was in Edinburgh to ask. She returned to Lady Anne, who was arranging for her purchases to be delivered to the Princess Hotel.

Since the shops were closing for the mid-day dinner hour, Lady Anne and Dinah walked back to the hotel. They were joined shortly by the commissioner who escorted them into the dining room, explaining that Alexander was making arrangements for a cargo and would meet Dinah later.

After dinner, the commissioner and Lady Anne left to return to the Dockyard. Dinah went to a terrace on the harbor to sit and read a London magazine as she waited. The time went quickly. The harbor was busy, filled with all types of small craft skimming the water and providing public transportation from Hamilton to the opposite shore. With their white sails, the darting boats were like a flock of gulls scavenging the clear blue water for food.

Alexander arrived at tea time, exuberant over his success. A cargo of cedar would be loaded the next day, and in two days they would be on their way to Scotland. Dinah smiled, happy for him and happy he had lost his dourness of the night before.

"Dinah," Alexander leaned across the table to take her hands, "you've brought me luck again. There's good business here. Why, we could build a ship just for the Bermuda-New York trade alone—with more room for passengers than on the *Star of Scotland!* But," he smiled, "you're not interested in that."

"I am," Dinah insisted. "I'd like to learn more about ships and what you do . . ."

"Business isn't for women," Alexander chided with a laugh.

"Then, what is?" Dinah challenged. She could not imagine sitting and doing needlepoint all day. Besides, the world, which had seemed so wide before, was even wider now. Dinah was confident that there was nothing now that she could not do.

"To be attractive to men," Alexander replied softly, wondering at the change in the girl. Last night, she had been as composed as if she had been going to formal dinners all her life. And today, she had a self-confidence that he had not noticed before. If the shy, frightened girl had attracted him, this woman fascinated him. He looked into her eyes, seeing a new boldness in them. Perhaps there was something to what Ian MacKie had said about growing up fast at sea, he thought.

Chapter 6

TWO DAYS AFTER the trip to Hamilton, the *Star of Scotland* sailed for home. Despite Alexander's wanting to spend a few more days exploring the island—and teaching Dinah to ride—he had given in to Captain MacKie's urging that they leave. It was the hurricane season, and the captain wanted to sail while the weather held. He had been caught a few times in sudden savage storms, such as the one that had wrecked the Virginia supply ships on the Bermuda shoals. The story of that storm, he had heard from the local sailors, had been the basis of Shakespeare's play, "The Tempest."

Once they were at sea, the routine of the voyage set in. The two young women, with little to do, found time heavy on their hands—especially Molly, as Geordie had little time to spend with her. There were only so many ways they could fix their hair, so many hours they could spend dressing for dinner. There was only so much they could ask about Scotland. Still, whenever they had the chance, they asked Alexander, Captain MacKie and Geordie, endless questions about Scotland, most of which the men could not answer since they were about what Dinah would do during the day. Alexander had little idea how his sister Margaret spent her time, except for going to the theater in the evening or to dinner parties and balls; the other men were at sea too much to know what the waiting women did.

Suddenly, the monotony of the voyage was broken. Two weeks out of Bermuda, Dinah and Molly were awakened abruptly as the ship seemed to crash around them. Planking that had been creaking before seemed to be shrieking. The heavy chairs on which they sat to eat their meals were sliding and scraping along the deck of the cabin to bang against walls as if they were being thrown by a giant. Anything that was not nailed down was being tossed about—including Dinah and Molly. As the ship plunged and rolled, she was bouncing on the bunk like a baby in a wildly rocking cradle. One particular wallow seemed to send the ship almost on its port side, and a small scream escaped from Dinah's frightened lips.

"Dinah," Molly called from the cot where she was clutching the frame, "are you all right?"

"I-I think so!" Dinah struggled to the edge of the bunk, trying to sit up. Her stomach was in her throat, tainting her mouth with a bitter acid taste. Sitting up, however, helped, to her relief. The taste was still there, although her stomach had returned to its normal position.

Molly groaned as the ship slid into another plunge that sent her stomach churning. "I'm going to be sick," she managed to say. "We're going to die! I wish I were home!" she wailed.

Molly's distress made Dinah forget her own. She felt around for her robe and pulled it on. Hanging onto the bulkhead for support, she inched her way across the cabin floor to where Molly lay huddled in the cot. The cold floor reassured Dinah with its solidity. The nausea receded in her desire to help Molly.

"Get up, Molly," Dinah urged. "You'll feel better. It's only a storm," she said soothingly.

Molly was not to be comforted. A roll of the ship that sent Dinah tumbling off balance onto the cot brought another scream from Molly, but under Dinah's urging she managed to sit up and did feel better. The two girls, wrapped in a blanket, clung to one another, listening to the ship's groaning protests against the wrath of the storm, protests so loud they never heard the pounding on the door. Then they saw Alexander opening the door and holding a lantern high.

But it was an Alexander who was a stranger. Any vestige of the well-dressed, cultured gentleman who had been so at home in Mrs. Bradley's parlor had been torn from him by the gale winds raging outside. He was Heathcliff returned from a rampage on the desolate moors in "Wuthering Heights," Dinah thought, seeing his black hair matted to his forehead by the rain and his eyes sparkling with the excitement that the storm roused in him. The swaying light broadened his cheekbones, flaming like fire along them. Dinah stared at him, at the naked power and life in his face, her heart beating a pounding counterpoint to the storm. If they were sinking, she would be with Alexander.

"You're all right, then," he said with relief, seeing the two girls sitting up and watching him. "It's just a bad storm."

"We're sinking!" Molly wailed.

"No!" Alexander laughed. "It's a sturdy ship, a good Scottish ship with a good Scottish captain and crew. You've naught to worry."

A crash overhead made him pause to listen. The shouts he hears sobered him, and he said, "I must go on deck. Stay below—I'll send Johnny with a light and some food." He started to leave, turning back to add, "Don't worry. The storm isn't the end of the world, although we are in for some rough weather."

The cabin boy arrived shortly. Once the lanterns were lit and the young women had dressed they felt a little better, and the tea and bread and butter that Johnny had brought helped lift their spirits.

For Molly, the recovery was brief. The pitching of the ship sent her back to bed, this time with a basin. Dinah tried to comfort her, but all the girl wanted was to be left alone. Dinah, ashamed of herself, left the maid to her misery. Still, she knew if she stayed in the small, stuffy sleeping cabin much longer, she would be sick as well as Molly. And one of them had to be well enough to take care of them both.

Despite Alexander's warning about staying below, she knew she had to have some air. She made her way slowly along the companionway, holding tightly to the railing and taking her time when the ship seemed to be tossed high on the crest of a wave before plunging into the sea-trough with a wobbling roll.

The sight on deck made her legs go weak. Rolling waves crashed over the rails, washing the deck midships, and she could barely see the foredeck for the foaming, forthy, curling water that obscured it as the helmsman attempted to keep the ship headed into the wind. If the water from the sea were not bad enough, rain was lashing the decks. The crash that had sent Alexander on deck must have been the ship's lifeboat. It was swinging dangerously in its davits, half freed from them by the screaming wind, while sailors worked frantically to lash it secure.

Dinah knew it was too dangerous to go on deck. Yet, she could not bear to retreat to the cabin where she felt trapped by the storm and Molly's illness. She began to understand the wild expression in Alexander's eyes. The storm excited her, too, and she raised her face to the sky, ignoring the rain beating into the companionway. It was impossible to tell what time it was. The sky was filled with black clouds, as rolling and enormous as the waves of the ocean, and so low she felt she could reach up and touch them.

"I thought I told you to stay below!" Alexander appeared out of the storm, looming over her.

"I needed some fresh air," Dinah screamed over the wind. "Molly's sick."

"The decks of a ship are no place for a woman in a storm," Alexander replied. He took her arm roughly, intending to push her back into the companionway, as the ship, carried on the crest of a wave, plunged into another trough. The two of them were thrown together, and Alexander held her in his arms to steady them both. The perfume in her hair mixed with the salt spray made him feel drunk. His arms tightened, and he could feel her heart beating in her slender body pressed against his chest.

Dinah could see the pulsing of a vein in Alexander's temple and the ripple of a muscle along his jaw.

91

The motion of the ship made it impossible for her to free herself—but she didn't want to. Her whole life seemed to be condensed into the wild passion of the storm and the pressure of Alexander's body against hers.

"My God," Alexander murmured, seeing the expression on her face. A momentary break in the storm gave him the chance to lead Dinah below. He stopped at the door of the master's cabin.

"Molly's sick," Dinah objected, wanting to stay outside. "She's sleeping."

"In here, then." He took her to the captain's cabin, which was empty, his eyes on her face and the amber eyes, wide with excitement, reading into that excitement a response to his own. He knew the captain would remain on deck until the storm abated. At the moment, anyway, he was busy directing the securing of the lifeboat.

"You're cold," Alexander said, seating Dinah on the bench under the sternlight, while he poured her a glass of cognac.

The strong brandy burned Dinah's throat, but it tasted good, warming her, chasing away any fears she might have about being alone in the cabin with Alexander. Alexander himself was standing in front of her, warming her hands holding the glass between his, his body graceful on his spread legs as he rolled with the ship.

Dinah smiled at him. She felt safe with him to protect her from the storm the way he had on deck that first day when the roll of the ship had torn her fingers loose from the rigging. If he had not been there, she might have gone overboard and no one would have known.

When Alexander refilled the glass with cognac and sat beside her, she leaned against him, letting him put his arm around her, despite the warning that flashed in her brain. The storm and the cognac had dulled the sharpness of the warning. Alexander had saved her life, he couldn't—wouldn't—hurt her.

Alexander's eyes took in the trust in the girl's face.

She was so relaxed that she was almost asleep. He had to go back on deck to help if he could, but he could not leave her sitting there in MacKie's cabin. On an impulse, he picked her up and carried her to the bunk where he laid her down, starting to rearrange her cloak to cover her.

The young woman's blouse was open. In her hurry to dress, her fingers had missed half the buttons and the ivory swell of her breasts shone luminously in the half light of the cabin. Alexander hesitated, before starting to fasten the buttons. His breathing was ragged as he yielded to the impulse that had been mounting since the first time he had kissed Dinah.

Dinah's pleasant drowsiness faded, when she felt Alexander's mouth brushing her nipples. She struggled against his kisses on her breasts, her throat, her mouth.

"Alexander!" she cried out, trying to push him away.

The man did not hear her. His mouth crushing hers smothered her calls for help, as his hands tore at her clothing until he could feel the warmth and softness of her thighs.

Dinah, twisting frantically under him, realized her struggles were only exciting him more in the same way that the raging storm had aroused him. One of his hands was between her legs, rubbing ever so gently and stirring a sudden yearning in her body, a yearning that was increased by her attempts to get free. She moaned, half in agony and fear, half in pleasure. Alexander's own clothes were loose, and she could feel the coarse, curly hair of his body tickling along the length of her own body.

Then his hands encircled her hips, pulling her body upwards to where his erect, hard male organ waited eagerly. When the ship crested another wave, plunging downward, Alexander plunged between her thighs.

Dinah screamed in pain, her teeth biting Alexander's lower lip until she could taste his warm, salty blood. His half-closed brown eyes were black, his face hungry with eagerness. He submerged himself into Dinah again and again. Her pain was gone, swallowed up in a frantic heat and desire of her own that over-flowed inside her and left her limp. Alexander groaned, pouring himself into her until his body relaxed and he became aware of the chill cabin and where he was.

The man stumbled to his feet. He was overcome by guilt as he looked down at the almost naked girl, her clothes torn and her blood staining the pale skin of her thighs red.

"My God!" He touched the girl with shaking hands. "Dinah . . ."

She recoiled. Now that it was over, all she could think of was her naked body. She wrapped her torn clothing around her, hiding herself in her cloak, and ran from the cabin. Alexander started to follow her, forgetting his own half-clothed body.

Dinah stumbled to her cabin. Molly, thankfully, was sleeping. Dinah struggled out of her clothes, wanting only to get clean. The water in the pitcher was cold, but she did not feel it. She scrubbed and scrubbed herself, trying to cool her hot body, before she dressed in clean clothes. That left the clothes she had been wearing, the ripped blouse and the blood-stained underwear and skirt. Dinah bundled them together, thrusting them in the back of a drawer. When the storm let up, not that she cared now if the ship sank, she would drop them overboard.

The girl went into the small sleeping cabin. It was filled with the stench of Molly's vomit, and she tried to ignore the foul smell as she took a cool cloth to bathe Molly's hot face.

What was she going to do? How could she face Alexander again? Much less Captain MacKie—and Alexander's father and sister whom she had never met?

Dinah brushed away the tears scalding her cheeks. What made her even more ashamed was that one moment, that one glorious moment when she and Alexander had been joined together in ecstasy, she had known such pleasure as she had never have imagined. Despite her life's being ruined, that one moment seemed worth it—at the time. Now, she wanted to run out into the storm. It would be so easy from the storm-tossed decks . . .

No, Dinah told herself. Regardless of what had happened, she must go on. She was a woman now. A woman. Her body grew hot with the remembered joy and the overwhelming desire. And a longing such as she had never known or imagined before.

Chapter 7

FOR MORE THAN two days the storm raged relentlessly, the whole wrath of nature seeming directed against the barkentine that tossed helplessly on the heavy seas. The ship would groan to the crest of a wave, only to slide into its trough. No canvas was raised, for not even a jib could withstand such a gale. The ship fought back gallantly, every timber screaming in protest with each fresh assault, the captain and crew—just as gallantly—fighting to save her.

The two young women were left to themselves, with only Johnny to tend to their needs. The diet of hardtack and salted beef with an occasional pot of hot tea was not of the sort to resuscitate Molly. Even Dinah, struggling to care for Molly as she tried to retain her own strength, found it hard to stomach. She thought longingly of New York and Bermuda.

The storm, nevertheless, was a blessing in one way: Alexander was far too busy to pay her any attention. Two or three times a day, he would check to make sure the two girls were all right and would vanish almost immediately, to Dinah's relief. Captain MacKie, immense in oilskins, looked in when he could, too. The mere sight of the broad-shouldered man, his blue eyes bloodshot with lack of sleep, was enough to re-assure Dinah. As for Geordie, he also found time to stop in for a few minutes, more worried about Molly, who weakly attempted a smile, than about Dinah.

Dinah's fears, despite her reassurances to Molly, grew as a new sound joined the creaking of the timbers—the sound of pumps. Every man not needed on watch now manned the pumps night and day.

Dinah slept when she could. She had forced Molly, too weak and sick to protest, to move into the bunk, taking the cot for herself. Captain MacKie saw to it that the cot was firmly bolted down and had rails raised to keep Dinah from being thrown out. Yet, Dinah, more often than not, huddled in the armchair, a quilt wrapped around her. She was afraid that if she were to lie down, she might be overcome with seasickness, and one of them had to be as fit as was possible under the circumstances.

Dinah lost track of time. No light came through the portholes that had been battened down against the furor of the waves. As a result, the only light came from a lantern overhead, whose swinging was as dizzying as the waves. She watched it for what seemed hours at a time, until the motion mesmerized her and she managed to doze off.

Her sleep was no more tranquil than her waking hours. In her dreams she was locked in an embrace with Alexander, her breasts burning for the coolness of his kisses, her loins trembling with desire. She would awaken wondering if it would hurt so much the next time. She was no longer worried about what would become of her for what she had done and no longer ashamed. The longer the storm went on, the more she feared for her life—and the loss of the untold joy her body had revealed to her.

Yet, there is a limit as to how long a young, healthy girl can go without sleep. Dinah reached her limit on the third day. Curled up in the chair, the doze gave way to sleep, sleep so deep that she passed beyond the dream barrier.

How long she slept, she did not know but she

awakened with a start, her eyes wide and her heart pounding, sure the ship had sunk. After the noise of the storm, an unearthly quiet had descended. Her eyes sought the lantern, swaying slightly but no longer swinging wildly to and fro. Dinah sprang to her feet, listening. No, the ship was not sinking. It was still afloat, silent only in comparison to the creaks and groans of the past few days.

Making sure that Molly was sleeping soundly, Dinah took her cloak. No one now could object to her going on deck. She opened the door, invigorated immediately by the freshness of the air that greeted her after the closeness of the cabin. As she hooked the door open, she decided that fresh air was what Molly needed most of all.

Few sights are more beautiful than the sea after a storm. The clouds had broken completely, baring a naked heaven clothed only in a few wisps of mist. In the west, the sky was flushed pink with the promise of a flaming sunset. Overhead, sails had been raised, billowing whitely against the blue vaults of the heavens. The water sparkled in the last of the sunlight, the surface marred only here and there by a wave more stubborn than the rest. Loveliest of all to Dinah was the sweetness of the air. She raised her head, breathing deeply again and again, only gradually becoming aware that someone was near her, watching. She turned, hoping and yet fearful to see Alexander.

It was Ian MacKie, fatigue etched in heavy lines in his face, in the puffiness of his eyelids, the drooping of his broad and usually erect shoulders. Tired as he was, his smile lit up his face and his blue eyes sparkled, as he saw she had seen him.

Dinah smiled, too, happy that the storm had passed and happy that it was Captain MacKie and not Alexander who stood there. "Good afternoon, Captain. It's all right to come on deck now, isn't it? I mean the storm is over . . ."

"Of course, Miss Murray. You must want to stretch your . . ." he paused, a flush rising in his face.

Dinah laughed. "My legs, Captain?" She was too

97

exuberant at being released from the cabin to care about the niceties of language. She tilted her head, letting the hood of her cloak fall back. During the wildness of the storm, she had done little except to brush her hair and tie a ribbon around it, leaving it to hang in a curly mass about her shoulders. "Yes," she laughed again, "I do have legs—or limbs, if you prefer."

"In Alexander's absence then, may I escort you on a turn about the deck?" The captain offered his arm to her, his fatigue forgotten.

Dinah took it, her eyes darkening at the mention of Alexander. Her heart pounding, she asked, hoping it sounded casual, "Where is Alexander? I should think he, too, would be on deck."

"Getting some rest. I sent him below along with Geordie as soon as the sails were set. Neither of them slept much at all," he commented, "not while the storm was raging."

"And you? Did you?" Dinah looked at the captain, noticing for the first time the heavy lines in his face. "How tired you must be!"

"The ship is my responsibility," MacKie said simply. He nodded at the sunset, at the ball of fire descending into the ocean and shooting flames of red and orange into the darkening sky. "Besides, as soon as it is dark enough, I must take some sights and lay a course. During the storm, the best we could do was hold our own."

"Are we lost then?" Dinah asked, perturbed by his words.

"Oh, no, not quite." The captain laughed. "I did not mean to alarm you. Soon enough, all too soon, we shall be off the coast of England."

"England," Dinah mused. "And then?"

"And then, in a few days we shall be home in Scotland," he said slowly, as if he were not eager to be home.

At the mention of Scotland, the young woman shivered involuntarily. Scotland meant Sir Robert and

Lady Margaret, the new life she had been promised, and leaving the ship that now seemed like home.

MacKie misjudged the shiver. "You're cold, and here I've been walking you around . . ."

"Oh no, I'm fine," Dinah said hurriedly. "The fresh air feels so good after those days in the cabin." She hesitated before adding, "The only problem is that suddenly I am ravenously hungry."

"Well, tonight you shall have a good hot meal. I have already given the cook his orders. Perhaps you shall not dine like a princess, but you will have a decent repast," he said apologetically.

"I am not used to dining like a princess." Dinah turned to him with a worried look. "In fact, I don't even know how princesses dine."

"Nor do I, Miss Murray." He looked down at the lovely face, its forehead wrinkled in a frown. "If one day you find out, you must let me know," he murmured.

The frown was erased in a smile, and Dinah squeezed his arm. "You shall be the first to know. In the meantime, do you think it would be possible to have some tea?"

"Of course. I should have thought of that myself. I'll have it sent to your cabin." He started to lead her toward the companionway.

"Won't you join me, Captain?" She glanced at the sunset, noticing only a few stars were out. "By then it will be time to take those sights."

MacKie accepted with alacrity. While he went to find Johnny, Dinah checked on Molly. The maid was still asleep, breathing heavily and evenly, and Dinah closed the door between the sleeping cabin and the small outer cabin. In her absence, Johnny had straightened the room and opened the hatches over the portholes. It was as neat and spotless as it had been the first evening she saw it.

Over tea, Dinah studied the captain. They had not been alone since the first morning when he had shown her around the ship. The excitement of sailing, the newness of life aboard ship, and the attention Alexander had paid her had kept her from giving much thought to him. That was a mistake, she decided, and one she must rectify, if she were to have a friend, whom she well might need, in Edinburgh.

As she poured the tea, Dinah asked him to tell her about Edinburgh. The man helped himself to sugar, stirring it thoughtfully into the strong brew. "You'll find it different from New York, Miss Murray, if that's what you're thinking. More quiet, smaller." He leaned back, seeing the city in his mind, with the castle on the hill dominating the narrow, twisting streets at the base.

"I can't imagine it," she sighed. "The only castles I've seen have been in books. The city must be very grand."

"Not all of it. Where my mother lives, is a small house in a lane off the street that leads from the castle to Holyrood Palace," he said with a smile.

"Then, I fear I should feel more at home there— in your mother's house," she added hastily, "not the palace. Oh, dear, a castle *and* a palace. Whatever will I do in such a place!"

"Miss Murray," the man leaned across the table and took her hands between his large ones, "you will have Alexander and his family to see after you. I'd not worry so about such things as castles and palaces."

Dinah smiled, reassured by the warmth and the steadiness of his blue eyes, by the strength of those capable hands holding hers. "And you, Captain?" she asked.

"Yes, of course. I shall be there, too, until I have to go to sea again. If you ever need me, Miss Murray, I am yours to command," he added earnestly.

Dinah flushed, both in embarrassment and pleasure at the captain's words. "I feel much better knowing I have such a friend to rely on," she replied as earnestly.

"That's settled then." The captain rose reluctantly, glad she had lost the worried lines between her eyes. He knew all too well that once they landed, chances were that their paths would rarely, if ever, cross again.

High as he might stand in Sir Robert's esteem, they were not of the same social class. Any business the two would have would be contracted in Sir Robert's office, not his home. In New York, life might be different. There, perhaps, he might have been able to woo Dinah and win her hand, but not in Edinburgh. In Edinburgh, under the aegis of Sir Robert, she would be surrounded by eligible young suitors, not the least of whom was Alexander. His jaw tightened.

Standing, looking down at Dinah, he tried to smile. "I must go now. The ship's sights . . ."

"Of course." Dinah sprang to her feet. "And you must sleep, too. How tired you must be and here I am, rattling on about Edinburgh."

"It was my pleasure." He walked to the door, giving her a last smile before he left, closing it behind him.

Dinah returned to her chair. Until Captain MacKie had mentioned Alexander, she had almost forgotten him—almost but not quite, not even when he had taken her hands in his. Yet, her heart had beat faster, not with the rushing of blood pulsing through her veins that was enough to make her tremble at Alexander's touch, but more with a pleasurable sweetness. She sighed. Well, she had better put both men out of her mind and see to Molly.

When she opened the door to the sleeping cabin, Molly was wide awake, dressed, and putting her hair up. "Feeling better?" Dinah asked.

Molly laughed. "I really think I am going to live, although I wasn't sure there for a while that it was worth it." She shook her head. "How you managed to stay on your feet, I don't know!"

"One of us had to," Dinah said, staring at herself moodily in the mirror. Now that Molly was up and about and the storm over, she felt oddly let down.

Molly went on chattering, too relieved to feel well to notice Dinah's mood. "Who were you talking to? I heard voices. Did Geordie . . ."

"Captain MacKie."

"Oh ho! And what will his lordship, Alexander,

101

have to say about that?" asked Molly slyly. "It seemed to me he had pretty well monopolized you for himself."

"Oh, Molly, do be quiet! Remember, Alexander is my cousin," Dinah said, reminding herself at the same time.

"A distant one." Molly gave a shrug. "Much too distant for his attention to be cousinly courtesy."

"True," Dinah agreed.

"Well, it doesn't do any harm to let a man think he isn't the only one. It heats the blood, I've heard, and . . ." Molly stopped. Dinah had blushed a deep red. "Oh, dear," Molly said in amazement, "what did I say?"

Dinah sat down in the chair, recalling the torn and bloody underclothes she had hidden in the closet. The secret she had meant to keep with her to the end spilled out, as Molly's eyes grew wider and wider. "Molly," Dinah cried at the end, "Whatever am I to do?"

"Oh, dear," Molly whispered, "oh dear, oh dear." Somehow, although what had happened between Dinah and Alexander had been the same as what she did—and enjoyed—with Jim and Geordie, it had never occurred to her that it was the same with someone raised as a lady as Dinah had been and a gentleman like Alexander. Oh, he might have his way with a maid—he was a man and men had appetites—but not with . . . with a lady.

"Molly?" Dinah whispered.

Molly made up her mind in a hurry. As she saw it, Dinah had no choice. "You have to marry him. You must tell him that," she said firmly. "He . . . he . . . he took advantage of you, of your youth and innocence," she added pompously, sounding distinctly unlike Molly.

"Marry him?" Dinah stared as Molly. "That's easy to say, but how do I go about that, especially if he won't have me."

"You must make him," Molly insisted, sounding far

more sure of herself than she was. "We'll think of something, you'll see."

Thinking was one thing, doing was something else, as the two young women discovered. After one calm night, the weather gradually worsened again, giving little opportunity for intimate strolls on deck. All three men were busy, Captain MacKie and Geordie with the ship and Alexander with checking the cargo in the hold. The cozy dinners, too, seemed a thing of the past, the young women more often than not dining alone. Molly, her thoughts on Geordie, was no less restless than Dinah. As a result, both were quiet and moody as, standing on deck, they watched the ship make landfall off the Isle of Wight in a swirl of mist. The ship was forced to heave to, and they spent the night in a heavy fog, haunted by the ringing of a bell to warn off other ships.

The fog lifted with the dawn and slowly the ship moved down the English Channel. Off Dover, the sun broke through giving the passengers their first view of land since Bermuda. Chalk cliffs rose from the water and gleamed white in the sun. Beyond were green fields, here and there a cottage, and once in a while a village in a cove, the harbor bobbing with small fishing boats.

Dinah had had plenty of time to think. Regardless of what Molly had said about her marrying Alexander, she wasn't sure it was the right thing to do. If her mind was filled with doubts, however, her body was not. The mere sight of Alexander on the bridge was enough to send that fire of desire rushing through her body. A touch made her heart pound, although the touches were few as Alexander kept his distance. Sadly, she decided that Alexander had no use for her, not after what had happened. Then she remembered the urgency of his passion, how eagerly he had possessed her, withdrawing so slowly. Perhaps, though, it was different for him. It had obviously not been his first time. She frowned, not knowing what to conclude. The waves, cleaved by the bow of the ship, took her attention.

Raising her head, she saw Alexander standing on the foredeck, watching her. The sight of him and the pounding of her heart made up her mind. If he would not come to her, she must go to him. Head held high, her hair pulled loosely back by a ribbon, her cape flowing from her shoulders, Dinah moved gracefully toward him. As she approached, she saw his dark eyes burning in his face above the wide cheekbones, his skin flushed as with a fever.

She paused at the foot of the gangway, one hand on the rail, one foot with bared ankle on the rung. The halt was deliberate, if not planned. Dinah was well aware of the sun on her hair and the white cliffs behind her. As she looked up at him, Alexander released his grip on the rail and walked toward her, descending the gangway to meet her.

"I owe you an apology," he said stiffly.

"And I, you," Dinah retorted.

Alexander raised an eyebrow. "It seems we should have a talk." He glanced around the deck, noticing the helmsman had been joined by Captain MacKie and that Geordie had come on deck on his way to relieve Captain MacKie, although the watch did not change for at least an hour yet. Then he saw Molly with Geordie. "Perhaps your cabin," he suggested, "as we seem to have an audience here."

Dinah nodded. Head still high, she took Alexander's arm. Seeing Molly start toward her, Dinah shook her off with a slight nod of her head. The young woman frowned, but made no move to follow.

Once they were in the master's cabin, Dinah's courage flagged momentarily as Alexander closed the door firmly behind them. Leaning against it, his face still flushed, he eyed Dinah.

Neither spoke. In the silence, the young woman removed her cloak, folding it over a chair by the table. She was wearing a simple green wool dress with a close fitting bodice, the top few buttons open. The skirt clung to her hips, revealing the firm body beneath. Normally she would have been wearing several petticoats. For comfort at sea however, both Dinah and Molly had given up the voluminous under-garments for a single petticoat that did little to conceal the shapeliness of the body beneath.

Dinah realized that Alexander had every intention of waiting for her to speak, regardless of how long that might take, as if his earlier, brief apology had been enough. She could feel the veins in her temples pounding and a sinuous heat in her loins, the same heat that memories of that morning aroused. She must make him like her again!

She move toward him, taking his cold hands in her hot ones. "Alexander," she began.

"Dear God!" The words seemed wrenched from him. "Don't look at me like that," he whispered hoarsely. "Don't you know what you are doing to me?"

"I?" Dinah was puzzled. Didn't he realize what he was doing to her? "You are angry with me," she said innocently, "ashamed to bring me home to your father." She leaned her head on his shoulder, taunting him.

"Angry? Ashamed? My God, Dinah, if I am, it is only at myself." He put his arms around her, holding her close, his mouth crushing hers, expecting her to pull back.

Instead, Dinah's mouth sought his, her lips parting to accept his tongue. Her body pressed against him, and she did not pull her hand away when he placed it on his swollen member. A faint smile on his mouth, he drew away from her to lead her into the sleeping cabin. This time, he removed her clothes gently, Dinah helping him with the buttons. Then, lying on the bunk, she watched him undress, surprised at how hairy his chest was and admiring the muscles in his arms that flexed as he sat down beside her to remove his trousers.

"What beautiful red hair you have," Alexander murmured.

Dinah's smile turned into a gasp as she realized what hair he meant. He buried his face in the soft fur between her legs. Gently he pressed her lips apart with his fingers as his tongue caressed the soft flesh inside, His mouth was hot, breathing fire into her. Her body quivered with pleasure, a pleasure that numbed her brain to everything except the rapture of his lips and teeth and tongue, giving her such exquisite joy. She moaned slightly as he stopped, but it was only to take her breasts in his mouth, sucking them gently as he placed her fingers around his rigid shaft. Half unconscious of what she was doing, Dinah massaged it with one hand, the other losing itself in his dark hair as she pressed his head closer to her breasts, the pink nipples now hard and aching.

When Alexander finally mounted her, she spread her thighs willingly, her hips pressing upward to receive the first thrust. This time, there was no pain, only an ecstasy that consumed Dinah. Her body tingled, her thighs and hips rising to meet every stroke, exploding too soon in the hot liquid of a climax. She wanted more, wanted to feel him even deeper inside her. Her hands pressed against his spine, her legs entwining his legs. Her passion excited Alexander so much that he couldn't tear his eyes from her face, her slightly open mouth and her eyes shut as if in pain.

Dinah moaned. "Don't stop, not yet, she said as he paused for a moment, raising himself on his elbows to see her radiant face.

"You little vixen," he muttered with a smile, driving inside the warm, luscious darkness of her body.

All of Dinah's senses combined into one feeling of shattering, blazing joy. She watched the desperate hunger on Alexander's face with wonder as she listened to his breathing become sharper and faster. He brought his face down over hers, opening his mouth wide on hers and drinking in the sweetness of her kisses, his lips and teeth preying so hard she could scarcely respond. He slowed his movements and stopped for a moment. A thrilling shiver shook her involuntarily.

Then he began to move again, so gradually that she felt her entire body had gone numb except for the exquisite sensation of his almost withdrawing. She gripped his back and hips, digging her fingertips into his flesh, feeling his bones move in her hands. She wanted him deep inside, deeper than anything could ever be, totally inside her. He seemed to stiffen a little to resist her, and then a strange, almost sad cry escaped from him.

Dinah had never heard such a sound before and her first impulse was terrible worry—was he alright, in pain? She sought his eyes and was surprised to see a look of simple, incredible happiness. She sighed with pleasure and relief, trying to hold him closer, to keep this moment as long as she could.

They lay together, soaked and exhausted. She listened to her own ragged breathing and realized that her gasps now slowed in rhythm with Alexander's. He rolled back from her and a sudden coolness fluttered over her body, feeling delicious and yet somehow threatening.

Alexander sat up, flexing the muscles of his shoulders and running a hand over his dark hair to brush it back from his forehead. He stood up, naked before Dinah who lay watching him.

The wonder of what had happened still suffused her in a warm glow that was not diminished by the sight of the man standing over her. She thought he was the most beautiful creature she had ever seen. How broad his shoulders were, how curly his dark hair, how small his waist and narrow hips. His heavily muscled thighs were those of a fine horseman. She reached up to touch the coarse dark hair between his legs.

"To think," Alexander, marveled, "I was about to apologize to you for what . . . the way." He shook his head.

Dinah frowned. With Molly, she had agreed that she had to make Alexander marry her, to save her from the shame of what had happened. As a result, she decided to give herself to him again, not resisting this time but eagerly to show him that she was not afraid of him, that she loved him. It had been so simple, seemed so simple, during the nights she had lain awake, tossing in the bunk, wondering why he was ignoring her. The reason had to be that she had disappointed him the first time.

He was pulling on his trousers, his eyes still feasting on the feminine delights revealed to him. "My dear, you had better dress yourself. I hardly think Molly will remain on deck for long after Geordie has relieved MacKie."

Dinah sat up, suddenly ashamed of her nakedness at his remark. True as it was, it seemed callous after her—their—delight in one another. Her whole body seemed to blush as she reached for her chemise.

Alexander watched her, other thoughts taking hold of him, thoughts of his father to whom he was responsible for both Dinah and the ship's safety. Yet, it was not of that responsibility he was thinking as much as it was of himself and his own passion. "When we get to Scotland," he said moodily, his mind so much on himself and his own thoughts that he was heedless of how Dinah's blush gave way to a ashen paleness, "I must talk to my father."

"Talk to your father!" Dinah sprang to her feet, staring at him. Oh, she thought, what would this man who had sent for her think? If Alexander told him about the two of them, he could only believe that she—and her mother—were no better than those women who walked the streets by the docks on the lookout for sailors.

"He has to know," Alexander insisted stubbornly, surprised at her vehemence and still lost in his own thoughts. "Marriage is not . . ."

Dinah turned icily cold at the words. Alexander had used her. All his attentions had been with a single purpose and had nothing to do with his caring for, loving, her. He did not intend, had never intended, to marry her. Not waiting to hear the words from the lips that had kissed her so passionately and intent only on her own thoughts, she spoke quickly with a bitterness new to her. "Of course, marriage is not possible now."

Her words startled Alexander out of his own contemplation. He stared at her, seeing her fully for the first time since he had started talking. Not believing

108

what he had heard, he asked in amazement, "Marriage not possible?" The words he had meant to say about marriage not being impossible between cousins as distant as they were completely forgotten. "Dinah, what are you saying?"

Her only resolve was to protect herself and Molly. If Sir Robert turned the two of them out, she did not know what they could or would do in a strange country. Above all, regardless of what Mrs. Bradley had said, she could not write the woman for help, not after the woman's kindness and hopes for her future. Sure that Alexander could never understand what she was thinking, she insisted stubbornly, "You must not talk to your father. If you do, I will tell him you are lying."

Alexander's lips thinned in a straight line at her threat. He had differences enough with his father, and he could not afford her adding to them. "Very well," he agreed, "I shall say nothing to my father. Have no fear," he added sarcastically, "he intends to welcome you as a daughter regardless of me or my sister."

Dinah grabbed at the straw of the mention of daughter. Now, more than ever, she needed to know about Sir Robert, to know what to expect. What was more, only Alexander could tell her what she needed to know. Captain MacKie, after all, knew Sir Robert only through business dealings and as an employee. Her resolve firm, she stepped in front of the door to prevent Alexander from leaving. "Tell me about your father," she demanded, softening the words the moment they were out of her mouth. "Please, Alexander. You have said nothing during the voyage—and now we are so close to Scotland."

When Alexander only looked at her silently, Dinah raised her face, letting him see the tears in the corners of her eyes. "Don't you," she asked, "at least owe me that? To tell me about your father?"

Alexander shook his head, not understanding the reason for the change in her or the fears that had been so strong for her to try to keep him in the cabin a while longer. "What a strange girl you are," he marveled. "It will be very difficult to forget you, this voyage. All this," he motioned at the bunk, the bedclothes rumpled and half on the deck, "and you dismiss me so lightly for my father."

Once again, Dinah who was now completely caught up in her own thoughts, misunderstood his meaning. "I am only thinking about what is best. And it is best that you do not talk to your father—for both our sakes," she added pointedly, "yours and mine."

The last argument was one with which Alexander was in total agreement. "In the last respect," he said grimly, "you are quite correct as far as I am concerned. Still," his dark eyes glinted, "I shall miss you."

And I, you, Dinah thought. Her body grew cold with the realization of the pleasures she would know no more, but she kept her silence.

The silence lengthened, as Dinah still barred the door. Both were fully dressed, with only the red fullness of Dinah's lips betraying the passion of the desire that had carried them both to such heights moments before.

Alexander's eyes caressed her, as if taking a long farewell, the softness in them disguised by the cruelty of his cold words. "Well, then, as long as you are quite dressed, let us go on deck and I will tell you about my father, about this proper family from whose loins," he smiled in selfish pleasure at the blush the word inspired in Dinah, repeating, "from whose loins, as I said, you are sprung."

He escorted her to the deck. To Dinah's amazement, Captain MacKie was still on the foredeck, not yet relieved, while Molly and Geordie were standing in the lee out of the cold north winds that was filling the sails to hurry the ship to its destination. It had seemed to her that she and Alexander had been below for hours.

Alexander sniffed the wind, looking around and finally selecting a spot in the sun along the starboard rail, sheltered from both the wind and the hearing of the sailors holystoning the deck. He seated Dinah on a chest in which extra mooring lines were stored.

"Yes?" Dinah asked meekly, afraid at the way his

mouth suddenly twisted in what passed for a lopsided smile, not realizing that the way her head, with its wealth of red hair, had tilted on her long, graceful neck as she looked up at him provided him with an impulsive inspiration.

"I assume that your mother, being of good Scottish blood, has told you of Mary, Queen of Scots?" he asked, ignoring her blush of anger at his sarcasm.

Dinah nodded, trying to remember the history she had learned in the house on Washington Square. She recalled that James V had been king of Scotland at the time Henry VIII was king of England. James had died when Mary was only a few weeks old. Although she was anointed queen, her mother served as regent, sending Mary to France, the land of her own birth, to be raised at the French court.

She told Alexander, who said, "You are quite correct that Mary was his only child by his wife, but James had not Henry's scruples about marrying his mistress. The great love of his life," he used the words deliberately, "was Margaret Erskine, by whom he had several sons who were excluded from the throne by reason of their illegitimacy."

Dinah had to smile. "Oh, Alexander, that was so long ago. What does that have to do with you—or me?"

"You shall see, my dear. To begin with," he went on, never taking his eyes from Dinah's face, "Margaret married a Sir William Douglas, to whom she also bore several sons, and it is this Clan Douglas to which the present-day Douglases, my father and myself, trace our lineage."

"And me?" Dinah asked eagerly.

"Not quite." Alexander, warming to his subjects, was determined to tell the story his own way, increasing Dinah's confusion as he returned to the story of the impetuous willful Queen of Scots.

The young queen was wed to the Dauphin, the heir to the throne of France, at 14, becoming queen of France two years later. She also had a claim to the throne of England through her grandmother, Margaret

Tudor, and it was this claim that resulted in the life-long enmity of Elizabeth I of England. Her role as Queen of France ended with the death of King Francis a bare year later. Her loneliness at the new court and the illness of her mother who had continued to rule Scotland in Mary's stead impelled Mary to return to the land of her birth and take her rightful place as Queen of Scotland.

"She landed," Alexander told Dinah, "at Leith in the Firth of Forth, where we too shall land, and made her way by horseback to Edinburgh—as we also will, although by coach."

Dinah interrupted him. "I find this all very interesting, but I do not understand what it has to do with me."

A cloud had passed over the sun, casting Alexander's face in shadow and giving him a sinister air. Alexander was determined to tell the story in his own way. "As I told you, you will see, if you will only let me tell you. Mary was a good queen, far better than many give her credit for. She chose wisely, at least at first, in selecting her ministers, one of whom was the Earl of Moray, her half-brother and the son of Margaret Erskine—or Douglas, if you will—and James V. And Scotland was not an easy country to rule, with the various clans and lords all too willing to go for each other's throats. She was also a young woman, only 18, two years older than you," Alexander said with a grin, "and by all accounts of a passionate nature."

Dinah blushed, partly in anger and partly in pleasure at being compared to a queen. Yet, she could not see what this had to do with her, especially when Alexander skimmed lightly over Mary's marriage to Henry Stuart, Lord Darnley, a distant cousin who also had a claim to the English throne through his mother. Darnley, a handsome and dashing young man, turned out to be a scoundrel, so much so that he was murdered shortly after the birth of his and Mary's son.

"Some people," Alexander went on, "believed Mary ordered the murder. By that time, the alliance among the clans began to fall apart with one faction backing

Mary and another, a regency until her son became of age. Mary married again, this time to James Hepburn, Earl of Bothwell, who some say raped her to force the marriage." At Dinah's gasp, he interrupted the story to interject, "Even queens are human, Dinah," watching her face.

Dinah lowered her head, biting her lower lip. Illogically, she wondered whether Mary had found any pleasure in the act, whether unwillingness gave way to delight. At the same time, she was angry at Alexander. "Oh, this is all too ridiculous. You are making fun of me." She started to rise. "This has nothing to do with me!"

"But it does." Alexander placed his hands on her shoulders, refusing to let her leave, until she resumed her seat. "Mary, carrying Bothwell's child, was forced to fight the dissenting clans. Her side lost and Mary was captured, with her captors giving her to Sir William Douglas and his wife, Margaret Erskine to guard."

"And the baby?" Dinah asked, intrigued for the first time.

"Well, there are those who say she was never with child, and those who say she miscarried and the baby died." His eyes narrowed. "Douglas family history provided a third theory. Margaret was a clever woman and one who enjoyed power. Aided by the secrecy surrounding the pregnancy, when the baby was born, she let Mary believe he—it was a son—had died. She then took the child to her son, the Earl of Moray, to hold as a kind of trump card. You see, Moray had been appointed regent for Mary's son by Darnley. Infant mortality being what it was, the two thought that if anything happened to the Darnley child they could bring forth this baby. Margaret, if necessary, could provide witnesses to his birth. In that way, Moray and Margaret, of course, would be the powers behind the throne, the real rulers of Scotland.

"While this plot was going on, Mary herself was plotting her escape from the clutches of the Douglas. She did escape and eventually fled to England for help

113

and protection. Instead, Elizabeth had her beheaded after nineteen years of imprisonment. Her first son—and as far as she knew, her only son—became James VI of Scotland and James I of England after Elizabeth's death." The man deliberately drew out the end of the story, waiting for Dinah to ask the question she was sure to ask.

Dinah took a deep breath. "The . . . the second child?"

"There was, of course, never a need for him. Moray raised him as an illegitimate child of his, a bastard, until he was assassinated a few years after Mary fled to England. Then Margaret took the child and raised him, marrying him off to one of her daughters."

"I still don't understand what that . . ." Dinah stopped, raising her eyes to Alexander's face, to the smile that played over his lips and the dark eyes watching her closely. "Moray," she said slowly, "Murray. Is that it?"

He opened his mouth, then closed it, surprised at the expression on her face, a mixture of pride and sorrow. Clearing his throat, he spoke softly. "Yes. So you see, we are distantly related by virtue of the marriage of Moray, or Murray, if you prefer."

"And I, I am a . . . a descendent of Mary, then!" The idea fascinated Dinah. She, the daughter of an immigrant Scottish governess, a descendent of a royal queen of Scotland! Then, she remembered that the story of the second birth was only rumor and added hastily, "I mean, if the story you tell me is true."

Alexander smiled ruefully. "Had I any doubts before, I had none the moment you walked into the room at Mrs. Bradley's."

The words took Dinah by surprise. "When I walked . . . what do you mean?"

The man hesitated, recalling her refusal of what he had intended as a proposal of marriage. "You," he said brusquely, "are the very portrait of her. She was tall as you are, with a long neck. Her hair was red, her eyes amber." With those words, he turned on his heel abruptly to mount the gangway leading to the foredeck.

Dinah sat where he left her, barely noticing his departure. Her mind was spinning, a whirlpool of thoughts, of questions answered and unanswered. Surely, Sir Robert had not summoned her to Scotland merely on the basis of a tenuous relationship more than 300 years old, although what Alexander had said of a Moray/Murray marrying a Douglas was undoubtedly true. No, there had to be a closer relationship than that, one that either Alexander did not know or did not tell her.

And what of Alexander himself? She could not account for his early attentiveness any more than she could his more recent apparent coolness. She recalled sorrowfully those moments in the cabin. He had seemed pleased enough with her then—but again the passion had been followed by a coldness, one that this time was infinitely worse. How could he possibly have thought to tell his father unless he were out to destroy her! Dinah shuddered, only hoping he would keep his word. She would have to be very careful, keeping her distance yet at the same time watching that she did nothing to make him turn his back on his word.

As if those thoughts were not enough, there was also the thought of Molly. She recalled her happiness at the suggestion that Molly accompany her to Scotland. Life had seemed so simple then, an adventure. Now, she had to consider Molly in any decision she was called upon to make, for she was responsible for her, although that might not have been what Mrs. Bradley had intended. Whatever happened to her, she would have to make sure that Molly was safe and taken care of.

Last of all, there was Dinah herself. All her life she had been taken care of, her needs tended to, decisions made for her. Even the decision to go to Scotland had not really been hers. It had been made for her by her mother and Mrs. Bradley, first of all, then by Sir Robert and Alexander. The only decision she had really made on her own had been to force—yes, there was no other word for it—to force Alexander to marry her, to make him love her, to please him as she had evidently not pleased him the first time. Whether the decision was right or wrong was not important. What was important was that she had failed. From now on, she would have to be strong, strong enough to take care of both herself and of Molly. She must guard against her impulses.

With a faint smile, she remembered hearing or reading about the differences between the two queens: that Mary had let her heart rule her head, while Elizabeth had let her head rule her heart. Well, if she were a descendent of Mary, she was also distantly related to Elizabeth, and she would be far better off to take the latter for her example than the former. Let me resemble Mary in looks, if I could believe Alexander, she told herself, but let me emulate Elizabeth.

Chapter 8

🌹 🌹 🌹

WHEN DINAH RETURNED to the cabin, she found Molly sitting at the table in the little sitting room, a bit of sewing in her lap. At Molly's eager smile, she suddenly remembered the rumpled bedclothes on the bunk. Wondering whether Molly had been in the other cabin or not, she waited for the young maid to say something.

Molly, noticing the solemnity in the other girl's expression, said uncertainly, "Did you have a talk with Alexander?"

Dinah nodded, relieved at the question and trying

to think of an excuse to go in the other cabin. Molly, unwittingly, gave it to her by saying, "Oh, dear. Don't tell me yet. Wait until I get more thread."

"I'll get it," Dinah said quickly. "There's no reason for you to get up. It's in the chest, isn't it?" Without waiting for a reply, she hurried into the other cabin, opening the door and closing it quickly behind her. She straightened the covers quickly, hoping Molly would not notice the bunk was not made up with Johnny's usual nautical neatness, and dropped her cloak on it. Fortunately, the spool of thread was where she expected it to be.

Returning to the other cabin, she handed the thread to Molly, prepared to lie about having to look for it should Molly ask about what took her so long. Molly, however, her thoughts half on Dinah and half on herself, hadn't noticed. "Well, did you?" Molly repeated.

"Yes. " Dinah sat down opposite Molly, wishing she had her mother's needlepoint to work on so she would not have to look at Molly.

"And? For heaven's sake, Dinah, don't keep me on pins and needles," urged Molly.

Dinah took a deep breath. She had never deliberately lied before and she tried to convince herself that what she said now was not a lie either. Briefly, skimming over much of what Alexander had told her about the tragic queen, she told Molly about the history of the Douglases and her own origins. Molly's eyes grew rounder and rounder, her hands motionless in her lap.

"Oh, my!" Molly sighed when Dinah had finished. "Do you believe it? Is it really true?"

Dinah had to laugh. "How do I know, Molly? I see no reason for him to lie, however, as I can quickly enough find out from Sir Robert."

"True,'" Molly agreed. "I wonder why your mother never told you."

Dinah shrugged. The same question had been on her own mind. "I don't know, unless she thought I was too young—or maybe she simply wanted to wipe out everything about Scotland from her mind. She did look on New York as a new life, and that, I know, was why she wanted to have me there." She sighed. "I'll never know now."

Molly picked up her sewing again. Dinah had not really answered the question, at least not the question she had on her mind. "Did you talk about anything else?" she asked casually, far too casually for Dinah to miss her meaning.

"No. I was . . . was much too overcome." Dinah avoided her friend's eyes. To change the subject, she queried, "What did you and Geordie talk about?"

"About Edinburgh. He said we would be landing in two days." Tears welled in the girl's eyes. "Oh, Dinah," she wailed. "In two days, this voyage will be over. I will have to start calling you Miss Dinah. It will be 'Mr. Alexander,' and Lady this and Lady that. I will be a maid again, and you . . . we won't ever be friends again."

Dinah smiled at her. "Molly, whatever happens, we will always be friends. It may be that you will have to call me 'Miss Dinah' in front of others, but when we are alone we will be the same 'Dinah' and 'Molly.' "

"No," Molly insisted, "it won't be the same. It can't be. Don't you understand? Geordie told me all about the fine house that the Douglases live in, about how everybody is a lady or a lord, much finer than even Mrs. Bradley and her friends. Even Captain MacKie is not invited to the house!"

Dinah's resolution that she must be strong wavered, until she saw the fear on Molly's face. "Well, I am not going to worry about that. At least now. It is far too late to change my mind. Come, Molly, cheer up," she urged. "If I am not worried, why should you be? Besides, I'll take care of you."

"You'll take care of me?" Molly laughed, her innate humor bubbling to the surface at the thought of Dinah taking care of her. Slyly, she offered, "Perhaps, not for long. Geordie . . ." She stopped, pressing her lips together. It was bad luck to say such things.

118

"You and Geordie," Dinah mused, "I should like that." Happy as she was for her friend, a new stab of loneliness cut her heart.

"Well, not yet," Molly conceded. "I mean, he hasn't said anything definite, except to ask whether I thought you would mind if he called on me in Edinburgh."

"Of course I wouldn't mind. What a thing to ask, as if he needed my permission!"

"I told you, Dinah," Molly soothed, "Geordie said it's different in Scotland from New York."

Dinah wished that Alexander had said as much about the present as the past. "We'll see," she compromised, reluctant to let Molly know how ignorant she was about the new life ahead of her.

The next few days passed quickly. The two young women spent much of the time packing. After six weeks at sea, they had worn most of their dresses and these now had to be carefully folded in tissue. Their meals were served in their cabin with the excuse that the men had far too many details to see to before docking. When they did meet, Dinah and Alexander, as if by mutual agreement, avoided one another.

On the second afternoon, their traveling clothes laid out, with only the gowns they were wearing left to be packed, they took a last turn on deck. Geordie approached them, his eyes on Molly, to tell them they were to dock in the morning, entering the Firth of Forth with the early tide. Dinah and Molly looked at one another, anxiety showing in their faces, their hearts pounding.

"Miss Dinah," Geordie's timid voice broke into Dinah's thoughts, "Miss Dinah, might I have a word with Molly? That is," he added hurriedly, "if you have no need of her for the moment?"

Dinah smiled at him, uneasy at the new note of subservience in his voice. "Of course, you can have a word with her—several, if you wish." She glanced around, noticing Captain MacKie on the foredeck. "Besides, I would like to talk to Captain MacKie while he has a moment, to thank him for his courtesy to us."

She left the two and joined the captain, unwittingly comparing him to Alexander. The broad shoulders and deep chest and the solidly planted, wide-spread legs gave the captain a stolid look that was enhanced by the square-jawed, deeply tanned face. His demeanor was altogether stern until one looked into his blue eyes, which had the clear true blueness of a rare sapphire, and a sparkle that betrayed a lively sense of humor. In Dinah's presence, moreover, his eyes had softness to them that would have surprised the crew to whom he was an exacting, if just, taskmaster.

"Mr. Campbell has informed us that we will be docking at Leith in the morning, Captain," Dinah began.

"Aye, Miss Dinah," MacKie agreed. "It has been a pleasant voyage for me, no thanks to the weather."

Dinah laughed. "Captain MacKie, you may be captain of this ship, but I fear neither you nor any man is captain of the weather."

"True enough, alhough I regret that it caused you discomfort."

"My regret," Dinah replied, choosing her words carefully, "is that the voyage is at an end. I will soon be among strangers in a foreign land. I feel I have lost one set of friends only to gain another, whom now I am forced to lose as well."

MacKie was puzzled, although pleased. "To me, it appears you will be gaining a family— and you know Alexander, who will surely be the guide you feel you need."

"Yes, of course, Alexander." Dinah tilted her head, clasping her hands in front of her. "I have been raised simply. I worry sometimes, that he must find me much too simple—just as I will find this new life much too grand."

The captain had been aware of a strain existing between the two distant cousins. His suggestions that the two ladies join them for dinner had been summarily dismissed by Alexander, first on account of the continuing bad weather and then because of the work that had to be done before landing. Whatever was on the girl's mind, he did not know, but he did know he had to reassure her.

"Miss Dinah, if I may speak bluntly, whatever worries you have, you can forget," he said earnestly. "I have known Sir Robert for many years, and you will find no finer gentleman—or man—anywhere. Once you meet him, you will see how groundless your fears are."

Although Dinah, her eyes on the captain, believed him, she was still afraid. MacKie, after all, was unaware of what had happened between Alexander and herself, and it was fear of what Sir Robert should do, were he to find out, that drove Dinah to forge a friendship with the captain that would persevere after she left the ship. "I believe you," she said suddenly allowing the fear to be spoken. "But what . . . what if . . ." she turned her head away, thinking of her mother whose death had left Dinah alone in a cold world where her only salvation at the time had been Mrs. Bradley.

MacKie laid a gentle hand on her shoulder, attempting to comfort her as best he knew how. "I don't understand, Miss Dinah. I would like nothing better than to be your friend, to help you if I can, but you must tell me first what it is that so bothers you."

Dinah took a deep breath. "I was thinking of my mother. She was only forty, not really old, and yet, she—God called her. You have been gone a long time, more than three months altogether—and what news have you had of Scotland. Perhaps Sir Robert has changed his mind, or worse . . ."

"And you will be alone again," the captain concluded. "I doubt that you have to worry. Sir Robert is a vigorous man, but with your mother's death so recent, and you so young, I do understand. If it wil make you feel better, I will give you my mother's address in Edinburgh. Whether I am at home or not, you and Molly will always find a true Scottish welcome, I can assure you."

"And you," Dinah looked up at the man, wishing he would take her in his warm arms, hold her close and protect her against the ill fortunes she was sure lay ahead, "you will be my friend."

"You need hae nae doot on that score," he assured her, lapsing into the dialect of his childhood, "I am your friend."

Dinah smiled, taking his hand in hers. How large it was, so capable and strong. Such a man would not take her and then desert her with such unfeeling alacrity. Yet, warm as her feeling was toward him, there was none of the hotness, the pulsating of the blood that Alexander always stirred in her. "I shall treasure that promise."   ,

Impulsively, Dinah lifted her mouth and kissed the man's cheek. "Will we see you for dinner? After all, it is our last night aboard the *Star of Scotland*."

"Aye. It will be my pleasure to entertain you and Miss Molly—and I am sure that Geordie will join us, too."

"I shall look forward to it, Captain. And now, I must see whether I can help Molly in any last-minute packing." Dinah left him, fully aware of his omission of Alexander's name. It must be a mistake, she thought, or else he had taken Alexander's presence for granted.

Dinah stopped in the companionway outside the door to her cabin, not wanting to interrupt Molly. She could not go back on deck lest the Captain wonder, without an excuse. She was saved from having to make one up, as Geordie left the cabin. He saw her and blushed a deep red. Dinah smiled at him and went into her own cabin.

Molly was standing in the center of the room, her lips still warm from Geordie's kiss. Determined to win Geordie, she had made up her mind not to let what happened the night of Dinah's dinner party in Bermuda happen again. Although she had drawn the young mate down on the settee next to her, had let him fondle her breasts until she could feel them growing hard and flushed with blood, she had drawn back from further advances, asking him about Edinburgh. On his promise to call on her, Molly had pressed her

122

soft body against him, her mouth teasing an ear and then his mouth, her tongue darting between his lips until he began to breathe heavily.

"When, Geordie," she had asked. "Will it be soon?"

"Soon as ever I can make it, within a week, Molly, love," he replied, his hands fumbling with the buttons on her dress.

"A week, Geordie?" His hand was cool on her hot breasts, and her heart began to pound as he pressed his lips on them, kissing first one and then the other, his tongue seeking out the firm, red nipples.

"A fortnight at the most," Geordie hedged, his mouth still filled.

Molly pushed him away, taking his face in her hands. "You! First a week and now a fortnight—I thought you a man of your word!"

"Oh, Moll, Molly love, I am, I am!" Geordie flushed, looking like a little boy ready to cry. "I canna promise a day and an hour. First, we must see to the unloading of the ship, arrange with the chandler's, pay off the crew . . ."

"I thought a first mate was a man of prominence," Molly teased, "and now you sound no better than a seaman."

"You dinna understand. Both MacKie and I will be the last to leave, as we are the first to board." Geordie was thoroughly miserable. "I'll send you word and come to you soon as ever I can. I canna promise more."

"Nor can I," retorted Molly. "For I too have obligations, Di . . . Miss Dinah," she amended, "who might any moment step through that door." She started to button her dress, relenting to give Geordie a last kiss.

"Oh, Molly," the mate whispered, "at this moment I would wish to be aught but a sailor. How willingly I would change places with a footman or a coachman to be with you."

"Oh no!" Molly stared in consternation at Geordie. "You would not like that life, always waiting on others, your betters but no better than you are." She laid her cheek on his shoulder.

"You won't be a maid all your life, if I have my way." Geordie laid his cheek against hers. "You'll wait for me, not fall for one of those fancy liveried gents?"

"I'll wait," Molly promised, turning her head to kiss his cheek, her body suffused in a warm glow, "a week, ten days at the most." She giggled. "Now you must go before Miss Dinah returns."

Geordie left reluctanty, realizing how right Molly had been at the sight of Dinah. Dinah, for her part, saw the smile on Molly's face. She had been smart to plead for the captain's friendship. Sooner than she realized, he might be the only friend she had in the world.

The captain had summoned the last of the ship's resources to put on as fine a dinner as possible. He and Geordie greeted the two young women in their best uniforms, the brass buttons of their double-breasted, navy blue jackets polished to a golden luster. Alexander was not there, and his absence made Dinah uneasy.

Even as she smiled, accepting the glass of sherry from the captain, she felt tears rising in her eyes. How like home this ship had become. She had felt no regrets, except a faint twinge, on leaving New York, where there had been too much excitement, each day bringing new experiences, the buying of a new wardrobe and more clothes than she had ever dreamed of owning—with cost no object, the dining in fine restaurants, the carriage rides. She had had no time for reflection, even at night in her own bed, as she had been too exhausted to lie awake and think. The ship, and her life aboard it had been different. After leaving Bermuda, despite the storm, life had assumed a lazy routine. In a way, she felt as if she belonged here, with the captain and Geordie and Molly in the warm glow of their companionship. She avoided the thought of Alexander, for it was due to him that she dreaded the disembarking in the morning and feared the welcome she would find, despite the captain's high regard for

Alexander's father—especially now with Alexander missing.

The arrival of Alexander did little to dispel her gloom. His mouth was set in a thin line and his eyes almost black, as he bowed curtly to Dinah and Molly.

"I apologize for my tardiness," he said with exaggerated courtesy, pouring almost half a tumbler of whiskey, "but business with the cargo has kept me below."

"At least you are free now and can join us," Dinah murmured, trying to match his courtesy.

His dark eyes studied her, and he raised his glass in salute before emptying half of it. "My pleasure, my dear, although I fear you will have quite enough of me tomorrow to last you a while—if my company has not already become a burden."

Dinah flushed in anger. If his intention was to put her in her place, she would show him that he failed. "Quite the contrary, Alexander," she said spiritedly. "It is you who I fear have found me dull in comparison to the company to which you are accustomed. For who am I but a poor American, with none of the culture . . ."

Alexander laughed, his cheeks flushed from the whiskey he had just finished. "You are mistaken—quite mistaken. American women are the vogue, the toast of London, one might say. It's reported that your Jennie Jerome, Lady Churchill, has captured the heart of the Duke of Wales, if not his favors."

With a shock, Dinah realized his meaning, that Jennie, whom she had innocently raved about in New York, was the Prince's mistress. She dropped her eyes, speechless at such an idea.

MacKie relieved her of the necessity of a reply, obviously feeling that Alexander had passed the bounds of good behavior. "Alexander, you mentioned the cargo. Was there more storm damage?"

"No. I was merely checking the invoices. I made a few purchases in New York that I want to be sure are loaded on the dray with the luggage." He poured himself more whiskey.

MacKie frowned, his eyes turning to Dinah with a worried look. He was saved from having to carry the conversation himself by the arrival of Johnny.

Dinner was as festive as was possible on a ship that had been at sea for a month without access to fresh supplies. There was a chowder, thick with fish and bits of carrots and potatoes, followed by a ragout made from the salted beef that had been simmered with dried apples and potatoes. Dessert was a tart baked of the last of the flour and the apples, topped with carmelized sugar.

As Johnny removed the last of the dishes before serving the coffee, Dinah and Molly lavished praise on the captain for the dinner. He smiled, thanking them and adding, "By tomorrow evening, it will seem poor fare, although I hope it will leave you with pleasant memories of the voyage."

"Indeed it will," replied Dinah. She wanted to say more, to impress again on the captain her need for a friend in Edinburgh, a need that was growing with the nearing of the time when she must leave the ship. She glanced at Alexander who had eaten in silence. His attitude this evening frightened her, and yet every time she looked at him her body burned with eagerness for his touch, for his hot mouth, for the ectasy he aroused in her. "I hope, Captain," she flung caution to the winds, "that we will have the pleasure of seeing you in Edinburgh. I would hate to think that I would not see you again."

Alexander gave Dinah no opportunity to reply. "I am sure my father will be glad to receive you, Ian, long after Dinah has forgotten the pleasures of the voyage as she quickly will in her new life."

Once again, Dinah realized the meaning behind the words, that what Alexander was saying was that she had forgotten *their* pleasure. Tears came to her eyes again. As if she could ever forget Alexander! How wrong he was! She would remember him always with a desire time could not change, willing to make any sacrifice if only that would make events turn out differently.

PART II

Scotland and London—
1895-1896

Chapter 9

🌹 🌹 🌹

MORNING LEFT LITTLE time for more than hasty goodbyes. Dinah had risen early, dressing quickly in a heavy traveling dress and cloak, to hurry on deck for her first glimpse of her mother's native land. She saw nothing. A heavy fog had set in during the night, shrouding the shore in swirling mists. MacKie could barely be seen on the foredeck, shouting orders, while Geordie saw to the furling of all but the necessary sails. The deck was alive with sailors, those not busy with the sails standing at the hatches. Dinah had gone below to her cabin to get out of their way.

Molly had risen in her absence, and the two young women looked silently at one another over the tea Johnny had brought them. The ship was buzzing with excitement and activity, with even Johnny filled with elation at being home again to have time for his usual gossip.

"We're here," Molly said in a small voice.

"Almost," Dinah agreed, knowing that Molly was as frightened as she, the enormity of their decision, so lightly made, now hitting them full force. They would be as much at the mercy of the whims of virtual strangers as the ship had been at the mercy of the storm.

"Are you frightened, Dinah? I mean, was it right to come so far?" Molly asked, her round blue eyes pools of fear.

Molly's fear instilled courage in Dinah's lagging spirits. She must remember from now on that she was a descendent of queens and act as they would have in her place. Mary, she was sure, was not afraid as she stepped on her native land for the first time in thirteen years—or, at least, she did not show it or admit it to anyone. And neither would Dinah.

"We have no reason to be afraid, Molly," she said as calmly as possible. "Haven't both Alexander and Captain MacKie assured us of Sir Robert's welcome?"

"Then, you think it was right . . ." Molly was still dubious.

"Yes." Dinah talked to reassure herself as much as Molly. She took the little maid's hand, saying earnestly, "What did either of us have in New York? I would have stayed on with Mrs. Bradley as her secretary, you as her maid. We could never hope for much more, whether it were with Mrs. Bradley or another. And now, you have met Geordie, and I . . ."

Molly smiled, remembering Geordie's promise to call on her in a week or ten days. She could envision a future with him, a future with more promise than what lay behind.

Before they could say more, they heard the sound of lines being run out, great thick hawsers as large as a man's arm, and the creak of wood against wood as they docked. Once more, they looked at one another.

Alexander came to get them. He was dressed in the heavy tweeds that he had worn on the day Dinah first saw him. The sight twisted a knife in Dinah's heart, and she couldn't help but think of the joy now lost to her forever. Silently, the two young women donned their cloaks and picked up their small traveling bags to follow him on deck where only a few warehouses and a ship's chandlery was visible in the fog.

"Oh, dear," Molly wailed.

Alexander ignored her, leaning down to whisper in Dinah's ear. "Mary landed in a fog, too, and it was said that she brought with her 'only sorrow, dolor, darkness, and impiety.'"

Dinah had no chance to reply. Captain MacKie and Geordie were waiting for them at the gangway that had been let down. While Geordie renewed his promise to a tearful Molly, MacKie slipped a paper in

129

Dinah's hand. "My mother's address, should you need it," he murmured, a sharp eye on Alexander to make sure he could not overhear, before he kissed her hand.

A dray was already being loaded with their trunks, as Alexander helped them into a closed coach. Johnny rushed up with a basket containing refreshments for the journey, and Alexander climbed into the coach, sitting himself opposite the two young women. No sooner had he sat down than the coach lurched forward, amid the screeches and screams of the gulls invisible in the fog.

As the cobbles gave way to the smoothly packed dirt of a road, Dinah leaned forward to peer out the window. The fog, if anything, was thicker than on the water. Disappointed, she leaned back.

"It's not much of a welcome, I'm afraid," Alexander said, regretting his earlier malicious remark. He tried to atone for it, saying, "Don't worry. It will make my father's welcome all the warmer."

Dinah pulled the cloak more closely around her to ward off the chill. "The climate is not always like this, is it?"

Alexander had to smile. "I'm afraid Scotland has more than its share of fog, although it is worse here along the Firth, and it is November."

Dinah thought of the cool, crisp, yet sunny days of New York in October. Even there, now, it would be chill and damp. She realized she had lost track of time during the weeks aboard ship. "I had forgotten it was November," she admitted sheepishly.

"Days and weeks do lose their meaning aboard ship," Alexander agreed. The carriage was rolling smoothly now, and he took an insulated jug of hot tea out of the basket on the floor beside him. "Perhaps some tea will help." He poured another cup for Molly and finally one for himself. "There are sandwiches, too, to make up for the lack of breakfast."

"Thank you, but the tea will be fine. I don't think I could eat right now," Dinah apologized, admitting to her own fears.

130

Alexander nodded, rubbing a temple with his free hand. "About last night. I'm afraid I was rude, ruder than I had cause to be. The whiskey must have gone to my head."

Dinah studied him levelly, her eyes clear, as she recalled his insinuations. Evidently, Alexander had his own fears, fear that she might mention the drinking to his father. A saying of her mother's came to mind, and she said with a twinkle in her eye, "Wasn't it a Scot, Robert Burns, who said, 'With whiskey, we'll face the devil'?"

Alexander returned her gaze. "It was, my dear, but do you mean yourself or my father by the devil?"

Dinah damned him in her thoughts, feeling her face flush. "Take it as you wish." she replied stiffly, looking once more out the window, where the fog swirled as thick as ever.

Alexander took the cup from her hand, his own hand lingering on her knee, as he told her in a low voice, "And it was Shakespeare who wrote, 'I am slain by a fair cruel maid.' You are fair indeed . . ."

Dinah refused to look at him. "Trading quotations is one way to pass the time, but I meant nothing personal."

Alexander removed his hand as quickly as if he had touched fire. "You make it damned difficult for a man to apologize, Dinah. If your mother were as stiff-necked as you, I wonder at my father's eagerness to take her daughter into his home."

Nothing Alexander could have said could have struck at Dinah's heart as his mention of her mother did. The tears that had been swelling in her eyes since the last evening spilled over. Ashamed of herself, she scrabbled in her reticule for a handkerchief.

"Oh, Di . . . Miss Dinah!" Molly cried, trying to find her own kerchief. Lost in her own thoughts, she had barely paid any attention to what was said. Now she turned on Alexander in fury. "What have you done to her?"

Alexander was as surprised at the sudden tears as Molly. He shook his own handkerchief from his sleeve, handing it to Dinah who was forced to accept it.

The young woman ignored her maid's efforts to comfort her. "Stiff-necked, am I," she sputtered through her tears. "And you are not, I suppose. You are the very . . . very essence of . . . of gentility."

"Hardly, although I cannot face a woman's tears. For God's sake, Dinah, please. I would take back everything I have said and done if only I could, if only you would stop crying," he pleaded. "We will soon be there," the coach had given a sudden lurch, once more being drawn over cobblestones. "Whatever will my father think, to see you weeping so."

The mention of Sir Robert stopped Dinah's tears as quickly as that of her mother had started them. She wiped her eyes, sniffing a little.

Alexander smiled in relief. "Now blow your nose like a good girl."

Wordlessly, Dinah obeyed before returning the handkerchief to him. "Thank you. And I'm sorry. I did not mean to cry like that."

The carriage drew to a stop. Alexander descended first before raising his hand to help Dinah. Their eyes met. "Dinah," he said slowly, "whatever you think of me, let us start afresh. We cannot change the past, but it need not taint your future."

Dinah opened her mouth to agree, closing it at the sight of the house. Regardless of what Alexander had said, it was every bit as grand as the Jerome mansion. The front door was now open, and a man was standing in the glow of the hall. "Oh, dear," she said, "how very grand it is, Alexander . . ."

The man squeezed her hand, helping her to the ground. The coachman meanwhile had assisted Molly, who joined Dinah. Alexander escorted them to the front door.

The man in the doorway could only be Sir Robert. The lines from his nose to his mouth and at the corners of his eyes were deeply engraved, and his hair was iron gray. He was stockier than Alexander and shorter. His manner and bearing were that of a successful man, used to command.

"Father," Alexander drew Dinah forward, Molly following, as a butler shut the door behind them, "here is Dinah Murray."

"My dear," Sir Robert took her cold hands in his, his eyes probing her face as if in search of her mother, "welcome to Edinburgh and my house. It is your home now, as it is mine."

"Thank you, Sir Robert." Dinah smiled, the hood of her cloak falling back to reveal the crown of curly red hair and the long, graceful neck.

Although Sir Robert's eyes clouded slightly as he glanced at his son, his smile did not fade. "Excuse my staring, Dinah," he said in a deep voice roughened with emotion. "You are lovelier, more grown up, than I imagined. In my mind, I saw you looking like your mother at her age. You are taller than she and more beautiful than she ever was."

Dinah flushed. How childish and needless her fears had been.

Sir Robert released her hands, turning to Molly. "Who might this be?"

Quickly Alexander explained about Molly, adding graciously, "Molly has been friend as well as maid, Father."

"Mrs. Bradley was quite right to suggest your accompanying Dinah. Indeed, I should have thought of it myself. You, too, are welcome, Molly, and you have a place here and with Dinah for as long as you wish."

"Thank you, sir," Molly replied, dropping a curtsy.

"Now, I am sure you could use some hot food after that cold journey in the fog. First, though, you will want to freshen up." He nodded to the butler. "Jamison, please have Mrs. Jamison show the young women to the room I ordered prepared." He smiled at Dinah. "I am sure you will not mind sharing quarters for a while longer until I can have a room made ready for Molly."

The house was obviously run with an efficiency that Mrs. Bradley would have appreciated. Within seconds, a middle-aged, plump, rosy-cheeked woman appeared whom Sir Robert introduced as his housekeeper, Mrs. Jamison.

"Mrs. Jamison," Sir Robert told her, "please show Miss Murray and Miss Carew to Miss Murray's room and then come to the library."

The girls were led up a grand staircase that spread its arms from the center of the hall to the second floor. What Sir Robert had called a room turned out to be two rooms, a small sitting room decorated in blue and gold, and a large bedroom. On the floors were blue and gold Brussels carpets, thick and soft underfoot, and the large canopied bed had a matching blue coverlet and canopy.

Mrs. Jamison smiled, checking the large pitcher and wash basin on a stand. "The water's good and hot. I had it brought up as soon as we heard the carriage stop. If you want more, just ring." She motioned to the bell cord by the bed. "Is there anything you need before I leave?"

"No, thank you, Mrs. Jamison," Dinah smiled.

With the woman's departure, both girls looked at one another. "Oh, Molly," Dinah burst out, "have you ever seen the like! Why, these rooms alone put Mrs. Bradley's house to shame."

"I know." Molly, practical, went to the bed and bounced up and down on it. "Just feel this. You'll feel like you're sleeping on a cloud."

"I just don't believe it. I'm afraid I'll awaken and find this is all a dream," Dinah sighed, Alexander forgotten for the moment.

"Pinch yourself," Molly laughed. "I just did and it's still here."

"And see," Dinah went to the fireplace that graced one wall with a handsome white marble lintel. "There's even a fire lit."

While Dinah warmed her hands and removed her cloak, Molly poured hot water in the basin, saying, "Well, you had better wash and clean up, or Sir

Robert will be sending up to find out what's happened to us."

The two girls washed quickly, leaving on their traveling dresses. Until the trunks arrived, which would be later in the afternoon according to Alexander, they had nothing else to wear. They were soon ready to go back downstairs. After leaving the room to walk to the top of the grand staircase, they took a few minutes to look around them. The hall was as large as a ballroom. By the door was a mahogany table, polished to a fine brilliance, with a silver candelabra and tray. Along one wall was an equally polished and fine sideboard and matching candelabra and a few chairs for guests to use until they were announced. The staircase itself was marble. Everywhere they looked they saw signs of a wealth for which Alexander had hardly prepared them.

Descending the staircase, they hesitated, not sure which way to go. Jamison appeared, seemingly from out of nowhere, to tell them that the gentlemen were waiting for them in the library. He ushered them into a magnificent book-lined room, so large that the fire in the grate and the candles by the chairs and settee in front of the fireplace did little to dispel the shadows in the rest of the room where the heavy draperies were drawn across windows to keep out the damp November chill.

Sir Robert saw that they were comfortably seated and then asked Jamison to have the tea brought in. "My daughter, Margaret, is sorry that she could not be here to welcome you. She had made arrangements to visit friends this afternoon. She will be joining us for dinner, Dinah, and you shall meet her then."

Once Dinah saw the meal that was to be served them, she wondered how she would be able to eat again. The butler and a footman brought in trays, which were set on tables in front of the girls. Under the covered dishes was steaming lamb and barley soup, warm freshly baked bread, and a finnan haddie, creamed smoked fish that Dinah recalled her mother making. For dessert, there was a hot fruit pastry topped

135

with thick cream. Both girls ate with a good appetite, finding themselves hungry. Neither had had any breakfast, and they had been too excited to eat the sandwiches.

After they had eaten and Jamison had removed the trays, Sir Robert himself poured tea for them. The cups and saucers of thin china seemed fragile after the heavy mugs to which they had become accustomed on the *Star of Scotland*.

Alexander had satisfied himself with sandwiches and brandy. As they sipped their tea, he lit a cigar.

Sir Robert, pouring a cup of tea for himself, sat in a chair opposite them, regarding them with a thoughtful expression. "Dinah, I realize it is much too soon to talk about the future. Alexander told me that your mother had only recently passed away before his arrival. Between your loss and the voyage, not to mention your discovery of a family whom you never knew existed, you must be confused. And now you are in a strange country.

"Nevertheless, this is your home, and I want you to feel as if you are the member of the family you actually are. All of us, and I speak for my daughter, too, will do whatever we can to help make you feel at home. Feel free at any time to come to me. Now, if there is anything you need or anything I can tell you to enlighten you about your new life—or," he smiled, "reassure you, please tell me."

Dinah shook her head. There were questions she should ask, but the combination of little sleep and hot food made her brain feel drugged. As Sir Robert said, so much had happened and was happening, that even if she had all her wits about her she would not know where to begin. Still, she had to say something because he was expecting it, and she fell back on the little courtesies her mother had dinned into her from childhood. "You have done more than reassure me, Sir Robert. As you say, all is so new . . ." She lifted her hands helplessly.

"You are a wise girl, wise beyond your years—as your mother was," Sir Robert said with a sigh.

Dinah dropped her eyes, the only questions she wanted to ask were about her mother, why she had left such a fine place, and about the father Dinah had never known. Yet, these could hardly be asked here and now. There were other questions, too, that Alexander had raised in her mind. She had noticed the frown on Sir Robert's face when her hood had fallen back and had heard his comment about her mother. She had always assumed that she took after her father until Alexander had raised the ghost of Mary Stuart. There was that question to be answered as well.

Sir Robert stood up. "And now I am sure both of you could do with a rest." He said to Molly, "Jamison will take you to Mrs. Jamison who will see to your comforts. If she does not, let me know. Once you are settled and have a chance to get used to us, we will talk about your future, that is, should you decide to stay with us. I want you to know, Miss Carew, that I appreciate the sacrifice you have made. If your wish is to return to New York, I will see to it that you lack nothing."

"Thank you, sir." Molly dropped a curtsy, with a side look at Dinah. "My wish is to see to Miss Dinah. I am a good maid . . ."

"Now, now," Sir Robert interrupted, "I meant to cast no shadow on your qualifications. I am sure from what my son has told me that Mrs. Bradley would not have suggested your accompanying my . . . my cousin if you were not capable. But you, too, will need time to adjust, and I want you to know you have it. In the meantime, my daughter's maid will see to Dinah with your assistance, if that is agreeable to both of you."

At their nods, Sir Robert pulled the bell to summon the butler, saying to Dinah, "Dinner is at eight. It will be only the four of us, and we will not be dressing."

Chapter 10

🌹 🌹 🌹

DINAH SAT AT the small inlaid rosewood desk in her
sitting room. In front of her was a heavy sheet of
paper bearing the Douglas crest, addressed to Mrs.
Bradley. Her pale brow furrowed as she tried to think
of how to begin the letter. In the two weeks since she
had arrived in Edinburgh, so much had happened that
Dinah found it difficult to organize her thoughts.

She thought back to the first night and the dinner
en famille at which she had met Margaret, Alexander's sister. Although the trunks had arrived, there
had been little time to press any of the gowns. Since
Sir Robert had said they would not dress, she had
worn a simple dark green gown that she had worn on
shipboard with the petticoats that went with it. The
fitted bodice had set off her figure, and the white collar had flattered her complexion and hair. Joining the
men in the library for before-dinner sherry, she had
found them wearing tartan trews and smoking jackets. The sight had filled her with the realization that
she was really in Scotland, but her initial pleasure was
spoiled by the meeting with Margaret. Margaret, in a
heavy watered silk gown with a deep-cut neckline,
long sleeves lavished with Alençon lace, and a fashionable bustle, made Dinah seem definitely the country cousin.

The evening, despite Sir Robert's attention to Dinah, had not gone well. Margaret had engaged in conversation, pointedly bringing up social occasions and
dropping names and places that meant nothing to Dinah. One particular name kept recurring, that of the

Anguses and of a Mary and James Angus in particular who were coming to call the next day, anxious to hear all about Alexander's voyage and, of course, to meet Dinah. As if that were not bad enough, Dinah had been forced, still full from the tea, to sit through a long dinner, listening to Margaret's prattle about how "foreign" the food must be and how "alien" the customs.

The remarks had become more pointed in the library where the two women waited for the men to finish their port and cigars and join them for coffee. Dinah had held her tongue with difficulty, pleading fatigue to return to her room as soon as she courteously could. To her relief, she had found Molly laying out her nightclothes. After Dinah had changed, the two friends had settled in front of the fire to talk.

Molly, despite Sir Robert's instructions to relax, had done anything but. She had immediately set about making friends with Mrs. Jamison, who was responsible for the house and staff with her husband, and with Margaret's maid, a girl of Molly's age called Parker. From her bits and pieces of conversation with them, Molly had learned that the Anguses belonged to the nobility. Like much Scottish nobility, however, their wealth lay in the lands which were heavily entailed. The Douglases, at least this branch of the family, could claim no titles, the "sir" in front of Sir Robert's name entirely due to his having been knighted by Queen Victoria.

Molly had giggled as she told Dinah about Margaret Douglas and Mary Angus being the best of friends, so much so that they were fellow conspirators in encouraging a match between Margaret and James Angus on one side and between Mary Angus and Alexander on the other. Sir Robert, however, had refused to take James into his shipping company and was opposed to a match between Margaret and James on the grounds that James was a ne'r-do-well. As a result, James had been forced to go to the Army.

"Alexander," Molly had said, eyes covertly watching Dinah, "is a willing enough escort. But, Dinah,

Parker says that he tells Margaret that he has no intention of marrying Mary—or anyone else."

Dinah had learned the accuracy of Molly's intelligence when the two young Anguses paid their call. After Dinah was introduced as "our young cousin from America," the three had ignored her to question Alexander in detail about his trip, what he thought of New York, and the side trip to Bermuda. Alexander had answered briefly, making no attempt to conceal his growing boredom. When Mary had coquettishly suggested a ride in the park in the morning, he had ostentatiously gone to Dinah's side, seating himself casually on the arm of her chair and taking one of her hands in his.

"I am afraid, Mary, I have a previous engagement, do I not, Dinah?" He raised Dinah's hand to his lips and hurried on to prevent her from answering. "I have already promised to show our cousin the castle."

Dinah, unable to control the emotions that Alexander still aroused in her, had suggested that he could take her to the castle another day. Alexander insisted that he could not disappoint her. He had not, although he had kept his distance when they were alone.

The emotions he had aroused in her, in fact, grew stronger in Edinburgh. On the ship, she had had Captain MacKie to turn to. Here, she had no one, and in those first weeks Alexander had been her constant escort to the small dinners given in her honor by Sir Robert's friends.

At the same time, Dinah was lonely as never before. She had always been a solitary and independent child, able to amuse herself, but she had always had her mother to run to, or the cook, or, more recently, Molly. Here, life was so formal. To see Molly, she had to summon her by pulling the bell rope, and often Molly was busy as both she and Parker had duties other than serving their mistresses. As a result, the only real time they had to talk was when Molly helped Dinah prepare for bed.

Nevertheless today was different. Last night, Sir Robert had told her that Captain MacKie had been to the offices of the shipping line and had asked if he might call on Dinah. Sir Robert had given his permission, and MacKie was to arrive shortly. Dinah sighed, laying down the pen. For the twentieth time she went to the mirror to be sure she looked attractive.

How plain the gowns purchased with such excitement in New York now appeared. They were, moreover, unfashionable. Margaret and her friends favored fitted gowns, the full skirts drawn up into a bustle and the low necklines filled in with lace or frills for daytime. In contrast, Dinah's dresses were fitted to the waist where they blossomed in fullness, depending on the number of petticoats worn. Even worse, with the exception of a few dresses that bared her shoulders for evening, all had high necks with little Irish lace collars, more appropriate for a school girl than a woman of society. Dinah grimaced at her reflection. Other than school girls, the only woman who wore such modest gowns was Queen Victoria, a thought that depressed her even more. This gown, a flattering rust fabric of silk and wool, at least rustled like silk when she moved.

Still, the neckline was hideously plain. On an impulse, she went to the dressing table, opening the drawer in which was the silver brooch that had been a prized possession of her mother's. Dinah held it up to the neckline, deciding the heavy silver and smoky stone made her appear more mature. Upon hearing a rap on the door, she fastened it quickly and went to open it, her heart beating at the thought of MacKie waiting for her.

Molly told her excitedly, "They're here—the captain and Geordie. Do hurry. I've shown Captain MacKie into the library, and Geordie is waiting for me in the back parlor."

"Don't keep Geordie waiting, Molly." Dinah pushed the other girl toward the rear stairs. "I can find the captain myself."

Ever since Sir Robert had told her about MacKie, Dinah had realized how much she missed his company. At sea, she had taken his presence for granted.

Besides, he had seemed so staid in comparison to the excitement that the mere sight of Alexander roused in her—much as she hated to admit it. At the same time, she had a curiously passionate need to see this man she had asked to be her friend.

The man was standing, hands behind his back and back to the fire. The sliding doors opened soundlessly, and for a moment the man did not notice her watching him, giving Dinah a few seconds to compose herself. How different MacKie was from Alexander, his father, and the men she had met at the various dinners. Tall and slender or short and heavy, they had an almost feminine grace emphasized by the richness of their clothes. MacKie with his broad shoulders and big chest emphasized by the simplicity of his uniform was their opposite, just as the directness of his blue eyes and his smile of genuine pleasure at seeing her was the opposite of their flattering appraisal and assumed airs. He approached her, hands out in a straightforward gesture of welcome.

"Ian!" Dinah burst out, running into his arms and not realizing she had called him by his first name for the first time.

"Dinah, my dear." Ian responded to her overture, holding her close for a moment before releasing her to take her hands. "Let me look at you and see how Scotland is treating you."

Dinah laughed delightedly, her shyness of the past two weeks disappearing. "How marvelous to see you! You have not changed at all!"

"In two weeks? But you, you are lovelier than ever, although you have lost those rosy cheeks that bloomed with your turns about the deck," he smiled. Hesitating, he added, "Are you happy? Your welcome was all that you had been led to believe?"

"Oh, yes. Sir Robert has been so wonderfully kind, just as you said," Dinah told him. "I have been introduced to so many people that I can hardly keep the names straight."

MacKie's blue eyes studied her so closely that Dinah had to drop her own eyes. There was no need for him to know about Margaret's coldness or Alexander's apparent ignoring of her. "You are quite happy, quite content here?" he asked again.

The young woman was unable to lie to the blue eyes that she could feel watching her, despite her lowered lids. "It . . . it is all so terribly new, so much grander . . ." She raised her eyes, "There are times when I yearn to be back aboard the *Star of Scotland,* where life was so much simpler."

"That is understandable." Ian glanced around the room. Although he had seen the house many times, this was the first time he had been inside. The size, the grand style, and the elegance made him uncomfortable, and he could easily imagine how Dinah must feel.

"Do you think so?" Dinah sighed, wanting reassurance. "There are times when I think of those small rooms I shared with my mother and wish I were back —and then I think of my mother, leaving all this. How she must have longed to have rooms and rooms to walk through."

Ian had no answer, although he did have a ready solution. "Perhaps, then, you would welcome an opportunity to join my mother and me for tea, unless you have other plans. I realize that the invitation is sudden, but I returned to Edinburgh only yesterday. It would give her great pleasure. I have told her about you, and she is eager to meet you. It was her idea to invite you."

"And you?" Dinah could not resist playing the coquette, as she tilted her head, looking at him flirtatiously from under her eyelashes.

The captain's tanned skin turned darker, as he admitted honestly, "It would give me great pleasure, too, Dinah."

Although he wanted to call a carriage, Dinah preferred to walk as soon as she found it was only a few blocks from Princes Street, and the Douglas mansion, to the lane below the castle where the small house that Ian had bought for his widowed mother was. After taking her cloak and informing Jamison she would be out for tea, she let Ian lead her to the street.

The day was unexpectedly warm and sunny for late November, the equivalent of October's Indian Summer in New York. The days of fog and rain made Dinah appreciate the sun all the more, which was her reason for wanting to walk. She seemed actually to be seeing Edinburgh for the first time, to see the walled ancient castle set on its rock like a crown in the sun. Even the dull gray mansions lining the street seemed less cold and forbidding.

Dinah chattered happily like a child, as she told Ian about New York and Washington Square, how on days such as this she would often walk there, perhaps sit on a bench to watch the mothers and nursemaids taking their apple-cheeked charges for their breath of fresh air. "I would like to do that here, but there seems to be no place to walk and everyone is always going about in carriages."

Ian frowned, recalling how Dinah had enjoyed going on deck in all weather. "Surely you are not confined to the house all day?"

"Oh, no. I didn't mean that. Alexander and Margaret and their friends ride when it is possible in the park beyond Holyrood Palace. They keep horses there."

"Then you could join them?" Ian pressed.

Dinah looked at the ground, a blush rising. "Ian, I have never learned to ride. Alexander has promised to teach me," she lied, for she had never mentioned it to him, "but I am afraid of horses. Not the poor old things who draw the carriages," she added quickly, "I mean those handsome sleek creatures that are always tossing their heads and pawing the ground. I would feel quite helpless on one. Still," she raised her head with a laugh, "I must try, mustn't I?"

"Aye," Ian agreed. "Anyone who can learn to walk on a rolling deck as you did has all the courage and ability to ride the wildest stallion."

"Do you really think so?" Dinah asked, eager again for reassurance.

"I know so." Ian took her arm to steer her down a narrow street.

Dinah immediately felt at home. It resembled the mews where she had lived for as long as she could remember, except it was even neater. At every window, moreover, was a window box filled with late-blooming fall flowers. Ian stopped at a small, three-story house with green shutters and a green door. Although he rapped the brass knocker, he opened the door without waiting for an answer.

The hall was narrow. Doors on the right led to the rooms on the ground floor, a flight of stairs toward the rear led to the second story. At one side was a sea chest and a coat rack. No sooner had Ian hung his cap on one of the arms and helped Dinah remove her cloak then a woman bustled out from a room at the back of the stairs. All Dinah needed was to see her eyes, which were of the same startling blue as her son's, to like Mrs. MacKie immediately.

Ian kissed his mother's cheek, saying, "Mother, here is Miss Murray."

Mrs. MacKie took Dinah's hands, studying her face. "The least you could have done, Ian, was to tell me how beautiful she is. Welcome, Miss Murray." She led them into a small sitting room, with a coal fire burning cheerfully in the grate. "Make yourself at home, while I tell the girl to bring the tea."

Dinah looked around the room curiously. Grouped around the fire were a small sofa and two comfortable arm chairs. To one side was a roll-top desk, the top up to reveal neatly arranged pigeonholes. By a window was a straight chair with an embroidery frame in front of it.

Ian was about to apologize for the smallness, as Dinah said, "How cozy this is. I am so grateful to you for your invitation." She sat on the sofa, carefully drawing her skirts to permit Ian to sit beside her.

"Well, Miss Murray," Mrs. MacKie joined them, "we shall have our tea shortly, if you do not mind waiting for hot scones."

"Indeed not. What a lovely room this is, Mrs. Mac-Kie."

Mrs. MacKie smiled, thinking of the grand house on Princes Street. "It is small but more than enough to care for, Miss Murray."

"It is larger than what I was used to in New York." She hesitated before adding, "Please call me Dinah. I also find 'Miss Murray' more formal than what I am used to."

"Of course, Dinah. Your mother was Scottish, my son tells me. I ask because I notice the brooch you are wearing. Was that hers, may I ask?"

"Yes, it was." Dinah fingered the brooch before unclasping it to hand it to Mrs. MacKie. "The stone is a cairngorm, I believe."

"It is that. It is the badge that has me curious, the oak and the thistle around which the silver is worked. Surely, you have noticed them?" Mrs. MacKie raised her eyebrows.

"Of course. I assumed they were merely decorative. Aren't they?" Dinah asked in puzzlement.

"In a way." Mrs. MacKie looked from Dinah to her son and then back to Dinah. "Perhaps I am speaking out of turn, for your mother obviously told you little of your heritage for reasons of her own. Still, you are here now, and I . . . I would dislike you to be . . ." she glanced again at Ian, "to be surprised."

"Surprised?" Shaking her head, Dinah said, "I don't understand."

"Dinah," Mrs. MacKie began firmly, "you know about the clans, which are really families and those who paid allegiance to them. Each clan had its own tartan to be worn only by members of the clan." At Dinah's nod, she went on, "Each clan also has its own coat of arms and badge or brooch. Traditionally, the badge was silver and worked with the symbol of the clan, with or without a cairngorm or other stone. The purpose of the badge, originally worn in battle, was to identify members of the clan to each other, as many came from far places and could be strangers.

146

The penalty for wearing a badge of a clan to which one didn't belong was death."

Dinah's eyes widened, but Mrs. MacKie continued. "The badge had another purpose. It guaranteed the wearer a proper burial, with the person finding the body to take the silver badge in payment for that courtesy."

"I still don't see . . . I mean, the pin is of the Murray clan, isn't it?" asked Dinah.

"No." Mrs. MacKie handed her back the badge. "It bears the oak and thistle, the badge of the Stuarts."

Dinah seemed deaf for a moment, blood pounding through her veins, as she recalled Alexander telling her of her heritage and how she resembled the Queen of Scots. "Dear God," she murmured, saved from having to say more by the appearance of a young maid with a tea tray.

No more mention was made of the badge. Mrs. MacKie asked, instead, about the voyage, basking in Dinah's comments about the ability of her son. Too soon, it was time to leave. The early winter dusk had fallen, and Ian insisted on a carriage to take them to the Douglas house.

He saw her to the door, where Dinah thanked him for the afternoon, asking him to thank his mother again for inviting her to come for a visit any time. "I'll see you again, Ian, won't I?" she asked anxiously.

"If you wish. As a matter of fact, Sir Robert has invited me to dinner on Friday, although he mentioned a party to which you had been invited," Ian said with a smile.

Dinah knew the reason for the smile. Ian MacKie, captain of a ship or not, was hardly the social equal of his daughter—or Dinah now. "I shall see you then," Dinah promised. "I have had quite my fill of parties." Especially, she thought, those where I am left to sit while Margaret and Mary go off with their friends.

She let herself into the house. Passing the doors to the library on her way upstairs, she heard voices and paused. Although she did not mean to eavesdrop, what she heard made her listen more intently.,

147

"Damn you," that was Sir Robert's voice raised in anger, "had I another son, I would send you to the Army as Malcolm Angus did with James. Oh, yes, don't tell me again about your successes in New York and Bermuda—you did well enough even if you refused to listen to MacKie or the advice of the commissioner."

"Father," Alexander's own voice was raised, "if Ian . . ."

"Ian said nothing against you. As a matter of fact, he defended you. His major concern was for Dinah, whom he feared you had done little to reassure about her welcome. From what I have heard, those fears were not groundless. I have been told how you escort her to these affairs, only to leave her for the gaming tables."

"Margaret . . ." Alexander tried to say.

"I have every intention of speaking to Margaret, too, but you are a man and you have friends who would be more than willing to have her for a dancing partner and escort her to supper. As if those reports were not bad enough, now I find you owe over a thousand pounds. I had hoped that MacKie would set you an example. After all, he is close to your age, not a man old enough to be your father whom you would surely ignore. Instead, you have acted the fine gentleman—and I have had reports of that, too, including your drinking. Well, sir!"

The voices were drawing close to the door, and Dinah fled upstairs. Reaching her room, she pulled the bell rope before remembering that Molly might still be with Geordie. It was Molly she wanted to talk to, which meant she would have to invent an excuse should Parker arrive. But it was a radiant Molly who entered the room.

Mrs. Jamison had told Molly to use the back parlor where she and Geordie could talk undisturbed. In the few weeks she had known Molly she had come to like the young American who always had a smile and was so willing to help, despite her relationship with Dinah. She also admired the courage it had taken to leave

148

family, friends, and country to accompany her young mistress and come so far to a foreign country. A courage that Molly's hair-raising tale of the storm at sea had only further attested to. At the same time, Molly deferred to Parker in all matters except Dinah's comfort, never trying to make herself out as any better than the other servants.

Then, there was Geordie. He had arrived in Edinburgh several days before the captain, who still had to see to matters pertaining to the ship. Geordie's first stop, even before he had gone to his sister's, had been Molly, an attention that completely won over Mrs. Jamison's romantic heart. After that first brief visit, he had stopped by the house almost every day, either in the afternoon when Molly was free before dinner, or in the evening. Despite the frequent visits and the use of the back parlor, however, there had been no intimacy between Molly and Geordie with the exception of long kisses and a few caresses.

That afternoon, in view of the weather, Molly and Geordie had gone for a walk. As they ambled down Princes Street toward the fine shops, Molly had brought up the one subject that had never been discussed between them and that puzzled Molly. For all his attentions and declarations of love, Geordie had never mentioned his family or marriage, leaving Molly uneasy and afraid that he did not think she was good enough for him.

As they paused in front of a shop window filled with the various clan tartans, Molly said, "Your family must be happy to have you home again, although what do they think of your going out so much?"

"I only have a sister, Moll, love. My parents died when I was small, and she raised me, but she's married now with so many bairn that she's glad enough to have me out of the house."

Molly nodded, recalling her own family. She had actually been glad to go into service where she would have a room of her own. "Doesn't she ask where you go, what you . . ."

"Oh" Geordie flushed red, "You mean, have I told her about you?"

"Yes." Molly blushed, too.

"Of course I have, love, and told her, too, that I want to marry you!"

They were in the middle of the street. Molly stopped abruptly, just as a coach, the driver urging the horses to greater speed turned the corner. Geordie grabbed her arm, pulling her to safety, as the horses clattered past, hooves sparking the cobblestones.

"Are you sick?" Geordie asked.

"Oh, Geordie!" Oblivious to their surroundings, Molly threw her arms around his neck, smothering him with kisses as passersby stopped and stared at the couple, smiles on their faces. "Do you mean it?"

"Naturally." Geordie was bewildered. "You canna think I would come to see you every day, satisfy myself with a kiss or two and a fond pat, if I were not intending to take you to wife!"

"Then," Molly floundered, angry at him, "why have you said nothing?"

"I thought you knew, especially after the ship . . ." Geordie sounded miserable, his blue eyes clinging to Molly's face.

"A woman likes—needs—to be told, to be asked, I should say," Molly replied more haughtily than she felt.

"I meant to. I was going to. Your next day off, I wanted to take you to meet my sister; it's a fair distance from here. If you liked one another, I would then ask Dinah for your hand."

"Does it matter that your sister and I like one another? It is you and I who matter. As for Dinah . . ." They were still standing at the curb. Geordie shook his head at the vagaries of women, whom he did not understand in the least.

"I wanted it all proper," he said. "Besides, Moll, what will you do when I go to sea? I would not want you to be staying in service."

"Oh!" It had not occurred to Molly that marrying Geordie would mean leaving Dinah, at least not until Dinah was settled in her new life. As they walked on, Molly's thoughts were on the future. Surely Geordie would not insist she leave Dinah. Yet, "all proper" could only mean that. With a cheerful optimism, she decided that perhaps Dinah would be settled soon, and then she and Geordie.

"There's a small house near my sister's, Molly. One more voyage and I can buy it for us." He talked on earnestly about his sister, making plans to take Molly to meet her the following week on Sunday, when Molly would have the whole day free.

As Molly listened, she forgot about Dinah, thinking about the life Geordie was offering her, a little house of their own with a garden. She had never had a garden in her life. Happily, she took Geordie's arm, holding it close.

The happiness lasted during the rest of the walk and over tea. Only when she saw Dinah's face and the thoughtful expression on it did her own happiness fade. She could hardly tell Dinah her news right now. She would have to wait. She knew Dinah would insist that she marry Geordie as soon as possible.

Dinah, too wrapped up in her discovery about the meaning of the brooch and what she had overheard to notice the glowing expression on Molly's face fade, was seated in the small sitting room. Her brow was wrinkled in thought.

"Miss Dinah, is anything wrong?" Molly hurried to her side.

Dinah smothered what she had been about to say about Alexander. It would not do to discuss an overheard conversation that she might have misinterpreted. "Not really." Dinah tried to summon a smile, as she told Molly about the afternoon with Captain MacKie and his mother and the charming little house under the shadow of the castle.

Molly listened. She knew Dinah too well not to be aware that she was disturbed. "Dinah," Molly seated herself at Dinah's feet on a small footstool, "if it was all so pleasant, why are you frowning so? You will get wrinkles before your time!"

.. Dinah smiled slightly. "You know me too well, Molly." With that, she told her about the brooch, finishing with, "you don't really think that what Alexander said about Mary Stuart could be true, do you? I mean, it is all so fantastic! Besides, no one else has mentioned any such likeness. Yet, now this brooch," she said it in her hand and she showed it to Molly, pointing out the oak and thistle.

Molly, clever as she was in many respects, could not conceive of the past, of events that did not concern her and that she had not experienced. "I wouldn't worry my head with such things," she declared. "Even so, what difference does it make? Three hundred years ago!" She shook her head at the number of years.

Dinah took the brooch back. "You're right. Why should I bother with such things?" She decided to change the subject, and an idea came into her head. "I have decided to ask Alexander to teach me to ride. What do you think?"

"That's a good idea," Molly agreed, concealing her own thoughts about horses. Having grown up in the city, she was used to seeing them on the streets. In addition, she had often watched Jim groom the carriage horses in the stable down the mews and had offered them tidbits. Once, Jim had playfully put her on its back. Looking down on the ground, which had seemed so far away, she had insisted on dismounting immediately. Still, she had seen the fine ladies riding in the park and had heard servants talk of hunts at country estates where their families went for the season.

Besides, there was Alexander. To Molly's mind, he was the perfect match for Dinah. Anything that would bring the two closer together was to be approved—and the sooner the better, she thought.

For once, the Douglases were all dining at home. Dinah drew Alexander aside at the first opportunity. He agreed enthusiastically to her suggestion, offering to give her the first lesson the next day. As a result, Dinah asked to borrow a riding habit from Margaret, who could hardly refuse outright with her father looking at Dinah in approval. Sullenly, she offered to let Dinah try one on.

The jacket and white frilled blouse were a good fit, as were the boots. Although Dinah was taller than Margaret, she had small, narrow feet, and the boots were even a little large. The skirt was the only problem because of the length.

"It will never do," Margaret said curtly. "The skirt is much too short. You might as well take it off."

Dinah surveyed herself in the mirror. Granted, the skirt was short, but the boots kept the costume within the bounds of modesty. "I am not so sure," Dinah said stubbornly, determined to ride as soon as possible. "Perhaps we should get Sir Robert and Alexander's opinion."

The other young woman was derisive about the suggestion. "They're men! They would agree to anything, especially," she added pointedly, "if it showed more than a bit of ankle."

"Well, I intend to ask them anyway." Dinah tossed her head and left the room before Margaret could stop her, with Margaret following in order to give her opinion.

As Dinah modeled the riding habit for the men in the library, she spoke quickly to forestall Margaret's objections. "Margaret feels it is too short—and, of course, I am taller. What do you think?"

Alexander chuckled, with a glance at his father. "It certainly looks modest enough to me."

"I agree. Dinah, it will serve until you decide if you like riding enough to have one of your own fitted," Sir Robert confirmed.

"My opinion is that it is much too short," Margaret insisted angrily. "One simply should not show so much ankle. It's not decent."

"Come, come, Margaret. When Dinah is on the horse, no one will notice. I never knew you were such a prude," Alexander jeered.

"Then the matter is settled." Sir Robert stepped in swiftly to avoid the unpleasantness going any further.

"Very well. Let Dinah make a fool of herself,"

Margaret sulked. "At least, I shall not be there to watch, as I have a fitting at the dressmaker's. Dinah would do better to come with me and . . "

"I disagree. The weather is far too fine to last this time of year," Alexander put in smoothly, glancing at his father and remembering their earlier conversation. "I think we should take advantage of it.'"

"I am afraid for once I agree with Alexander," Sir Robert conceded, recalling the same discussion and giving his son a thoughtful look.

Chapter 11

THE STABLE AT Kirk o' Fields was beyond the old city walls, not far from Holyrood Palace. Although the morning had been overcast when they left Princes Street by carriage, Alexander had been right to insist that the lessons not be delayed, as the sun broke through the clouds by their arrival at the stable.

The young man had a gentle bay mare saddled for Dinah. While his own black stallion was being saddled, he assisted Dinah in mounting the horse. "Her name is Duchess," he explained, showing her how to hold the reins with her clasped hands upright. "If you pull the right rein, she will turn to the right. If you pull the left, to the left. So try to keep your hands as steady as possible. Hold tightly enough that you need only pull back slightly to stop her, but loosely enough not to ruin her mouth." He held her hands, showing her what he meant.

Dinah nodded, trying to concentrate on his instructions. The emotions that she had held in check since their last episode and angry words on the ship now rose again, as she felt the touch of his hands and saw the eager expression on his handsome face. Her seat was doubly unsteady from the awkward position of the side saddle, and she was glad he was there to catch her if she fell. The idea, in fact, had a certain appeal, for she ached to feel those arms, steady and gentle as they had been as he had lifted her into the saddle, around her again.

Alexander, seeming to guess her thoughts, looked up at her, tall and straight in the saddle. "Dear Dinah," he murmured, "I feel you will make a fine horsewoman. Are you comfortable?" At her nod, he moved to the horse's head to take the bridle and lead the beast forward.

Dinah gasped at the sensation, at the slight sway that made her want to drop the reins and grab the horse's neck for support. "Alexander . . ."

"Steady," Alexander urged. "Keep your hands steady."

"I . . . I feel like I'm going to fall!" Dinah cried in alarm.

"No, you're not. You're perfectly safe. Think of—" Alexander tried to think of a suitable simile, "a rocking horse. Surely you had one as a child?" He added, "and relax a little. Sit straight, but not so stiffly."

Under Alexander's encouragement, Dinah began to lose her fear of the horse and to enjoy the ride. Before long, she felt confident enough for him to let go of the horse's head, calling out directions. Then, he mounted his own horse. In a nearby ring, riding beside her, he gave her further instructions to accustom her to the horse and the reins.

After a while, Alexander suggested she try trotting the horse, "Unless you have had enough for one day," he added.

"Not yet. I mean I haven't had enough." Dinah's eyes were sparkling. "I'm just starting to enjoy it."

"Good for you. Hold on, and remember to pull back on the reins any time you want to stop." Alexander nudged the stallion with his heels, and the horse broke into a trot, Dinah's horse following suit.

Dinah's heart jumped into her mouth. Her body stiffened, tightening up on the reins. As Duchess started to slow her gait, however, Dinah eased up on the reins and the horse resumed the graceful pace. The young woman's eyes had been firmly fixed between the horse's ears, but as her exhilaration mounted, she turned her head to smile happily at Alexander. "And to think," she marveled, "I used to be afraid of horses."

Alexander laughed. "My dear, I do not think you are afraid of anything. You have more courage than many men I have known."

"Why, Alexander!" Dinah stared at him in surprise, exhilarated now by the admiration in his voice.

"Surely you know," Alexander went on as he slowed his horse to a walk, "how much I admire you and always will. I would do anything to take back those words that hurt you so much."

Dinah's hands tightened slightly on the reins. A yearning that she could not suppress rose in her. To take her mind off the memories of those precious hours with him, she tried to concentrate on Ian MacKie and the cozy tea she had enjoyed with him and his mother.

"I know few women," Alexander went on, "who would so willingly have left home and family to voyage to a strange land and a life that must seem as alien as the moon."

Dinah smiled. The answer to that statement was easy. "You forget I had only my mother in New York. With her death . . ."

"You had Mrs. Bradley, too, who was and is far fonder of you than you may realize," Alexander interrupted to spare her the pain he knew the memory of her mother always aroused in her.

"Yes," Dinah said, almost forgetting the horse under her. "Still, I did not have much to look forward to, did I? A life as a companion or governess, one day a small cottage somewhere. You gave me no choice," she said in a determined voice.

Unwittingly, Dinah had tightened her hands and

changed her seat slightly. Duchess took the slight pressure as a signal for a gallop, breaking gait with a pounding of hooves that left Alexander behind. All thoughts except trying to stay on the horse flew from Dinah's mind, as she attempted to remain upright and keep her knee tight around the horn of the side saddle. She would have dropped the reins in her panic, except the only other thing to hold on was the horse's mane and the mane with the horse's neck stretched out seemed impossibly out of reach.

Behind her, she could hear Alexander's horse thundering to try to catch up with her. That sound, at first a comfort to Dinah, turned out to be a signal for Duchess to decide on a race. The normally gentle mare thrilled to the chase, increasing its speed. Without even thinking about it, Dinah pulled back on the reins to help her maintain her balance. As she tightened them, she felt the horse slow a little and she recalled Alexander's instructions. Somehow she managed to wrap the reins around her gloved hands, tightening them even more and forcing the horse to bring its head up. As it did, it dropped into a trot. Dinah quickly wrapped the reins around her hands again, bringing the horse to a standstill so suddenly that she almost went over its head.

Although her heart was pounding furiously and her lungs were gasping for air, the young woman felt a thrill of excitement at controlling the horse. Frightened as she had been at first, the ride had given her a confidence in her abilities, as if she knew she could do anything. Her face was flushed and her eyes sparkled in golden flashes when Alexander stopped beside her.

"Are you all right?" he asked anxiously.

"Of course!!" Dinah assured him.

"You had quite a ride. I must say you frightened me a little."

"I frightened you?" Dinah, her eyes still sparkling, turned her face toward him, noticing how pale he seemed, his dark eyes almost black. Her heart, after calming a little, began to pound again, to beat as frantically as her horse's hooves had beaten only moments earlier.

"My dear Dinah, you could have fallen off and have been badly hurt or worse," the man told her, his voice rough with emotion. "I would never have forgiven myself had you been hurt—and my father would never have done so either," he added.

At the mention of his father, Dinah felt her heart slow immediately. Still, Alexander did say that he would never have forgiven himself. Yet, why had he had to mention his father in the same breath? "Well, I'm quite all right, thank you!" She tossed her head, feeling the hat give a sudden slip. Still holding the reins tightly, she could do nothing except let the hat, the veil loosened, fall off. She blushed furiously, her new-found dignity lost in the childish toss of her head.

Alexander's burst of laughter did not help. "Dear Dinah," he murmured, dismounting from his horse to pick up the hat. After he had remounted, he placed it on her head and tied the veil, his hand brushing her cheek tenderly and a little longer than was necessary. "If only you knew," he said softly.

"Knew?"

"Nothing." The man touched her hands. "Loosen the reins a bit, my dear. I think you have had quite enough of a riding lesson for one day. We'll walk slowly back to the stable. By the way," he added, "you had better order a nice hot bath the moment we are back at the house—or you will be quite unable to sit through dinner this evening. Since I seem to recall the Anguses are coming, it will be unsuitable for you to eat off the mantelpiece."

Dinah smiled, although a little grimly, recalling Margaret's reluctance to lend Dinah the riding costume. What fun she and Mary Angus would have over that headlong gallop. "You won't tell anyone about . . . about the horse running away, will you?" she asked anxiously.

"I shall brag about it," Alexander told her firmly. "I have never seen a novice ride a horse so well. You are as much a born horsewoman as you are a sailor, neither of which is any mean accomplishment. You have nothing to be ashamed about. Still," he hesitated, thinking of what his father would say about his being careless enough to let the horse run away, "it is probably best that we do not mention it."

"Thank you, Alexander," Dinah said gratefully, misunderstanding the reasons for his agreement.

Both were silent until they were in the carriage again. As the carriage passed Holyrood on its way into the city, Dinah summoned up the courage to ask what had been on her mind. "Alexander?"

"Yes?" He had been staring out the carriage. Now, he looked at her for the first time since he had helped her into the carriage, noticing the flushed cheeks, the full mouth, the unconsciously graceful tilt of her head on the slender neck. His hands ached to reach out for her. Instead, he put his hands in his pockets, leaning back against the seat of the carriage with a casualness that was the opposite of what he felt.

Dinah noticed his movement, taking it for a dismissal of her. She bit her underlip. "Nothing." She turned her head away.

"Well, you must have had something in mind," Alexander said, adding as if he thought she might blame him, "and Duchess is gentle. I certainly did not want, do not ever want, anything to happen to you."

"Does that mean that you won't take me riding again?" Dinah asked anxiously.

"Oh, my dear!" The young man took his hands from his pockets to take her hands in his, squeezing them gently. "If that is what is worrying you, don't give it a thought. Of course, I will take you riding again, anytime you wish, as a matter of fact. Did you enjoy it—you weren't too frightened?"

"I loved it!" Dinah enthused.

"Then, tomorrow you must be measured for your own riding habit. A few more lessons, and you will put both Margaret and Mary to shame."

Dinah fell silent again, knowing all to well that such

a compliment would not be taken kindly by the other two young women.

As soon as they reached the house, however, Dinah followed Alexander's advice. A metal tub was carried into the bedroom, where Molly carefully supervised the adding of hot and then cold water until the bath was just the right temperature. Even so, Dinah had to lower herself carefully into the water, where Molly encouraged her to lean back and relax.

The hot water relaxed Dinah. The fresh air and the exercise had given her the same feeling of delight in life that the days at sea with the brisk wind in her face had imparted, the same feeling of life being wonderful and filled with still unimagined and untasted joys, and the same yearning to know and taste life to the fullest.

Dreamily, she let her mind drift to Alexander who always seemed a part, a very vital part, of this discovery of herself, of her body and the desire that she had never known existed. Her hands drifted over her body, the ripe breasts and nipples, the flat stomach, the slender thighs, to the soft hair of the most intimate part of her body. How wonderful it would be to rise from the hot water, to dry herself with a soft towel scented with delicate perfume, and then to be wrapped in the warmth of Alexander's arms, to feel his body close to hers, his manhood rising to meet her.

As she thought of Alexander's body, so hot and big and strong, so gentle and urgent between her legs, Dinah awakened herself. That was in the past. She must forget it, thought that was easier said than done. As Molly wrapped her in the scented towel, she could feel her body aching for the pleasures she had known on the ship. If only she could know that joy once more, just once more, she would be satisfied. No, that was not true. One more time and she would want one more time after that and still another . . .

"Dinah?" Molly's voice brought her friend back to the present. "You're all right? The riding . . ."

"I'm fine, Molly. It was so exciting, and I am so eager to go again," Dinah assured her friend. "I guess the hot water relaxed me, maybe too much." She gave a fake yawn. "I would much rather have a sleep than have to have dinner with the Anguses."

Molly wrinkled her nose in distaste. From Parker she had heard all too much about Lady Mary and Margaret and their planning. She wondered whether to say anything more to Dinah, even though Dinah had said very little about Alexander recently. Perhaps she would have a talk with Geordie about it. Besides, Dinah had been so eager to see Captain MacKie again. Yes, Molly decided, it would be best to wait for a while. The *Star of Scotland* was to sail for America again soon, and by then Dinah might be more settled in her mind. Life here was still new and exciting for the both of them and much more so for Dinah.

Dinah wore the gown that she had worn to the dinner party in Bermuda, insisting that Molly do her hair the same way. Thus, remembering the success of that night, she went to dinner with more confidence than she had felt in a long time, hoping that the overheard conversation and the gown would recall the shipboard attentiveness in Alexander.

Sir Malcolm Angus was a florid-faced, stocky man, always running a finger between his collar and neck. To Dinah, he seemed a typical country squire whose major conversations consisted of his horses and his dogs, both preceded and interspersed with "Damn me!" He obviously missed his home at Kinross, near the Douglas estate. Lady Janet, on the other hand, was a small thin woman with a sharp face, alert to the needs of her son and daughter and especially to the prospects of a good marriage for each. To that end, she had encouraged Sir Malcolm to borrow heavily in order for them to rent a fine house in Edinburgh, again not far from the Douglases. Dinah had been there several times to small dinner parties and evening soirées at the suggestion of Sir Robert who had wanted to introduce Dinah to Edinburgh and its society slowly. As far as the rest of her knowledge of the Anguses was concerned, she was indebted to Molly whose open, friendly manner had encouraged confidences from

Mrs. Jamison as well as Parker, neither of whom was fond of the overbearing ways of Lady Janet and Mary, for all their titles.

James was handsome if effeminate, at least to Dinah's eyes. He seemed far more at home in an evening suit and tails than in his Guards' uniform. Mary was as small as her mother but more buxom, favoring low-cut dresses to show off her plump white bosom. Like her mother, she had a gift for making light conversation that Dinah could not help admire. Dinah also admired the way the short young woman had of looking up into a man's eyes, a seeming helplessness that instantly brought all the young men to her assistance. This was a feat impossible for Dinah, whose height had her at eye level with most men. Alexander, in fact, was an exception. Dinah arrived in the library just as the Angus carriage stopped at the door, giving her little opportunity to talk to Alexander, who had been telling his father about the riding lesson. Sir Robert greeted Dinah with a kiss on the cheek.

"My son tells me that with a few more lessons you will be riding as if you had been on horses all your life," he told Dinah. "Perhaps you have inherited the talent from your mother, who was a fine horsewoman."

"Was she?" Dinah was surprised. Having known her mother only in the confines of New York and as a governess and companion-secretary, she had still not realized that her mother's early life must have been much as hers was now.

"Indeed she was." He gave her hand a squeeze as he left her to welcome the Anguses.

Mary immediately went to Alexander, pouting up at him, "Margaret told me at the dressmaker's that you went riding this morning. Naughty lad! To think you did not tell me."

Over her head, Alexander winked at Dinah. "I fear you would not have enjoyed the ride. It was a lesson for Dinah, as she has decided to improve her horsemanship."

"Improve?" Mary turned to stare at Dinah. "According to Margaret, you had never been on a horse before today."

"It is talent that counts," Alexander said smoothly, "not the number of times with which a person has been on a horse. Dinah rides as if born to it."

"How fortunate. Then, we must all go riding—at least as soon as Dinah has suitable clothes," Margaret added sarcastically.

Sir Robert, who had heard only the last part of the conversation, said, "She shall have whatever she wants. That brings up another subject, one which is a major reason for our dinner this evening." He turned to Alexander. "First, get some sherry for the ladies and whisky for us."

Dinah accepted the sherry with a mounting curiosity about what Sir Robert had to say. As she glanced at the others, she saw they were as puzzled as she.

Sir Robert took a place in front of the fireplace, studying his son and daughter and his friends before taking Dinah's hand. "I think the time has come for Dinah to be formally introduced to society. I, therefore, propose a ball in her honor. Although a year of mourning has not passed, the circumstances—and Christmas coming—seem to suggest that this is the proper time. You are a woman, Janet, what do you think?"

Lady Janet's lips had tightened in a thin line. Looking at Dinah, her hand in Sir Robert's, she frowned slightly. "I am not sure, Robert. There are customs to be observed."

"I am fully aware of that, Janet. Yet, considering that Dinah is new to Edinburgh and New York is so far away, I feel the circumstances alter the situation. Then, there are the holidays, a time for rejoicing, the rejoicing of life and," he nodded at Dinah, "youth."

"She will be invited to parties, Robert," suggested Lady Janet.

"It will not be the same." Sir Robert sought Sir Malcolm's support. "What say you, Malcolm?"

Sir Malcolm sipped his whisky, his eyes roving between his wife and his friend, loyalties obviously torn.

He cleared his throat, finally saying somewhat pompously, "I agree with you, Robert. A ball in her honor is just the thing."

"So say I," murmured Alexander, "from a man's point of view."

"That leaves James. James, what say you?" asked Sir Robert.

James shifted from one foot to the other. He had seen the flush of anger on Margaret's face. Whatever he said, it was obvious, would bring wrath down on his head from one quarter. As his father had done, he cleared his throat and watched Sir Robert. "Aye, Sir, whatever you say."

The agreement from that quarter did not please Sir Robert, as Dinah could tell from the way his hand tightened, holding hers. She had also seen Margaret's face, and she knew James would pay later for his agreeing so meekly with the other men.

"Then, that is settled," said Sir Robert in a tone of voice that intimated it had been settled from the beginning. "Now, Jane, I would like to ask your help. Both myself and my daughter will need your assistance, as a woman with experience, to make sure that all is done in the best way. Besides, you have served in that capacity before, both with Mary and with Margaret at their introduction to society. If you will draw up a plan, I will go over it with you. Needless to say, money is no object. You are not to consider cost at all in your plans."

At the mention of money, Lady Janet relaxed slightly. "Very well, Robert. First, we must decide a date. It must not be too close to Christmas, and it cannot interfere with the New Year."

"Quite correct. I had in mind December 20th, which, if I am not mistaken, Dinah, is your birthday?"

Dinah looked at the older man in surprise. "Why, yes, it is. How did you know that?"

Sir Robert smiled. "I asked Molly, as I knew it had to be about then. That's another matter. And so, you see, Janet, it is quite proper: the holidays, Dinah's birthday, and her introduction to society."

The rest of the evening was passed in discussing the party, a ball to be followed by a supper. Dinah, of course, was to have a new gown, several gowns, in fact, as would the other young girls. They were to go to the dressmaker the next day with Lady Janet. Sir Robert had thought out his plan well in advance. Although he asked for and welcomed suggestions, there were few that anyone could make to improve on his original plan. Any that lessened his grand plan were immediately dismissed.

Dinah listened to the plans in a daze, unaware of the growing fury and jealousy in Margaret's face. Nothing in Dinah's life had prepared her for such an event. She found herself looking at Alexander, whose eyes seemed constantly to be on her face, telling her to keep up her courage, the courage he had praised that morning. More and more as the evening passed, she yearned to be in his arms, to feel his kisses hot on her mouth and to feel his hands caressing her body. After the thrilling ride, the hot bath, and now this evening, that was all she needed to feel she was living in a dream.

She was so lost in her fantasy, in fact, that she totally forgot Molly's warnings about Mary and Margaret. Both were fully aware of Alexander's attentiveness, and their eyes met in resolve. They had no intention of seeing their plans go awry because of this outsider in their midst. Lady Janet, too, felt threatened, and her thin lips grew even thinner, as she looked at Dinah and listened to Sir Robert.

Chapter 12

❀ ❀ ❀

IF DINAH HAD thought the days of shopping with Mrs. Bradley were busy, they had given her little idea of how busy she would be now. First, there were the designs of the dresses to be selected. Originally, she had left the selection to Lady Janet until she realized that the gowns being chosen for her were more conservative in style and more suited to simple fabrics than the silks and satins that were being reserved for Margaret and Mary's gowns. After a conversation with Lady Janet succeeded only in her receiving a lecture on her lack of appreciation for all that was being done for her, she enlisted Alexander's help.

Alexander took one look at the designs, and his lips tightened. "Let me show my father," he suggested. After that, Sir Robert gave his approval not only to the gowns and designs but also to the fabrics and the colors. He gave orders, too, for a riding habit for Dinah and several costumes for day to take the place of the school-girl outfits that Mrs. Bradley had thought best. He seemed determined to make Dinah the most elegant young woman in Edinburgh, not noticing that his determination bred a growing strain in Margaret's demeanor. Dinah blossomed under it, and once again she found herself under Alexander's spell. And he, no matter how busy his days, found time to take her riding.

Then, there was Ian MacKie. The evening that he had come to dinner, Alexander and Margaret had been to a party with James and Mary Angus. The two men had deferred to her in their conversation about ships and sailing, asking her advice about New York and discussing Bermuda. The latter Dinah knew more about than New York because of her day spent shopping with Lady Anne.

After dinner, Sir Robert had excused himself for a short while in order to go over some papers before giving them to MacKie. As a result, Dinah and MacKie had coffee alone in the library.

Once more Dinah was wearing what she called the Bermuda dress, her hair worn up in back with the small curls framing her face. MacKie's eyes had been on her all evening, even during his conversation with Sir Robert. Now, as he watched her pour the coffee, however, his eyes lingered over her in silence.

Dinah, too, was silent, as she recalled the obvious respect and affection between the two men, reluctantly comparing that feeling to the one between Sir Robert and his son. It was almost as if the elder man wished Ian were his son, especially in the way he deferred to Ian's judgment. Was it, she wondered, that the father expected too much of the son or had the son in some way unknown to her disappointed the father? She could not guess, and she could not ask.

Ian broke the silence. "Dinah," he said softly, "as you must have gathered, I will be sailing soon again."

The girl nodded. "I will miss you, Ian."

"You are happy here? You don't wish to return to New York?" the man asked, leaning forward.

Dinah's eyes widened in surprise. "Leave? Oh no! As you said, Sir Robert has been most kind, almost like the father I never knew. And he's planning a party for me."

"I know." MacKie put the cup on the table and stood up, hands behind his back, to move to the fireplace. To Dinah, he seemed to be pacing a foredeck. "It's only that I felt I had to ask." He paused. "Have you any letters or messages that I could deliver to Mrs. Bradley for you? I know you must have written her, but perhaps a personal message . . ."

"Oh yes!" Dinah put her own cup down and sprang lightly to her feet, going to Ian and taking his hands in hers. "How thoughtful you are. I should have thought of that myself."

The man smiled at her, his blue eyes seeming to pierce through her. "You would have, Dinah, as you are the most thoughtful person I have ever known." He let her hands go to take her face in his hands.

Their eyes were almost level, and yet Dinah felt small in the presence of the man with his broad shoulders and deep chest. How could she have ever thought him stern? The thin line of his lips had a tender curve and the sun-curved lines at the corners of his eyes smiled at her. Dinah let her body lean against his. His arms enclosed her, his sun-bronzed cheek resting against her ivory one. She had never felt so safe in her life as she did in the protection of his arms, and she raised her lips to meet his.

Their kiss was long and tender, broken only when Ian, breathing hard, broke away from her. "Dear Dinah," his face was flushed beneath the tan and his voice, rough with emotion, "I have no right . . . I apologize."

"Oh, Ian, do not apologize, please, for I am as much to blame." She followed him to take his hand and raise it to her lips. "It was only a kiss," she went on, not noticing the look of pain that crossed his face or the pleasure that followed as she added, "and surely we are permitted that."

The man smiled at her, his blue eyes even deeper in color with the intensity of his emotion. "Then, you will let me see you again before I leave?" he asked.

"Of course! How else am I to get my messages for Mrs. Bradley to you?" Dinah smiled back, thinking how much she enjoyed Ian's company. There was none of the passion that rose in her with every touch of Alexander's, and yet there was a warmth in her body, a glow that suffused her from the most intimate point between her thighs to her breasts where her nipples tingled for the touch of his lips. A curiosity to know him better, to lie naked in his arms and to know his body, sent a flush to her cheeks. She knew she should not feel this way, not think such thoughts, but she could not stop them.

"Perhaps Monday we could have tea again or go for a walk if the weather is clear?" MacKie's voice was still rough with emotion.

"Let's see." Dinah tapped her full lips with a slender forefinger. "I must go to the dressmaker for a fitting in the afternoon, although I could meet you at your mother's house after that, if you like."

No sooner was their appointment settled than Sir Robert entered the room. He joined them for coffee, pouring a brandy for himself and MacKie. Once again, he apologized for his absence, although Dinah was sure that he had noticed the flush on her cheeks.

Sir Robert handed some papers to MacKie, saying, "Ian, here are the letters of instruction that I mentioned. I would like you to read them over and feel free to make any suggestions. You will note that I have given you absolute authority, and full credit with which to buy any cargo you think best, as I had given Alexander on the last trip." As he mentioned his son's name, his lips tightened. "I would have done better . . . Well," he shrugged, leaving the rest of his sentence for Dinah and MacKie only to guess at, "what is done is done."

"Thank you, Sir." Ian took the folded papers and put them in his pocket. "I will look them over, and we can sign them next week, as I am sure that any arrangement you make is fair." He rose to his feet, extending his hand to Sir Robert. "I must take my leave now, but I thank you for a most enjoyable evening."

"It was our pleasure, mine and, I am certain," he glanced at Dinah, "Dinah's too. You are most welcome any time. Is he not, Dinah?"

Dinah nodded, adding, "I will always be happy to have you call, Captain MacKie."

MacKie left, Sir Robert himself seeing him to the door. As Dinah waited for Sir Robert to return, she thought about the young captain, recalling the tenderness of his kiss and the warmth of his arms, both so gentle and yet both concealing a passion that she could

169

hardly have guessed. She stood up restlessly, her young body yearning for the fulfillment she had known with Alexander but suddenly curious to know what such fulfillment would be like with Ian. The two men were so different that it surely could not be the same. With a slight smile, she wondered whether Margaret or Mary ever had such thoughts, if they, especially Mary—she felt a twinge of jealousy at the thought of Mary with Alexander—had ever known that particular ecstasy.

"Well, Dinah," said Sir Robert, interrupting her thoughts, "thank you for joining us. I hope our male talk did not displease you."

"Oh, no, Sir Robert!" Dinah smiled at him. "I quite enjoyed it. Often at dinner on the ship, the men —Captain MacKie, Geordie Campbell, and Alexander," she added hurriedly, "talked of the problems of the day. I am afraid, in fact," she admitted truthfully, "that I find that talk much easier than much of what is usually discussed."

With a laugh, Sir Robert put his arm around the girl. "I wonder if you realize how refreshing it is to me to have you here. I am also often bored by society, necessary as it is."

"Sometimes I don't know what to say, and I feel so, so clumsy," Dinah sighed. "Life in New York was quite different." The thought of her mother came into her mind for the first time in weeks. Impulsively she asked, "My mother, was she as at home in society, as you call it?"

Sir Robert took the girl's shoulders in his hands, looking down into her eyes and yet not seeming to see her. He appeared more to be looking beyond her into some past that troubled him. "Your mother . . ." He shook his head, as if trying to clear his mind, "You are very like her in some ways. You don't look like her, although you have her eyes and her nose, but you have the same spirit, the same courage. Do not," his voice was gentle with intensity, "be so headstrong as she was. Do not leave those who love you. Above all, dear Dinah, do not let your heart rule your head," he added.

Dinah stared at the older man, seeing lines of unhappiness in his face that she had never noticed before. She did not know how to answer him, and she did not want to make promises that she might not be able to keep. So she attempted a weak smile.

Sir Robert, lost in his thoughts, seemed not to notice her silence. He kissed her gently on the cheek. "Now, off to bed with you—and once more accept my gratitude for your company tonight and the pleasure you constantly give me."

Dinah went to her room, lost in her own thoughts. As she started to ring the bell pull, she recalled that she had given Molly leave to go to Geordie's sister's house for the weekend. Thus, it would be Parker who would answer her call, and it would not do for Parker to see her in such a state of confusion. With a smile, she started to undress herself. After all, it had not been long ago that it would never have occurred to her to ask for or need help.

Once in bed, she thought back to the strange conversation with Sir Robert and then to her mother. How little she had really known the woman who had borne her and raised her! Her mother had always seemed so quiet and so steady. She had seemed to have a reserve that prevented her from showing affection or speaking of love, although all her actions were those of a loving mother. The courage, Dinah understood. After all, it had taken courage for her mother to leave home and family for a strange country across a dangerous sea. But spirited and headstrong were not words that Dinah had ever associated in any way with her mother. It seemed that the woman Sir Robert had known and the mother she had known were two different women. Try as she might, as hard as she might, she could not imagine her mother as a person who let her heart rule her head. Dinah sighed, drifting off to sleep with the picture of her mother, careworn, thin, and wracked with pain, before her eyes.

As a result, her sleep was far from easy. Her mother and Sir Robert floated past, younger somehow, changing and becoming younger until they faded into Dinah herself and Alexander. The two reached out to touch, only to slip past one another in a grotesque dance, never in one another's arms. Or was it a dance at all? For there they were, naked, bodies arching and longing for one another—and still unable to touch, even though Alexander seemed to reach out for her, until Dinah awakened, crying softly in her yearning. Her body was hot and damp with perspiration and her legs ached as if she had been gripping Alexander, her thighs wrapped around his buttocks.

The high-necked white nightgown was soaked and seemed to be choking her. Dinah sat up, staring at the shadows surrounding her. They seemed to be alive with ghostly figures of her mother, Sir Robert, and Alexander. How she longed at that moment for that sweet warmth that had possessed her in MacKie's arms. Or was it only that Ian had not been in her dreams and, therefore, seemed a haven from all the ghosts?

With a shudder, Dinah slipped out of bed and lit a candle. The shadows retreated, but only a little. Still crying softly, Dinah lit all the candles in the room. The nightgown was too heavy on her body. Impulsively, she took it off. After all, it would never do for Parker to find it in the morning, still damp, she thought as she hung it over a chair. In that instance, she saw herself in the pier glass between the windows.

Her red hair was tumbled about her shoulders in a wild, curly mass. Her sleepless eyes were wide, flecked with gold, while her full lips were parted and red with a passionate fire. Still, it was not her face that held her gaze; it was her body. Of course, she had seen herself naked before but never in a mirror—and what she saw in the mirror was what Alexander had seen. Young as she was, it was the body of a woman, with softly rounded shoulders, full and firm breasts, the nipples rosy pink, the torso slender and small-waisted above the curve of her hips and buttocks. Her thighs and legs were shapely and long, the hair at the mound of venus, red and as curly as on her head.

Dinah crossed her arms over her breasts, noticing

the cleavage between the ivory mounds. She ran her hands over her hips, tilting her head. No, seen this way, her neck was not too long. She was still too tall —nothing could change that, but all in all her body was a good one, she decided, the equal of Mary's even if she was much more slender.

The candle flames flickered as a gust of wind against the windows sent a draught through the room. Dinah shivered, aware of what she was doing and where she was. Hurriedly, she picked up the nightgown and pulled it on, one arm catching in a sleeve. She struggled angrily with it, finally feeling the fabric tear under the arm. Then, she blew out the candles and went back to bed, pulling the covers up to her neck, squirming between the silken sheets, her head resting on the lace-trimmed pillow. She realized, with a faint twinge of surprise, that she was not ashamed as perhaps she should be, as her mother would have been of her had she known. Or would she? She wasn't sure any more, not after what Sir Robert had said, even though she still could not reconcile her picture of her mother with his. With a sigh, Dinah turned out, pulling her legs up, and slept, this time dreamlessly.

The morning light scattered the last remnants of her bad dream. Instead, she found herself thinking more and more of Ian MacKie. She had always known he would be leaving Edinburgh again, and although she had not seen him that much, she began to realize how much his presence meant to her. His departure would mean the loss of a friend, the cessation of the friendship that had grown on shipboard and that she had taken for granted. She started to look forward to Monday with an impatient eagerness.

First came the fittings. With her new awareness of her body, Dinah studied the gowns with an intense interest—especially the ball gowns. The first she tried on for Lady Janet and Margaret's scrutiny, Mary having gone riding at Kirk o' Fields with Alexander, was the white satin one for her introduction to society.

The off-the-shoulder neckline was trimmed with creamy Alencon lace that provided a flattering contrast to her ivory skin. The bodice was tightly fitted, forcing her breasts up to display that round fullness that Dinah had noticed crossing her arms in front of the mirror. While the skirt seemed slender and molded to the lines of her body in front, the back had a fullness that was gathered up into a form of bustle, allowing more than enough movement for a sweeping waltz.

Lady Janet and Margaret examined her critically, as Dinah turned her head trying to see herself in the pier glass almost behind her back. The dressmaker, accompanied by an apprentice of about fourteen, stood nearby.

"The skirt is much too snug," Margaret commented to Lady Janet. "She will never be able to dance properly in it."

"I agree. What do you think about the neckline, Margaret? With her long neck, it is much too low to be flattering," added Lady Janet.

"Perhaps a little more lace to fill it in would do," replied Margaret dubiously, "although, I'm not sure."

"Madame LaPorte," commanded Lady Janet, "do try loosening the skirt."

Dinah had listened without interrupting, although she was angry that they were treating her as a statue or a mannequin. What was more, she had been deliberately posed in a way that she could not see herself in the mirror, although the others always stood in front of the pier glass. Before the small, dark Frenchwoman could touch the dress, Dinah shook her off, ignoring the others as they had ignored her.

"A moment, please, Madame. I should like to see for myself." She stepped quickly to the glass, studying the reflection, her anger mounting at what Margaret and Lady Janet had tried to do to the dress. Not only was there already enough lace, there was too much, so much that it almost succeeded in concealing completely the rise of her firm young breasts. The skirt, on the other hand, was perfect. Although it was molded to show off the slenderness of her hips and thighs, there was ample material in the back to allow her to move freely.

"I find the skirt perfect, Madame. I will not have it touched. As for the neckline, I agree with Lady Janet that it will not do at all." In the mirror, she could see Lady Janet and Margaret exchange glances. Margaret was frowning, while the older woman's mouth had tightened into a grim line. She would have an argument on her hands. Yet that was their fault and of their making, and she would call upon Sir Robert for a final decision if that should become necessary.

The young woman took a deep breath, feeling her breasts expand against the smooth satin. As Madame LaPorte's hands fluttered to the neckline, Dinah said to her, "No more lace. In fact, I would prefer that you remove it all. It seems much too fussy for a ball-gown and it does emphasize my neck. Perhaps no lace would be best. What do you think?"

The little dressmaker's eyes twinkled, as she quickly snipped the basting thread and removed the lace before the others could speak. "Mademoiselle has an eye for *la mode*," she murmured. "With your figure, you have not the need of such reticence."

As the lace fell away, the gown came into its own, the simplicity of its lines more than enough to show off the elegance of Dinah's figure and height. The effect to Dinah was of a princess in a story book, and she smiled in pleasure at the sight.

"Magnifique," whispered Madame. "Do not let them change it."

Dinah turned to face the others, their faces grim. "I think it is perfect now, don't you?" She was amused at their expressions, which told her all she needed to know and made her determined to stand her ground.

Lady Janet bit her lip, as if pondering what to say. Finally, she said carefully, "You are much too young for such a dress. It needs the lace. If you feel you can dance in the skirt," she compromised, "I will give in on that point. The neckline, however, is totally unsuitable."

"I agree," Margaret put in firmly. "It must be changed, Dinah. Father would never approve."

Dinah smiled. "Well, I think the gown is perfect as

it now is. If it is a matter of Sir Robert's approval, then I think we should leave the decision to him. In the meantime, Madame, not a stitch is to be changed."

Madame nodded, and the apprentice hurried to help Dinah take that gown off and put another one on. The rest of the fitting went smoothly, as Dinah mentioned Sir Robert and his approval at any mention of a change. The final fitting was for the riding habit, which had been finished.

Since Margaret and Lady Janet still had fittings, Dinah took her leave, pleading a visit to the bootmakers. Instead, however, she found a hansom cab and ordered it to the small lane and the MacKie house. As she left the cab, she realized she was much too early for tea, so early in fact that it was possible no one was at home. Hesitatingly, she pulled the bell.

MacKie, in shirtsleeves, opened the door. "Dinah!" he said in surprise.

"I am sorry, Ian," she apologized, "but I didn't realize how early it was. The fitting was finished, and I didn't want to wait for Margaret and Lady Janet . . ."

"Don't apologize. Come in!" He ushered her into the house and the small sitting room where a coal fire burned cheerfully. After he had taken her cloak, he put on his jacket. "The fittings went well?" he asked.

Dinah told him about the disagreement over the ball gown, purposely making it amusing. "Sometimes," she said with a sigh, "I fear I am not made for this life and the wealth that goes with it. All those parties! Whatever will I do?"

"Be yourself," advised the captain. "If I am any judge of men, you will find yourself with a score the moment you enter the room."

"Do you really think so?"

He laughed at the anxious tone in her voice. "I know so, my dear Dinah, and I envy all of them the pleasure of your company." He looked away from her for a moment, his blue eyes darkening. "I shall be thinking of you at sea, remembering our dinners."

"What fun they were! I think of them often, wishing I were back aboard the *Star of Scotland.*" That was not quite the truth, although she did remember the trip, wanting to relive it—both to relive what had happened between her and Alexander and to wipe out those events, not make the mistakes she had.

"Do you?" MacKie was pleased. Her words encouraged him, and he went on, "Dinah, we sail sooner than I expected. The cargo that Sir Robert arranged is being loaded now, and tomorrow I must go to Leith."

"Oh, Ian!" Tears started in Dinah's eyes. She looked up at him standing in front of her at the fireplace. "Then, how happy I am I came early, to have this chance to talk to you, to see you again." Impulsively she rose to her feet, taking his hands in hers, her amber eyes drinking in the sun-bronzed face, the steady blue eyes, the stern mouth that had been so tender on hers.

MacKie's arms went around her, holding her close. Dinah rested her cheek against his, pressing against him until her breasts grew hard at the closeness of his broad chest. She could feel his heart beating faster as he kissed her cheek. She turned her face, her lips meeting his, desire for him warming her body. Her loins were hot with the pressure of his manhood growing large and strong between her legs. How she wished he would pick her up, carry her somewhere and fill her with that exquisite passion that she had known with Alexander. She ached to run her hands over his body, to feel his capable hands caressing her. What would it be like with him, she wondered, nestling in his arms.

MacKie was breathing hard, his mouth urgent on Dinah's. He groaned as if in agony, before reluctantly letting her go and moving to the window. "Dear God," he whispered to himself more than to Dinah, "dear God." He ran a shaking hand over his hair.

Seeing the intensity of his emotion, Dinah was ashamed of herself, of the desire that had sent her into the man's arms. She sank into a chair, too weak to stand, angry at him for not satisfying her and yet angry at herself for what she must have done to him. "Ian," she whispered tentatively. "Ian."

He turned to look at her, the lines in his face deeply etched. "You are so beautiful," he murmured, "so young, so innocent . . ."

Dinah grew hot again at the mention of innocent, knowing he was blaming himself for what was her fault. He was wrong in thinking her innocent, but he was right she was young, far too young to know what to say now.

"I am sorry, my dear," the man apologized. "I should not have." He took a deep breath. "Dinah, you must know how much I care for you, that I love you and have loved you since you walked aboard my ship."

"Ian, oh Ian . . ."

"No, let me finish before you say anything. I had hoped that we would have more time to get to know one another, that I would not be sailing until after the first of the year. Now, that is changed." He left the window to stand above her and take her hands in his. "Sir Robert knows how I feel about you, and he has not discouraged me. Rather, he feels your future is your own, your decisions yours to make, although he hopes you will not be rash. Perhaps that is why we are sailing so soon."

Dinah looked at him, her heart beginning to pound again. She was sure she knew what he was going to say, to ask. She did not want to hurt him, but there could be only one answer. If only she could stop him now! Yet, he was so dear to her, and the emotion she had felt earlier had been genuine. Her mouth was dry, and she licked her lips slightly as she waited for him to go on.

"Dear Dinah," MacKie's blue eyes darkened with emotion and the stern mouth softened, "what I am trying to say is that I love you, that I want to marry you, to ask you to think about it until I return, my love."

Dinah, much as she wanted to avoid his gaze, could not tear her eyes from his face. Inside her chest, a knife seemed to turn. How she wished she could tell him about Alexander, but she knew how angry he would be and she was afraid of what he might say to Sir Robert. As she felt tears welling once more in her eyes, she finally managed to wrench her eyes from his face to stare at interlocked hands.

"Oh, Ian, you are so very dear to me," she said softly. "I wish . . ." she hesitated, taking a deep breath, "I wish I were older and wiser. I could not marry . . . promise myself . . . to—to anyone right now."

MacKie read into her words what he wanted to hear, twisting the knife even deeper in Dinah's heart. "I understand, my love. All I want is that you will think of me, think over what I have said, while I am away. When I return, you will be older and will know your heart and your mind better."

"Yes, that is true," Dinah agreed, knowing that time would not change what had happened between herself and Alexander.

There was no time to say more, as Mrs. MacKie returned from her shopping. Over tea, she exacted a promise from Dinah to visit her now and then while Ian was away, a promise Dinah could make willingly out of a fondness for the woman, a fondness that had nothing to do with Ian. Mrs. MacKie, cheerful and smiling, reminded her of her own mother. After tea, Ian insisted on getting a cab and seeing her to the Douglas' door, where once more he declared his love for her, kissing her tenderly on the cheek, before saying goodbye.

Dinah, confused as she was, said goodbye reluctantly, knowing it would be many months before she saw him again. Still, a lot would happen in that time. She had spoken the truth when she said she would miss him.

After Jamison let her in the house, she went to her room to dress for dinner, preparing herself to face Sir Robert over the question of the ball gown. Her hand on the bell pull, she hesitated, not wanting to face Parker's curious eyes. Parker undoubtedly would run with any news about what she said or how she acted to Margaret.

As she hesitated, however, she heard a light tapping on the door and went to open it. A radiant Molly was standing there. Dinah pulled her into the room, and the two old friends hugged one another happily. Dinah was spared from talking, as Molly prattled eagerly about Geordie and his sister.

The weekend had been a busy one, filled with new adventures for Molly, including her first train ride. From the station, a hour's ride outside Edinburgh, it had been a short walk to the cottage on the outskirts of the village. Molly, who had never been in the country before, had fallen in love with everything at first sight. She had helped the sister's two children feed the chickens and gather the eggs, and Geordie had taught her how to milk the gentle cow. Then, there had been the walks with Geordie across the cold brown winter moors, as he told her how they would be purple with heather in the spring. Afterward the fire had felt so good, and the tea, freshly baked bread and newly churned butter seemed more delicious than the finest delicacies. That morning, they had gone for a walk through the village, with Geordie's pointing out the cottage he wanted to buy for Molly.

Standing in front of it, he had taken Molly's hand, asking her to marry him before he sailed. Although the captain had to go to Leith the next day, Geordie had another week before sailing, according to the message that had been delivered as they left the house.

As Molly told Dinah about the proposal, she saw the shadow on Dinah's face as Dinah asked, "And what did you say?"

Molly hesitated. "I said I would think about it," she said cautiously. "Now, tell me about you."

Dinah, who had only half been listening to Molly's recitation, shrugged her shoulders. "Not much," she lied, as she told Molly about the fittings.

Molly was not satisfied. From Dinah's face and demeanor, she knew something else had happened and her immediate thought was that Alexander had something to do with it. Could he have possibly asked Mary Angus to marry him, she wondered. That thought was dismissed almost as soon as it came into her head. Had that been the case, Mrs. Jamison or Parker whom she had seen in the kitchen would have told her. She would have to find out, as she could not leave Dinah for Geordie as long as Dinah needed her. Not only were they friends—and Molly was sure she was the only genuine friend Dinah had—but they were also strangers together in a foreign country. With a sigh, she realized that she would have to tell Geordie that she could not marry him, at least not now as he wished, and her usual optimism deserted her as she tried to tell herself that it did not matter. After all, Geordie was sailing in a week's time and would be gone for months, so what difference did marriage now or on his return, when Dinah was settled, make to her?

"Come, Dinah," Molly said as cheerfully as possible, "enough talk for now. You must dress for dinner. I am certain," she added, watching Dinah's face, "that Alexander will be on your side."

"Do you think so?" Dinah asked, doubtful that Alexander's being on her side would help where his father was concerned.

"Of course!" Molly's happiness faded completely. Since Dinah had never told her about the overheard conversation, she took Dinah's doubt for new trouble between Alexander and her. Under those circumstances, she would certainly have to stay with Dinah.

Chapter 13

🐿 🐿 🐿

ON THE AFTERNOON of the party in Dinah's honor, Sir Robert came to Dinah's room. She was only recently out of the bath, and her skin had a rosy flush to it. The man smiled at her, moved by the sparkle in her eyes and the red hair tumbling about her shoulders that made her seem younger than she was.

He motioned her to sit down, glancing around the room as if seeing it for the first time. "Did you know that this was your mother's room?" he asked.

"Was it?" Dinah was surprised, wondering even more how her mother could have left such luxury, could have lived in such luxury without a word about it to her daughter.

"Yes. We had many a talk here, but that is not why I am here," he said quickly, as if not wanting to be reminded of the past. He took a small velvet case out of his pocket and handed it to Dinah. "These were your mother's too. They were a gift on her sixteenth birthday, and it seems fitting to me that you should have them on your birthday."

"My mother's?" Dinah frowned, looking at the brushed velvet of the case. New questions rose in her mind, questions that would be brushed aside along with the others to increase the enigma of her mother. The box told her nothing, however, and she opened it, giving a gasp of surprise.

Inside the case on a bed of white satin lay a magnificent double strand of pearls, what was called a dog collar, from which was suspended an emerald sparkling with green fire. In the center of the circle formed by the creamy white pearls was a pair of earrings, each earring consisting of a single emerald from which was suspended a tear-drop pearl, perfectly matched in color to the pearls in the necklace.

"How beautiful!" Dinah finally managed to say.

"They are yours now, my dear." Sir Robert was amused by her wonderment. "Aren't you going to try them on?"

His words brought Dinah to her feet. She went to the mirror over the fireplace to hold an earring up to her ear. With a laugh, Sir Robert took the necklace to clasp it around her neck. Her long, slender neck displayed the jewels to perfection as Dinah turned her head this way and that. Impulsively, she kissed Sir Robert's cheek.

"Oh, thank you, thank you!" she said. "I shall treasure them always."

Sir Robert looked at her and smiled. Patting her on the cheek, he told her to get dressed. Only later, as Dinah sat before the mirror in her bedroom did she recall the sadness and the pain on his face as she thanked him. Uneasily, she wondered whether her mother had said the same words in thanks. She soon forgot her mother, however, in the light of Molly's admiration. The neckline had been left exactly as Dinah had wanted it. Sir Robert, in fact, had been amused at the disagreement and had told Margaret that it was Dinah's dress and her choice whether or not to have the lace at the neckline. And so the gown had been left alone, for which Dinah was glad once she had the necklace and earrings on. They were decoration enough, adding the perfect touch to her statuesque beauty.

And Molly had succeeded beautifully with her hair—parting it in the middle, and drawing it back smoothly in waves over her ears and twisting it in a knot at the back. To wear it on top of her head, as Parker intended to do with Margaret's hair and Margaret had suggested to Dinah, would only have added to Dinah's height.

"Well, Dinah," Molly told her, "if you're not the

most beautiful woman at your party, she will have to be a queen. In fact, all *you* need is a crown and you could be a queen yourself."

"Now, Molly, enough is enough. I shall be quite happy to have my dance card filled." She turned away so that Molly could not see her face. If her words had brought pain to Sir Robert, Molly's words about the crown reminded her of the only jewelry she had known her mother to have, the clan clasp with the coat of arms of the royal Stuarts.

At the head of the sweeping grand staircase, Dinah stopped. Musicians were tuning up on the balcony. Holly and mistletoe had been entwined with red ribbons around the balustrade. The great hall below was lit by hundreds of candles in sconces on the walls and in enormous branched silver candelabra. The floor had been cleared, but chairs lined the walls. The sliding doors leading into the library and the formal salon stood open, through them coming the light of more candles.

The young girl caught her breath at the scene. As she did, Alexander came out of the library and saw her. He smiled, coming up the stairs toward her, taking two steps at a time, and holding a hand out to her.

As he reached her, he caught his breath in his turn. "You are a vision, Dinah. No princess could be lovelier. In fact, you are a princess tonight."

He escorted her down the stairs to the library where his father was waiting with Margaret and the Angus family. The other girls' dresses were white also, but of an iridescent silk. Imported French silk roses decorated the low neckline of Margaret's dress, and matching flowers adorned the curls piled high on her head. Mary's dress was trimmed in blue velvet, and Parker had done her hair even higher than Margaret's in an attempt to give her some height. Both girls were outdone by Dinah, whose height and grace were accented by the wisdom of her utterly simple gown and Molly's skill in dressing her hair in such a plain style. The jewels added a perfect touch, but even without them Dinah would have caught any man's eye.

With the exception of James, the men wore formal black suits with white skirts. James, however, to Dinah's surprise, wore the formal kilt, jacket and plaid of his regiment, giving him a new dignity and stature.

Sir Robert immediately claimed Dinah's first dance, Alexander the second and last, and James the third to Margaret's dismay. They left the library then to form a receiving line at the foot of the staircase, as the guests would be using the library and two small rooms beyond for their coats and the dressing room.

While they were still in the library, however, Sir Robert had a word of warning, meant equally for Alexander and James. "I realize that by custom there are usually tables at which the men can play cards. I do not agree with such pleasures, as you know. Besides, this ball is in Dinah's honor. There will be no cards and no wagers."

"Of course, Father," Alexander agreed, his mouth set in a grim line, looking like a little boy who had been scolded in front of his elders.

Dinah had no chance to consider the implications of the warning. Guests began arriving and for the next hour she was introduced to more people than she had met in her whole life. The names and faces faded into a blur, although she could not miss the admiration on every man's face and the jealousy on more than one woman's.

Once the dancing started, Dinah was claimed for dance after dance, with only the dance with Sir Robert being passed with one partner.

Alexander bowed to her before taking her in his arms. "Well, my dear," he murmured, "you will not lack for partners or callers from now on. Or for riding masters. I fear you will be too busy to remember old friends."

Dinah smiled, a little giddy from the dancing. Although champagne had flowed freely, she had had little chance to drink more than a sip before a partner appeared. "I would not like to think I would forget old friends, Alexander. As for riding, there is still too much for you to teach me."

Alexander's eyes were serious, dark and mysterious in his saturnine face. "This evening is truly the beginning of your new life, Dinah. I know it has not been easy for you. Indeed, with the exception of my father, I fear we have all been remiss. And I, unkind."

Only Alexander's arm firmly around her waist kept Dinah moving in time to the music. "Unkind?" Dinah asked in puzzlement. It was true that he seemed to alternate between devout attention and utter abandonment, but she had not thought of that as being unkind, more a concern with his own life.

"Unkind," he said firmly. "Still, seeing you tonight, I wish you would give me another chance, let tonight erase how much I hurt you."

"Oh, Alexander, I would like nothing better than to have us be . . ." she hesitated, not sure of the word she meant. As always, when she was near him, she could feel the familiar warmth in her loins, the desire to be in his arms, his lips on her mouth and then her breasts.

"Yes?" The dance had twirled to a stop, with partners bowing to one another before taking their partners to supper. That honor tonight for Dinah was to be Sir Robert's.

"As . . . as we were," Dinah finished, hoping he understood her meaning.

"You are a puzzle, my dear Dinah. You say too much and yet say nothing." Alexander shook his head as he led her to his father.

The supper was a feast of delicacies. There was game, pheasant and squab and grouse, all artfully presented and adorned with their feathers in a colorful array; fish in aspic; a whole pig roasted with an apple in his mouth; other meats; a variety of velvety mousses; and tarts, both hot and cold. Sir Robert filled a plate and poured a glass of champagne before leading her to a small table set up in the salon.

As Dinah sat down on the small gilt chair, she realized it was the first time she had rested all evening and yet she was not tired. Still too excited to eat, she nibbled at the delicacies and sipped the champagne, grateful to be alone for a few minutes. At least with all the dancing, she had had little opportunity for conversation. Now, however, she would have to talk, and that was difficult for her. To make the light, coquettish chatter that came so easily to Margaret and Mary was hard work. To her surprise, even that came easily. She was surrounded by too many men to do more than smile at them, as they issued invitations to show her Edinburgh or to take her riding.

Finally, the guests started to drift reluctantly home. The Anguses were the last to leave, Lady Janet pointedly asking Dinah about the party to give Mary a chance for a last chat with Alexander. Although Alexander had danced with Mary, far more of his attention had been given to Dinah and he had also danced with many other of the young women at the dance. Margaret went upstairs immediately after saying goodnight to James, who then approached Sir Robert. Although Dinah could not hear the conversation, she could tell from Sir Robert's face it was not to his liking.

After they, too, had departed, Sir Robert said goodnight, telling Dinah to sleep as long as she wanted, and Alexander escorted her to her rooms. In the small sitting room, he took her hands, studying her.

"I was thinking," he said slowly, "of that first afternoon I saw you at Mrs. Bradley's. Do you remember, Dinah?"

Dinah nodded, as the same thought had been going through her mind. "What a child I was. Yet it was only a few months ago!"

"And now you are a woman," he put his arms around her, his mouth kissing her cheek and then her mouth.

Dinah's arms went around him. And now, I can never go back, she thought, not after tonight, not after . . . Her lips responded to his, their tongues meeting and sending fire throughout her body. He dropped his head, his lips seeming to brand the pale mounds of her breasts, one hand seeking out her buttocks beneath the flounces of her skirt.

Her heart was pounding. "Alexander . . ." she murmured.

The sound of his name startled the man. He drew quickly away from her, taking his leave with a curt goodnight.

Dinah clasped her body in her arms, trying to contain her longing for the man. How her body ached for his touch, for the fulfillment of the delights he had once shown her. Tears in her eyes, she went in to the bedroom where Molly, asleep in a chair, was waiting for her.

Dinah's party heralded the start of the holiday season. Balls, parties, and dinners followed quickly one after another, with Dinah lacking neither invitations nor partners. At first she noticed only that everyone seemed to dance with everyone else, that partners for suppers or at dinners were sometimes the same and sometimes different. As the busy round became less of a novelty, Dinah began to pay more attention to the people. There was one pair in particular, a charming young married couple, who would arrive together and then drift to different partners, and always the same partners. The arrangement seemed to be taken for granted among the hostesses, who obliged by seating the couple with their chosen partners at every occasion. And they were not the only ones.

As a result, Dinah began to listen more to the conversations going on around her. Victorian society for all its seeming decorum had its own rules. A woman, recently returned from London, for example, spoke of the Prince of Wales who had been seen rather more often than social propriety required with Dinah's idol, Jennie Jerome Churchill. There was also talk of some indiscreet letters on the part of Jennie's brother-in-law to a very prominent lady and a successful attempt to avoid a scandalous divorce. Other liaisons were also mentioned, taken for granted and discussed with amusement rather than the raised eyebrows of condemnation.

The people—the women—were married, which in

some way seemed to make the liaisons more permissible. Dinah, nevertheless, began to wonder whether what had happened on the ship was as sinful as she had thought. London, even Edinburgh, seemed far more permissive than New York. Then, there was the matter of gambling.

The Prince of Wales was an ardent card player, despite Queen Victoria's disapproval. The problem was that his zeal did not match his skill, with wealthy friends often having to pay his debts. Again, although the whims of royalty were far beyond Dinah's understanding, she tried to relate what she heard about the prince to those she knew, particularly Alexander as well as to James. Both, it seemed, were as zealous card players as the Prince and both, as unsuccessful. The first time that Sir Robert had paid off Alexander's debts had been a warning, one that the son did not take. As the debts recurred, Sir Robert's disapproval had mounted, leading to his sending Alexander on the *Star of Scotland* as his emissary to Dinah in the hope that months at sea would give him a new perspective.

James was a different matter. Sir Malcom was not rich, and James was not only heavily in debt at the tables but also to his friends. As a result, he had gone into the army to avoid prison. The army had been a means, too, to get Sir Robert's approval of his marriage to Margaret. Sir Robert, however, had refused to discuss even an engagement until James had proven himself by paying off his debts and stopping his gambling. If filial duty required him to pay off his son's debts, it did not mean he would accept a son-in-law whose debts were even more profligate. All Margaret's pleadings and declarations of her love for James had done nothing to soften her father's heart toward him even though he might accept his son's marriage in hopes that it would give him a sense of responsibility. Alexander, on the other hand, had shown little inclination to marry, despite having been a favorite escort of Mary Angus before Dinah's arrival. Now, to Dinah's consternation, she learned wagers were being made due to the alternating of his attentions to her and Mary.

To Dinah's relief, the round of social events began to ease with the coming of Lent. One evening, the first time in weeks that the Douglases were dining at home alone, Sir Robert brought up a new subject.

"Dinah," he said, "have you had enough of Edinburgh for a while?"

"Of Edinburgh?" Dinah repeated, confused.

"I was thinking, that with spring coming, we might journey to Kinross-shire. You know that I have a home there, and it is still early enough to get a little hunting in."

"A capitol idea," declared Alexander. "You would like it there, Dinah. The moors are beautiful this time of year, and you could practice your riding—for which you have had so little time, thanks to the parties and the weather."

The winter had been cold, with snow often blustering in from the northern highlands. Although the weather had not interfered with social life, it had prevented Dinah from riding very much.

Sir Robert looked at his son with amusement, wondering about Alexander's motives. As far as he knew Alexander had behaved himself admirably during the season and had not incurred any debts, although he had not given up cards. At the same time, he knew that his son had always enjoyed the country and the life that went with it. "At least you agree with me that it is time for a change," he said indulgently. "What about you, Dinah?"

"I will do whatever you suggest, Sir Robert," smiled the girl. "Having never seen Kinross-shire, I can have no opinion."

Margaret, however, was not so sure about the suggestion. "It's early yet and it is bound to be cold," she hesitated, "but perhaps we could go to Stirling first —it is on the way. James would be only too happy to show Dinah around the castle." she added, trying to tame her sarcasm.

Sir Robert studied his daughter. "I would like to see how James is doing with the regiment myself. In that case, perhaps the Anguses would join us, as I am sure all of them would like to see James, too."

Sir Robert drew up his plans with his usual dispatch. They would leave the 15th of March to be away for about six weeks. In the meantime, servants were sent ahead to help the caretakers at Kinrossshire prepare the house. There were country clothes to be ordered for Dinah, too, including a riding habit in the Murray tartan.

Shortly before they left, Dinah received a letter from Ian MacKie that arrived in a bundle of dispatches from New York. She studied her name in the neat, precise writing on the envelope carefully as she tried to remember the captain. So much had happened that she had difficulty in recalling his face until she thought of the blue eyes and then all the features appeared in front of her. Yet, she had not forgotten him. Often during a dance or at a party, she had seen a face that reminded her of him, although none of the young men whom she had met had had his broad shoulders or big chest. Often, too, as she made light, flirtatious conversation with her partners, she had longed for the simple, straightforward honesty that had marked all her talks with MacKie.

Now, reading his letter, it was like that afternoon he had held her. It was as if she could feel his lips on her cheek, against her mouth, his chest rousing her nipples, and she sighed for the warmth she had felt, not the burning passion that Alexander could excite, but desire's comforting warmth.

"My dear Dinah," he wrote, "how often I have thought of you on this crossing, recalling my last voyage with you as a companion. The voyage has been uneventful, despite a storm shortly before we arrived in New York. Unfortunately, I fear the transactions here may take longer than we expected. Still, business has been successful and I have hopes of sailing for Bermuda within the next few weeks.

191

Should all go according to plan, we should arrive in Edinburgh about Easter."

He added, "I hope you have been as happy as I know you have been busy with the social season over the holidays. Even so, I like to think you have thought of me a little, that you will still consider me a friend on my return. My feelings for you have not diminished and, in fact, are stronger than ever. I love you, Dinah. Whatever you decide, please know that I will never hesitate to assist you in any way I can."

Dinah read the letter several times before she noticed the post script at the bottom, asking her to call on his mother and tell her when he expected to return. She realized that he had enclosed the letter with the business dispatches in order for her to receive the letter as soon as possible. She decided that she would call on Mrs. MacKie the very next day. It was a visit that was long over due, and one that she had intended to make long ago.

In fact, she thought impulsively, why not go right now? She had fittings the next day, after which the Anguses were coming for tea. Putting on the heavy cloak she had worn at sea and taking a small bonnet, she went downstairs to tell Jamison she would be back later. The day was cold but sunny and a walk would do her good.

As she walked, her eyes sought the castle towering over the city. What a familiar sight it had become, as familiar as the arch in Washington Square had once been. For the first time in months, she thought about her mother and the urgency that had sent her from a life of luxury to that hard, penurious life without family or friends in the New World. What had driven her to leave those lovely rooms, once hers and now Dinah's, to leave behind the jewels and fine clothes, taking only the sterling silver Stuart brooch and the Murray plaid that had been Dinah's baby blanket? Alexander and certainly Margaret, she was sure, knew nothing, while Sir Robert—whatever he knew—avoided her questions. Probably, she sighed, she would never know, unless in some way she herself could unlock the mystery. The word unlock reminded her suddenly of her mother's dying words that she had almost forgotten, "Rabbie," and what was it? "Lock" and "eleven"? She should really ask Sir Robert, she supposed, except she was not sure that he could answer, or would.

She had reached the small house. Hand raised to pull the bell, she hesitated, wondering whether she should not have sent a message ahead. Well, she was here. She pulled the bell, giving her name to the little maid who answered and stepping inside the house.

Mrs. MacKie bustled out of the small kitchen at the rear of the house immediately to greet her, apologizing for the apron. She was in the middle of baking, she explained, insisting that Dinah go into the small sitting room where a fire would warm her up in no time.

"I would prefer the kitchen," Dinah asserted, recalling the Bradley kitchen on baking days. Besides, the small front room held memories for her and she had had enough of memories for one day.

"You're sure?" the older woman asked dubiously.

"I am—and I promise not to get in your way."

"Very well," smiled Mrs. MacKie.

The kitchen was as cozy as the rest of the house. At one end was a big iron coal-burning stove; at the other, a small table where tea things were set out. In the center was a large wooden table, now set out with bowls and rolling pins. Dinah was seated at the small table, while Mrs. MacKie set a kettle on to boil and was told about her son's letter.

"Thank you for coming," replied Mrs. MacKie, grateful for the news. "Sir Robert usually sends around word he is safely arrived, but to hear it from you is much more pleasant. One worries so . . . I shall never get used to that."

"You don't regret his decision to go to sea?" asked Dinah curiously.

"Oh no! It was what he wished and what makes him happy. It is only," she sat down opposite Dinah,

193

letting the maid prepare the tea, "that it is a hard life, even harder for a woman, I think, than a man. He is doing what he loves, while a woman can only wait."

"I had not thought of it that way," Dinah said slowly.

"You should, my dear. One of these days you will marry, perhaps my Ian who loves you, I know," Mrs. MacKie responded as Dinah flushed. "Oh, he hasn't told me anything, but I knew the first day he came home from the last voyage and mentioned you. That's not what I meant to say, however. All I mean is that whomever you marry, you must consider what he does —and you must love him, in spite of that."

Dinah thought of what she had seen and heard at the parties. "Marriage sometimes doesn't mean very much, it seems."

"That depends on the man and the woman. But you are right in that people often marry for reasons of their own, especially in the gentry. There are marriages of convenience. I am afraid you may have your choice—to marry for love or for fortune."

The young woman thought of her mother. Had the moments of love that had resulted in the conceiving of Dinah been worth all her mother had had to give up? That was one thing she would never know, as only her mother could answer the question and her mother was gone. Yet, somehow Dinah did not think that her mother had ever had any regrets. If there had been, surely there would have been some bitterness and resentment at her change of station in life, and there had seemed to be none.

"Well," Dinah tried to smile, "I am young yet, and marriage . . ."

Mrs. MacKie smiled, too, and got up to get the tea. Shortly afterwards, Dinah left, insisting on walking home. She needed time to think. No one before had ever talked to her of love and marriage as if they were two separate things, as if the two could be separated. She had always assumed love meant marriage and vice versa, that regardless of what she had seen and heard she would have both. Yet, perhaps that was not necessary. Perhaps she could love Ian and marry Alexander or love Alexander and marry Ian. For that matter, what, in fact, was love—the burning passion she felt near Alexander or the quiet warmth when she was with Ian?

Chapter 14

THE CLIFF ON which Stirling Castle was built was far more precipitous than the one in Edinburgh. The castle itself reared soaring, crenelated walls above the ground mists at sunset, as the coach rattled toward it. To Dinah, it seemed that all Scottish castles must have been built on such crags.

The ride had seemed montonous and jolting, although the coach was comfortable. The party had used two coaches, with the Douglases and Dinah traveling in the first, followed by the one with Lady Janet, Sir Malcolm, and Mary. Both coaches, however, had been loaded with traveling trunks. Then, there was the fog, which had never let up during the thirty-five-mile ride, covering the countryside with a white mist and forcing the horses to move more slowly than otherwise. The castle, outlined against the sunset and standing above the fog, in fact, was the first scenery Dinah had seen since leaving Edinburgh.

The town was scarcely more than a village, with a few inns for visitors and a scattering of houses where families of the regiment lived. As the coach pulled up at the largest inn, James, who had been waiting for them, came out to help Margaret step down. Alexander offered his hand to Dinah, and she took it.

They hurried inside, past a noisy public room and

into a private dining room where a fire blazed in the fireplace and candles cast their golden friendly light. Dinah stood in front of the fire, warming her hands, until the chill of the ride was dismissed by the fire.

Alexander joined her, taking her cloak from her shoulders. "I hope tomorrow will be a better day," he said. "You couldn't see much in the fog, but there really wasn't too much to see."

"I'm sure the fog won't last," Dinah told him optimistically, knowing by now that it could last all winter in Scotland. She stretched her back. "Ohhh, I'm stiff. My legs are too long for riding in a coach."

"If it's any comfort, Mary doesn't appear any more comfortable," pointed out Alexander as the Anguses entered the room. Mary was moving stiffly, her face puckered in a pout.

Like Dinah, she hurried to the fire. "Alexander, the least you could have done is ride part way with us in that terrible coach. Just feel my hands." She offered them to him.

Alexander patted the hands before taking her cloak. "I am afraid, my dear, I could have done little to keep you warm. Surely you had a warm robe as we did?"

Dinah turned her face away, recalling how Alexander had tucked the robe around the two of them, as Sir Robert and Margaret sat opposite. During the ride, he had had no hesitation in pressing his leg against hers. Even through their clothes, her skin had warmed to the touch. Later he had put his arm around her, to make it easier for her to put her head on his shoulder for a nap. She had closed her eyes, but she had not slept for the enjoyment of being so close to him. Indeed, one reason for stiffness was due to her attempt to keep from pressing against him even more in front of the other two.

She was relieved when a maid appeared to take the three girls to clean up in the room they would share. It was a good-sized room with two double beds and a fire blazing in the fire place. The maid had already brought basins of hot water and clean towels for them. Dinah let the other two wash up first. The maid had reminded her of Molly who had gone on ahead with the other servants, leaving Parker behind to care for Dinah and Margaret. Parker was to meet them at the Kinross-shire house with a few other servants in a few days. Dinah smiled, suddenly eager to see Molly, whom she knew would be happy to see her and happier to see the letter from Geordie that was in Dinah's handbag.

The supper that James had ordered was ample and simple, although the best the inn could offer. There was a roast joint of mutton, a shepherd's pie, a vegetable of cabbage boiled with carrots and potatoes, and a compote of dried fruits in brandy. As they ate, James told them of his arrangements, a tour of the castle in the morning, luncheon with the commanding officer, and an invitation to watch a review of the troops in the afternoon if they wished.

Sir Robert looked with new approval and respect at James, as Margaret smiled happily. "You have done well. I am sure we will enjoy our visit."

"I hope so, Sir Robert," said James with a sidelong glance at Margaret. "Colonel Forbes is eager to meet you. There is talk that the regiment may be posted to Africa, and he is anxious to talk to you about the country."

The group discussed Africa and the next day, before James had to leave promising to meet them the next morning at ten and escort them to the castle. The travelers, tired from the journey, were only too happy to go to their beds.

Mary and Margaret helped one another undress, while Dinah managed for herself, neither asking nor being offered help. As she slipped into the double bed, her toes found the warmth left by a warming pan, and she snuggled down under the feather comforter. As she fell asleep, she could hear Mary and Margaret whispering to each other and giggling now and then, as if making some kind of plan. Dinah dismissed them from her mind, feeling sure they were discussing Sir Robert's new approval of James.

Breakfast was huge, bowls of oatmeal, followed by

platters of eggs, rashers of bacon, grilled kidneys, and kippers. No sooner were they finished, than James was at the door with the carriages.

The road leading to the castle was steep, barely wide enough for the carriages, a solid wall of rock on one side and a deep drop on the other. Dinah could well understand how the castle had never been defeated in battle, as Alexander had revealed. The only way up to the castle was the road, which would accommodate only a narrow file of soldiers, easily defeatable by a small company at the castle. The only other way was up the sheer cliffs on the other sides of the castle, an almost impossible feat. As a result, the castle was superbly preserved. In the center was a large open area used for drills and parades, surrounded by out buildings, their backs a part of the high walls where cannons till peeped through the openings.

Two kilted soldiers stood guard at the gate, snapping to attention as the carriages entered. Dinah could not help staring at her first sight of Scots in full dress. The knee-length kilt was topped by a scarlet doublet. A plaid, blanket length in size and in the same tartan as the kilt was draped over the left shoulder and fastened at the shoulder with a brooch bearing the regimental badge. A sporran was suspended from the waist, to serve as purse and pockets, its original purpose being to carry a day's rations. Plaid hose were folded just below the knees above jackboots. A small dirk or knife was held by the right garter. On each soldier's head was a glengarry with the crest and motto of the regiment.

Alexander took Dinah's arm, James and Margaret leading the way. "They are rather impressive, aren't they?"

"Very," Dinah agreed, picking up her skirts to climb a narrow staircase to the walls.

The day was sunny and clear, with mountains to be seen in the distance. Alexander pointed to the road, which they would take next morning leading west to Kinross-shire, adding, "Queen Mary stayed here more than once, first as a babe when a number of clans rose against her and were defeated by loyal clans under her mother. Later, when whe returned to rule, it was said to be one of her favorite places for hunting. It was here, too, Mary saw her son, King James VI of Scotland and I of England, for the last time after sending him here for his own protection."

"Did she live here, then?" asked Dinah curiously.

"No, her main residence was Holyrood Place, but she often made 'progresses,' as they called them, to visit parts of her realm. Stirling was a favorite one, being only a day's journey from Edinburgh. And then, too, it was considered a fortress, where she would be safe. It's said she spent her last night here before leaving for England to ask Elizabeth for protection. There's no proof of that, and Stirling was in the hands of her enemies by then. As you can see, it's as impregnable as possible, and a secret visit without anyone's knowing would have been impossible."

"Poor Mary," sighed Dinah, "to be welcomed with such fervor and then to be hunted by her own people."

"And to die virtually alone in a foreign land," mused Alexander.

Dinah shuddered at his words, at the fate that had been Mary's, but more at the memory of her mother and now the thought of herself. Unconsciously, she stepped closer to Alexander. As she did, Mary, who had been following them with her parents, came up and inserted herself between them, taking Alexander's arm.

"Dinah, you have had Alexander to yourself for long enough. And whatever were you talking about so seriously?"

"About Mary, Queen of Scots, and her unhappy life," said Dinah deliberately to see the effect on Mary.

"Just think, Alexander." Mary siezed on the subject, "since you are related to the Douglases, if she had married a Douglas, you might be king of England."

Alexander laughed. "Not I, although perhaps my father. In that case," his eyes glittered, "I would be Prince of Wales, surrounded by the most beautiful ladies in the realm, all eager and willing." He stopped abruptly.

"And we," Mary pouted, "are not beautiful?"

Alexander's eyes sought Dinah's over the top of Mary's head. He left Mary's question unanswered.

Mary, however, was determined to have an answer. "Well, are we not beautiful enough for you to share your life?"

"You misunderstood me, Mary. If I were Prince of Wales, sharing my life would be one thing and not a matter of my choice. It was who shares his bed I was thinking of. Jennie Churchill, Lily Langtry, Lady Dudley . . ."

Mary dropped Alexander's arm as if it were on fire. "You cad!" she sputtered. Her face was flaming. "No gentleman would mention such a thing to a lady."

Dinah, although she was surprised at Alexander's statement, had to suppress a smile at Mary's tantrum. From what she had heard discussed in front of and between Mary and Margaret, Alexander's statement was common knowledge. Still, she was angry at him for the mention of his bed, as she knew that was aimed at her. Looking at Alexander, therefore, she said to Mary, "Perhaps Alexander is not the gentlemen he pretends."

"Then, we shall have nothing to do with him, at least until he changes his attitude, shall we, Dinah?"

To Dinah's surprise, Mary took her hand, forcing Alexander to follow them. The alliance was so unexpected that all Dinah could manage was a smile.

Luncheon was in the officer's dining room, a high-ceilinged room paneled in a dark oak. The colonel, resplendent in Highland kilt uniform, sat at the head of the table with Lady Jane on one side and Sir Robert on the other. At the foot of the table was James with Dinah and Margaret. Alexander was seated between his father and Dinah and opposite Mary and her father.

As he held her chair, Alexander whispered in Dinah's ear, "I apologize for what I said on the wall. Mary will have her way, and I spoke without thinking of the consequences," adding, "as I do, all too often."

Dinah nodded, waiting for an opportune moment to say softly, "You must apologize to her, Alexander, even if you said nothing that she had not talked about with Margaret."

"Aha, I thought you ladies could hardly be as innocent as you pretend, you excepted, Dinah," replied the young man.

"You must still apologize," Dinah insisted.

"Since you ask, I will—but only because I wish to please you." Alexander picked up his wine glass, glancing around the table. Margaret was hanging on every word of James at the foot of the table. At the head, his father and the colonel were engaged in a serious conversation. Across the table, Sir Malcolm had turned from talking to Mary to his wife, and Mary was looking at Alexander with a pout on her face. He opened his mouth, then closed it.

Dinah, expecting the apology, was surprised at the silence. To fill it in, she said, "It is very imposing, Mary, isn't it? All those kilts . . ." she motioned to the officers, mostly dressed in kilts, sitting at tables around the room.

"To an American like you, I suppose. I have seen it before," Mary lied.

Dinah's sympathy dried up. If that alliance of the two young woman had only been for effect, then let Mary wait for the apology. Besides, apology or not, Mary would soon be throwing herself at Alexander, she suspected.

She did not have long to wait. As they went outside to watch the afternoon drill, Mary immediately placed herself in such a way that Alexander had to take her arm. Dinah found herself with Sir Robert, who was happy to escort her to the stand where the colonel was waiting for them.

First came the pipers, the drum major elegant in a high feathered hat with the hackle of the regiment and carrying a big baton. As he raised the baton, the pipers blew into their pipes, emitting a wild swirl of sound skyward. It was less music to Dinah than a screeching, ferocious sound, well suited for its intended purpose of scattering an enemy in fright. Yet, it was a thrilling sound, too, in the open air, beneath the glowering battlements, especially as the pipers stepped out at brisk pace that sent their heavy skirts swinging in the rhythm of the parade. Then came the regiment, marching in time to the pipes, their kilts swinging, too.

The parade was over much too soon for Dinah, who watched until the last of the soldiers had marched back to barracks. Cheeks rosy with excitement, Dinah squeezed Sir Robert's arm.

James escorted them to the waiting carriages, promising to join them for a traditional high tea at six. In the meantime, they were to have time to rest, as they would be up early in the morning to finish the journey to Kinross-shire.

At the inn, Dinah removed her dress and lay in the bed, listening to the chatter of the other two girls. This time, they did not whisper, and Dinah could not miss the fact that they were ignoring her presence. In front of Sir Robert, Margaret might pretend a friendship, but the pretense had become less and less since Dinah's party, especially when Mary was with her. The pleasure of the day faded, and the thought of the weeks ahead at Kinross-shire with Mary and Margaret began to take on a sense of foreboding. She turned on her side, trying not to listen.

She would not let them see her cry. Indeed, she would not cry at all. If she had not been able to cry at her mother's death, why should she weep because of two silly girls? She would simply have to be strong. At least, she would soon have Molly to talk to, Molly whose ever-present optimisim would soon banish that feeling of approaching doom.

Chapter 15

DINAH HAD ASSUMED that the journey to where they were going was farther than from Stirling to Edinburgh because of Sir Robert's insistence on an early start. Instead, it was only a little more than 20 miles, and the reason for the early start was due to Sir Robert's desire to reach his country house in time for luncheon.

As they approached their destination, Dinah looked curiously out the window. She was sitting next to Sir Robert, as Mary and Margaret between them had urged Alexander to ride that day with the Anguses. "You must share your company," Margaret had said. "You rode with us yesterday. Today you should accompany Mary." Alexander had demurred, saying that he had to point out the sights to Dinah, and Mary had pouted until finally he gave in, one reason being the morning fog that obscured the countryside, a fact he could not deny as Margaret indicated.

The sun, however, had dispersed the fog shortly after they started out. Now, in the distance, Dinah could see an ice-blue lake, or loch as Sir Robert called it, with islands dotting it. The surrounding moors were still brown, although here and there were purple patches of early heather, and the cold air was filled with a freshness that was sweet to Dinah's city-bred senses. She was entranced by the loneliness and the isolation, the scattered cottages and the villages they had passed through and the distant hills shimmering in the mists that clung to them.

She recalled the days at sea, the utter emptiness once they passed the limit of the sea birds' flight.

There, the vastness of the sea had filled her with a sense of her own mortality, of the power of nature and the helplessness of man, especially as the ship had rolled, wallowing and tossing on the waves. Here, she was filled with a sense of life, hidden as it was. Wisps of smoke rose from distant cottages, and birds were flushed from the gorse by the sound of the carriages, twittering and wheeling high over their nests. Here and there, a male pheasant darted farther into the gorse, its plumage vibrant in the brown of the hillside. A flock of long-haired white sheep, still in their winter wool, scattered skittishly from a graze near the road, baaing in panic.

The coach came to a crossroads. As it turned to the left, descending toward the shore of the loch, Dinah saw the signpost indicating that the other turning led to the village of Lochleven.

"Lochleven!" Dinah's voice rang out over the clutter of the coach's wheels, and she shivered.

"Are you cold?" Sir Robert tucked the blanket solicitously around her.

Dinah shook her head. "Lochleven—is that where we are going?"

"Of course." Sir Robert was puzzled. "Where did you think . . ."

"Kinross-shire. Isn't that what you called it?"

"Dinah, this is Kinross-shire. It's what you would call a county," he explained patiently. Across from him, Margaret, who had been half asleep and who had been awakened by Dinah's cry, listened avidly.

"And Lochleven?" Dinah asked, aware of Margaret's attention. She wanted to wait until she was alone with Sir Robert, but her heart was pounding with impatience from the sight of the word and the sound of it in her mouth.

"Lochleven," Sir Robert pronounced it the Scottish way, the "ch" a swallowed guttural, "is the name of the lake, loch and leven. It is also the name of the castle that you can see on that large island out there." He pointed to the island he meant. "The village nearest the house is called Lochleven, too, but I always think of the house as being in Kinross-shire," he added.

"Perhaps Lochleven means something else to Dinah," suggested Margaret. "Does it, Dinah?" Her eyes glittered with curiosity.

Dinah shook her head, thinking quickly. "It's such an unusual name, at least to me."

"You've never heard it before?" persisted Margaret.

Dinah shrugged, ignoring the question and turning to look out the window. She was glad her hands were hidden under the blanket, because she could feel them shaking. Her mind was reeling. Lochleven was what her mother had meant, not lock and eleven as Dinah had thought she had said, never having heard the word before. What did the place mean, what had it meant, to her mother that she should call it out with her last breaths? Even then, did she mean the loch itself, the castle, or the town? Dinah could not guess, and the more she thought about it the more confusing Lochleven, the Lochleven of her mother, became.

What a mysterious woman her mother had been! What secrets she had kept to herself even at the end, secrets that were still locked in the past and that Dinah could not even guess at. Yet, something terrible must have happened to drive her mother from the luxury in which she had been raised to the genteel poverty in which she had died, to force her to seal her lips and keep her heritage from her own daughter. Dinah was sure that whatever it was that happened to drive her mother away had happened at Lochleven. If so, then perhaps she would be able to uncover the secret. She forgot her sense of foreboding of the night before, as she began to look eagerly toward the visit here. Then, she saw Margaret still watching her.

The carriage fortunately had arrived at the house, which was actually an estate. Wrought iron gates opened onto a wide drive that led through a broad lawn to a gracious entrance with a Georgian porte cochere. The entrance hall was virtually a room, with other rooms leading off from it. It rose three stories high, with balconies leading around it on the other floors. Off to one side was a circular iron staircase. The house, built by Sir Robert's father in the early 19th century, was based on the small palace at Greenwich that was built during the reign of Mary Stuart's son.

Jamison and his wife, Molly, and the personal servants of the Anguses were lined up to greet them. Dinah hurried Molly off to her room. Although smaller than her bedroom in the house on Princes Street, the room was equally luxurious and furnished in the same colors. Dinah paid little attention to it or to the view from the windows of the formal gardens at the rear of the house that led to the shores of the loch.

She hugged Molly, as she had not been able to do before. "I have a present for you," she declared opening her traveling bag to hand Molly the letter from Geordie.

"From Geordie? Oh, Dinah!" Molly hugged her back and started to open it, hesitating as she asked, "Do you need anything? Can I help you?"

"No," Dinah laughed, taking off her cloak. "I can manage quite well. You read your letter."

Dinah took her time washing up and changing clothes for the luncheon in the dining room, watching the other girl's face. Molly, as Dinah had done with MacKie's letter, read it through quickly at first, before sitting on the bed to reread it more slowly, her face glowing more and more with each word. With a twinge of guilt, Dinah realized that she had been so wrapped up in herself that she had failed to recognize how much Molly loved Geordie.

"You love him, Molly, don't you?" Dinah asked as Molly laid the letter aside and went to Dinah's side to help her with her hair.

"Yes, I do. Every time I think of him . . ." Molly sighed, remembering the proposal and the marriage she had put off.

"Did he want you to marry him before he sailed?" At Molly's nod, Dinah asked, "Why didn't you?"

"I couldn't, Dinah, not then. He wanted me to move to a cottage near his sister, to leave you," Molly admitted miserably.

"Oh dear! You didn't say no because of me, did you?" Dinah was dismayed at the thought.

"I had to. I . . . what would I do in the country all those months at sea, when you needed me!" Molly said cheerfully, optimistic as always.

"I-I would have managed," affirmed Dinah, not at all sure what she would do without Molly.

"With Parker?" Molly laughed genuinely. "Geordie can wait a bit."

"Still, when he gets home again, I think the two of you—"

"I'll think about it. I am not sure I am quite ready to retire to the country yet," Molly said, sounding surer than she felt.

"You're certain? The ship should return about the time we get back. You could be married at Easter." Dinah looked anxiously at Molly's face.

"We'll see, Dinah." Molly patted the last strand of her hair into place. "Or do you want to be rid of me?"

"Of course not." Dinah sprang to her feet. "I am not sure what I would do without you, Molly, but I want you to be happy. After all, you have given up so much for me."

"If it hadn't been for you, I wouldn't have met Geordie," Molly pointed out. "So, let's just see what happens, shall we," she added firmly.

Dinah nodded, leaving the room as the coachman carried in her traveling trunk. Luncheon was in a dining room overlooking the loch and the formal gardens. From where Dinah was sitting, she could see the castle a few miles distant on the island, and her eyes were drawn to it, time and time again, despite Margaret's sitting opposite her.

Margaret obviously noticed the direction of Dinah's gaze, as she said, "Father, as soon as it warms up a bit, we should take a picnic and go to the castle. I am sure Dinah would be interested."

"Would you, Dinah?" Sir Robert asked. "If so, I can arrange to hire a few boats in the village."

Dinah, thinking of her mother, said, "Yes, I would like that."

"Of course, she would," put in Margaret conversationally. "After all, if Dinah is to live in Scotland, she should know more about its history, including good Queen Mary.' "

"What has Mary to do with Lochleven?" Dinah, her mind on her mother, had only half been listening.

"After Mary had her first husband poisoned, she married James Hepburn, Earl of Bothwell. Of course, she had to because she was carrying his child . . ." Margaret began.

"Margaret, that's enough," interrupted Sir Robert. "Dinah, her husband was murdered, although Mary was cleared of any knowledge of it. At the same time, Bothwell was one of the plotters and she did marry him as he represented a powerful faction of lords. There were rumors that he . . . forced her . . . to marry him. That may be true or not."

"Does it make any difference how or why she married him?" Margaret said airily "The fact remains that she was forced to give up the crown in favor of her son, and was sent to Lochleven until they decided what to do with her. She also had her second baby there, according to family history."

Alexander stopped his sister, saying in a gentle tone of voice, "I think I told you that aboard ship, about the Earl of Moray and the Douglases."

Dinah's color rose. She remembered all too well the story and the circumstances, just as Alexander must have. "Yes. Yes, you did. And that was where . . . it happened? Lochleven?"

"Oh, yes," Mary Angus but in eagerly, with a glance at Margaret. "And Mary is supposed to haunt the castle, too, crying at night for her baby, isn't she, Margaret?"

"Enough!" Sir Robert interjected. "You girls are as filled with stories as a book of tales. There is no such thing as ghosts."

"Spirits, then, if you prefer," Lady Janet said innocently. "Everyone at court quite freely admits that

Queen Victoria consults a spiritualist to get in touch with Prince Albert."

"Janet," Sir Malcolm was as disdainful of the idea as his friend, "you women are foolish to put such stock in stories. Ghosts, spirits, call them what you will, are figments of the imagination. Now, let us talk about something else. Some hunting, perhaps, as I saw more than a few plump birds beaten out by the carriages."

To Dinah's relief, the subject was immediately taken up by the men. Alexander suggested that he ride to the village the next morning, at which time he could arrange to hire some beaters and to find out about boats to take them to the castle. They had lingered so long over luncheon, he pointed out, that it was too late that afternoon. "Perhaps," he added, "Dinah would like to go with me."

"Oh yes," agreed Dinah.

"What about Mary and me?" asked Margaret.

"I intend to leave early. Dinah is an early riser, or was on shipboard," he said with a smile. "You girls sleep much too late and take much too long to get ready." He turned to Dinah. "Can you be ready by nine—or is that too early for you, too?"

"I'll be ready," Dinah promised.

With that, everyone rose from the table, Dinah and the other women going to their rooms, while the men went into the library to discuss their prospects for hunting. Dinah, who found Molly busily ironing the packed clothes, decided to go for a walk in the formal gardens. To her surprise, she was joined by the other girls who had found their maids equally industrious and their rooms filled with clothes.

In the gardens, with the castle in the distance, the subject obviously came up again. Dinah herself brought the subject up, more out loud to herself than to anyone else and instantly sorry for the words. "However did she get away from that island?"

"They certainly didn't let her go," laughed Margaret, "not with Lady Douglas guarding her interests and those of her sons, legal or not!"

"Then, how . . ." puzzled Dinah. The castle, despite the walls that had fallen with time, seemed formidable with watch towers that overlooked the loch and its approaches, and with only a narrow beach between them and the waters.

"Two of Lady Douglas's sons fell hopelessly in love with Mary. She was supposed to be beautiful and quite charming, even if she had too long a neck and was too tall," Margaret said pointedly. "Between them, they managed to steal the keys to the door to Mary's room and to bribe boatmen from the village. Then, on a moonless night, one son put holes in all the boats save the one and Mary, wearing a servant's dress, was rowed to the shore, right about here, I would imagine, where the older son had horses waiting. Mary went from castle to castle, where she knew she had support, gathering some of the clans. There was a final battle, after which Mary fled to Elizabeth's protection."

Dinah shivered, as much from a cloud passing over the sun as from the idea of the queen's flight across the dark waters of the loch with only a few stars to guide her. Incongruously, she wondered whether her mother, too, had fled from here.

Mary had seen the shiver. "Truly, Dinah, Mary's ghost is supposed to haunt the castle, regardless of what Sir Robert and my father say. I wonder what she's like!"

"Why not go there and see—some moonless night, that is?" Dinah laughed.

"Perhaps she would only appear for you," Margaret murmured. "After all, you are supposed to be a descendent."

"It's growing cold. I think I'll go in. I'm sure Molly is finished by now." Dinah turned abruptly on her heel, leaving the other girls behind. She tried to dismiss the suggestion, but it kept recurring to her during the rest of the day and that evening. The last thing she did before going to bed was look at the castle. There was a moon, and the night was clear. It must have appeared the same, much the same because the light was not bright enough to see where the walls had fallen, when Mary was a prisoner there and bore her child. It must have appeared the same, too, when her mother was here, Dinah was sure, just as she was sure that this had been her mother's room some eighteen years earlier, before her mother, too, had run away.

Dinah had been sure she wouldn't sleep with such thoughts in her head, but she did, deeply and dreamlessly, thanks to the country air. Molly, in fact, had to awaken her to get her up in time for the ride into the village with Alexander.

Dressing hurriedly, she rushed to the breakfast room where Alexander had told her to meet him. To her delight, she was there ahead of him. By the time he arrived, she was sitting calmly, drinking a cup of coffee and nibbling some toast.

"Good morning, Alexander," she said sweetly.

"Good morning. I wasn't sure you'd be up." He went to the sideboard to help himself to the hot dishes warming there.

"I said I would be. Didn't you believe me?"

"I always believe you, Dinah." Alexander sat down, the words hanging enigmatically between them. "Haven't we both kept our word?"

Dinah flushed, as she, too, recalled the circumstances of his telling her about her heritage. "Yes."

He ate silently, saying no more until they were mounted on their horses and riding into the village. "That silly sister of mine and Mary didn't give you bad dreams with that chatter of theirs, did they?"

"No. I slept very well, thank you."

"I'm glad of that. I had visions of your rowing over to the island, just to see for yourself," he replied. "Promise me, Dinah, you will not go to that damned island unless I am with you."

Dinah was surprised by the vehemence of his tone. "Why? Surely in broad daylight you don't expect to find ghosts on the island."

"I don't want you going there alone," he insisted.

"I have no intention of that! But I wouldn't be alone if I were going for a picnic with Mary and Margaret, would I?"

"Never mind that. Just promise me that you won't go without me. If you don't, we will go back to the house right now," he added slyly.

"You don't mean that!" the young woman protested.

"I do, if that's the only way I can make you promise that you will go to the island only if I am along. Furthermore, I won't take you riding anymore—and you know, whatever else I am, I keep my word," he reminded her savagely.

"Very well, then. I promise I will not go to the island without you, although I do wish you'd tell me why."

"I will when we are there." He spurred his horse. "Now let's see if you remember what I taught you."

Both horses broke into a trot. At first, Dinah tensed, her body jolting against the rhythm of the horse. As she relaxed, her body began automatically to move with the horse. She was almost sorry when they reached the first houses at the outskirts of Lochleven and they slowed the horses to a walk.

The town was small, a cluster of white-washed, thatched-roof cottages facing on a dirt road. In the center was the steeple of a granite church. Near it was an inn called the James First, with a livery at the back.

"We will leave the horses here and have a cup of tea while I talk to the proprietor."

He dismounted and went to Dinah's side to help her down. As he held his hand up, a flock of geese rounded the side of the inn. The waddling, hissing and angry mob, necks extended, darted angrily at the intruders, spitting in attack. The horses reared. Dinah felt herself falling, but fortunately she had not yet started to dismount. As Alexander tried to grab the bridle, Dinah struggled with the reins, her bones jarring as the horse dropped on its forefeet, trying to kick out with its rear feet at the geese behind.

The noise brought the proprietor out. He shooed the geese away and hurried to the horse to help Alexander. "Better'n a watch dog, them geese are," he noted with satisfaction. "That's what the Romans useter keep 'em for, so the Reverend says."

"Damn the Romans!" Alexander handed the horse's head to the proprietor to help a thoroughly shaken Dinah to the ground. "This girl could have been killed!" He put his arm around her. "Are you all right, my dear?"

Dinah nodded, taking a deep breath. "I'm fine." Now that she was on the ground, she realized that she had been less frightened than startled. The horse's rearing had given her the same sense of exhilaration that she had felt when Duchess had run away accidentally, not that she was going to tell him that as long as he was holding her close.

"You're MacNab, aren't you?" Alexander asked, going on without waiting for an answer. "Do you think you can get us a cup of tea?"

"Aye, sir, Mr. Douglas." He eyed Dinah curiously, not recognizing her as he did Alexander.

Inside the inn, he settled them in the bar, apologizing that the other room wasn't cleaned up from a party the night before. He left them alone, returning in minutes with a pot of tea intended for his own breakfast and setting out brandy, "for the lady's nerves."

Alexander poured tea for the two of them, lacing both cups liberally with brandy. "Drink that," he ordered, "you must need it."

Dinah drank it meekly, sipping it slowly and listening to Alexander discuss their reason for coming to the village.

The proprietor, a short, wiry man with a fringe of greasy red hair and a several days growth of beard, listened. Dinah distrusted him immediately, disliking the watery, pale blue eyes, one of which had a milky cast.

When Alexander had finished, MacNab wiped his mouth with the back of his hand. "Well, sir, Mr. Douglas, the beaters I kin manage. I'll speak to the lads tonight. If it's tomorrow you want 'em, tis all you want you'll have."

"Agreed. And the boats?"

"Them's not my business. Some of the lads, they has their own. Your best bet is ol' Tom. Lives back there," MacNab nodded at the shore of the loch. "You can't miss him. Him has several boats—builds 'em himself, being an old sailor. Got a couple sons, strapping lads, who knows the loch like I know me ale."

"Very well. Have the beaters at the house by seven. The cook will give them breakfast." Alexander stood up.

"Aye, sir, Mr. Douglas." MacNab wiped his mouth.

Alexander turned to Dinah. "Do you want to wait here while I speak to the boatman?"

"No. I'd rather go with you. I'm fine now," Dinah added. She wanted to get away from MacNab. All during the conversation with Alexander, his good eye had shifted to her, studying her with unconcealed curiosity that almost amounted to fear. A mere lifting of the cup to her lips was enough for his eye to fly to Alexander, only to shift back to watch her seconds later. As she stood up, he scrambled to his feet, wiping his mouth in relief, his eyes on her face.

"Aye, speak to ol' Tom. Him and his boys, they ain't afeared of the loch—nor ghosts either," he muttered.

As Alexander held the door for her, she glanced back. The little man was crossing himself furtively. She hurried outside, taking a deep breath and glad to be out of the bar with its odors of ale and whiskey long since drunk and pipes long since smoked.

"Why such a hurry?" Alexander was amused. "MacNab seemed quite taken with you, my dear. Why, he couldn't take his eyes off you."

Dinah thought of telling him about the sign of the cross and then decided not to. She was sure he would think she was mistaken, though the gesture had been clear and unmistakeable. "He's a strange little man. He could do with a wash, and so could that inn."

"It did smell rather stale. I just hope he comes through with those beaters," muttered Alexander.

"Then, you don't trust him, Alexander?"

"He's always come through before." Alexander laughed. "But I always have the same feeling, that men will agree to anything in front of you." He held out his hand. "Here, let me help you. This path must lead to 'Ol' Tom,' as he called him."

The path was narrow, steep, and muddy, and Dinah lifted her skirt, glad for the boots she had on. She had to step carefully, nevertheless, to avoid the waste left behind by a cow that had recently been led to a shed behind a cottage.

"What did he mean about their not being afraid of ghosts, Alexander? Is the lake, loch I mean, haunted, after all?" They had reached the shore, and the graveled beach made walking easier.

"Ghosts, again? Listen, Dinah," Alexander said firmly, "I have never heard of ghosts before—and neither has Margaret or Mary. They made it up to impress you."

"And MacNab?" persisted Dinah.

"Oh, I have no doubt he sees ghosts every night. He probably drinks too freely of his own brew. Then he sees 'ghosties and ghoulies and things that go bump in the night,' as Robert Burns put it. Look at those moors," he waved a hand at the brown, gorse-covered hills. "Not a tree in sight. To live here, one would have to be mad—or a poet."

Dinah, although still not satisfied, let the matter drop. She was sure he knew what MacNab had meant from the defensive tone in his voice. His attitude, however, made her determined to find out the truth about the ghost or ghosts or whatever it was that MacNab had meant, even if it meant she had to spend a night in the castle of Lochleven. If Alexander would not talk to her, she had no one else to whom to go, as Sir Robert had made quite clear where he stood on the matter of ghosts and spirits. Thus, it was up to Dinah herself.

Ol' Tom was a gnarled gnome of a man with white hair and a neatly trimmed white beard. His face was brown and wrinkled; his hands, large and capable. They found him planing planks for the keel of a boat that was perched in a homemade sling.

After Alexander introduced himself, he nodded. "Sailed on yer father's ships. I did. Ship's carpenter. Best ships I ever sailed. Aye, he knows how to pick his cap'ns, he does."

"My father will be pleased to hear that," Alexander said.

"Good vittles and plenty of 'em, no worms in the biscuits," recalled Tom. "No one ever pulled drunk out o' a grog shop neither, and waked up to find himself at sea. Yer signed sober." The old man noticed Dinah standing behind Alexander for the first time. His bright eyes studied her. "If yer wife would care for a cup of tea, won't take a minute. Kettle's still hot."

"I'm sorry. This is Miss Murray, a distant cousin. Dinah, tea?"

Dinah smiled, hesitating and not sure whether the tea was offered out of politeness or not. She liked the old man and did not want to hurt his feelings.

"I'll get it then," Tom said, taking her smile for acceptance. "Help yerself to some chairs." He pointed to a table by the door of the small cottage, at which were placed three sturdy chairs undoubtedly from the same hands as the several boats pulled up on the gravel.

Dinah sat down, watching the gentle waves of the loch lap the shore. The sun glittered on the water and on the castle. The castle with its formidable history seemed peaceful, locked in the tranquility of the scene. Right now, she could hardly believe in ghosts.

Over tea, with whisky for the men, Alexander explained about the reason he was there. "We'll need two, maybe three boats. If your sons can row two, perhaps I can row the other."

"When was yer thinkin' of goin'?"

216

"Whenever you like. We want a nice day, of course," explained Alexander.

"I was thinkin' that. I'll tell yer what, I'll have the boys row down, leave a boat there in the next coupla days. After that, the first nice day, they'll be on yer doorstep bright and early, to give yer time to get ready. Won't take long to row to the island. Only thing, they say come back, yer come back. The loch can kick up mighty fast when the wind turns."

"Fine." Alexander took the hand the old man offered and shook it to seal the contract.

"It's done. I'll speak to the boys tonight. They're off in the hills with their dogs," apologized Tom, "or I'd interduce yer to 'em."

"I'll take your word." Alexander stood up. "We'll be on our way."

"Take the path here by the side of the house." He pointed to Dinah's boots. "It's easier walking for the lady. Miss Murray, eh?" he smiled, offering her his hand, too. "Yer welcome any time, the two of yer."

On their way back to the inn and the horses, Alexander remarked, "Now there is a man I trust."

"He was charming, wasn't he? We must go back sometime, Alexander."

"I would rather do business with him than Mac-Nab," he hesitated, adding, "remember what I said. Just because there is a boat at the house, don't go wandering off to Lochleven Castle by yourself."

Alexander's persistence was increasing Dinah's curiosity about what was on the island. It had to have some importance for him to make such a point about her not going. "Why ever should I? I promised, but," she added, "what is there in the castle that makes it so imperative for you to be with me?"

They had reached the horses, and Alexander took a good look around to make sure the geese were nowhere in sight before helping Dinah mount and then mounting his own horse and answering her questions. "First of all," he said slowly, "you heard what Tom said about the Loch and the wind."

"And second?" she asked when he didn't go on.

The man sighed, realizing he had to say something that would sound valid to Dinah. "Well, no one has lived in the castle for years, although there is a care-taker who looks after it. From here, it looks in good condition. Inside is another matter. I wouldn't want you falling and hurting yourself or getting lost."

Dinah let the subject drop, feeling she would get no more out of Alexander and still sure there was something more to the castle than what he had said. "Oh, look!" she cried, pointing to a small bird with a ruff of feathers around its neck that took erratically to wing in front of the horses. "What is it?"

"A grouse. You can see why we need beaters. The colors are so similar to the gorse that you can't see the birds on the ground."

"That doesn't sound fair," objected the girl, "to flush them out just so you can shoot them."

"That's the way it's always done. Besides, they are small enough that they are difficult to shoot." He chuckled. "That's one skill Sir Malcolm has, other than going into debt."

The conversation lapsed, as Alexander spurred his horse into a trot and Dinah followed. The day was perfect for riding, a rare March day with a warm sun that hinted of spring. Only when an infrequent cloud passed over the sun did it seem that winter was still in the wings, waiting, making Dinah sorry when they reached the house.

Chapter 16

🌹 🌹 🌹

THE FINE WEATHER continued through the next week.
The men went hunting in the mornings, while the
women slept late. Luncheon was filled with talk of the
bags of game. In the afternoons, Lady Janet supervised the young women in needlework, with Dinah
once more taking up the tapestry that her mother had
started. As often as she could, she made an excuse and
went for a walk, preferring the fresh air to the endless
discussions of what they were missing in Edinburgh.
Sometimes, too, depending on how tired he was, Alexander took the three girls riding.

With the weather as fine as it was, Dinah wondered
where Ol' Tom's sons were. One boat had been delivered as promised and lay pulled up on the gravel of
the shore. On her walks, Dinah looked at it longingly,
her curiosity to go to the castle increasing impatiently
with the passing of each day. Only the thought of the
two mile walk into the village and back—she was still
not sure enough of herself to go riding alone—kept
her from going to the village to ask Tom. Finally,
one day at luncheon, Alexander announced that the
picnic to the castle was set for the next day. One of
the beaters was Ol' Tom's son. Preferring the moors
to the Loch, he waited to suggest the outing until the
men, with the exception of Sir Malcolm, had decided
to take a rest.

Now the day was here, the other girls seemed unin-
terested in the excursion. Their shrugging off of her
questions increased Dinah's curiosity and excitement.
During the afternoon and evening, she anxiously

watched the sky for any sign of clouds rolling in over the hills that would foretell the ending of the fine weather. The sunset, however, was glorious, the last golden rays touching the castle in a halo of light before the sky turned a rosy red shot with orange arrows. The violent hues touched the castle itself, making it seem afire. Then, night set in and the castle loomed tantalizingly close, a dark shadow in the starlight of a moonless night.

Preparing for bed, Dinah took a last look at the castle and scanned the sky. The stars were twinkling brightly, and there was not a suggestion of clouds in the sky. Reassured, she went to bed to find that she could not sleep for thinking about the castle. She tossed and turned, trying to imagine what it was in the castle that had made Alexander exact that promise from her. She thought of MacNab, too, his shifty-eyed gaping at her and furtive making of the sign of the cross. Finally, she dozed off into an uneasy sleep, only to be awakened by Molly.

She dressed as Alexander had suggested, in a loose skirt with a heavy jacket and boots, to make getting in and out of the boat easier and for walking on the island. There was time for breakfast, as Alexander loaded the boats along with the two boys who were as big and husky as their father was short. Alexander was to row Dinah and Mary in one boat, while Tom Jr. was to row a second with Margaret and Lady Janet, with Bob rowing the third, in which were blankets and picnic baskets.

By the time they had reached the boats and were staring on the journey, Dinah realized why Tom had waited and Alexander had suggested heavy jackets. The sun was warm, but the air rising from the cold waters of the lake was cool, despite the spell of warm weather. The earlier they had gone, the cooler it would have been.

To Dinah's surprise, Alexander was no amateur at the oars, pulling with as much energy as the much huskier Tom and Bob. Sitting in the stern of the boat, facing him, she watched the castle draw nearer. The closer they rowed, the more forbidding the castle became, as imposing rising out of the waters of the loch as Stirling had been on its cliff. The difference was that Stirling had been filled with life and sound. The ancestral castle of the Douglases, on the other hand, was silent and brooding, all life gone with the passing of the centuries and the need for such a fortification. It seemed to have grown in upon itself, embracing its memories and secrets.

They landed near what had been the main gate where the beach was the widest. The gate itself was long gone, leaving only a huge arched opening in the moss-grown walls. Bob, in rubber boots, beached his boat first. Wading back in the water, he picked a giggling Mary up in his arms and went back for Dinah. Leaving them standing on the shore, he held the boat to permit Alexander to climb out over the prow and the two beached the boat, repeating the process with Lady Janet and Margaret.

Alexander took advantage of the opportunity, as they waited for the other two, to murmur in Dinah's ear, "Now we're here, don't go wandering off."

Dinah nodded, moving to the gateway to stare inside at the large cobble courtyard. The castle was much larger then it had appeared from shore, rising several stories high with a maze of buildings erected against the walls. There was room enough for a small garden, now overgrown with nettles, where Queen Mary must once have walked.

When everyone was ashore, he sent the boys to look for a sunny, dry spot for a picnic. Dinah was amused and a little amazed at the way he had taken charge of the expedition in a manner that brooked no argument, not that there was any. Margaret and Mary, now they were here, seemed as intimidated by the castle as Dinah. So, there was no discussion when Alexander told them to wait in the courtyard while he searched out the caretaker, going toward a building near the garden where a small wisp of smoke rose from the chimney.

Lady Janet looked around with a shiver. "What a

hateful place. Just imagine the drafts in those rooms and the dampness from the stone and the loch. It makes me eager to return to Edinburgh!"

Mary grimaced. "One could never have a party here!"

Margaret laughed. "Who would ever come calling! No wonder Queen Mary was sent here. It must have seemed safer than a prison."

"She did escape," pointed out Dinah.

Alexander came back alone with a big ring of keys. "The caretaker is having his dinner. He told us to look around. That," he pointed to a round tower, "is where Mary was held prisoner." He started toward a nearby square keep. "Let's start here."

"No," Dinah interjected. "I want to see the tower."

"Me, too," chorused the other two girls.

"Lady Janet?" asked Alexander, evidently hoping she would agree with him. "What do you say?"

"Go where you like. I, for one, have no intention of going inside. It will be damp and cold. I shall wait on the beach." She left them, walking back toward the boats.

Alexander gave in, leading them to a large oak door. He had to try several keys before finding the right one to twist in the stiff lock. The door opened with a protesting creak.

The rooms were empty, as damp as Lady Janet had promised and far more unpleasant. Spiders had spun a network of webs that brushed ghostly fingers unexpectedly against Dinah's cheek, despite Alexander's attempts to whisk them away. A faint skittering betrayed the presence of mice. In the fireplaces, charred wood had fallen into ashes and decay. Here and there lay a broken chair and a bit of torn fabric to betray the inhabitants who had once lived there.

Margaret and Mary soon dropped back, while Dinah pressed on with reluctant Alexander.

At the head of a stone staircase, its treads worn and damp, Alexander finally put a firm hand on Dinah's arm. Ahead of them was another corridor, the doors open to allow a faint light to pass through.

"Enough, Dinah. As I told you, there is nothing here any more than in the other rooms. Surely, you yourself recognize that."

"Yes, I do now." Still, she could not resist peering into one more door, one more room as empty as the others.

"Then, let's go back."

If Dinah was disappointed as she joined the other two girls in the courtyard, Alexander was relieved. He started toward the caretaker's house to return the keys, but Dinah laid a hand on his arm. "Can't we look is some of the other buildings?"

"What for? They will be as deserted as these. Dinah, there is nothing here. Those two," he nodded at a now meek Margaret and Mary, "were only teasing you, taking advantage of your ignorance."

"Well, I still want to see more," Dinah insisted.

"Oh, Dinah, don't be so stubborn," said Margaret. "At least, let's have some lunch."

Dinah was forced to give in. That did not mean she had given up. In one way or another, she was determined to look around some more before they left the island.

The boys had found a pleasant spot on the beach, fully in the sun, and had spread out the blankets. No one said much as they ate the cold sliced chicken and meats and sipped white wine. While they were straightening up, Dinah slipped away from the others, despite her promise.

Standing in the courtyard alone, she stared around, trying to see within the walls, to feel some aura that remained of the long-ago inhabitants. On an impulse, she started toward an oaken, metal-barred door that appeared to be slightly ajar. Cautiously, she pushed it open, heart pounding, expecting the room to be as filled with cobwebs as the others were and yet hoping that the secret of Lochleven lay here.

The room had evidently been used as a chapel from the altar-like arrangement at one end. What's more, unlike the other rooms it was relatively free of cobwebs. There were also a few pieces of furniture, a pair of spindly chairs and a large chest with an iron lock. Dinah pushed the door open wider, to let in more light. As she did, she noticed a picture on one wall and went closer to look at it.

Her first reaction was a gasp of surprise. It was a portrait of a woman, a woman with a long, slender neck around which was a jeweled necklace with a pendant. The golden-red hair was dressed close to the head and covered with a jeweled chaplet. Dinah's eyes absorbed these details, her brain still refusing to take in the face, for the face was enough like her own for the portrait to be of her. The complexion was white, luminous through the dirt of the centuries obscuring and dimming the finger lines; the nose, slightly aquiline; the forehead, high; and the eyes, amber and almond shaped. Dinah's mouth was larger and fuller than the delicately curved, small mouth in the portrait, and her ears were smaller, but given the same hair style and the dress of the day, she herself could have sat for the portrait.

Here was the reason for MacNab's crossing himself, Dinah was sure. Whether he had seen this portrait or a similar one, in the dim light of the shuttered inn, he must have felt he was looking at Mary, Queen of Scots, come to life again. Here, too, was foundation enough for the truth of the family legend about the baby of Mary being spirited away. Dinah's heart was beating so hard that she thought she was going to faint, first with the shock of recognition and then with anger, anger at Alexander who had noticed the resemblance, anger at his father, too, and the others, all of whom must have seen other portraits of Mary.

Dinah studied the portrait more closely, to make sure she was not mistaken. As she did, she noticed fine gold lettering at the bottom and took a step closer to try to read it. With difficulty, she made it out: "In my end is my Beginning." The words engraved themselves on her heart with a branding iron, and the pity she had felt for the tragic queen grew.

So lost was she in her thoughts about the queen and her scrutiny of the painting that she did not hear the voices calling her until Alexander burst through the door.

"Dinah, didn't I ask you, tell you . . ." he exploded. "Damn you, you frightened me half to death."

"Did I?" Dinah turned to face him, her jaw set and her eyes flashing fire. "Then you should have told me, not let me find . . . this."

"This?" He noticed the picture for the first time and came to Dinah's side to look at it. "Oh, God!"

"Why, why didn't you tell me, Alexander?" Dinah blazed, more furious than before at the stupefied expression on his face.

"I didn't know it was here. Truly, I swear I didn't." He took her cold hands in his. "Believe me, Dinah."

"Perhaps not, but you did know about the resemblance, Alexander—you told me that. There must be other pictures in Edinburgh," Dinah insisted.

"Please, Dinah."

"It was very cruel of you. That's why Margaret and Mary, the story about ghosts . . . Your father, too!" She cried with dismay.

"No, Dinah, not my father," Alexander said gently. "The first time he saw you, all he saw in you was your mother. I am sure he still doesn't see this likeness."

Dinah turned back to the picture, studying it once more. "It could be, has to be, just a coincidence," she murmured, trying to convince herself.

"Perhaps," Alexander agreed, trying to reassure her. "I don't know, my dear. I just don't know at all."

"Me," Dinah laughed, "to be descended from a queen."

Neither of them had noticed Margaret and Mary enter the small room. At Dinah's last words, the two glanced at one another. "What is it, Dinah? What did you find?" asked Margaret eagerly.

"What?" Dinah was startled. She moved away from the portrait. "An old painting," she said, trying to be casual.

"Oh? Let us see, too!" Margaret, Mary beside her, crowded around the painting, looking from it to Dinah, their lips tightening in dismay.

Dinah, head held high, walked outside, trying to conceal her excitement. When Alexander followed her, she ignored both his presence and his entreaties to listen to him, maintaining her silence in the boat on the way back to the mainland. She broke it only to tell Molly about the portrait as she dressed for dinner, wishing she could pretend a headache to avoid the conversation she knew would occur over the meal. That, however, would only postpone the subject.

Molly, after her first surprise, was distressed. "Oh dear, Dinah, you're sure it wasn't the light? Or maybe Margaret planted it there, as a joke," the maid suggested.

"No, I don't think so, not the way Alexander acted. I mean, he knew about the resemblance, that's all. And I don't think that Margaret knew about the picture. If she had, she wouldn't have been so willing to have lunch instead of looking around the castle some more."

"Do you think," Molly's American background refused to let her believe that her friend could be royalty, "I mean, you don't really think you are descended from Mary, do you?"

"I don't know what to believe, Molly. It all seemed a very charming, romantic legend," said Dinah miserably, "because there was no proof that the child lived. After seeing that picture, I'm not sure. You should have seen it, Molly! It was almost like looking into a mirror, except for the hair style and the clothing."

Molly shook her head. "Well, my advice to you is to forget it. It all happened so long ago. What difference does it make now?" Molly laughed, "You certainly aren't going to be asked by Queen Victoria to assume the throne of England. Even if she doesn't much care for Bertie, she has too many other children!"

Dinah had to laugh, too. "Oh, Molly, what would I do without you!"

Molly averted her face, her thoughts on Geordie. "I don't know, Miss Dinah," she answered primly, her voice sincere.

Dinah missed the meaning behind Molly's words.

She was too busy thinking about that evening, about what she would say when the subject came up at the dinner table. Her best tactic, she decided, was to make light of it and avoid giving Margaret and Mary any satisfaction about her true feelings on seeing the picture. As a result, she deliberately joined the others just as they were going in to dinner.

Sir Robert studied her solicitously, already informed by Alexander of what had happened. "Dinah," he started to say.

"Father," Margaret interrupted quickly, "we had the most marvelous day, and Dinah made the most startling discovery, didn't you?"

"I suppose you could call it startling," Dinah said carefully, adding, "there was a picture, a painting, in a small room of Queen Mary. I must say it did rather resemble me."

"Resemble!" Mary burst out. "Dinah could have sat for it!"

"I do wish you girls had told *me* about it, but Dinah was in such a hurry to leave," put in Lady Janet. "Honestly, Robert, I'm not sure that I believe them."

"I do." Sir Robert's voice was thick. "Alexander told me about the painting. He said it was of Mary as a young girl, about Dinah's age. Where it came from, I can't imagine."

Lady Janet, sitting opposite Dinah, studied her frankly. "Well, she really does somewhat look like Mary, the height, the neck, the nose—and of course, the color of her hair and eyes. So do a lot of women, Robert. I, for one, believe that old story is rubbish! Dinah, a descendant of Mary, Queen of Scots!" Lady Janet was disdainful.

Sir Robert chuckled in spite of himself. "Janet, I do believe you are a snob. Dinah may have been born in America, but remember her mother was born in Scotland and was a distant cousin of mine."

Dinah listened to the conversation with amusement. Although she was still angry with Alexander, she was relieved in that she was sure from his father's tone of voice that all Sir Robert had seen was the resemblance to her mother because that was what he had been looking for. Perhaps, even Alexander had not been sure and it took someone like MacNab to notice it.

"If it is true," Mary said airily, "then Dinah is just the one to see Mary's ghost, spirit, I mean," she added hurriedly, to get in the more acceptable word. "Just think, Dinah," Mary leaned across the table eagerly from where she was sitting next to her mother, "if Mary would come for anyone, it would be for a descendent of hers. Of course," she tossed her head, "you have to be very brave . . ."

"Rubbish!" Alexander exploded. "For God's sake, Mary, you are not suggesting that Dinah spend a night on the island in that room!"

"Why not? I would in Dinah's place," Mary said, "just to see . . ."

"So would I," chimed in Margaret. "It's her baby that Queen Mary is supposed to cry for though, and so Mary and I would not do. Dinah, on the other hand . . ."

"Father," Alexander appealed, "make them stop. It's not a joke. Dinah, don't listen to them."

"I agree. I will have no more of this talk," Sir Robert said firmly. "At the next mention, we will return to Edinburgh."

"Now, Robert, don't be hasty. We've still got more huntin' ahead of us. Why, one of the beaters was talkin' about some deer he had seen in a copse in the glen . . ."

"And James is supposed to visit us over the weekend," wailed Margaret.

"Very well. Then, Malcolm, you take your daughter in hand, and Margaret, you stop this nonsense for once and for all. Alexander," he turned to his son to change the subject, "you said the boys mentioned some fine trout in the lake and the nearby streams?"

The conversation shifted to fishing, with the women remaining silent. Dinah knew, however, that the subject was not finished, regardless of what Sir Robert said. Neither he nor Alexander, much less Sir Malcolm, was around all the time. During those hours of needlework and the walks in the garden, one or another would certainly bring up Lochleven—and Lochleven itself, looming on the landscape, was not easily forgotten.

Dinah herself had no intention of going to the island again, at least not to wait for a ghost. Regardless of what Mary and Margaret said, of what the queen herself might believe, she did not believe in ghosts and spirits. Yet, the castle haunted her, and as the date for their departure grew closer, she wanted to see the castle and the picture again. When she mentioned it to Alexander, he refused to listen to her. She knew she could not possibly row to the island by herself. The small, well-made boats were much too heavy for her to maneuver, unless, she thought, she could get one of the boys to row her there. That might be possible, too. One or the other of them stopped by the house every day or so, to find out whether Sir Robert had need of a beater or someone to show him and the other men the trout streams. With that in mind, she started to keep an eye out for them, despite the fact she knew both Margaret and Mary were watching her closely.

This was one plan she had to keep from Molly. Molly, who secretly believed in spirits, would try to stop her, even if it meant her going to Sir Robert. So Dinah watched and waited, growing more impatient as the days went by.

One day after the boys had taken the men trout fishing, Dinah was in the garden alone as they returned to the boats they had left on the shore. Regardless of their preference for the moors, they always rowed to the Douglas house as the quickest means of getting there and back.

Dinah waved to them and approached them to ask about the fishing, which had been good that day. When Dinah made her proposal to go to the island that evening, they looked at one another uneasily.

"Please," Dinah begged, "it's important." She tried to think of a means of appealing to them, suddenly recalling her mother's brooch. "You see, that day on the picnic, I was wearing a brooch—it was my mother's," Dinah sniffed into her handkerchief, "and I lost it. I think I know where it is."

Tom Jr. exchanged glances with Bob. "The old man," Tom objected.

Dinah thought quickly. "It's worth a pound to me." She knew it was far too much money, more than either made in a week working for Sir Robert, and she hoped the money would make the offer irresistible.

"Why not!" Bob said quickly. "He doesn't have to know. I'll say I'm going to the pub. He'll be asleep soon enough."

They agreed on a time, early enough for Bob to have the last rays of light for the row across. Promising not to keep him waiting, Dinah returned to the house. She would have to plead a headache that night as an excuse for not going to dinner, and she would also have to invent an excuse to keep Molly from checking on her. As she glanced back, although she saw the boys talking earnestly between themselves, she paid them no more attention, sure that Bob would be waiting for her.

Molly was dubious about the headache, especially when Dinah told her to take the evening off, that all Dinah wanted to do was sleep. As for the others, Dinah didn't care. Margaret looked at her, saying nothing.

Alone, Dinah changed into a heavy dress that she had worn on shipboard and had brought to the country anticipating colder weather than that year's mild spring. She would need it that night, however, that and the heavy cloak she had also worn at sea. In a small handbag, she tucked some candles and a flint along with the biscuits that Molly had brought her in place of dinner. Dressed and waiting for the sun to start to set, she turned to the bed, arranging the covers and the pillows in such a way that it looked as if she were sleeping.

As the last rays of a blood-red sunset touched Lochleven, Dinah left her room, slipping down a side stair. At this hour, she felt sure that she would not be discovered, as the others would be dressing for dinner.

Once outside, she avoided the garden, which could be seen from the rooms at the rear of the house, for a path at one side. Hurrying down it, she began to have her first doubts. What was she doing, going to the island? She really did not believe in spirits, and yet Mary's constant taunts had tantalized her. Besides, she really did want to see the painting again.

Bob was waiting for her. He nervously helped her into the boat and pushed off, rowing more quickly than he had on the first visit. At the island he helped her out, finally breaking his silence to tell her he'd be back at dawn.

"Dawn!" Dinah was dismayed. "I only wanted to look . . ."

"Dawn," he repeated, looking around uneasily as if he really did believe the island were haunted. "I ain't stayin' here with no one around."

"There's the caretaker," Dinah suggested hopefully.

"Nay. He's off to Kinross to see his folks," said Bob.

Before Dinah could protest any more, he had pushed the boat off. She watched him rowing with a firm stroke to the mainland. She had counted on the caretaker's being on the island. Now she was totally alone and destined to spend the night. like it or not, in the castle of Lochleven. She decided she would have to make the best of it. The first thing to do was find a place to stay out of the wind, as the crisp breeze had picked up and she would soon be chilled through.

Inside the walls of the castle, the air was still except for a gust that found its way through the steep, thick stone walls. Dinah glanced longingly at the caretaker's rooms. She picked her way carefully across the courtyard to the small room in the round tower. What would she do if the door were locked? It might have been only an accident that it had been open the time before. Heart pounding, she pressed the latch, pushing against the door. As it had the first time, the door's hinges protested but it opened easily enough. Dinah left it slightly ajar and lit a candle, drawing a deep

231

breath of relief at the wavering brightness of the flame, she examined the room.

This time, she knelt in front of the chest, dipping the candle to get enough wax on the floor to stand up the candle and free her hands. The heavy iron clasp and lock looked more imposing than they actually were. She twisted the padlock experimentally. To her surprise, the clasp gave way.

The trunk itself was rectangular, bound in embossed leather in an intricate design of fleur-de-lis, the insignia of France. Dinah breathed faster. The trunk could have belonged to Mary herself, she decided, examining it more closely for any initials or other indication of its ownership. There was none, and Dinah opened the lid with trembling hands, not sure what she hoped or expected to find. Taking a deep breath, she lifted the candle to look inside. The trunk was empty, as empty as the rooms in the round tower that had been Mary's prison.

Disappointed, Dinah picked up the candle and went to the picture. It, at least, did not disappoint her. The likeness was as striking as Dinah had remembered it. She stared into the amber almond eyes, trying to search out some answer in the calm expression. Whoever had painted the portrait, however, had not believed in painting feelings. The eyes were blank, surveying the world without fear or happiness or any of the other emotions that one might have expected to find on the face of a woman who had been a queen of Scotland almost from birth, a queen of France at sixteen, and a widow at seventeen. The most touching part of the picture, in fact the only part that revealed what Mary might have been thinking, was the motto: In my end is my Beginning.

Dinah was not sure how long she had stared at the portrait when she first became aware of a sound. She tilted her head, listening. In the distance was the murmur of the loch, of waves ceaselessly caressing the the stony beach. Somewhere, a night bird called, its piping echoing in the walls of the empty castle, but that, those sounds, was not what had caught Dinah's attention.

232

She blew out the candle, pressing herself into the corner of the wall, listening even harder until she heard it again, the sound of a pebble striking a stone and a muffled, careful footfall.

Her eyes scurried around the room. The only place to hide was the altar, if that was what it was, at the other end of the room. Using the faint starlight filtering through the windows of the room, she edged toward the altar, thinking to conceal herself there. Another stone struck against a cobble, closer this time, and Dinah could hear the sound of boots. Whoever was out there was no ghost. Uneasily, she remembered how eager Bob had been to leave. Had that been an act and had he returned for reasons of his own?

Once more she edged along the wall, stopping again, this time halted by a faint glimmer of light as if a lantern had been lit. Her lungs were aching, and she realized that she had been holding her breath. With a sigh of relief, she let the air out, reassured by the lantern. Whoever was out there was obviously not trying to conceal his presence. It was probably the caretaker, returning early from Kinross, she decided. In that case, however, the lantern would be moving away from her, not coming closer. Once more she started toward the altar.

She was too late. The door was pushed open, the lantern held high to fill the room with light. Dinah stared into it, trying to shield her eyes to see who was there.

"Dinah!" Alexander called, lowering the lantern, his face still in darkness. "Thank God, I found you. You little fool . . ."

"What are you doing here?" she blazed, furious at him for frightening her and angry at herself for her first thought had been that the castle really was haunted by a ghost.

"You thought you were so clever, didn't you?" Alexander ignored her question. going on in a hard voice. "You thought you'd come here without anyone's knowing, to commune with Mary's spirit, I assume."

"I do not believe in ghosts! I wanted to see the pic-

233

ture again. You wouldn't take me . . ." Dinah said defensively.

"And so, clever girl that you are, you secretly bribed Bob," replied the man, his voice sarcastic.

"What do you care? It's not your business!" His tone aroused her anger again.

"I am fully aware of that!" He shot back grimly, as he put the lantern on the floor. "Perhaps I should have left you alone here for the night as Margaret and Mary intended, but I could not do that." He ran a hand through his hair. "Come, my dear, be reasonable." He took a step toward her.

The young woman backed up, forgetting how close she was to the raised platform and struck her ankle against the step. A sharp pain brought tears to her eyes.

Alexander, seeing the tears, rushed to her to take her in his arms. "Dear Dinah, I didn't mean to make you cry."

Dinah rested her head against his shoulder, enjoying the feeling of his arms around her. Her anger dissolved. She felt too good in his arms. But she still wanted to know how he knew where to find her. "Then tell me what you are doing here," she whispered.

"Gladly." He stroked her hair, his lips kissing her cheek, "Later . . ."

The girl tried to ignore the hotness of her body, the hotness that made thinking so difficult when she was this near to him. Reluctantly, she pushed him away. "Now, tell me now."

Alexander told her the story briefly. Margaret and Mary had missed neither her fascination with the portrait nor her earlier interest in the castle. They had, in fact, encouraged her with the intent of getting her to the island alone at night, as they felt sure she would do with enough teasing. After the picnic, they had bribed the boys to tell them, should Dinah try to rent a boat. Thus, after Dinah had spoken to the boys that afternoon, they had immediately gone to the kitchen, sending word to Margaret who, in her turn, had bribed Bob to leave Dinah alone on the island for the night.

"As for me," Alexander went on, "I found out from Molly. I wonder if you know what a friend you have in that girl."

"Molly knew nothing . . ." replied Dinah in confusion.

"My dear sister," Alexander continued, "along with Mary, could not help gloating in front of Parker who told the other servants. Molly came to me." He smiled, adding, "And I came to you."

"Thank you, Alexander." Dinah was genuinely grateful.

The man put his arms around her, his mouth hot on her neck. "There is the caretaker's cottage," he murmured. "I doubt it's locked, for who would come to this place?"

Dinah started to protest, tried to withdraw from his arms, but her body was hot with desire, her breath coming faster against his cheek. Her mind told her she could refuse him, force him to row her to the mainland in the boat he had used. As before, her body cried out, refusing to obey her brain. She wanted him, wanted to feel the sensuous pleasure of his body next to hers, of his kisses . . . "We have the night," she whispered, yielding to her desire.

Alexander looked into her face, a faint smile on his lips. He picked up the lantern and Dinah's case with one hand, his other arm around her waist as he led her to the cottage. The latch opened easily. Inside, he set the lantern on a table and lit the fire laid on the hearth before taking some blankets from a bed and placing them on the floor.

"My love," Alexander whispered, kissing her again, his hands removing her cloak, one by one undoing the buttons of her gown. The gown fell to the floor, and Alexander lifted the loose chemise she was wearing over her head. He cupped her firm young breasts in his hands, lowering his mouth to cover them with kisses, his tongue igniting her nipples until they were deep red and hard.

235

His hands impatiently freed her from the rest of her clothing until she stood before him naked. Kneeling in front of her, he kissed the inside of her thighs and the soft hair between her legs. Her body tingling from the fires he had lit inside her, Dinah pressed against him, her hands fondling his hair.

He stood up, his hands now fumbling in the eagerness to be free of his own clothes. Dinah watched, sitting on the blankets in front of the fire. The flames turned her skin to gold, her hair to fire, as the tongues of light licked in shadows over Alexander's body. He stood before her, naked, his manhood strong and hard. Dinah touched it with a forefinger, wondering at its size and how it ever found its way into her. Impulsively, she touched her lips to it, feeling the silken smoothness grow tighter.

"Dinah, my darling." Alexander sank to his knees beside her, pressing her back gently on the blankets.

The caretaker's cot was hardly more than a wooden pallet; so hard that as he moved on top of her, she felt pushed toward him, nothing in her able to resist his movement. He kissed her face and her breasts tenderly, slowly, stopping momentarily to look into her eyes and see how openly she wanted him, how eager she was to feel him inside her. He buried his face between her breasts, inhaling deeply the scent of her skin and her light perfume. Dinah shuddered, both with the sensation of his breath on her skin and with the thrilling newness of opening her eyes to see him sucking her nipple. The pressure of his lips was as sweet as a baby's might be, but the hunger in his face a man's.

Now he entered her in one deep stroke that took both their breaths away. He stayed very still for a moment and Dinah tensed, her entire being intent on responding to him. Then he began to thrust very hard and fast. Dinah moaned, knowing that it was useless to try to hold back. The heat of him inside her, the strength with which he pressed her against the hard mattress, opening her until she thought she would have to cry out, made her throw herself back against him, meeting each of his strokes with her own suddenly violent energy. Finally, when it seemed that to hold each other any closer they would have had to tear into each other's skin, they both began to tremble and the long, sweet moment of culmination held them practically motionless. She clutched him tightly, wanting to be this close to him forever.

Their bodies relaxed and their breathing slowed. How handsome he was in the firelight, Dinah thought, studying the planes of his face, the dark eyes glinting with an animal fervor in the light. And how much she loved him! She belonged to him, would belong to him forever, regardless of what the future held. She wanted to tell him that she loved him, but the memory of what had happened the night she had tried before to tell him stilled her tongue. Instead, she held him closer, trying to drink into her tissues the feeling of his body. What was he thinking, she asked herself. Was he, in his turn, thinking of her?

Alexander raised himself on an elbow to look at her. "You are magnificent, Dinah, the most delightful woman I have ever known."

"Am I?" She smiled at him, her full lips quivering with the remnants of the passion still in her, passion aroused at the thought of the "other women."

"You know you are, you little minx." His tone was half amused and half bitter, as he reached for another blanket and pulled it over them. "I can't have you catching cold."

Dinah smiled, cuddling her body against him. "You'll have to keep me warm."

His arms tightened around her. Dinah, thoroughly satisfied and tired now, relaxed into a half sleep. The tingling of her left arm falling asleep under the weight of Alexander's body awakened her. He was sleeping so peacefully that she tried to move it without rousing him. After she had succeeded, she was too wide awake to fall asleep again.

How ironic it was that here in this castle where Mary, Queen of Scots, had been imprisoned and where her ancestor was born that she should fulfill herself with Alexander. The words on the painting, "In my end is my Beginning," seemed prophetic, as true for her in this place called Lochleven as they were for Mary, as perhaps they had been for her mother for whom the place had had such a meaning that she recalled it with her dying words. Why? What had happened to her mother here? Surely, it had not been a prison for her, or had it? No, from the way her mother had uttered it, Lochleven held a sweeter meaning.

Alexander muttered in his sleep, and Dinah looked at him, a new possibility coming to mind, one she was sure was the correct one. It was here, must have been here, that her mother had come with her father, here that she was conceived in the shadow of the castle to which they both owed their existence.

Chapter 17

🌹 🌹 🌹

THE ISLAND WAS still wreathed in darkness when Alexander went to get the boat. While she waited for him, Dinah straightened the cottage and laid a new fire for the caretaker.

By the time she was finished, she could hear Alexander calling to her and she hurried to the boat. In the first faint streaks of light in the east, they could see Bob coming for her. Alexander waved him back and rowed them to shore. It was still too early for anyone to be astir, as Alexander kissed her gently in front of her door. Only after she had slipped quietly inside did he go to his own room.

Alexander and Dinah were the first up, as they had planned. In the breakfast room, he had time to kiss her quickly before his father entered. Sir Robert said "good morning" to them, his face inscrutable although he must have noticed how close they were to each other.

As they helped themselves from the hot dishes on the sideboard, Sir Robert said, "You both seem to have a good appetite this morning."

Dinah flushed. Usually she had only tea and some toast. This morning she had taken scrambled eggs, several rashers of bacon, and even a broiled kidney. Recalling she had had no dinner the night before, she said, "I guess I am quite hungry, although I had no appetite with that headache last night."

"You're feeling well then, my dear?" Sir Robert asked solicitously.

"Very well, thank you." She looked at her plate to avoid the amusement in Alexander's eyes.

The next to join them was Sir Malcolm, whose wife always had breakfast in her room, a luxury she could enjoy here but not at home where the Anguses had only the minimum number of servants. He was eager to go trout fishing again, having hooked and lost a particularly large trout the day before. Sir Robert declined, having received a case of papers that he had to go through. Alexander hesitated, wanting to go and wanting to delay going until his sister and Mary joined them.

The girls arrived just as Alexander had run out of excuses. Both were sleepy-eyed, looking covertly at Dinah every chance they had. Dinah, still filled with the pleasure of her night, smiled brightly at them.

"You look tired, Mary," she said, trying to sound concerned. "You haven't caught my 'headache,' have you?"

"I say, Margaret," Alexander put in, winking at Dinah, "you look a little pale, too."

"I'm afraid neither of us slept very well," Margaret replied haughtily.

"Really? Perhaps it was something at dinner, as Dinah seems fine." Alexander was enjoying himself. "Still, I ate the same things and slept very well."

"Alexander, you are impossible," snapped his sister. "Men have much stronger constitutions than women."

"So I've heard. I rather think, however, all that talk of ghosts and spirits went to your heads. You both look as if you have been seeing ghosts," added the young man.

"Rubbish!" Sir Malcolm stood up. "I say, Alexander, are you coming fishing with me or not? I'll lay a wager I get that fish today."

"I'll take that wager, Sir." Alexander rose and went to the door, turning back to add, "Why don't you follow Dinah's suggestion and go for a brisk walk this morning, as she is going to do?"

"Ass!" Margaret screamed, throwing her napkin at him. "Get out of here, before . . . before . . ."

Alexander laughed and left the room. Dinah followed as quickly as she could, having had the satisfaction of seeing that she and Alexander had really turned the tables on the other two girls.

The walk, however, was put off. A cold wind had blown up, bringing with it rolling billows of dark clouds. By afternoon, a steady drizzle had set in. After three days in which hardly anyone left the house and then not for long, Sir Robert decided to return to Edinburgh. The trunks were packed and sent off in a cart, with Jamison and his wife and the rest of the servants following, leaving Molly and Parker to tend to the needs of the Douglases and Angus for one evening. The two maids were to return with their mistresses. With an early start, Sir Robert hoped to make it to Edinburgh in one day.

The long, tiring ride, with two stops to change horses and to get something hot to eat, found all the passengers exhausted by the time the coaches pulled up in front of the house on Princes Street, where the Anguses were to spend the night. The Jamisons and the other servants, however, had quickly put the house in order. Fires were lit in every room and a hot supper was waiting for them. Better yet was the news that the *Star of Scotland* had arrived safely at Leith.

Dinah found herself looking forward to seeing the young captain again.

It was three days before Geordie arrived on the threshold, taking Molly eagerly in his arms and murmuring endearments in her ear. After Molly had kissed him thoroughly, she seated him on the couch in the servants' sitting room, studying his face anxiously.

"A few more freckles, Lass. Otherwise, I'm still your Geordie," he told her, amused at her scrutiny.

"Oh, Geordie!" Molly threw herself in his arms. "Just to see you again! It's been so very long, and I . . ." She fell silent, unwilling to admit she had missed him as much as she had.

"Missed me, did you?" he asked gently after a few moments. "Well, no more than I missed you. It's a thing you will have to get used to, Love. I'm a sailor."

"I know." Molly covered him with kisses again. "But let's not talk about your leaving. You're here now, and that's all I want to think about."

"You thought about me, about us?" He looked around the room. "If only we had a place to go to be alone. I want you so much."

"Shush, Geordie, I'm hot enough as it is. And Mrs. Jamison is kind enough to let us be here," said Molly, who had had the same thought on her mind.

"You'll marry me, then? As soon as we can . . . ?"

"Oh, Geordie, darling." Molly kissed him to silence him and give herself time to think. How she wished Dinah and Alexander would make up their minds, Alexander anyway, as she was sure that Dinah was still in love with the young man. She had hoped the trip to the country, where they would be together so much more than here in Edinburgh, would decide him. She was sure that he loved her, too. How angry and worried he had been when she told him what she had overheard about Lochleven and about Dinah's being missing. And then to spend the night together! She had checked Dinah's room several times during the night and had been awake in the dawn as they had slipped upstairs. They had not spent the night talking, that she knew from Dinah's face, although Dinah had tried to tell her that.

"Come now, Lass, have you thought about it, about us marrying?" Geordie gently drew back and took her face in his hands. "Answer me, now, and we'll have plenty of time for kissing afterward."

Molly nodded as well as she could. "I have, Geordie, love. First let us get to know one another again." Her voice was unsteady, although her round blue eyes held his.

She left Geordie to help Dinah dress for dinner, insisting on staying even when Dinah tried to dismiss her. "You need me, Dinah," she said.

Dinah laughed. "I don't know what I would do without you, Molly. You are the only friend I have." She said the words lightly, as she had so often in the past, not noticing the effect they had on Molly this time.

Molly paled, biting her lip. Despite the lightness of the tone, she heard the ring of truth under it. The result was that she felt torn apart. She could not leave Dinah as long as Dinah needed her, but she could not keep Geordie waiting forever either. Well, there was Captain MacKie, too, and Dinah had always liked him. MacKie, in fact, she decided, would be better for her than Alexander with his gambling and obviously unsteady ways.

"Captain MacKie should be back soon, I expect," she told Dinah. "Geordie said probably by the weekend."

"Truly?" Dinah's eyes brightened. "It will be good to see him again." She meant the words, although not in the way Molly took them. The night on the island had renewed her love for Alexander who had been very attentive to her ever since.

"You like him, don't you?" probed Molly.

"Of course! How could anyone not like Ian? He's a fine, gentle person," stated Dinah, thoughtfully, thinking how wonderful it would be if only he and Alexander were the same person. Then, she could enjoy the passionate embraces of Alexander and the steady honesty of MacKie and not feel guilty in thinking about either. Well, they were not the same person, and she would have to resolve the conflict within herself that thinking of the two of them aroused in her.

She saw MacKie on Sunday. He arrived in Edinburgh on Saturday, no sooner arriving than sending a message to invite Dinah to tea at his Mother's on Sunday. Dinah accepted by the same messenger, no longer feeling the need to ask Sir Robert's permission. She found she was looking forward to seeing him, despite the attentions of Alexander. Besides, attentive as he was, he never spoke to her seriously or called her his darling or his love. Once again, she found herself losing hope for anything more than those few hours of ecstasy.

On Sunday, Dinah drove in the carriage with the Douglases to the Angus house where they were to have high tea. Dinah had declined, because of MacKie. Sir Robert had seemed pleased with the invitation, although Alexander had raised an eyebrow. In the meantime, she had given Molly a few days off to go with Geordie to visit his sister.

Alexander was the last to leave the carriage, which was then to take Dinah to the MacKies. "Have a good time, Love," he said.

"I intend to, Alexander," murmured Dinah so the others could not hear. "You do not mind, do you—will you miss me?"

"With Mary to entertain me? No. I was thinking of you and our dour captain."

"Dour? I would hardly call him that!" She giggled. "Or are you jealous that another man may find my company pleasing?"

"Don't be coy, Dinah. It does not suit you!" He got out of the carriage. As he closed the door, he added, "I can't imagine a man who would not find your company pleasing."

His words rang in Dinah's ears during the rest of the short ride. He had to like her and like her very much to say that, she decided. Yet, if he did, why did he not make some declaration of love to her? He was really an obstinate, selfish creature—that was the only explanation she could find for his words and actions, so often at odds.

MacKie was waiting outside the small house for her. The moment he saw her, his face lit up, the blue eyes sparkling with happiness. "My dear Dinah, how good to see you," he said as he helped her from the carriage. "Let me look at you."

She smiled warmly under the glow of the blue eyes. "Have I changed, Ian? Indeed, you are so tanned that you must have had a good voyage home."

"You are more beautiful than ever. I had forgotten how lovely you are," he mused.

"Thank you, Ian, but I think you are prejudiced. And how is your mother? Did she tell you I stopped in after I received your letter?" asked Dinah, wanting to change the subject from herself.

"She did, and I thank you for that." He opened the door for her and helped her with the light cloak she was wearing. She was wearing a pale green dress with a fashionable bustle and a high neck trimmed with lace. He took her hands, admiring the trim figure and firm breasts under the tight bodice. "Indeed, you are more beautiful than ever."

"I have changed then." Dinah sighed. "I am not sure that I want to change as much as you seem to find."

"Oh, my dear!" He dropped her hands and put his arm around her to lead her into the small sitting room. "When I met you, you were a frightened and brave girl. There, on the ship I saw you change, becoming more assured, blooming in the sea air. All I meant is that you are no longer a girl, a lovely girl to be sure, but a beautiful young woman."

"Yes," Dinah agreed, "I have grown up. I can see that, feel that . . . Still, I think I was happier as I was on the ship."

Mrs. MacKie bustled into the room to greet Dinah and kiss her cheek. The little maid followed with tea. It was simpler than what was served at the Douglas house, a plate of hot scones, dripping with butter; freshly baked mince tarts; and a cake. Dinah ate eagerly, enjoying the simplicity of the small repast. Too often, there was too much food to eat or to enjoy. Over tea, MacKie insisted on hearing everything that had happened, and Dinah told him about her birthday party, the many other parties, and the trip to Lochleven.

Seeing the interest in their faces and relaxing in the warmth of their company, Dinah said impulsively, "My mother, when she was dying, mentioned Lochleven. I did not know what she meant. I still don't, except it had to be that place, didn't it? There isn't another Lochleven?"

Ian glanced at his mother, saying gently, "No, there is no other Lochleven. You're sure that's what she said?"

"Oh, yes, Ian, except at the time I had never heard of the place, and I thought she said 'lock' and 'eleven,' but now I know . . ." She hesitated, adding, "there was another word."

"What was that?" Ian set the cup down.

"Rabbie, I think, something like that. Do you know what that means?" asked Dinah innocently.

The captain leaned forward, his blue eyes clouded. "Are you sure that's what she said? It couldn't be anything else?" At Dinah's puzzled nod, he glanced at his mother before turning back to Dinah and taking her hand. "Dinah, Rabbie is a nickname, a Scottish nickname for Robert."

Dinah's heart skipped a beat, as she connected "Rabbie" with Sir Robert. She recalled the night at Lochleven castle with Alexander, when she had wondered whether she had been conceived at Lochleven. That idea had been wrong, a fantasy. After all, Dinah's father had been unacceptable to her uncle and Sir Robert's father and would not have been invited to Lochleven, even though his name could well have been Robert or Rabbie. No, her mother's calling out of Lochleven and Rabbie, whether Sir Robert or another man, had to be a memory of happier days, of her youth, an evocation of a time of pleasure.

"Dinah?" Ian said softly, interrupting her thoughts.

"I'm sorry, I was thinking about what you said," she said, explaining her conclusions.

Ian listened, finally agreeing with lowered eyes. "That sounds like the most reasonable explanation."

Mrs. MacKie was more practical. "Regardless of what it means, Dinah, does it really make any difference now? It was all so long ago," she pointed out.

"I know," Dinah smiled, "and you are right, of course." She thought a last time of her mother, thin and weak, more unconscious than conscious and talking as if Dinah were a baby or a child again. "Tell me," she said to Ian, "did you see Mrs. Bradley?"

"Aye, and I delivered your letter. She wanted to hear all about you." He took a letter from his pocket. "She asked me to deliver this to you."

"And you waited until now! Shame on you, Ian, you forgot about it," Dinah scolded.

"Only for a while. You dazzled me, and I forgot about everything except how lovely you were."

Dinah laughed. "Now tell me about your voyage."

Mrs. MacKie excused herself to go to evening chapel, leaving the two alone. After she left, an awkward silence fell between them, each remembering the last time they had been alone in the sitting room. Finally Dinah prompted Ian about the voyage, and he told her about it: storms all the way to New York, a delay over loading, and the voyage home, as sunny and breezy as the outward voyage had been stormy.

"And your next voyage?" asked Dinah, suddenly wanting Ian to stay in Edinburgh for a while.

"Please, Dinah! I am barely a week home." He went on, "Sir Robert has promised both Geordie and me several months off, even if it means the *Star of Scotland* sailing under another captain on its next trip."

"She is yours!" Dinah cried. "He would not give her to another captain, would he?"

"Just for one voyage. After all, he cannot have

her out of service for several months, and Geordie and I have had little time ashore the past year," he explained.

"True. Speaking of Geordie, has he spoken to you of Molly?" Dinah asked eagerly.

"Only that he wishes to marry her, as you must know," said Ian. "For some reason, she has put him off. He hopes that with enough time ashore this time, he can convince her."

"I am afraid, Ian, I am partly to blame," Dinah said guiltily. "You see, Geordie insists that Molly leave service, and Molly feels I need her. She is a friend, above all." Dinah left unsaid that despite her successes she had no friends. Margaret had resented her from the beginning, so any friendship there was out of the question. Margaret and Mary, in addition, had been close friends for years with no room for a third. Besides, after the affair at Lochleven, Dinah had lost any desire to have them for friends. "Still, I will do all I can to encourage her. I know she loves Geordie, and she deserves her chance at happiness."

"And you, have you thought about marriage?" asked Ian.

"I am not as sure as Molly that I know what love is." Dinah's voice was soft. Once more, she thought of Alexander and the relationship that kept her from considering anyone except him.

"Dinah," Ian stood up and moved to stand in front of her to take her hands. "you know I love you. You would not have all the luxuries and comforts that you have now with Sir Robert . . ."

"Oh, Ian!" As she kissed his hands, he drew her up. Their eyes were almost level. She took a deep breath, "When I decide to marry, luxury will not enter into it. I am still too young." Her voice trailed off, and she kissed his cheek, unable any longer to meet his eyes. "I had better go now."

"Dinah," Ian put his arms around her, "remember I am your friend, too. Whatever you decide, in fact, I will always be your friend."

"Yes, yes, I know." She let herself relax, encompassed by the warmth she felt, even as her heart beat faster. Her mouth sought Ian's. As their lips met, Dinah pressed closer to his broad chest, her nipples tingling with the excitement of the embrace. The memory of the night with Alexander was still too fresh, and she broke out of the circle of the Captain's arms.

Ian sighed. "Come, I'll see you home."

In the carriage that he sent the young maid to get, Ian asked a favor of Dinah. His mother's birthday was the following week and he wanted to buy her a new tea set. Would Dinah, therefore, help him select it? Dinah agreed willingly, agreeing also to come to dinner on the day.

As she left the carriage, she kissed Ian again, murmuring, "I do care for you, Ian. Will you give me time?" She knew she was not being fair, but just as she needed Molly, she needed Ian, at least for a little while longer. She wished she could tell him the truth about Alexander as easily as she had told him and only him about Lochleven. Yet, even if she knew how to tell him without hurting him, she did not know the words.

The birthday dinner for Mrs. MacKie turned into a party. Geordie and Molly had returned to Edinburgh, with Geordie staying at the MacKies in order to see Molly. After dinner, Ian brought out a bottle of champagne while the others brought out their gifts, to Mrs. MacKie's complete surprise. Dinah had a small brooch; Molly, a lace collar; and Geordie, an Irish linen handkerchief.

"Oh, dear," Mrs. MacKie smiled happily, "I don't know when I have had a nicer surprise. I thank you all." She sipped the champagne. "And champagne, too. You will spoil me, son."

"You deserve it, Mrs. MacKie." Dinah held up her glass. "Here's to many more, even happier birthdays."

"Thank you, Dinah. The only way I could be happier would be to see Ian married. He is at an age where he needs a wife, not a mother."

Dinah flushed, looking at Ian who was as embarrassed as she was.

Geordie took advantage of the mention of marriage to glance at Molly and squeeze her hand. As he opened his mouth ,she shook her head. He ignored her, saying, "I wish you would tell Molly that, Mrs. MacKie. I have been trying to get Molly to marry me, and she says we are both too young to be so serious."

"As long as you are serious, you are not too young." Mrs. MacKie looked at both Molly and Dinah. "Marriage should not be taken lightly. It is much more than merely being in love. It is caring for one another, wanting to care for and be with someone, through good days and bad. For all the joy, there is pain, too." She laughed. "Come, I am being far too solemn. I am old enough to have learned that no matter what one says to young people, they will do as they want."

Dinah smiled with the others, her mind on Mrs. MacKie's words. Before she could do what she wanted, she thought, first she had to know what she wanted. Even then, it was not up to one person. For example, she wanted Alexander, she was certain of that, although she was not sure that Alexander wanted her.

The girls went home shortly afterwards, with Geordie and Ian taking them by carriage. To their surprise Jamison opened the door as soon as the carriage stopped, calling to the captain. Sir Robert, he said, wanted to see him immediately. As a result, Geordie went with Molly to the servant's quarters, while Dinah entered the house with Captain MacKie.

Dinah had no time to say goodnight as Sir Robert said, "Come in, Dinah. I want to talk to MacKie, and you might as well hear it, too." He looked at the two of them, adding, "You may have feelings about what I say."

He explained briefly that he had received bad news about his business interests in East Africa. He would have to go there to try and straighten out some contracts that had to do with the railroad being built. "That is where you come in, Ian."

"Ian?" Dinah was startled. "Why?"

"Because all my ships are at sea, with the exception of the *Star of Scotland*. Ian, if I ask another captain to sail her, that will take time, both to hire the right one and for him to acquaint himself with the ship. As you have been captain since she was launched, I am asking you as a favor to make one more voyage, you and Geordie both. It is a lot to ask. You have both had two long and difficult voyages to New York and deserve several months at home. However, I will make it up to you. I have had papers drawn up transferring ownership of the *Star of Scotland* to you on your return. Naturally, my company shall continue to act as agent for you, should you desire that, but the ship itself will be yours."

Dinah looked at Ian, seeing the excitement in his eyes. A ship of his own had probably always been his dream and now it was being offered to him, with only the proviso he carry Sir Robert to Africa.

Ian took a deep breath. He looked at Dinah, trying to read her mind from the expression on her face. Dinah was no help. All she could think of was that she would lose both Sir Robert and Ian.

"I take it that the voyage is imperative?" asked Ian.

"Yes, and as soon as possible. I am already arranging the hiring of a crew and the taking on of ballast, as there will be no cargo outward bound, at least."

"When will we sail? I cannot speak for Geordie, but I will be ready as soon as you are."

"You are certain, Ian? It is not an order," replied Sir Robert. "You can continue in my employ as long as you like."

"Sir Robert," Ian was choosing his words carefully, "you gave me my chance at command at an age when I could have expected to remain mate for several more years. If you need me now, I would be more than ungrateful to refuse you. As for Geordie, I will talk to him."

"Thank you, Ian. Now for you, Dinah." Sir Robert turned his attention to the young girl. "Alexander will be taking my place with the company. I have no choice," he added grimly, "and I can only hope he listens to the good advice of others. As for you and Margaret, I have spoken briefly to Lady Janet who is willing to act as chaperone. You are both too young to leave on your own. Do you have any objections?"

Dinah shook her head, trying to conceal the dismay she felt. "No, sir," she whispered.

"I have suggested she take you to London. I had been making plans to have you and Margaret presented at court. There is no reason for those plans to be deferred, even though I am not here."

"The court? You mean to . . . to the queen, Queen Victoria herself?" Dinah was astonished.

"Yes," Sir Robert replied with amusement, "that is exactly what I meant. You would like that?" At Dinah's nod, he went on, "Then, there is no more to say tonight."

He said "goodnight" to them both, telling Ian to be in his office at eleven the next morning and to speak with Geordie. Dinah went to her room, her mind whirling with the rapid change of events. She could not imagine Edinburgh without Sir Robert, or life totally under the rule of Lady Janet. Then, she thought of Molly and felt ashamed of herself. Poor Molly! She was sure Geordie would choose to go with Ian for the same reason that Ian had chosen to go with Sir Robert, as Ian had given Geordie his first chance as mate. Dinah had resolved to tell Molly to marry Geordie, to make her plans and to enjoy the few months Geordie would have at home. Now, whatever she said would make no difference. There would be no time.

Dinah pulled the bell rope. She wanted to tell Molly about what was happening, to tell her herself before she learned about the events from Parker. Molly would be no happier than she was at the thought of Lady Janet in charge of the house.

Chapter 18

GEORDIE AGREED TO go on the voyage only after discussing his decision with Molly. They both decided he had no choice, especially because Molly would not leave Dinah until Sir Robert returned.

"I can't do it, Geordie love," Molly insisted, "not with that Angus woman running the house. She and Mary will be on Dinah like flies on a horse. I told you about Lochleven. And if they go to London . . ." Molly hated to admit even to herself that the prospect of going to London was tantalizing.

"And us? What about us? You'd put going to London with Dinah ahead of us?" asked Geordie miserably.

"Oh, London doesn't matter," Molly said quickly. "I mean, Dinah will need me there. We will have to wait. Besides, it won't be all that long. You said that, without a cargo and using the Suez Canal, you'd be there and back in no time."

"Depending on Sir Robert's business and how long it takes," Geordie warned. "MacKie will give me a reference, he's said so. Let's marry now. We can't wait for other people all our lives."

"No, Geordie. Dinah really needs me now. It has nothing to do with Mrs. Bradley, as you may think or any promises. I owe them something. If it hadn't been for Mrs. Bradley asking me to go with Dinah and for Dinah, we wouldn't have met, would we? And you, Geordie," she added, "you owe Captain MacKie something, too. Didn't he give you your chance as first mate?"

"Aye. You're right there," he agreed.

"You don't know that Angus woman!" Molly

smiled, her thoughts already on the time ahead. "It's all Mary, Mary, Mary." She shook her head in disgust.

Geordie had to give in. The next day, he left for Leith with MacKie to see to the ship.

The house itself was in a turmoil. Neither Alexander nor his father was there much, both spending their days at the office going over shipping contracts and cargos. One difficulty was a contract with the British East Indies Company that was up for renewal. It was decided that Alexander would accompany the others to London to take care of that.

Despite their absence, however, things were busier than ever with the Anguses starting to move in, having decided to close their house. Then, James arrived from Stirling Castle, with the news that he was being posted to Africa. In fact, he had come on the orders of the colonel to discuss with Sir Robert the possibility of a few advance troops and officers going to Africa on any ship Sir Robert might have sailing shortly. Sir Robert immediately offered passage on the *Star of Scotland* to Mombasa.

Over dinner that night, the men discussed the situation in Africa, particularly South Africa where the British, under Cecil Rhodes, were engaged in a struggle for power with the Dutch Boers who had first settled the country. The situation had been precipitated by discoveries of vast gold and diamond deposits, through which Rhodes had become a millionaire. Over the New Year, Rhodes, as Prime Minister of the British Cape Colony, had instigated a raid against the Boer Republic of Transvaal, whose president was Paul Kruger. The raid had been a disaster, and the German Emperor had telegraphed congratulations to Kruger, leading to the possibility that German marines would be sent to help the Boers. As a result, the British Army was being sent to reinforce South Africa, with some soldiers also going to British East Africa to keep an eye on German East Africa, which bordered it to the south.

"I must say," James said, "I would much rather be

going to South Africa. That is where the war will be, I am sure."

"But you could be killed," protested Margaret.

James laughed. "I could also get rich," explained James. "I've heard that the gold and diamonds are there for the asking, the picking."

"I'm afraid, James, with few exceptions, no one gets rich that easily," Sir Robert pointed out. "For one thing, the days of the Gold Rushes are over. Rhodes is most clever in controlling the exploitation of the mines. It is serious business there, with individuals having little chance to get rich. It is not like it is or was in America and the Yukon, or in Australia, every man for himself."

"Perhaps," James agreed. "Still, I find the idea of South Africa more inviting than East Africa, where we will only be guarding the railroad or keeping an eye on the Germans. If I must go on active duty, I would rather have it to a good purpose."

"That is estimable of you, James. I am proud of you." Sir Malcolm held up a glass of wine. "To James!"

"To James," the others chorused while James smiled.

Lady Janet stared at her husband. "I, for one, am on Margaret's side. I cannot see the honor and the glory of being killed."

"Mother! The war will not last long. What can the Boers or those Zulus do against the British Army?" protested James. "I would probably be home far sooner than I will be, going to guard a railroad."

"I do not see why you have to go," insisted Margaret. "There are other officers, with more experience, who would be better suited to such duty. Don't you agree, Father?" She appealed to Sir Robert.

Sir Robert smiled gently at his daughter. "I'm afraid, Margaret, that James—or any other officer— has little choice. He is a soldier, and soldiers, men and officers, go where the War Office sends them."

"True," remarked Sir Malcolm. "I only wish I were young enough to join them. From what I've heard, the huntin'," he sighed. "You will have a fine time, James. Elephants, lions, tigers . . ."

Alexander laughed. "Sir Malcolm, there are no tigers in Africa. That's India you are thinking of!"

"Well, there are elephants and lions and those strange creatures, rhinos, they call 'em," insisted Sir Malcolm, retreating to his wine glass.

Sir Robert studied James carefully, glancing from him to Margaret. "I hope you will take advantage of the opportunity, not waste it spending your time hunting or indulging in some of the other pleasures you may find." He knew from the reports of his agents that Mombasa was as much an Arab port as it was a British one, with a flourishing slave trade.

James colored. "I gamble very little, sir. On an officer's salary . . ."

"So I have heard. Your example is a good one." He stopped, avoiding the mention of Alexander and his debts which were mounting again.

Alexander looked at his plate, fully aware of what his father had meant to say. He raised his head to look at his father.

Dinah wished he would say something, but Alexander held his tongue, making no promises. Still, she saw the jaw tighten. Feeling sorry for him in the silence that had fallen on the table, she tried to think of something to say.

Instead, the silence was broken by Mary. "Well, I am proud of you, James, and of you, Alexander. You will have a lot of responsibility on your shoulders until your Father returns, and we all must do all we can to help you, mustn't we, Margaret?"

"Of course!" Margaret did not even look at Dinah. "All you have to do is call on Mary and me," she said pointedly.

Dinah bit her tongue. She had no intention of parroting Margaret and Mary. Still, she had to say something. "Sir Robert," she said slowly, "how long do you think you will be gone?"

"I have no idea, Dinah. Hopefully, when we get to Mombasa, it will take only a week or two. If not, I may have to go to Nairobi, which is the other end of the railroad." He smiled. "In which case, I will be able to get in some of that hunting that Malcolm mentioned."

"Ah, the huntin'!" Sir Malcolm sighed longingly. "What I wouldn't give to go with you, Robert!"

"I should say not!" Lady Janet stood up, putting an end to the conversation. "Come, girls, let us leave the men to their brandy and cigars. And no more talk of hunting, husband! If I am to lose my son temporarily, I will not lose my husband, too!"

She stalked from the room, the girls following her, each wrapped up in her own thoughts. Margaret was the most upset because of James's imminent departure. In a way, Dinah could sympathize with her out of her feeling about Ian's leaving.

"Margaret," Dinah said, "I'm sorry about James."

"Are you? I wonder . . ." Margaret looked at Dinah thoughtfully. "My father seems to listen to you. Perhaps you could talk to him to use his influence with Whitehall to keep James home."

"I couldn't do that! Besides, you know your father would not."

"Oh, Dinah, don't be so honorable! If it were you, you would try anything," said Margaret haughtily.

"Would I? I am not so sure," Dinah told her, thinking of MacKie. She had not tried to dissuade him from going at all, tired as she knew he was from the weeks at sea and from command. It had been his decision to make, and he had gone out of a sense of responsibility, as a means of repaying Sir Robert for the confidence placed in him, not for the ship that would be his on his return. For that matter, she was not that sure that James did not want to go to Africa, from what he had said. He might prefer South Africa, but she was sure he was going to East Africa willingly.

Margaret smiled. "You might be sorry, Dinah. One of these days, with my father gone, you might need a friend."

The threat was implicit and clear. Dinah wavered momentarily, not wanting to antagonize Margaret. Yet, just as Ian had had no choice, and Geordie too, she had no choice. "I cannot, Margaret, much as I might like to. You know as well as I do that your father will not interfere, regardless of what anyone says. Why should he listen to me, if he will not listen to you who love James?" Dinah pointed out.

The logic carried no weight with Margaret, who picked up her skirt to sit beside Mary on a small settee. Dinah sat opposite them, half listening to their talk about James and ways of keeping him home, as Lady Janet listened indulgently. Dinah was amused, particularly at the suggestion that James could fall from a horse and break his leg. She would like to be around when that was mentioned to James.

An idea came to her, and she said mischievously to Margaret, "Why not run him down with a carriage? James is far too good a horseman to fall off. Even then, he might not break his leg."

"A carriage? He could be killed!" Margaret shrilled.

"It was only a suggestion," Dinah said with a smile. "I tried, didn't I?" She settled back in her chair, waiting for the men to join them. Someway, she had to talk to Alexander, to let him know that she, too, would do all she could to help him.

As soon as the men entered the room, she stood up to take the cups of coffee that Lady Janet poured and hand them to the men. She noticed that Mary took her chair, to permit Margaret to signal James to sit beside her. Unwittingly, Mary had given her the opportunity she wanted to seek out Alexander.

She handed him a cup of coffee, saying, "Alexander . . ."

"Yes?" He smiled down at her.

"If there is anything I can do, I will. You know that, don't you?" Her eyes met his straightforwardly.

"I do, Dinah. Have no fear, I count on your support above anyone else's. You will not let me down, will you?" he asked, pleadingly.

Dinah glowed. It was as close as Alexander had come to saying he needed or wanted her, and she warmed to his need. "Of course not, Alexander. I would do anything for you."

"Dear Dinah," he murmured.

As far as speaking to Sir Robert about Margaret's request went, Dinah was glad that she did not try. Even if Sir Robert were willing, there was not time for him to do anything. The next day, he received word that the other officers and troops who were to accompany James were on the way to Leith. As a result, he and James made plans to leave the next day.

Despite Sir Robert's attempt to make the last dinner in Edinburgh a festive one, it was a failure. He had spent the day going over last minute details with Alexander, and the two arrived too late to change, striking a note of transition that the others could not ignore. Then, Margaret, Mary, and Lady Janet fussed over James with tears in their eyes until James grew restless, reminding them that he was only going to be guarding a railroad, not going to war. Sir Malcolm seemed the only one untouched, drinking his wine and eating his dinner as if tonight were nothing special.

Dinah, for her part, was anxious for a last word with Sir Robert. The opportunity came in the library. As she offered him a cup of coffee, she asked, "May I speak to you for a moment?"

"Naturally, Dinah." He sat on a sofa and drew her down beside him.

"I shall miss you," she began. "It will not be the same with you away."

He patted her hand. "Hopefully it will not be for long, and you will be too busy in London to think of me often."

"No," she said firmly and honestly, "I shall always think of you, of your kindness and generosity to me, for which I have never thanked you properly. Oh, Sir Robert . . ." Tears welled suddenly in her eyes. First she had lost her mother, and now barely a year later she felt as if she were losing him.

"Now, now, Dinah, no tears. No thanks are needed. I did what anyone would do under the circumstances.

My only regret is that your mother did not write me sooner, that she let those years go by without a word." He sighed. "Enough of that. You must enjoy yourself, my dear. London is an exciting place nowadays, with the Prince and Princess of Wales setting the pace for society. It will be one party after another, with the Diamond Jubilee coming up and royalty gathering from all over Europe."

"I wish you were to be there."

He chuckled. "And I will be, Dinah, before you know it. The *Star of Scotland,* by the way, will be stopping at London on the way home. For now, though, you must listen to Lady Janet. In a way, I think it is just as well. As a woman, she is far more aware of your needs than I am."

Dinah did not try to argue. Even so, she knew she would be more alone than ever in her life, with only Molly and possibly Alexander to help her. She recalled the argument over the dresses; life under Lady Janet would be a set of similar situations, with Lady Janet pressing her own daughter and Margaret forward.

Sir Robert noticed her silence and said quietly, "Lady Janet is a fine woman, Dinah. Otherwise I would not leave you and Margaret in her care. I have told her that you are to be treated exactly as if you were my own daughter. She is a woman of the world, moreover, and will be able to help you with any problems," he smiled, "problems that I as a man would undoubtedly be helpless to solve."

"Very well." Dinah smiled back. She would have to be strong, just as she had been in setting out from New York.

"And Alexander will be with you," Sir Robert went on. "He, too, will be there, to take my place." A shadow passed over his face, as he added, more to himself than Dinah, "I sincerely hope."

Dinah noticed the shadow and immediately defended his son. "I know he will do a good job, Sir Robert. Didn't he do well in New York and Bermuda? You were pleased, I know."

"Yes, I was. Still, he will now have a much

bigger responsibility on his shoulders and I hope he will let neither that nor the society in London go to his head." Sir Robert took her hand. "You will have to keep an eye on him, help him, Dinah. I think he may listen to you where he will listen to no one else."

"Yes, Sir Robert." Dinah felt a warm glow rising to her cheeks.

There was no chance to talk further, as James came up to ask about their departure the next day. In the morning, although everyone gathered for breakfast, even Lady Janet, no one had time for private conversations. Margaret, who valiantly tried to get James alone, was forced to kiss him goodbye in front of the others. Once again, Dinah felt sorry for her, as the women and Alexander and Sir Malcolm waved goodbye from the front steps to the departing coach.

Alexander immediately left for the office, while Sir Malcolm departed for his club. The women looked at one another, each sad for their own reasons, with Margaret now in outright tears. Mary took her to her room to comfort her, and Lady Janet went to speak to Mrs. Jamison. Dinah, left to herself, went to her room.

Underneath her sadness was a feeling of exhilaration at the challenge that lay ahead of her. She was older now than she had been on the ship, and she had had a little experience. She resolved to show Alexander just what a help she could be to him, how much she cared. A whole world of experiences lay in front of her. London! They were going by train in a private carriage. It was her first train ride, and the prospect excited her, despite Molly's saying that trains were noisy and dirty and not at all as comfortable as ships. Molly, after all, was only used to the short ride to the village where Geordie's sister lived, and to sitting in a crowded coach. A private car was surely different.

During the next two weeks and the round of fittings for new gowns, Dinah looked forward to the train ride. The women were alone much of the time, Alexander going to his father's office every day and often bringing papers home to work on in the evening. Sir

Malcolm, as usual, spent most of his time at his club. As a result, the women became increasingly anxious to get to London. Once again, trunks were sent ahead, with the Jamison's departing early to arrange for the hiring of servants for the London house in Sloane Square that was watched only by a caretaker and his wife who did what cleaning was necessary.

The day of their departure finally arrived. The train left at noon, and there was a flurry of last minute packing and preparations. The coachman took Molly and Parker to the station first, to ready the private carriage. Shortly afterward, the others crowded into the carriage and were taken to the station.

Chapter 19

THE DIN AND clangor of the railroad station assaulted Dinah's ears, the shriek of the locomotives' whistles in disharmony with the loud sighs of escaping steam. Amid the cacaphony, her eyes took in the high vault of the roof, paned completely in soot-stained glass. The place seemed full of people rushing to and fro, except for a refreshment bar in the corner, where women elegantly gowned in dark clothing sat sipping tea while their men stood at a bar, whiskey in hand.

She stared openly at the huge black engines with their conical stacks spewing blacksmoke. She had seen trains before, although never this close. As she peered into the coaches of the train that they were to take, she began to wonder whether Molly wasn't right. The third-class coaches had stiff-backed wooden seats. Overhead, metal racks were filled with an assortment of bundles and cases that threatened to tumble down with the starting of the train. The cars had no compartments, with doors only at either end. Next came the second-class coaches, with upholstered seats and doors leading into compartments. The first-class coaches were similar, only more luxurious. Nevertheless, on a long journey, such as the one to London, it would be far from comfortable for six of them, not to mention Molly and Parker, to sit facing one another. The prospect was not one Dinah looked forward to, and the excitement of making her first train journey began to fade rapidly.

The coach into which Alexander led them, however, was quite different. Dinah had heard and read about the ornate private cars of people like the Vanderbilts and Astors in America. This car, she was sure, was their equal. The rear section, or the front—she was not sure which was which—was luxuriously appointed with upholstered chairs set around gleaming mahogany table that could be folded up against the matching paneling of the car. Overhead, a mythological scene of Paris and the three goddesses was painted in glowing colors. Lighting was provided by gilt oil lamps set at intervals along the walls and an equally ornate chandelier. Dinah was speechless, and even the usually sophisticated Lady Janet was obviously impressed.

Lady Janet cleared her throat. "Your father has provided generously for us, Alexander. And the rest of the car?" She nodded toward the double mahogany doors at the other end.

"The sleeping compartments. There are four. Sir Malcolm and I, of course, shall share one. I leave it to you ladies to make your own arrangements, whether, for example, Dinah and Margaret share one or they may prefer the company of Molly and Parker," Alexander suggested.

Dinah smiled, sure the last statement was for Dinah's benefit. She seized the opportunity to make her own arrangements before Margaret had a chance to open her mouth. "Molly and I are used to close quarters from the ship," she pointed out. "That arrangement suits me very well."

Margaret glared at Dinah, obviously not happy about sleeping with her maid and not eager for Dinah's company either. "That will suit me, too, as I will have need of Parker, and the compartments are much too small for three at the same time."

Alexander bowed at his sister. "You are quite right, Margaret. That seemed the best arrangement to me, although I did not want to force it on you."

"You are much too kind, Alexander." Margaret turned on her heel toward the doors. "I shall talk to Parker now." She paused, flinging over her shoulder. "At least, I assume I have the opportunity of selecting my own compartment."

"By all means," Alexander agreed.

Once Dinah saw the compartments, she had to smile at Margaret's words. All four were identical, narrow rooms with a single bed along each wall. Behind the door was a washstand with a pitcher and basin in white chin with pink rosebuds. Overhead were two narrow hammocks in which the essentials for the journey could be conveniently placed. Molly and Parker, who had been waiting in the narrow corridor outside the compartments, looking at the passersby and waving, immediately set about laying out their mistresses' toiletries. As they did, Lady Janet and Mary gave them instructions for their own needs.

By the time that Dinah returned to the salon, the train was ready to start. She went to a window that Alexander had opened to lean out with him. Her eyes sparkled with excitement, and her cheeks were flushed.

Alexander put his arm around her waist. "Don't lean out too far. Once we start, you're apt to get a face full of cinders."

"I'll be careful. How soon will it be?"

"There's the clock." He pointed to a high, large white-faced clock above the gates through which passengers were still streaming. "If the train is on time, we should leave as soon as the hands stand at noon."

No sooner were the words out of his mouth than there was a warning: A piercing blast of the whistle accompanied the shriek of steam from the valves under the wheels. Dinah watched the clock in fascination, waiting for the two hands to meet. As soon as they did, the car jerked forward. Through the window, she could hear the sound of doors being closed and a conductor's whistle blowing. There was another jerk and a grinding of wheels, as the train followed its engine, seemingly unwillingly at first.

"Alexander," Mary had gone to his other side. "Do close the window. You're letting in all sorts of smoke and soot."

"Of course. I'm sorry." He closed the window promptly.

The first part of the journey was through the Scottish lowlands. While the other woman read the books they had brought along for the purpose, the motion of the train not being suited to needlework, Dinah watched the scenery. The hills or braes were green with gorse and grass, spring having blossomed forth in the few weeks since they had returned from Kinross-shire. Here and there were thatched-roof cottages with roses climbing the white walls. Sheep and cattle grazed calmly, barely raising their heads at the passing of the train. Now and then, a dog rushed from a cottage to bark furiously, racing beside the train for a few hundred yards. Once, a horse drawing a cart shied, and the farmer had his hands full to keep the horse from running away to race the train.

As the novelty wore off, Dinah began to wish for the freedom of a ship at sea. Walking on the train was difficult. Besides, there was no place to go. On ship, she could at least go on deck. She was starting to yawn when Molly and Parker served a cold lunch of sandwiches and wine.

The rest of the day passed similarly, although Lady Janet excused herself to lie down in her compartment and Sir Malcolm dozed in his chair. Alexander stayed by himself, going over some papers he was carrying. There was no tea, only an early supper of cold meats and sandwiches, with more wine. The train had stopped at a station long enough for Alexander to go off and return with jugs of hot tea.

The lamps had been lit by a conductor who came into the car to make sure they were comfortable. Under the yellow flames, the mahogany shone, lending an air of coziness to the car. In a way, Dinah thought, it was like being at sea. The motion, and now the lights, made the car seem an island of comfort in a sea of darkness. Lady Janet sent everyone to bed early, with the warning that they would have to be up early, too.

Alone in the small compartment with Molly, Dinah giggled as Molly tried to help her undress in the motion of the train. Fortunately, she was wearing a simple dark skirt with a matching jacket trimmed in military style with braid and a high-necked white blouse that buttoned down the front. It was far easier for her to undo the buttons herself than have Molly leaning against her with the motion of the train.

"I declare," said Molly, giving up trying to help, "it was much easier at sea, and we had more room." She looked around the tiny compartment, sighing.

"Are you thinking of Geordie?" asked Dinah. Molly had said little about the young man ever since the final decision was made about his going with MacKie.

Molly nodded. "Where do you think they are now, Dinah? Almost there?"

"Not yet. Maybe at the Suez Canal. Don't worry, Molly, he'll be back soon. Sir Robert told me that if it looked as if he would have to stay any length of time, he intended to send the *Star of Scotland* to London. London," Dinah's eyes sparkled, "just think, tomorrow we will be there. I wonder what it's like!"

"Noisy and dirty, according to Mrs. Jamison," Molly giggled, "but the country is too quiet."

"And Edinburgh?"

"Just right!" Molly laughed again. She slipped under the covers of the narrow bed, pulling the covers up to her ears.

Dinah smiled. Turning down the lamp, she got in her own bed, trying to get used to the motion of the train and the clack-clack of the wheels. As she listened, the wheels seemed to be saying "Alexander" over and over again. The sound was soothing, helping her to drift off into sleep. Once she awakened. The train stopped at a station, and she looked at Molly. Molly, her mouth half open, was snoring softly.

She was probably dreaming of Geordie, Dinah thought, waiting for the train to start and resume the soothing rhythm of its message. She hoped that message was an omen, wishing that it were Alexander in the other bed. What would it be like here, to be alone with him, their bodies naked and loving? At the thought, she laughed. Not only the bunks but the compartments were far too small. They would have to stand up. The idea intrigued her, the two of them standing, their thighs pressed together, his hands on her breasts and hers on his buttocks, his organ large and finding its own way between her legs. The thought made her hot with longing, and she fell asleep again only long afterwards, after the train had left the station and had traveled for miles through the countryside.

When Dinah awakened again, Molly was stirring to the accompaniment of similar noises from the compartment next door where Margaret had slept with Parker. Dinah let Molly get washed and dressed first, before she arose. Once she was dressed, she went into the salon to let Molly repack the nightdresses and toiletries. Alexander was alone, staring into the fog of a London morning. To Dinah's eyes, he seemed tense and worried.

"Are you worried about those contracts?" asked Dinah.

Alexander turned around, startled. "Dinah! I thought I was alone. You surprised me." He avoided the question, asking, "Are you eager to see London?"

Dinah met his eyes boldly. "Not if you are not with me," she said impulsively, "no more than I was to go to Scotland."

"Truly, Dinah?" He studied her face. "I sometimes

think that you do not like me. Yet," he shook his head, "when you are in my arms . . ."

"Alexander, of course I like you!" She flushed, thinking of the ship and Lockleven. "If I didn't . . ." She stopped, thinking only a moment before adding, "It is you. I don't know what to think about you!"

"Me?" Alexander laughed. "I can't blame you. Sometimes, I am not sure about myself, what I think, what I want." He took her hands. "You will help me, Dinah, won't you? I cannot let my father down."

"Oh, Alexander, you know I will do all I can. I promise, I have promised." Her lips sought his, her mouth hot on his, and her body pressing against him as it had in her fantasy the night before. His arms tightened around her.

"Miss Dinah!" Molly's clear voice interrupted them and they stepped quickly apart. "If you don't need me, I will see what I can do to help Miss Mary and Lady Janet. Sir Malcolm is already up," she warned.

"At least it was Molly," Alexander murmured.

By the time the others had gathered, the train was pulling into the station, to the waves of the friends and relatives of the passengers. Through the burst of steam, signifying the braking of the train, Dinah spied Jamison, stiff and formal in his black suit and overcoat, waiting for them. After welcoming them to London and asking about the journey, he led them to the carriages he had waiting. One was the carriage that the Douglases kept in London, into which the six squeezed themselves. The other was a rented carriage, which was to carry him, the two maids, and the traveling cases to Sloane Square.

While Jamison supervised the two maids, the first carriage set off to the hot breakfast Mrs. Jamison had waiting them. Dinah looked around eagerly for her first glimpse of London. There was little to see in the fog. What could be seen reminded Dinah of the area around Washington Square, streets of houses with front steps rising to a parlor floor. Then the carriage reached a large park, in the center of which was an awesome building enclosed by a high iron gate.

"That's Buckingham Palace," Alexander explained, "where Queen Victoria lives when she is in London."

"Is she there now?" Dinah tried to peer through the fog at the imposing structure.

"I don't know. If not, she will be soon, I expect, don't you, Lady Janet?" he asked, noticing Lady Janet also craning her neck.

"I expect so." Lady Janet settled back.

"And the Prince of Wales? Doesn't he live at Marlborough House?" Dinah looked around for another building.

"We passed it, Dinah, just before we reached the park. I was looking for it, but I missed it in the fog," apologized the young man. "I promise you, though, you shall have a good look at it—and from the inside."

He had no time to say anything more, as the carriage had reached Sloane Square. The house itself was just off the square, and it, too, reminded Dinah of New York. It was set in a row of similar style buildings, much as the Bradley house had been, with a flight of steps leading to the parlor floor. Another flight led to the basement and the servants' quarters. The house itself was white with white pillars on either side of the door that was open now to reveal Mrs. Jamison.

Dinah realized she was hungry, especially after the cold repasts of the day before. She was not the only one. Even Lady Janet helped herself amply to the hot dishes waiting for them. As they ate, Lady Janet discussed their plans. First of all, she would have to send a footman around to friends and acquaintances with their cards, she said. That would give them time to get settled. Dinah listened, confused by the social protocol, which seemed very complicated.

She was glad when the meal was over and Mrs. Jamison showed her to her room on the floor above. Waiting for Molly, she thought about Alexander on his way to the company's London office. She told herself firmly not to worry about him, that he would take care of any problems just as his father would.

Chapter 20

LADY JANET MADE sure they were seen. The morning after their arrival, she had the carriage take the ladies to Hyde Park and Rotten Row. It was along the wide bridle path that anyone who was anyone rode in their carriages or walked. A few rode horses, their tails fashionably bobbed and stepping out elegantly.

The morning was sunny and warm, and all the ladies had their parasols up to protect their complexions. The most popular costume, Dinah noted, was a suit with large leg-of-mutton sleeves. She tried to appear as sophisticated as the others, leaning back against the cushions of the carriage with her parasol at a graceful angle, but something was always catching her attention to make her sit up eagerly. Lady Janet, sitting opposite her with Margaret, finally told her to behave, that she was acting most unseemly in showing such curiosity.

"Who do you suppose all the people are?" asked Dinah meekly.

"I have no idea. It really does not matter," Lady Janet replied.

Dinah was puzzled. "But if people come here to be seen, it does matter that others recognize them, doesn't it?"

Lady Janet's face flushed under the parasol. "You are much too old to ask such silly questions. Let the others look. I prefer to be looked at," declared Lady Janet, refusing to admit her ignorance.

Dinah did not reply. If Lady Janet had disliked her before, she realized that her questions had now antagonized the woman. She resolved to ask no more questions, though she was terribly curious. She could not understand why they dressed every afternoon for callers who did not arrive or why Lady Janet examined the cards that were left by footmen at their house, with such attention. The names meant nothing to her, and she hesitated to ask Alexander. Even if she had wanted to, she had little opportunity, as he was at the house only at dinner. In the evenings, moreover, privacy was at a minimum.

The first Friday that they were in London, however, Alexander returned to Sloane Square before tea. He found Dinah alone in the small library writing a much-delayed letter to Mrs. Bradley. She was only too happy to put the letter aside when he suggested going for a walk.

"You look very fashionable," he said, noting the small, flat hat atop her head and the short cape she wore over a lace-fronted white blouse with leg-of-mutton sleeves, as he directed their steps along Lower Sloane Street past a tall iron fence.

"What's that," Dinah asked. The fence enclosed a number of large buildings of the massive stone architecture she associated with Buckingham Palace. "It looks very royal."

"It is. It's the headquarters of the Duke of York, a younger brother of the Prince of Wales. The buildings beyond, to the right and just before the Thames, are the Chelsea Barracks," he added.

"We have seen so little of London," Dinah mourned. "All Lady Janet wants to do is ride along Rotten Row in the morning and wait for callers in the afternoon."

Alexander laughed. "And here I was, about to propose we go for a ride there ourselves in the morning. I had arranged for some horses from Leopold Rothschild, a friend of the Prince's and as avid a collector of horses as he, to borrow two riding horses."

"That's different! I should love that!" Dinah enthused. "And you must tell me who people are, as Lady Janet never does."

"If I know them, I shall. By the way," he said casually, "do you remember my once saying that one day you should see Marlborough House?"

"How could I forget? You said I might meet Jennie Jerome there," Dinah reminded him.

"That, I cannot promise. She spends much time in Paris nowadays, with a friend, Bourke Cockran. However, Saturday week, we have all been invited to a party at Marlborough House."

"Alexander!" Dinah wanted to throw her arms around him. Instead, she squeezed his arm. "You are not teasing me, are you?"

"Hardly! Actually, Dinah," he went on soberly, "it is far more than a party as far as I am concerned. Lord Salisbury, the Prime Minister, and other members of the Government will be there. I cannot get anywhere with our contracts at the moment, using the Government channels. Rothschild, who is a friend of my father's, had promised to bring the matter to the Prince's attention. He is very interested in Africa."

"Is there anything I can do to help?"

"I am not sure. I am hoping that Joseph Chamberlain, Secretary for the Colonies, will be there, too. His wife is American."

"I will surely do all I can to be as charming and entertaining as possible," Dinah promised, her eyes sparkling at the thought that he had come to her for help and not to Margaret or Mary.

"That is all I ask." His eyes twinkled. "You can play Jennie to my Randolph Churchill."

"Now I know you are teasing me, but I don't mind." They had reached the Thames, and Dinah looked at the river. "The Hudson is wider, but it has piers along it. This is much prettier."

"Ships nowadays rarely come upriver this far, except for smaller boats. They usually moor at Greenwich, a few miles downriver where there are more facilities. That's where the *Star of Scotland* will arrive."

Both fell silent, each thinking of Sir Robert who should be arriving in Mombasa any day. Dinah thought, too, of Ian, wondering how long he would be away—how long until he would be home. Depending on how long they stayed in London, she would have little opportunity to see him unless he stayed on in London, which she doubted. She dismissed the thought. It was difficult to think of anyone or anything else with Alexander beside her, his arm around her waist, as they watched the outgoing tide sweep downriver. She must do all he asked, to help him and make his father proud of him, she decided, flushed with happiness that he had told her first about Marlborough House and not waited to tell them all together. How very much she loved him—she wanted to tell him that. She turned toward him, her cheeks glowing with warmth and her eyes sparkling.

"Dinah . . ." Alexander looked at her. "One of these days," he said slowly, "I hope you will change your mind about me, think better of me."

"But, Alexander," Dinah was puzzled, "I do think well of you. Don't you know that?"

"Do you? Do you, really? If so, then I know this business will go well. For now, we had better go back." He took her arm.

The pressure of his fingers sent fire running through Dinah's veins. Her body ached for him, and she was filled with such longing and desire as she had never known before.

They arrived to find an angry Lady Janet, who had to send for another pot of tea. "Really, Dinah, you are very thoughtless to wander off, without mentioning anything. I did not know whether to wait or not."

Before Dinah could apologize, Alexander said, "It was my fault entirely, Lady Janet. I asked her to go for a walk."

"That is no excuse for her not leaving word with Jamison! Now, sit down the two of you." She glanced at Mary, who immediately moved over on the settee where she was sitting to make room for Alexander.

The older woman forgot her anger, however, as soon as Alexander told them about the invitation to Marlborough House, although he did not give them the details that he had given Dinah. The three women immediately began to talk about what they would wear. Dinah had already decided. She would wear the dress from her birthday party, not one of the new ones. It was the symbol of her growing up, and the memory of her argument with Lady Janet over the neckline would give her the courage to help Alexander all she could. The party, nevertheless, was in the future. Tomorrow she would go riding with Alexander.

The ride turned out even better than she expected. Leopold Rothschild was waiting for them at the stables and joined them for a ride. Dinah found herself being watched attentively as she rode with the two men, who barely noticed, so engrossed were they with their conversation about Africa. As they approached a carriage, however, Rothschild reined in his horse.

"Jennie," he said, "how nice to see you. I didn't know you had returned to London."

"Only yesterday." The woman smiled.

At the smile, Dinah recognized her as Jennie Jerome Churchill from pictures she had seen in newspapers. She studied her closely. Even though she was now 42, the woman was still as beautiful as she had been in her youth, with her large eyes and sensual mouth. With her was a man of about her own age, with a full mane of blond hair, and a younger man. She introduced them as Bourke Cockran and her son, Winston.

Rothschild bowed from the saddle, introducing Dinah and Alexander, adding, "Miss Murray is a countrywoman of yours, I believe."

"Truly?" Lady Churchill turned a brilliant smile on Dinah. "Winston was in New York last year."

"I . . . I was born in New York," Dinah ventured.

"I, too," Lady Churchill laughed. "And now, you, too, are living in Europe, I take it?"

"Yes, although I have seen only Edinburgh and Scotland and now London."

"Well, you must come for tea one of these days, to Great Cumberland Place." To Rothschild, she added, "Yes, I have opened it again, despite the expense. But now, continue your ride. I am sure I will see you at Marlborough house on Saturday?"

"We will all be there, Jennie," Rothschild told her.

At Jennie's "I look forward to seeing you there, then, Miss Murray," Dinah's heart soared. She was glad now that she had not finished the letter to Mrs. Bradley. As the men resumed their conversation, her mind flew to the letter she would now write, about meeting Jennie Jerome and the party at Marlborough House.

Dinah's first impression of the Prince of Wales was of a large, florid fatherly man, whose size was enhanced by the slenderness of the Princess of Wales. When she dropped the curtsy she had been practicing all week, she glanced up at him from under her eyelashes. This was the man that everyone called Bertie, the one who was noted for his mistresses, despite his obvious affection for his wife and family. It seemed difficult to credit the stories, although the man exuded a charm that could be irresistible, she decided, noticing the way Lady Janet lost her stern demeanor in front of him.

Dinah found herself overwhelmed with introductions. Knowing she would never remember them all, she murmured polite responses hoping she was saying the right thing. At the same time, she could not help but be aware of the admiring looks she was getting from the men. Nor did she lack for dancing partners, most of whom were shorter than she. Alexander was definitely one of the tallest men there, and she thought him more attractive than ever.

At a pause in the dancing, she discovered herself standing next to Lady Churchill and smiled at her. Jennie motioned her to sit down on a settee near them, asking her about people whose names Dinah had only read in newspapers or heard Mrs. Bradley talk about.

"I'm sorry, Lady Churchill, I'm afraid I've never met any of those people." Dinah smiled, adding impulsively, "You see, all this—kind of a life—is very new to me."

"New?" The older woman was surprised. "You seem very comfortable here, I think."

"Do I?" Dinah laughed, proceeding to tell her how she had come to be here. "And that," she concluded, "is why I find all this quite a fairy tale."

Lady Churchill, who had listened with amazement, shook her head. "You look, as the saying goes, to the manner born." She stood up. "You must really come to tea, so we can talk some more. Now you must excuse me, I see some old friends."

Dinah smiled and looked around, enjoying the first opportunity she had had to examine her surroundings. In a corner, she could see Alexander talking to several men. She smiled fondly, hoping he was having success and wishing she could help him. Then she saw a means. Mary was making her way toward him. The young woman rose quickly to her feet, making her own way through the chatting couples, to reach Mary just before Mary had disturbed the men.

"Mary," she said quickly, "do you know where Lady Janet is?"

"Oh, in the other room, I think." Mary looked around, for the moment distracted in looking for her mother.

Dinah took her arm, leading her gently away from the men. "It's a lovely party, isn't it? Those gorgeous gowns and the jewels!" Dinah sighed. "Did you notice Princess Alexandra's tiara?"

"I did! And the diamonds on the Duchess of Bedford!" Mary looked enviously at the pearl and emerald jewels Dinah was wearing.

Dinah flushed, not knowing what to say. Alexander came to her rescue. He waltzed Mary off, leaving Dinah to Leopold Rothschild.

"I have been wanting to dance with you all evening," the older man told her. "In fact, I have been looking forward to this dance since our ride."

"Really?" Dinah smiled, not knowing what else to say. "I am flattered, sir."

"You enjoy riding?"

"Very much."

"Douglas tells me you have no riding horses here. I have left instructions for you both to use any of my horses at any time. I hope you will make use of the offer," Rothschild told her.

Dinah was so surprised that she would have missed a step had not the older man skillfully twirled her around in time to the music. "I don't know what to say, except 'thank you.' It is very kind of you."

"My dear," the older man bowed to her as the music ended, "it is tribute to your beauty." He glanced around. "I must speak to Bertie, to ask him to put in a good word about those contracts."

"Please do! They are very important to Alexander and," Dinah added slyly, "to me."

The man smiled indulgently. "If they are important to you, they are also important to me. Will you be riding next week? I had thought to ride myself on Monday, if you would care to join me."

After Dinah said she would try, Rothschild left her with a bow. Alexander had evidently been watching, for he appeared with a glass of champagne for her as soon as Dinah was alone. When she had told him about the conversation, Alexander smiled.

"If you wanted to help," he said, "you did. He is quite taken with you. By the way, he asked my permission to take you riding. It is your decision, Dinah, and Lady Janet can hardly refuse."

Soon after, guests began leaving and the Douglases and Anguses were with them. While Margaret and Mary chatted with Lady Janet about their partners and the gowns the ladies were wearing, Dinah stared out the window, thinking about the Prince of Wales and Rothschild, as well as her conversation with Jennie Churchill. Whatever the next months could bring, she decided, nothing could be as exciting as this night.

After the party at Marlborough House, however, invitations began arriving daily. Lady Janet sorted through them, choosing which to accept. She was not happy about the invitations to Dinah alone from Rothschild and Lady Churchill, but she let Dinah accept them because of Alexander's intervention on her behalf.

The contracts, meanwhile, were negotiated quickly.

Just as important, the contacts that Alexander was making through Rothschild were leading to new business, more than enough to keep the Douglas line plying the seas continuously. As a result, Alexander was considering asking his father to buy two more ships as soon as possible. The only shadow over their lives, in fact, was the lack of any word from Sir Robert. However, there was no word either about the arrival of the *Star of Scotland,* which reassured them. Alexander was certain that if there were any serious problems, his father would have sent the ship home in order not to lose revenue from possible cargos. For that reason, he said, the ship must be waiting, although the business was taking longer than had been hoped.

Dinah found the attention she received at parties very flattering. She never lacked for partners, either dancing or riding. Yet none of the other men aroused the desire in her that Alexander did. The more men she met, the more she yearned for Alexander, for the warmth of his arms around her, the touch of his hands. Aside from that first walk, moreover, they were never alone except when they were dancing and that was not really being alone.

Molly was on Dinah's mind, too, and increasingly so as the weeks passed. London did not have the excitement to it for Molly that it did for Dinah. For her, life was the same as it had been in Edinburgh, with no round of parties to distract her. She began to worry about Geordie and grow afraid that something had happened to the ship. Nothing Dinah could say would lighten the fears or bring more than a fleeting smile to her face.

It was Molly whom Dinah was thinking of on a warm July afternoon as she returned from luncheon at Great Cumberland Place. She was looking forward to a quiet evening at home for once, although Jennie had told her that London would soon be all too quiet as the Prince always went to Cowes in August for yacht racing. To her surprise, she found Alexander waiting for her.

Before she could get out of the carriage, he said, "Would you like to go for a ride in the Park? We've had no chance to talk."

"Yes," Dinah agreed. "It's much too lovely a day to waste inside." She raised the yellow parasol that matched her dress, waiting for him to say what it was he wanted to talk about, but he was silent, moodily watching the passing carriages.

When they reached the park, he signaled the coachman to stop, saying to Dinah, "Let's walk."

Again, Dinah agreed, her curiosity growing as he helped her from the carriage and took her arm. A reason for the silence suddenly struck her. She stopped, turning to face Alexander, the words catching in her throat. "Your father, Sir Robert! Has something happened, Alexander?"

"My father?" Alexander stared at her. Her face was white. "I haven't heard . . . Is that what you think I wanted to talk to you about? Oh, Dinah! I am so sorry." He smiled at her.

"You were so quiet. I was afraid you had bad news."

"I was trying to think what to say. Dinah, do you remember on the ship, when I said I wanted to talk to my father?"

Dinah nodded. "I do. I asked you not to. I was afraid."

"Why were you afraid?"

Dinah flushed, turning her head away. "I was afraid of what he would . . . would," she took a deep breath, "would think of me, of what we had done."

"My God!" Alexander turned her face to make her look into his eyes. "You thought I would tell my father about that?" At Dinah's nod, he leaned down to kiss her lips. "What a fool I was. How much time we have wasted because of a silly misunderstanding."

Dinah's heart leaped into her throat. Her tongue moistened her lips. She met his eyes boldly. "Then what did you want to ask?"

"I should have asked you first," he mused, "only I was not thinking quite straight. You had me quite enchanted." He smiled, "Dinah, I wanted to tell my father that I loved you, that I wanted to marry you."

"But you should have told me first! Asked me—" Her voice caught.

"I know. I told you I was a fool. Oh, my dear, I loved you then, and I love you even more now. I could never have made it through these past weeks without you, not only for the way you have made friends with Rothschild and others. All the while, I was so jealous, watching you smile and flirt with other men. How I wanted to take you in my arms, hold you all night as I did on Lochleven, growing afraid I had waited too long. But I wanted you to be proud of me."

"Alexander, you love me, is that what you are saying?" she repeated.

"Yes. I am talking too much, is that it?" He smiled again. "Dinah, I love you. Do you think you could care enough about me to marry me?"

"I love you, too." Her voice was soft, so low he could barely hear her. "I always have, I think. From the first day I saw you at Mrs. Bradley's. I have dreamed of marrying you." She took his hands, raising them to her lips to kiss them and hold them against her cheek. "Do you think I could have done what I did, if I did not love you?"

"No, you could not. Forgive me for being such a fool, Dinah. Now, will you let me talk to my father, ask his permission for us to marry, as soon as he arrives in London?"

"Yes, of course." She frowned, thinking of Margaret and Lady Janet, as well as Mary. "Do you think we should tell the others? You could talk to Margaret, I will have to talk to Lady Janet."

"Is that necessary?" Alexander's face darkened.

"Yes." Dinah's voice was firm. "You know that Margaret hopes you will marry Mary, and so does Lady Janet. It would not be fair to them, and I will have a hard time concealing my happiness."

"Very well. You *are* right." He glanced around at the late afternoon strollers, kissing her lightly. "Now, let's go home where we can be alone and I can kiss you properly."

They walked back to the carriage. Dinah put up her parasol to shield them, and Alexander put his arm around her, holding her close, his breath hot on her cheek. Her body throbbed with desire, her thighs tingling from the touch of his hand. At the house, as soon as they were inside, he led her into the library and took her into his arms. Their lips met, his tongue teasing her lips until she opened her mouth, welcoming him. She put her arms around his neck, as her body pressed against him, her legs slightly parted and waiting his rising manhood.

"What are you doing?" Lady Janet's voice was so icy that it forced them apart with a cold chill.

Alexander and Dinah looked at one another, their happiness still on their faces. This was not how they had wanted to break their news, but the fury on Lady Janet's face brooked no delay, nor did her voice.

"I asked you—and I expect an answer—what are you doing? Sir Robert left you, Dinah, in my charge. What shall I tell him about this . . . this . . ." She waved a hand.

Alexander's face darkened at the mention of his father. "I do not think my father will disapprove once—"

"You do not, do you? Then you do not know your father!" Lady Janet turned to Dinah. "Nor will he think very highly of you, whom he has brought as a daughter into his home."

"Lady Janet," Dinah drew herself up, her chin high and her amber eyes flashing with anger, "if you would let us explain."

"Very well, then, explain." The woman stalked to an armchair and sat down, her arms crossed. "I am listening."

"Alexander and I, we love one another." Dinah glanced at Alexander.

"I have asked her to marry me, and she has said 'yes,'" the young man concluded. "We intend to ask my father's permission as soon as he returns home."

"Love? Marriage? That is out of the question. If Sir Robert had had any idea, he—" Lady Janet stopped, her sharp eyes studying their faces. "You cannot marry."

"I hardly think you are the judge of that," Alexander snapped.

"I am, in your father's place." She smiled faintly, raising one hand to her lips. "Your father, Sir Robert, then, has told neither of you about Dinah, who she really is?" Lady Janet emphasized the "really", loading the word with foreboding.

Dinah and Alexander looked at one another. "My mother and he were distant cousins . . ." Dinah faltered.

"True. He had told you nothing else?" Lady Janet insisted.

Once again, Dinah and Alexander looked at one another, shaking their heads. "That's true, isn't it?" Dinah asked.

"Oh, that's true. If you and Alexander were only distant cousins, too, there would be no reason why you could not marry." Lady Janet smiled again, enjoying herself.

"Lady Janet," Dinah's voice was firm, "if Sir Robert has told you anything he has not told me or his own son, tell us. Otherwise, I have had quite enough of this talk and am going to my room."

"You are much too haughty, Dinah, for a girl your age. Sir Robert has spoiled you from the beginning. I knew, when you had that dress changed, when you appealed to him . . ."

Dinah started to leave the room, Alexander at her side. He put his arm around her.

"Take your hands off her!" Lady Janet hissed, rising to her feet. "Don't you ever touch her again." As the two stopped, too startled by the tone in her voice to move, Lady Janet stepped between them, slapping Dinah sharply on the face. "You are brother and sister, half brother and half sister, that is."

Blood drained from Dinah's head. White-faced, her eyes enormous in her face, she reeled as if she were

281

going to faint. When Alexander went to help her, Lady Janet pushed him aside, letting Dinah grope for a chair. "What are you saying?" she finally managed.

Lady Janet, still standing between them, folded her arms, looking at them, observing the shock on both their faces. Thoroughly satisfied, she told them the rest of the story. "Sir Robert told me before he left that in case he did not return, he wanted Dinah to know she was his daughter. He and her mother," she went on, ignoring Dinah as if she were not there and talking to Alexander, "were lovers. They had been raised together, but he was ten years older, already married with two children, when they fell in love. He never knew why she ran away, until the letter she wrote shortly before she died, arrived. Then, he sent Alexander, never expecting that the two of you . . ."

Dinah closed her eyes, thinking of her mother and Sir Robert—Rabbie and Lochleven. Her mother never had been married. There was no stern uncle to disapprove. She was illegitimate, a bastard.

"It's a lie!" Alexander shouted. "Damn you, Lady Janet, I will never marry Mary. Admit it's a lie!"

"You have only to ask your father. If it is a lie, it is his lie," Lady Janet told him. "I hope for your sake that this affair of yours has only been confined to a few," she smiled, "stolen kisses."

Dinah struggled to stand. Alexander moved swiftly to her side, but Dinah shook her head. "No. I have to think." Once she was standing, Dinah looked at Lady Janet, at the smug expression on her face. She had to get out of the room by herself, get to her own room and Molly before she fainted. She could not faint now, not in front of Lady Janet, although she was sure that was what the woman wanted. She took a deep breath, feeling her head clear a little.

Picking up her skirt, she walked slowly toward the door and opened it. The stairs seemed insurmountable, as insurmountable as the cliff at Stirling Castle, but she forced herself to climb them, taking one step at a time. At the head of the stairs, she paused, a heavy blackness seeming to surround her. With an effort, she made her way to her room. The last thing she remembered was her hand on the bell pull.

When she opened her eyes, she was lying on her bed, the high front of the yellow dress opened. Molly was standing over her, fanning her. She closed her eyes again.

"Dinah! Oh, Dinah, look at me again. Are you all right? What happened?" Molly's anxious voice pierced Dinah's consciousness.

"Oh, Molly!" Dinah raised her head on the pillows.

"Is it Sir Robert . . . the ship . . . Geordie?" Molly asked, picking up one of Dinah's cold hands and rubbing it between her warm ones.

Dinah shook her head. "No. Alexander . . . it's Alexander and . . . and me. We were going to be married, but we . . . we can't, not ever." Dinah closed her eyes again, trying to return to the empty blackness. Instead, she saw Alexander and herself, naked and in each other's arms, his mouth reaching for her breasts, his hand caressing the soft hair at the parting of her thighs. Her eyes opened again.

"Why? What are you talking about?" Molly, not knowing what else to do, was still rubbing Dinah's hand.

Dinah pulled her hand free and struggled to a sitting position, as Molly plumped the pillows behind her. Dinah's eyes burned, but no tears came even during her explanation to Molly, of Alexander's proposal and Lady Janet's revelations.

Molly's eyes grew wider and wider, her own problems fading into the background with Dinah's halting tale of her true history. "But why, why did Sir Robert tell her and not you? If you are his daughter?"

"I don't know." Dinah's head ached, and she raised her hands to let her hair down in a rich, red fall over her shoulders. "I guess because my mother and he were never married. He must have thought I would hate them both for what they had done. Oh God," Dinah moaned, "for what Alexander and I have done."

"All the more reason for you to know, I should

think." Molly's tone was grim, especially with the thought of what could have happened.

"What am I to do? How can I face Lady Janet, Alexander, the others . . ." She knew she would have to face them eventually, but not that night. If only she could talk to someone, someone who was older and her friend. More important, if only Sir Robert would return to tell her himself. An idea began to form, the only solution to the quandary in which she found herself. First, though, she would have to find out about Sir Robert—and to do that, she would need help. There was only one person whom Dinah knew who might be able to help her. She could not go to Rothschild, her first choice, because of Alexander. That left Jennie Churchill, who might be able to enlist the Prince of Wales in her cause without telling him the real reason. She would have to talk to Jennie as soon as possible. Recalling that Jennie, too, was planning a quiet evening, she struggled to her feet.

"Where are you going?" Molly cried. "You must lie down and rest. "I will get you some tea."

"No. Quickly, help me change to a suit and then go and hire a cab," Dinah told her firmly. "I must see Lady Churchill."

"Jennie Jerome? But what can she do?" Molly stuttered.

"I am not sure, but she is my only hope." Filled with determination, her fingers flew at the buttons of her dress.

Molly, her mind still a maze of anguished thoughts, stepped quickly to help her, reacting automatically to her training. Once she had changed her clothes, Dinah sent Molly off to hire the cab and fixed her own hair. The others would be dressing for dinner, and she wanted to get quietly and quickly away without anyone seeing her.

The maid returned to tell her a cab was waiting at the corner. Molly left the room first, making sure no one was in the hall or downstairs. Dinah, following, let herself out the front door. The cab was waiting as

Molly had said, and Dinah gave him the address on Great Cumberland Place.

Only when she was knocking on the door did her determination momentarily flag with the thought that perhaps Lady Jennie could or would do nothing, but it was too late to turn back. Although the butler was surprised to see her again, he let her in the house and sent a maid to give Lady Jennie the message that it was imperative Dinah see her.

To her relief, Dinah was led to Lady Jennie's private sitting room where the older woman took one look at her face, saying, "My dear! What has happened? You are pale as a ghost."

Without indulging in any preliminaries, Dinah quickly told her story, not holding anything back, including the night at the castle on Lochleven. "So, you see, Lady Jennie, it is imperative I speak to Sir Robert. Only he knows the truth with my mother dead—and if that is the truth, then I must live with it. First, I must hear it from his own lips, not second-hand."

"Yes, yes, of course." Lady Jennie shook her head. "But what can I do. I will do all I can . . ."

"Thank you. Here is my plan." Dinah leaned forward eagerly. "Perhaps you can have or ask the Prince of Wales to find out whether Sir Robert is still in East Africa. Couldn't he telegraph, I mean have the Colonial Office . . ."

Lady Jennie nodded. "He can do that, and he will." She pressed her lips together. "You say he went out and was planning to return on the *Star of Scotland?* Well, I shall have Winnie check around first thing in the morning for any news of it. The harbor master at Greenwich might know whether it has been sighted. It will take a few days," she warned. "What will you do in the meantime?"

"I don't know." Dinah realized that she had thought no further than finding Sir Robert. "I must go back, I suppose."

"You could stay here, at least tonight," Lady Jennie offered generously, "if you would prefer."

The temptation was great, not to see Lady Janet

again, not to see Alexander, not to have to face Margaret and Mary as well as Sir Malcolm, all of whom would surely know by now. Then she thought of Alexander, Alexander who had no choice except to have to face them. She could not leave him alone. Let the others take their amusement out on her, not on him. "No. Thank you, Lady Jennie. I must go back."

"Will you be all right? There is room here."

"I am. I cannot let them think that I have run away as my mother did." Dinah raised her head. The tears that wouldn't come before now welled behind her eyes, and she had to force herself not to let the fountain flow.

"Very well. First have supper with me. I was only going to have a tray sent up. It will be no trouble to have one fixed for you, too," Lady Jennie urged.

Dinah agreed, especially after Lady Jennie suggested they write a note to the Prince of Wales to be sent to him that night. The young woman's spirits began to rise under the influence of the older woman's ministrations, the food and the knowledge that they were doing everything that could be done that night. Afterwards, Lady Jennie sent her home with instructions to the coachman to leave the note off at Marlborough House.

To Dinah's relief when she reached Sloane Square, she found Molly waiting outside for her. Molly was in tears as she told her that Lady Janet had wasted no time in telling the others about Alexander and Dinah.

"You should see Mary," Molly moaned. "She is so happy that she cannot even pretend to be sorry."

"And Alexander?" asked Dinah apprehensively.

"After you went upstairs, he left the house. He hasn't come home yet." Molly was wringing her hands.

"Come, Molly," Dinah said calmly. "It will be all right. Let us go inside and I will tell you what I have done."

Molly nodded, leading her to the servants' quarters, telling her that the servants were on her side. None had any sympathy with Lady Janet because of her autocratic ordering them about. Mrs. Jamison, in fact, kissed Dinah's cheek, telling her if she wanted a tray she would bring it herself. Dinah thanked her warmly, telling her she had already dined. Then, using the back stairs with Molly acting as watchman, she slipped into her room without anyone except the servants knowing she had left.

Chapter 21

THE PRINCE OF WALES was so intrigued with Dinah's romantic dilemma that he threw himself into the cause with buoyant enthusiasm. One telegram was sent immediately from the Colonial Office to the British Consul at Mombasa, requesting information. Another telegram was sent to the Suez Canal Administration, inquiring about the *Star of Scotland*. Meanwhile, Winston Churchill had gone to Greenwich, where the harbor master agreed to inform them as soon as he had news of the ship.

Dinah could do no more except wait. She withdrew uneasily into the house at Sloane Square, where the first mood of gloating at her predicament had rapidly faded into strained silence. Even Sir Malcolm had lost his usual ebullience. Alexander was rarely to be seen, spending his days taking care of business and his evenings at one club or another in the company of men. From the servants, Dinah learned that he was usually drunk when he returned at night. Her heart ached for him, and she longed to talk to him and tell him what she was doing but he gave her no opportunity.

As a week passed, Dinah's apparent calm began to fray. Molly watched her, more and more worried, wishing that the *Star of Scotland* would arrive with

Geordie and Ian MacKie to rescue them from what had become a house of torture.

That afternoon, a note arrived from Lady Jennie for Dinah, telling her to come immediately to Great Cumberland Place. To make sure, she had had her coachman deliver the note, with instructions to wait for Dinah. Dinah had been dressing to go for a walk with Molly in order to get away from the oppressive atmosphere of the house. She finished hurriedly, her mind spinning as to what the note meant, afraid it held bad news that Lady Jennie had not wanted to write. On the drive, she began to fear the ship had sunk with all hands.

She was breathless with fear and anticipation as she finally entered Lady Jennie's sitting room. The older woman smiled at her, motioning her to sit down.

"Dinah," her voice was solemn, her face a mask, "I have news from Bertie. He sent it round, soon as he had it."

The young woman's heart pounded as she searched the older one's face for a clue to the news. "Tell me," she said. "I must know . . ."

"Sir Robert," Lady Jennie began slowly, "is still in East Africa, although he has left Mombasa. He has gone inland, to Nairobi, the town at the other end of the railway, because of a lack of information at the coast as to what is needed there."

"Then, he *is* alive," Dinah sighed, relief flooding her until she remembered the ship. "And . . . and the *Star of Scotland*," she managed to say, thinking of Molly.

"She has passed through the canal and is on her way home. She should be in Greenwich any day now," Lady Jennie concluded.

"You mean," Dinah said, "she is overdue."

Lady Jennie nodded. "I am afraid so." She looked at Dinah somberly. "I had hoped for better news. What are you going to do now?"

"Go to Africa," Dinah decided on the spot. "I cannot wait here, not knowing. I must hear the truth from Sir Robert as soon as possible. Will you help me again?"

The older woman sighed. "I cannot dissuade you? While the Cape Colonies are quite civilized, Cecil Rhodes tells me, East Africa is not. A woman alone, as young as you are . . ."

"If you will not help me, I will go to Greenwich and ask for the first ship going to Mombasa," Dinah said firmly.

"Yes, you are quite determined. I suppose I would be in your place, too." Lady Jennie smiled. "Well, I will have Bertie have the Colonial Office wire Mombasa to tell Sir Robert to wait, should he return before you arrive. He can also arrange with the East Africa Company for you to go out as soon as they have a ship sailing."

Dinah nodded. "Thank you, Lady Jennie. I don't know what I would do without you."

The older woman laughed. "You would have found another way, including going to Bertie yourself, I think, Dinah, if you had had to."

Dinah rose. "Thank you again, Lady Jennie."

Back at Sloane Street, she went directly to her room. As she was about to pull the bell to summon Molly, Molly burst through the door excitedly.

"Dinah, Jamison told me you were back." She threw her arms around Dinah, not giving her a chance to say anything. "Geordie's back. He's downstairs. He came here directly after the ship docked."

Dinah caught her breath. "And Ian? Captain Mac-Kie?"

"He's at Greenwich." She noticed the sober expression on Dinah's face. "What happened?"

Dinah told her briefly, adding, "Tell Geordie to get me a cab and give the driver instructions for getting to the ship. "I must see Ian immediately."

Molly's heart skipped a beat. "You're not going to Africa, are you?"

"Yes, I am. I have no other choice. I have to speak to Sir Robert and hear the truth from him. What would you do in my place?"

Molly sighed. "I don't know. The same, I guess."

Dinah smiled, hugging Molly. "Then send Geordie off. I won't need you the rest of the evening."

Molly nodded and hurried out. A few minutes later, Dinah descended the stairs and left, just as Geordie arrived with the carriage.

He helped Dinah into the carriage, saying anxiously, "Do you want me to go with you? The docks are no place for a woman alone."

"No, Geordie." Dinah was firm. "Go to Molly. You have been apart long enough." When Geordie still hesitated, she added, "I'll be all right, truly I will."

During the ride to Greenwich, Dinah had plenty of time to think. First, she would ask Ian about Sir Robert. Then, she would ask him to help her find a ship to Africa, unless, she thought with a beating heart, there was a chance she might convince him to make a return voyage. She smiled at the thought, dismissing it. She could not ask that of him. The ship was his now, and he must sail where he liked, most likely back to Scotland for any repairs necessary and a talk with Sir Robert's shipping agents before deciding on a new cargo.

The carriage entered the dock area. The ships riding at anchor, their sails furled, looked peaceful, but the docks were teeming with sailors on leave and dock workers, rough looking men all and many half-drunk and leering up at the carriage. Dinah pressed against the cushions, trying to hide her face, especially as one roughneck tried to stop the horse, shouting and cursing drunkenly. The driver whipped the horse into a trot that sent the man reeling backward.

When the carriage eventually stopped, Dinah peered out into the dusk. To her relief, there was the familiar mermaid on the prow and the gold letters reading *Star of Scotland*. Asking the coachman to wait for a moment and paying him only half what he asked to make sure he did wait, Dinah hurried toward the gangplank, holding her cloak tightly around her. A sailor stopped her as she tried to climb the gangplank, hesitation on his face about leaving his post as Dinah asked him to go for Captain Mac-Kie. At the hesitation, her heart beat faster. What if Ian were not here! That thought had not occurred to her before.

"The captain's here, isn't he?" she asked urgently.

"Aye, Ma'am, but he left word not to be disturbed," the sailor said with a dubious tone in his voice, obviously surprised at seeing a woman on the ship.

"He will not mind, I promise," Dinah pressed. "Tell him that Miss Murray wishes to see him."

"Aye." The sailor glanced down at the dock, where a curious crowd of ruffians had gathered. "You better come below and wait."

Dinah nodded, surprising the sailor, whom she had not recognized, with her familiarity with the ship as she moved toward the companionway. Just inside the doorway, she stopped, watching the sailor pass her to knock on the captain's door. What memories flooded back, the dinners in the cabin, the first passionate embrace with Alexander. Tears welled in her eyes and she knew she had to reach Sir Robert.

The sailor entered the cabin. Dinah closed her eyes, crossing her fingers. Within seconds, Ian was there in front of her. He took one look at her face and enfolded her in his arms.

"Dinah, my dear, how very good to see you!"

"Oh, Ian!" The unshed tears poured down her face, as she handed the sailor the money to pay off the carriage.

Ian took her into the cabin, seating her in his chair and getting her a small glass of cognac as he waited for her to pull herself together. Dinah sipped the brandy, studying his face, the blue eyes with the engraved lines at the corners, the sensitive mouth, the blond hair hastily brushed back with a lock falling down on his forehead.

She took a deep breath, telling him quickly about Sir Robert's being her father and about Lady Janet, omitting for the moment any mention of Alexander. "So you see Ian, I have to talk to Sir Robert, to find out myself, to find out why he couldn't tell me himself."

"I understand that." The blue eyes studied her. '"but why have you come here this evening? You could have sent a message. Not," he added hastily, "that I am not glad, happy, to see you."

Dinah avoided his eyes. "I must go to Africa. Sir Robert may be there for months . . ."

"Dinah, Dinah, Africa is no place for a woman. A few months can't matter," he said, puzzled at her intensity.

"I must go, Ian. Besides," she smiled, "the Prince of Wales is having the Colonial Office wire Mombasa to tell him to wait for me."

He shook his head, bemused. "I don't know what to say. What can I do? You must have some idea in mind to come here at this hour."

"Ian," Dina went to where he was standing and took his hands in hers, "help me find a ship going as soon as possible to Africa."

"No, that I cannot do." He put his arms around her, holding her close. "I am sailing to Africa in a fortnight's time, as soon as my cargo is unloaded and a new cargo is abroad. You will go with me—or you will not go at all."

"Oh, Ian!" Dinah kissed the cheek next to hers impulsively. "You mean it—you will take me with you?"

"On one condition." Ian took her shoulders and forced her to look into his eyes."

"Yes?"

"That you do not go alone, that Molly come with you—or someone else, if you prefer, as I am not sure Geordie is going to make this trip with me. He and Molly . . ."

"I know." Dinah sighed. "It's time for them to marry." She shook her head, "But I don't know anyone else, and I cannot ask them to wait to marry." Dinah protested.

"Then I will. After all," Ian pointed out, "they will

be together on the ship. Perhaps they could even marry first."

"I cannot ask Molly," Dinah said firmly.

"Then, I will ask Geordie." MacKie was equally firm. "Now, come, I will send someone to fetch a carriage and take you home."

"That's not necessary," Dinah protested. 'I came alone . . ."

"Which Geordie should not have let you do. No, Dinah, I will not let anything happen to you." He picked up his uniform jacket. "Wait here, and I will be back shortly."

After he had sent one of the men hanging around the ship off to fetch a carriage, he returned, telling her he had arranged also for a watchman for the ship. Then, he asked her about London.

Dinah's relating of the parties and of the people whom she had met lasted through the arrival of the carriage and all the way back to London. The captain was amused, shaking his head now and then at the easy way in which she mentioned the Prince of Wales, Lady Jennie, Rothschild and others in the same breath. At the house, he was about to tell the carriage to wait when Dinah insisted that he stay the night.

"Ian, there is plenty of room, and Alexander will be glad to see you." She omitted any mention of the fact that he was rarely at the house nowadays. "I will speak to Mrs. Jamison."

Ian hesitated, looking at her face. It was a pale circle in the light of the gas lamp flickering overhead. "You have not told me everything, have you, Dinah?" he guessed.

"No. Not quite. But stay with us tonight, Ian," she urged.

"Very well." He paid the driver and dismissed the carriage, while Dinah went to the front door and knocked.

Jamison opened the door. "Good evening, Miss Dinah." He glanced from her to the captain following her up the steps.

"Captain MacKie will be spending the night with us,

Jamison. Will you tell Mrs. Jamison to prepare a room?" Dinah's voice brooked no refusal. "Is Lady Janet here?" she asked, dreading that encounter.

"They have gone out for dinner. I will ask Mrs. Jamison to prepare something for you, if you like," suggested the butler.

"Please. We can have it in the library." She started for the room, stopping to ask, "Are Molly and Mate Campbell here?"

"Yes, Miss Dinah." The butler's usually imperturbably expression gave way to curiosity.

"Then, ask them to come to the library." Dinah hoped that Molly would forgive her for the interruption. "This way," she said to Ian, opening the door to the library.

While they waited, she offered Ian a whiskey and poured a sherry for herself. The only obstacle to her journey was Alexander, to whom she would have to speak. Of course, she would also have to tell Lady Janet, but she was no obstacle as far as Dinah was concerned. She had come this far, and no one as trivial as Lady Janet or Margaret was going to stop her now.

When Jamison returned with a tray, followed by Geordie and Molly, Dinah told Jamison to get a message to Alexander, telling him MacKie was here and she had to see him. Taking a deep breath, she turned to the others.

"Molly," Dinah began, "I am going to Africa to find Sir Robert. I have to hear from him that he is my father. Ian has consented to take me when he returns with a cargo in a fortnight, with the provision that I do not go alone."

Molly looked from Dinah to MacKie and then to Geordie, dismay and conflict showing in her face. "Dinah, you cannot go alone!"

"That's what Ian says." Dinah moved to Molly and took her hands. "Molly, I do not want to ask you to go with me, to ask you to wait."

Molly nodded miserably, "Dinah . . ."

Ian, to give Molly a chance to think, said to Geordie, "I know you were not sure about signing on as mate for another voyage, Geordie. If you do, I will make sure you have a bonus at the end that will provide for that house you want to buy."

"Oh, Moll!" Geordie put his arm around the young girl's shoulder. "Our house!"

Molly sighed. She looked at Dinah and then at Geordie. "Dinah, Geordie and me, we have to talk. You have your supper." She drew Geordie to a corner by the windows.

Dinah and Ian sat down by the table where Jamison had placed the tray containing cold meats and sandwiches and a pot of coffee. "You would do that for me, Ian," she wondered, "give Geordie a bonus to buy a house?"

"I would do that and more, Dinah." The captain picked up a sandwich. "Now, tell me what the real reason is for this urgency."

"I will, Ian, I promise, but not right now. Once we have sailed . . . I must speak to Alexander first," she added.

"Very well. I still am not satisfied, but . . . but I love you, Dinah, far too much to refuse the help you ask of me." He made the statement calmly, aware that its meaning would not be lost on Dinah.

Dinah's hand trembled as she poured the coffee. "Thank you, Ian." She raised her amber eyes to his. "You are a true friend."

Molly returned, sitting on the floor in front of Dinah with Geordie beside her. "Dinah, Captain Mac-Kie," she said slowly, "Geordie and I have decided we will go with you. I cannot leave Dinah, not now when she needs me so much."

"You could marry before we leave?" Dinah suggested.

Molly shook her head. "We'll wait. We have a lifetime ahead of us. Besides, I would like to be married in Edinburgh with Geordie's sister there." Tears welled in Molly's eyes.

"Then, so you will be," Dinah assured her. "In the meantime, you are sure about coming with me?"

Molly nodded. "I cannot leave you now. Both Geordie and I agree on that. Once this matter is settled . . ." She stopped.

After Geordie and Molly left, Dinah asked Ian about his voyage as they finished supper. Before they went to their rooms, Dinah spoke to Jamison again, repeating her message about Alexander.

At the head of the stairs, Ian kissed her goodnight. "Dinah, I will have to leave early in the morning to get back to the ship, long before you are up. Whether I will get into London again or not, I am not sure, but Sir Robert's agents and Alexander can give you all the information you and Molly need to know about the sailing. At least, I will instruct the agents to do that." He paused, adding, "There is nothing more you want to tell me now?"

"I cannot, Ian." Dinah laid her cheek against the man's face. "If I could, I would."

"Then, I will wait until we are aboard the ship." He kissed her again. "Sleep well, my dear."

Dinah went to bed, although she did not sleep. She lay awake long after the others came home, waiting for Alexander and finally falling into a fitful doze. When she arose in the morning, Ian had already left. To her dismay, she found Alexander had not returned home. With a sigh, she wrote a note to be sent to Lady Jennie to tell her of her new plans and then summoned Molly. Between the two of them, they decided what to pack for the journey. Dinah told Molly not to mention a word about where they were going. If any questions were asked, she was to say that she assumed they were returning to Scotland. "First," Dinah said, "I must tell Alexander. He must not find out from anyone else."

Yet, the days passed, and Alexander did not come to her. When Dinah could wait no longer, she told Jamison that she needed the carriage one afternoon and went to the company's offices in the City. A startled Alexander admitted her to his private office.

"Please sit down, Dinah," he invited.

Dinah sat down, studying him. She was filled with pity at the changes in him. His face was haggard; his eyes, bloodshot; and his hands, trembling. "Oh Alexander," she moaned, "what has happened to you?"

"Nothing. I—I have been working quite hard recently," he explained.

"And going to your club at night?" she asked.

"That, my dear, is my business. Now, what have you come here to see me about? There has been no word from my . . . our father," he said.

"But I have had word." Briefly, she told him what she had learned.

The young man leaned back in his chair, his lips twisting in a smile. "You have done that? Gone to Lady Jennie and asked her to talk to Bertie?" He shook his head. "You amaze me, although I should not be surprised any more at anything that concerns you. Why did you do that?"

"Because I must hear it from Sir Robert's lips."

"Surely, you do not think that Lady Janet would make up such a lie, knowing he might contradict it on his return?" His eyes narrowed.

"I don't know." Dinah hesitated, thinking of the ideas that had come to her during the long nights she had lain awake. "Alexander," she leaned forward, "what if she did not tell all the truth? I cannot believe that your father . . . mine, too . . . if you will, would encourage us to be together, that he would leave like that."

"How could he know I loved you?" Alexander's tone was bitter. "No, Dinah, you are going on a wild goose chase. I should forbid it."

Dinah stood up. "It will do no good. I am determined to go, Alexander. Promise me." How she wanted to go to him, to kiss him, to smoothe away the lines on his face! Instead, he took a deep breath, "Promise me, you will take care of yourself, stop this drinking . . ."

"I promise nothing!" Alexander turned his back on her. "If you have said what you came here for, please leave." When he turned around again he looked as though he were dying.

Dinah left, tears in her eyes. That evening, she informed Lady Janet of her plans. The woman protested vehemently, threatening to lock her in her room. Dinah laughed at her.

"Lady Janet, I am determined to go. Besides, Alexander knows I am going, and he is not the only one. So does Lady Churchill and the Prince of Wales himself!" Dinah smiled, seeing the astonishment and anger on Lady Janet's face. "I would like to hear what you are going to tell Bertie," she used the name deliberately, "after he has done so much to help me."

"Malcolm," Lady Janet appealed weakly.

The florid man had a slight smile on his face. "There is nothing I can do, my wife." He turned to Dinah. "I congratulate you, Dinah, you have laid your plans well. My wife will not stop you. If you are so determined, you will find another way. I wish," he added wistfully, "that you had taken me in your confidence and that I could go with you!"

"Well, Dinah," Lady Janet said, pointedly ignoring her husband, "I hope you realize you are being most inconsiderate—and of Sir Robert too. You were to be presented to Queen Victoria in a fortnight, along with Margaret and Mary. Surely, you do not mean to give up that honor?"

"I do." How could Dinah explain how little the honor meant to her in comparison to the truth she had to hear from Sir Robert.

Lady Janet was still not through. "Sir Robert will be most disappointed in you. The Queen rarely grants such privileges nowadays."

"When I explain to him the reason, I am sure he will understand," Dinah replied, hoping that he would.

Lady Janet laughed shortly. "You are more than inconsiderate—you are stupid. You will hear only what I have already told you. In your heart, you know that. Why would I ever make up such a story, if it were not true?"

Lady Janet was right, Dinah knew. The girl turned away, not wanting Lady Janet to see the doubt in her face. At the same time, she knew more than ever that she had to hear it from Sir Robert and know the reason why he had never told Alexander or her.

PART III

Africa and London—
1897-1898

Chapter 22

THE VOYAGE TO Africa had none of the air of excitement that had characterized Dinah's voyage from New York. Memories of that trip haunted her, filling her with apprehension, regardless of any attempt by the captain and the others to cheer her up. Every step, in fact, seemed haunted by the ghost of Alexander stalking just behind her. As a result, she retreated into silent communion with her own thoughts, leaving Ian and Molly to gaze at her with worried eyes.

The bleakness of her thoughts deepened as the ship passed through the Suez Canal. She had no interest in the skill required to navigate the locks and, instead, chafed impatiently at the time required to make the slow trip. Nor did she take any interest in the scenery. The distant temples and pyramids on the Egyptian side were one with the vast expanse of the Sinai Desert on the other.

Day after day, she stared moodily over the rail, paying no attention to the increasingly worried MacKie and Molly. By that point, she had given up thinking about the future or even the past and was concentrating on Mombasa where she hoped Sir Robert would be waiting for her. She had asked herself too many times whether Lady Janet had lied, tried too many times to guess what purpose such a lie, which could be all too easily shown for what it was, could serve. That left only the supposition that the truth was that she and Alexander *were* sister and brother. But in that case, why had Sir Robert not told them? It was far too late to protect her mother's reputation, leaving only the idea that Sir Robert was covering up his own weakness. Yet, that did not seem right either. Could he simply have ignored the letter from Mrs. Bradley about her mother's dying and her existence?

After the ship had traversed the Red Sea and rounded the hump of Africa to head south for Mombasa, Dinah's fears intensified. On the one hand she wanted the journey over, while on the other she wanted to sail on forever. They were in the Indian Ocean now, where Arab dhows plied the slave and spice routes to the Arabian peninsula. Even though slavery had been outlawed in British East Africa in 1890, the law had little effect on the Arab slavers who simply transported their African captives to Arabia.

At Mombasa, much to Dinah's dismay, they were forced to stand off the port overnight. Mombasa itself was an island with several harbors: one on the east side of the island; one on the west, Port Kilindini, a more sheltered harbor; a third, Port Reitz, an inland habor reached by a channel from Port Kilindini; and a fourth, Port Tudor, also on the east, which was landlocked and reached by a winding channel. The last was impractical for a ship like the *Star of Scotland*. For the moment, MacKie had chosen Mombasa harbor itself, as it was the closest to the town of Mombasa.

After he had anchored as close to shore as possible, MacKie turned to Dinah, saying, "As soon as I have a boat lowered, I will send a sailor to the office of the East Africa Company's administrator with a message. Do you want to write a note or shall I?"

"I will." Dinah went to her cabin. She had already prepared a note, telling who she was and what she wanted. Slipping it into an envelope, she also enclosed a letter of introduction from the Prince of Wales. As she did, she smiled. No one could ignore his request to lend her all assistance as a personal favor.

She returned to the deck so quickly that the boat was still in its blocks. "Here, Ian." She handed him the note. "Make sure the sailor waits for an answer. I have asked for an audience as soon as possible."

Dinah's face was cold, giving little indication of the turmoil inside her that made her heart beat chokingly fast. Watching the boat row to shore, there was little to see. Somehow she had expected a port much like the one at Bermuda.

What she saw was a low-lying coastline, studded here and there were palm trees. The town was made up of white-washed one and two story houses with flimsy roofs, and a few cultivated patches of green in an otherwise sandy landscape. Her heart sank at the dismal prospect that it seemed to offer not one of even minimum comfort. The climate was equally oppressive, hot and humid, and her clothes were clinging to her body.

She began to pace the deck, trying to catch any breeze that might be around. MacKie, meanwhile, had rigged a sail over the deck to act as a shade. Molly was seated under it, fanning herself, watching Dinah anxiously and waiting for Geordie who had gone ashore with the boat to arrange for the unloading of the cargo.

Time seemed endless, the ship suspended among gently slapping waves, the only sound the distant shouts in a language Dinah could not understand that carried across the still waters. "How long do you think it will take for an answer?" Molly asked, putting the fan down to wipe her face.

"I don't know. Surely, the administrator will not ignore the Prince of Wales." Dinah tried to put more confidence in her voice than she felt at that moment.

"No," Molly agreed, "he won't do that. Perhaps, too, Sir Robert is already here, and the sailor has gone to fetch him."

"Perhaps." Dinah refused to let herself even think of that possibility. At this point, it was better not to raise her hopes too high. She rose, going to the rail to look for the boat, hearing voices.

A dhow had pulled alongside and was offering fresh pineapples and coconuts to the crew. Dinah studied the occupants. They were wearing long-sleeved white robes, similar to an English nightgown, except the waists were belted with a rope. Into the belt-like arrangement was stuck a knife with a curved, evil-looking blade. The men were barefoot and wore white skullcaps that did nothing to protect their swarthy, leathery skin from the sun. As she watched, one man took a coconut, cracking it open in even halves with sharp blow of his knife. Dinah shivered and returned to her seat under the awning.

Fortunately, she did not have much longer to wait. MacKie, who had been on the foredeck going over arrangements for unloading the cargo once Geordie returned, came to tell her the boat was approaching the ship. Dinah went to the rail eagerly, as the sailor climbed up a rope ladder that had been slung over the side for him. He saluted the captain and Dinah, handing her a note.

Dinah took it, her heart now hammering in her chest and her hands shaking so that she had to hand it to MacKie to open it. "Please read it to me," she begged.

The administrator told her that he would help her all he could. He had had no word from Sir Robert, but he would be pleased to have her for his guest at luncheon. He would expect her at one, unless she sent word that it was inconvenient.

MacKie handed her the note, which she re-read. Now her fears were realized. "Oh, Ian, where is Sir Robert?" she cried.

"I don't know, Dinah." The man felt sorry for her, but he was reluctant to put his arm around her in front of the watching sailors.

Dinah straightened her back. "Well, I shall discuss that at luncheon." She hesitated, thinking of the men in the dhow. "You will go with me, won't you, Ian?"

"Of course. I had no intention of letting you go ashore alone." He looked at her solicitously. "Do you think you can manage the ladder?"

Dinah smiled for the first time in weeks. "If I must,

I can. First let me change to something simpler, then we can leave."

Dinah changed quickly to a dark skirt that did not require more than one petticoat and a loose blouse. Taking a big hat with her and a parasol for the sun, she returned to the deck where MacKie, having left word for Geordie to proceed with the unloading, was waiting. He climbed down the ladder first and took her hat and parasol from her. Molly and a sailor helped her over the railing on the ladder. It swayed under her, seeming very fragile and inadequate. But, Dinah thought, if it would hold Ian and the sailors, it would hold her, too. She groped carefully down the rope ladder, as a sailor steadied it from below and Ian held up his arms to help her as soon as she was in reach. Dinah reached the boat and seated herself with a sigh.

"Good lass," murmured the man.

The boat pulled into a small dock, where Dinah and the captain waited for a sailor to find some transportation. Mombasa, so far, seemed a city of men. Most were Arabs, wearing either the white gown or a looser black robe. All were carrying knives, and a few were wearing turbans instead of skullcaps. The rest of the men were black. To Dinah's eyes, used to New York and Victorian Edinburgh and London, they seemed naked in the single piece of cloth tied at one shoulder that they were wearing. She stared at the muscled, rippling black calves and arms in fascination. Although Ian had warned her, it was one thing to hear about their clothing and another to see it. Her face, flushed from the heat, flushed a deeper rose shade.

The sailor returned with a rickety cart. Dinah looked at it in dismay, as Ian climbed up to sit next to the Arab driver and then helped Dinah mount to sit beside him. She had already donned her hat, and now she raised her parasol as much to shield off the insolent stares of the men as to protect herself from the sun.

The administrator's house was a long, low building with a veranda. An Arab servant silently admitted them, leading them to a parlor with windows on two sides to catch as much of a breeze as possible. The windows were covered with narrow slatted blinds that not only kept out the heat of the sun but also prevented the larger insects from flying in.

The administrator, a short, wiry, middle-aged man with a leathery tanned complexion, joined them almost immediately. He offered Dinah sherry and poured whiskey for Ian and himself, before giving Dinah as much information as he had.

After he had received the cable, he had inquired from the Arab liwalis or headmen of any news they might have heard of Sir Robert. "As far as I know," he finished, "he is still at Nairobi. If you wish to write, I will arrange for the letter to go with the next group of soldiers or workers going that way."

Dinah frowned, thinking. The mention of soldiers reminded her of James Angus, and she asked, "There were some soldiers who sailed with Sir Robert. One, James Angus, is a friend of the family. Do you know where I might find him?"

"There is only a small garrison here, Miss Murray, and I know all of them, so I can tell you he is not here. As far as I know, the soldiers that arrived were sent to guard the railroad, as there had been a minor uprising among the Samburu and Masai. Sir Robert, in fact, took advantage of their orders to travel with them. I will send someone now, however," he added, "to ask the colonel for what news he has of Angus or Sir Robert, if you wish. It won't take long."

"Please do," Dinah urged.

Over luncheon, he asked Dinah about London. She answered as best she could, being fascinated by the dishes prepared by his Indian cook: Mulligatawny soup, followed by curry of lamb with chutney, and fresh fruits. Her thoughts kept her busy, too. Unless there were word of James Angus when the messenger returned, she resolved that she would have to go to Nairobi. She had not come this far to wait for several more weeks for an answer. Then, too, she could not ask MacKie to stay on with the *Star of Scotland* any longer than was necessary.

They were drinking their coffee when the messenger returned. James Angus was at Nairobi.

Dinah listened, glancing at MacKie whose face had a worried expression. Before either of the men could say anything, she said firmly, "I see. Then, I must go to Nairobi, too."

Both MacKie and the administrator gaped at her, before each came up with his reasons as to why it was impossible for her to do so: The trip was dangerous; it would take time to get bearers and the equipment necessary; it was impossible for a woman to go alone; Sir Robert could well be returning momentarily.

Dinah took the last objection first. "From what you have said, the route is a well-traveled one. If Sir Robert were on his way, we would meet one another, would we not?"

"True," the administrator admitted, "but I cannot be a party to such a trip. There are the natives to consider. The Masai, a very warlike tribe, constantly raiding other tribes for cattle and slaves, have been active. And then, there are wild animals . . ."

"I am sure there are responsible people who will make the trip for money. As Administrator for the Imperial British East Africa Company, you surely know one person at least," she said firmly. On an impulse, she added with a smile, "I would hate to tell Bertie, the Prince of Wales, I mean, that there is not one person—"

"Captain MacKie," the administrator appealed, "cannot you dissuade Miss Murray? You have been here before. You have seen the liwalis. They will promise anything, although living up to their word is another matter."

"So I have learned in contracting with them for men to unload. Dinah, please."

"Very well." Dinah rose to her feet. "If you will not help me, I must throw myself on the mercy of these liwalis."

The administrator paled at the suggestion. The

liwalis thought women only good for two purposes, the slaves to work on the shambas or plantations and their own women to be kept out of the sight of all male eyes except their own. He gave in, in the hope of delaying the trip long enough to give Sir Robert time to reach Mombasa.

MacKie immediately proposed accompanying Dinah, refusing to let her make the trip without him. He dismissed his ship with a heavy heart, insisting Geordie would be in command until they returned.

Before Dinah and MacKie left, the administrator promised to start making arrangements and to let them know daily, as Dinah insisted, how the plans were progressing. At the door, Dinah said with a smile, "I shall hope to leave in a week's time, and I shall be sure to let the Prince know how helpful you have been."

On the way back to the ship in the administrator's carriage, MacKie tried once more to dissuade Dinah. The more he talked, however, the more stubborn she became. Dinah, in fact, was barely listening to his objections. She was already thinking ahead, to the day of departure.

At first, Molly insisted on accompanying Dinah. "We've been together ever since we left New York," Molly told her tearfully. "I cannot leave you alone now!"

"No, Molly," Dinah said gently, "I will not let you go with me. If the trip is as dangerous as they say, two women will be in the way. It may be difficult enough to get bearers and guards for one. You must stay here with Geordie." An idea came to her. "I understand there is a minister from the Missionary Society near here. We could send word, and perhaps the two of you could be married before we left."

Molly shook her head. "Geordie and I have waited this long." She looked out at the long, low, alien country with a shudder. "We will wait until we are back in Scotland."

Dinah and Molly spent the next few days finding a wardrobe suitable for the climate. An Indian tailor made up lightweight cotton skirts and jackets that could be worn with their blouses. He also provided mosquito netting to be draped over their hats, as even on the ship the insects settled in with a vengeance at sunset. The same netting was used to drape over the bunks at night. From him, Dinah learned of a bootmaker who fitted both Dinah and Ian out with low boots that the administrator was sure they would need on their safari. In the meantime, a liwali whom he particularly trusted because of past services, lined up fifteen bearers and two askari, or native soldiers, as well as an interpreter and guide who would be in charge of the expedition. His office also saw to the buying of necessary supplies and tents. The most important item was trading goods for natives they might meet along the way. In addition, he suggested that Ian bring a rifle and carry a pistol.

On the morning that the safari was due to depart, Dinah rose early. At breakfast, aboard ship, Captain MacKie gave last minute instructions to Geordie. Afterwards, Molly bade Dinah a tearful farewell. Then Ian and Dinah climbed down the rope ladder into the waiting boat. As the sailors rowed to shore, Dinah, who was facing the stern, watched the *Star of Scotland* riding at its anchor.

The ship looked graceful in the morning light, as she swung gently from her moorings. Her masts raked the dawn light, the furled sails glowing pink. Dinah closed her eyes to hold back the tears. So much of her life was tied up with the ship and, she thought, with Mac-Kie who was sitting opposite her. As if guessing her thoughts, he took her hand in his and squeezed it gently. Dinah opened her eyes to smile at him.

When they landed, the administrator and the liwali were waiting for them, with the safari party just beyond. Again, there was a last-minute reviewing of the details of the march and instructions. The chief bearer was a tall muscular man with the bearing of a chief, named M'Doro. The guide who would lead the Safari was an Arab, Ali bin Jumah. Both greeted MacKie, refusing to look Dinah in the face, calling him Bwana, the Swahili word for master. Dinah, they referred to as Memsahib, an Indian word, making Dinah wonder whether there was a female equivalent to bwana in Swahili.

After the administrator had made the introductions, he approached Dinah, drawing her aside, "Miss Murray, once more, let me beg you to give up this trip. It is still not too late. You can pay the men off with a little money and the trading goods, and they will be satisfied."

"No." Dinah shook her head to emphasize her word of refusal. "Thank you for your concern, but it is imperative that I speak to Sir Robert as soon as possible. As you say, it is conceivable that we may even meet along the way."

"Very well. I hope sincerely that you will meet." The man shook her hand. "Good luck, Miss Murray, although I hope you won't need it."

His words struck a chill in Dinah's heart, as she turned to look at her companions. Ali bin Jumah had left off the traditional robe for English riding breeches and boots, although he still wore his turban. M'Doro, on the other hand, was wearing the native robe, tied at one shoulder. His one concession was a pair of sandals. The two askari were wearing a kind of uniform with khaki trousers and high-buttoned khaki jackets, although they were barefoot, and carrying a rifle apiece. Their black faces were shining in the rising sun. The bearers were dressed the same as M'Doro. As she looked at them, however, they bent down to pick up large bundles and boxes, which they balanced atop their heads with one hand.

Dinah smiled at MacKie who was watching her. "It's time to leave," she said softly.

Chapter 23

THE SAFARI FOLLOWED the route of the railroad
through the coastal lowlands. The sandy coast gave
way to lush tropics, palm trees growing in clumps
amid high grasses. Here and there, stagnant pools
of water provided ideal breeding grounds for the insects that swarmed around anything that moved. Dinah
quickly lowered the mosquito netting that Molly had
stitched to the wide-brimmed hat she was wearing,
wondering how the natives could walk at such a brisk
pace, never pausing to brush the flies and mosquitoes
from their faces and near-naked bodies.

The first night was spent at Makupa, a small town
at the western edge of Mombasa island. From there,
boats took them to the mainland itself, where the
administrator had several donkeys waiting. Both Dinah and MacKie gladly alternated between riding
and walking. Unlike the bearers and Ali bin Jumah,
they were not used to walking all day, especially over
uneven terrain. With the help of the donkeys, however, the group was able to reach Sungali, another
town on the railroad line, the second night.

The local liwali turned his small house over to
them. It was not much of a house even by Scottish
peasant standards, merely four walls of sun-baked
mud, painted white and a thatched roof. The main
room consisted of a hard-packed dirt floor around
which were scattered low benches and a wealth of
pillows. In the rear room was a large wooden bed
frame on which were piled none-too-clean covers,
over which was hung a mosquito netting. Distasteful

as the bed was, MacKie insisted she take it because of the netting that offered protection from the mosquitoes and other insects while he slept on a settee in the front room.

As Dinah and MacKie grew used to walking, donkeys or not, the length of the daily treks increased. On the third day, they opted to push on farther and spend the night in the bush, rather than in the village of Mwachi, even though they knew there would not be another village for many miles and Mwachi was the last chance to sleep under a roof instead of a tent. Besides, each additional mile covered meant one less mile to travel to Nairobi.

When they finally drew to a halt an hour before nightfall, the bearers quickly erected the tents and lit cooking fires while M'Doro went to a nearby stream for water to boil for tea. He was back with the water on the run, warning Ali bin Jumah, Dinah, and MacKie to beware of bathing in the stream and the lake into which it flowed because of crocodiles along the banks.

Ali bin Jumah suggested that MacKie and Dinah might want to have a look at them before the light faded. With both men carrying rifles, the three set out for the spot where the stream fed into the small lake. The bank had been eroded during the wet seasons until some of the trees had fallen into the lake. Until Ali fired a shot, all Dinah saw were the scattered logs. Then, one of the logs moved. The crocodile had been sunning itself in the setting sun. With the shot, the carved back of the reptile and its long snout rose on short, stubby legs. The mouth opened to reveal gaping jaws filled with sharp, wicked-looking teeth. The animal snapped at them before waddling to the water and slipping under the surface, leaving only the nostrils visible. Dinah shuddered, looking around and realizing that other logs were also actually crocodiles.

"Hippo, too!" Ali grinned as proudly as a magician making a coin appear from out of nowhere and pointed toward the center of the lake.

311

"Oh, Ian!" Dinah cried, as the water horse nearest the shore, pink mouth agape, swam curiously toward them. The small round ears wiggled innocently above the wide-set pop eyes. Behind it, other hippos rose out of the water, only to dive again beneath the surface.

The hippos stayed in the water during the sunlight hours, Ali explained, leaving it only at nightfall to feed voraciously on the grasses of the surrounding country side. Despite their huge size and lumbering gait, they often traveled many miles before returning to the water at dawn.

Walking back to the camp in the short dusk before the sun dropped quickly below the horizon, the impact of Africa—its vastness and the strangeness of its animals—finally struck Dinah. Here, animals were the predators and in control, invading the precincts of man. It was the opposite of Scotland where man was the predator, using both ingenuity and blunt means to capture his quarry. Here she felt insignificant, her problems unimportant against the background of the life and death struggle for survival around her. She sighed, reminding herself of the importance of the matter that had brought her here. She had to save Alexander from himself and to do that she had to know why Alexander, at least, had not been told about their relationship. And increasingly she could not still her fear that something might happen to Sir Robert before she found out.

That night, as she lay in the tent, she was aware that the darkness was far from silent in the wilds. There was a constant rustling of the grasses, accompanied by strange grunting sounds, both near and far, that she assumed were the hippos at their nightly feeding. Just as she was falling asleep, a distant coughing roar awakened her. Her body tensed, as she recalled Ali bin Jumah talking at dinner about lions. When the roar was not repeated, she gradually relaxed. She finally fell asleep with the hope that she would grow accustomed to the strange sounds.

The trail they were following climbed leisurely toward the highlands, the palms and dense tropic undergrowth giving way to plains. Here and there were clumps of acacias, the tops of the trees flat as if supporting the table of the sky. Now and again, they passed a baobab, a tree sacred to the Africans. Some baobabs were centuries old with huge gnarled trunks and branches reaching aimlessly toward the heavens. They also passed the remains of native shambas or villages, their bomas or thornbush fences half collapsed and the baked mud or grass huts teeming with insects. The days were hot now, the nights turning cool with the setting sun. The stars, even at sea, had never seemed so bright and so close. When she mentioned it to MacKie, he told her it was because they were so close to the equator.

The plains of the grasslands were alive with herds of grazing animals, from tiny, deer-like dik-diks to massive cow-like elands. Herds of gazelles leaped and frolicked amid the placidly feeding zebras which looked much like Scottish highland ponies, despite their black and white striped coats. Gnus stared at them with bearded faces. Every night now was punctuated by the roars of lions, their yellow coats fading into the grass as they slept the day away. Of the big cats, Ali told them, only the cheetahs hunted by day.

The cheetah was a solitary hunter, Dinah learned as they paused to rest one noon. Nearby a herd of small gazelles with black and white stripes along their golden flanks and tails that flicked with the regularity of metronomes was grazing. Suddenly, the herd raised its heads as one, peering around before leaping off in panic. As the gazelles raced away, a straggler fell behind. Dinah saw the reason for the panic. Lying flat in the grass was a cheetah, its small ears laid back on the blunt head. How beautiful it was, with black tear marks under its eyes, its powerful shoulders, and golden body with its tracing of spots. In that instant, the cheetah was on its feet, spurting in a flat, elongated leap after the gazelle until it caught up with it, bringing it down by the neck.

That afternoon, they also saw their first herd of

elephants. The huge gray beasts were plodding in a straight line at an angle to the safari, each elephant following the one in front of it, like their safari itself. A large bull paused to watch the safari. It fanned its huge ears out, lowering its head, its long, curved ivory tusks menacing them, and swinging its trunk as if annoyed by the scent it caught. Everyone froze into stillness. The elephant's small eyes studied them, seeming to measure the danger. It raised its trunk, bellowing at them, the bellow echoing out of massive lungs, as it started to charge them. While the bearers and the askari scattered, Dinah stood frozen. Both Ali and MacKie reached for their rifles, Ali shouting to MacKie to aim between the eyes.

Even before the men could raise their rifles, the charge stopped as suddenly as it had begun. The elephant, now a moving mountain of docility, padded off to take its place at the end of the line. The herd moved majestically off into the distance.

Ali grinned nervously, trying to tell them that there had actually been no danger, that elephants often made a false charge to frighten off danger before it could become dangerous. Dinah and MacKie glanced at one another and nodded, but MacKie walked close to Dinah the rest of the afternoon, offering her the protection of his broad-shouldered body.

In the evening, as night settled in with its noises and the stars and moon came out in equatorial brilliance, Dinah and MacKie stayed by the fire. Ali had shot a gazelle for their dinner and had left them to distribute the leftovers to the rest of the safari.

"It's so beautiful, so awesome," Dinah said. "I'm glad I came, whatever lies at the end of the journey."

"Aye, it's all of that," MacKie agreed, pausing to light his pipe as he watched the firelight flickering on her face and setting her hair aflame. "Dinah . . ."

"Yes?" She smiled at him. "Thank you, Ian, for coming with me, for today. You have been so much more than a friend, and I have treated you unkindly at times. That elephant . . . If anything had happened to you," her voice faltered. In that moment, the stead-

314

fastness of her purpose in coming to Africa had blurred in the surge of emotion that overwhelmed her at the fear of what might happen, not to her but to Ian.

The captain puffed on his pipe for a moment, watching her and trying to read her thoughts. When she didn't go on, he said slowly, "Surely, my dear, you are aware that it was not only out of friendship that I insisted on coming with you. I have told you that I love you, Dinah."

"Please, Ian," the girl protested, turning away her head.

"No. You asked me to wait, and now I have waited long enough. Once before, I asked you to marry me," he reminded her. "I was patient then, letting too much time and too many voyages come between us."

"I know. I remember," she whispered, looking at the fire and seeing the cozy parlor of the little house in the lane near the castle in Edinburgh.

"Over the past few weeks," he went on, "we have been together as never before. How I wish I had the words to express my admiration for your courage and determination, my love for you. But I am no Alexander."

"Please!" Dinah interrupted him quickly, trying to ignore the mention of Alexander's name re-opening the wound in her heart until it was as fresh as the day that Lady Janet had flayed her with the truth about her real relationship with Alexander. The farther she came, the more she realized that perhaps she would learn nothing more than what she already knew. At the same time, the reason why Sir Robert had concealed the relationship while encouraging them to be together became ever more important. That reason totally consumed her, forcing her to say, "Ian, now is not the time to . . . to talk of . . ." She could not go on, knowing whatever she might say could hurt him.

"It is, Dinah." Ian's voice was firm. "We will soon be at Nairobi. I want Sir Robert to know how much I love you and want to marry you. I want you to let me talk to him and ask his permission. Will you let me?"

Dinah stared into the fire, wishing Ali would return to put an end to the conversation. Still, that would make no difference. Sooner or later, Ian would ask the question again. Sooner or later, she would have to answer him. Perhaps it was better that she put an end to the subject now, for once and for all. With a sigh and still avoiding his eyes, she said, "Ian, I cannot marry you."

"I don't understand, Dinah. 'Will not,' yes, but not 'cannot.' I know you . . . care," he could not bring himself to say love, "care for Alexander. Still, as long as he is your brother, that's no reason for you not to find love with me. I will do everything I can to make you happy, to give you the happiness you deserve."

"Oh, Ian, please don't say such things." She raised her eyes, looking at his face and the steady gaze of his blue eyes that demanded an answer even more than his words did. "I am not worthy of you," she burst out, "and so I cannot marry you."

"Not worthy?" Ian was amazed. Whatever he had thought might be the reason, he had never considered that reply. He smiled, "Dear Dinah, if anyone is not worthy, it is I. What am I, my family, in comparison to Sir Robert and the Douglasses?"

"It has nothing to do with our families, Ian. That, in fact, has never crossed my mind. You must remember I was raised as the daughter of a governess. Had it not been for Sir Robert, I would have gone into some kind of service, much the same as Molly." Dinah smiled grimly, saying softly to herself, "And perhaps I would have been happier, too."

Ian, who had not heard the last, asked, "Then, what is it, my dear?"

"I am not sure I can ever marry anyone," Dinah replied miserably. "If I could, I . . ." Tears rose in her eyes.

"Cannot marry anyone?" He shook his head in utter confusion at her words. "Come, Dinah, whatever is troubling you, I think you had better tell me now. You are a lovely, a beautiful woman, far too young to dismiss marriage so lightly."

So lightly! Dinah buried her face in her hands, unable to find the words to tell him. Even if Ian moved in a different circle than the Douglases, he was a man and a man of the world who had undoubtedly heard the same stories about what went on in society as she had. He would understand, she was sure, that a woman would make love to a man who was not her husband. That she was not a virgin might surprise and hurt him, although the surprise and hurt would pass. Not to be a virgin might not be shameful. What she had done, however, was far worse, for she had committed the unforgivable sin: incest.

Ian studied her carefully, feeling sorry for her and knowing he had to have an answer now, for her sake as well as his. The only way he knew to get that answe was to fall back on the truth as he knew it. Once again, he said, "I have come this far with you, Dinah. I did not ask questions when you begged me to bring you to Africa, accepting only your word that it was imperative for you to talk to Sir Robert. Now, you say you cannot marry me or anyone. Surely, I, of all people, deserve a better answer than that."

The young woman raised her head, looking at the man sitting across from her, the blue eyes watching her so steadily and firm set of his mouth. She had met her equal in determination. She knew he would not let her go until he had the truth. "Yes," her voice was soft, "you do deserve an answer." Her full lips tightened, as she raised her eyes to the sky, to heaven. "Ian, you must believe that I did not know, that no one ever told me—or Alexander—that . . . that we were half-brother and sister. To me, he is . . . was . . . the most handsome, charming man in the world! I fell in love . . . infatuated . . . with him. On the ship . . ." she swallowed hard, trying to find the right words, "the first day of the storm, he . . . we . . ."

From her expression, Ian understood only too well what had happened. "I understand, Dinah," he said gently, wanting to spare her the agony she was going through. "Even so, that is no reason . . ."

"Oh, Ian," the words exploded from Dinah in a flood, "that was not the only time. There was another time aboard ship, too—and that was my doing—and we spent the night together at the castle at Lochleven. I loved him, wanted him, my own brother!"

"You did not know, Dinah. How can I, or anyone, blame you for what you did out of innocence?" he asked. "Out of ignorance, too," he added, thinking of Sir Robert. "What I don't understand is why Sir Robert did not tell you, never told Alexander either, for you say he was as shocked as you." Anger at Sir Robert rose in him.

"Perhaps because he could not, and did not want to, tell us about my mother." Dinah sighed. "He probably did not want me to think badly of my mother because I was illegitimate."

"That's no answer," Ian's voice was furious. "Yes, it would be difficult to tell you under the circumstances. But not to tell his son, the son he had raised, is another matter. There is no excuse for that! He should have told Alexander when he sent Alexander to get you, to bring you back to Scotland. Damn the man! Damn him, too, for coming to Africa without telling you, leaving it to someone else. What kind of a man is he to do that?" Ian was incensed at Sir Robert and angry at himself for having respected Sir Robert so much.

"I know. I asked myself those questions all too many times." Dinah closed her eyes. "That's why I'm here. I have to know how and why he could tell a stranger, Lady Janet, what he could not tell me or even Alexander. I will have no peace until I know that!"

Dinah's misery was so acute that Ian put aside his anger in his desire to comfort her. He rose and went to her, kneeling in front of her and putting his arms around her to draw her close to him. The girl rested her cheek against his, savoring the tenderness of his touch.

"Ian, dear Ian," she murmured, kissing his cheek gratefully.

His arms tightened around her. "Dinah, whatever happened in the past is over. Nothing could change my love for you, do you understand? What happened happened out of innocence and ignorance. I won't ask you to marry me again, not now, not until you have spoken to Sir Robert, but then . . ." he let the words trail unspoken in the ar.

Dinah touched his face, tracing the broad cheekbones with a gentle forefinger, his lips, the line of his dark eyebrows. She kissed his forehead, wanting him to pick her up and carry her into her tent, wanting to spend the night in his arms, knowing from the expression in his eyes that he wanted the same. Yet, Ian was not Alexander. Ian was a man of pride and honor, and she could not accept the warm shelter of his arms without forcing him to compromise that pride and honor. She had hurt him enough without doing that to him. "Yes," she whispered, "I must talk to Sir Robert."

Ian released her and helped her to her feet, kissing her cheek. "Get some sleep, my dear. We still have a long journey ahead of us."

Chapter 24

🌹 🌹 🌹

NAIROBI WAS A sprawling cluster of roughly built structures. The largest bulding was a two-story hotel with a wide veranda. Near it was an assortment of stores that catered to newly arrived settlers, mostly farmers who were establishing coffee and sea plantations in the highlands. A Missionary Society had built a small church, near which was a primitive hospital. Just beyond the town itself was an Army barracks and a parade ground, distinguished by a flagpole from which flew the Union Jack.

Dinah and MacKie went immediately to the hotel to inquire about Sir Robert, while Ali saw to the bearers, promising to come by that evening. Dinah's heart beat faster. She was almost afraid that she would find Sir Robert gone, that somehow they had missed one another between Mombasa and Nairobi, or worse . . .

"Ian," Dinah asked, "will you?"

"I had every intention of asking, my dear." He took her arm leading her toward the desk filling one corner of the small lobby. He rang the bell on the desk.

After a second ring, a tanned, fair-haired Englishman appeared through a narrow door. He looked at the two of them, his eyes returning to Dinah and the unexpected sight of an Englishwoman.

"We are looking for Sir Robert Douglas," Ian explained. "Is he here?"

The man nodded. "He was—"

"Oh no !" Dinah cried. "Has he gone?"

"No. I mean, he's not at the hotel. You'll find him at the missionaries. They took him in when he got sick."

"Sick? Oh, Ian, we must hurry." Dinah started to leave.

Ian stopped her, arranging quickly for two rooms for them, and asking about the missionaries. "They are a Mr. and Mrs. Harrison," he explained as they walked toward the church.

Finding the church empty, they turned toward the small house next to it. A young black girl, her hair plaited in numerous braids over her head and wearing a loose cotton print dress, answered the door.

"We are looking for Sir Robert Douglas," Dinah told her. "The hotel said he was here."

The girl, who had opened the door only a crack, opened it wider, letting them into a small front room.

320

She motioned them silently to wait and left the room. Somewhere a clock ticked loudly.

The man who entered the room within a few moments was dressed in the solemn black of a minister. Like the desk clerk, he glanced from Dinah to Ian and back to Dinah again. "You are looking for Sir Robert Douglas?"

"Yes. I . . . I am Dinah Murray, his . . . his . . ."

"His daughter?" Harrison finished. "And you, Sir, you are not his son, by any chance?" he asked MacKie.

"No. I am Ian MacKie, one of the captains of his shipping line. I have accompanied Miss Murray here, after bringing her from England," MacKie explained. "Sir Robert, how is he?"

"He is sleeping right now. I have ordered tea, and my wife will be here shortly, too. Please sit down. I would like to talk to you before you see Sir Robert."

After his wife, a plain-faced, big-boned woman, had served the tea, the couple told Dinah that Sir Robert was very ill. He had contracted malaria. The first attack had been relatively mild, but each succeeding attack had become worse. "I am sorry," Mrs. Harrison finished softly, "there is little we—anyone—can do for him now. He is in God's hands."

"May I see him? Is he conscious?" Dinah asked anxiously.

"Sometimes, but he is very weak. I have told the girl to watch him. As I told you," Mr. Harrison explained, "he is sleeping now. As soon as he awakes, she will let us know."

Dinah nodded. She recalled suddenly that James had come here with Sir Robert. "Do you know anything about a James Angus? He is with the regiment here."

"Yes. He is at the barracks now, althought he comes every evening to see your father. In fact, it was who asked us to take Sir Robert in, as he did not feel he could get the proper care at the hotel."

There was nothing more they could do except wait. Ian suggested that he go to the barracks and talk to James, first making sure that Dinah was in good hands.

After he had left, Dinah told the couple briefly about her journey without going into the reasons for her making it. She said simply that Ian had had to come to East Africa with a cargo and she had sailed with him, hoping to make the return journey with her father. The Harrisons glanced at one another, but they did not question the story.

Finally Sir Robert awakened, and Dinah went into the small bedroom where he was staying. The room was small, although it had good ventilation from the mosquito netting-covered windows. Dinah sat down on a straight chair beside the bed.

"Sir Robert," she said softly, unable to call him father.

"Dinah." Sir Robert was a gaunt shadow of his former self. Feverish eyes peered up at her from a haggard, unshaven face. "Dinah . . . daughter . . ." He closed his eyes again.

Dinah caught her breath, her heart seeming to stop beating. It was true, then, just as Lady Janet said. The slight hope she had never let herself breathe vanished. Her legs felt heavy, too heavy to carry her out of the room. Tears in her eyes, she took her father's hot hand in her cool ones. More than ever, she needed to know why.

"It was not . . . not what you think." Sir Robert had opened his eyes again. "I should have told you myself. I . . . I could not . . ."

"It does not matter now," Dinah told him.

"It does . . . you . . . Alexander. I would like to see you happy . . ." Sir Robert sighed.

"Me? Alexander? I don't understand. If we are half brother and sister—" Dinah began.

"Is that what you think?" Sir Robert's hand tightened. "Lady Janet did not tell you?" The effort was too much for him, and he leaned back against the pillows.

Dinah let him rest. When Mrs. Harrison came into the room to tell her James was waiting with Ian to see her, she left the room only after Mrs. Harrison promised to let her know as soon as Sir Robert awakened again.

From James, she learned that her father's first attack of malaria had struck shortly after he had left Mombasa. Because of the need for the troops at Nairobi, Sir Robert had insisted on continuing the safari without any rest. He had seemed to recover at first and had even signed new contracts with the company building the railroad from Nairobi to Nyanza in Uganda. James, meanwhile, had been sent with a company of soldiers on a military expedition to find a group of Masai who were raiding the settlements close to Nairobi. When he returned, he found her father ill in the hotel with no one to care for him. As a result, he had spoken to the Harrisons who had taken him in. Despite the care, however, Sir Robert's condition had deteriorated.

"Then, Sir Robert is dying?" Dinah asked, heart broken.

"It is in God's hands, Dinah, as the Harrisons say. The company surgeon has looked at him, at my request," James added, "and says that they are doing as much as he could."

Dinah remained with the Harrisons to nurse her father. At first, he seemed to recover and her hopes were raised, despite the lapses into delirium when he seemed to think she was her mother or Margaret. Gradually, too, she learned the rest of the story.

Sir Robert was ten when Dinah's mother's parents had died in an epidemic and she had come, a baby, to live with the Douglases. As she grew up, Sir Robert had taught her to ride and they had been together constantly until his marriage.

"I loved your mother, Dinah. I wanted to marry her, but my father disapproved. For one thing, she was only fifteen and I was twenty-five, an age when he felt I should marry. He had my wife all picked out, in fact, the daughter of a friend of his who also owned several ships. We were both only children, and our fathers saw our marriage as the ideal business arrangement. Unfortunately, I loved your mother and never loved my wife, although my wife loved me—too much. I am afraid, despite knowing about your mother. My wife became pregnant. It was a very hot summer, and she went to Lochleven to escape the heat and have the baby, while I stayed in Edinburgh. After the child, a son, was born, she became very ill and the child was given to a wetnurse."

"Alexander," Dinah mused.

"Yes, we named him Alexander after my father." Sir Robert closed his eyes, before going on. "I loved him. He was a good baby, and by the time Margaret was born two years later, he was a sturdy, fine boy. In the meantime, your mother and I were more deeply in love than ever. That's why my wife insisted on having another child, despite the doctor's advice that she give up any thought of another pregnancy because of the difficulty with Alexander's birth and her illness. She refused to listen. After Margaret's birth, infection set in. The doctors could do nothing.

"She knew she was dying. Poor woman," Sir Robert sighed. "It was then she told me the truth, that Alexander was not my son."

Dinah gasped. "Not your son, not my . . ."

"No, not your brother. Her baby had been born dead. She had been so ill that the midwife had substituted the baby of the wetnurse who had been hired to nurse her baby, thinking to calm her. The midwife had meant well, hoping to give my wife the will to recover. When my wife did recover, she insisted on keeping the baby. The wetnurse agreed, unwillingly at first, but she had seven other children at home. Thus, my wife returned to Edinburgh with the baby as our son. When my wife first told me, I didn't believe her. Then I realized how much she loved me and how much she feared losing me to your mother."

Dinah tried to get him to rest. She could see that telling the story and the painful old memories were wearing him out. He insisted, however, on finishing the story he had started.

After his wife's death, he had gone to Lochleven to try to find the wetnurse or the midwife or both. Dinah's mother had followed him. She had been worried about him, too worried to leave him alone. They found that the wetnurse had died in childbirth the year before. Finally they found the midwife, who denied the story at first. But she had eventually admitted the truth. Alexander was not Sir Robert's son.

"Your mother and I stayed on at Lochleven. It was a lovely summer. We went riding on the moors and took a picnic by boat to the castle. You have to understand, Dinah, we were alone. My father was back in Edinburgh, as were the children. There were few servants, and we were alone all the time . . ."

"And," Dinah whispered, "you loved one another."

"Yes. When we returned to Edinburgh in the fall, I threw myself into the business, determined to be a success and to win my father's approval for your mother and me to marry. After all, the children did need a mother. In addition, I adopted Alexander secretly. Even if he were not my flesh and blood, I thought of him—think of him—as my son. Then, just as I was succeeding with my father, I had to go to London on business. When I returned six weeks later, your mother had left. No one knew where she had gone. Both my father and I had tried to find her, to no avail. We did trace her to Glasgow, where the trail disappeared."

"She told me that she had sailed from there to New York," Dinah told him.

"I gave her up for dead. I had no wish to remarry." Sir Robert closed his eyes. "I have written it all down in a letter to you and Alexander. I told Lady Janet, too, thinking it would be kinder for you to hear it first from her, but I see I was wrong, that she told you only half the truth."

"Yes." Dinah studied her father. "Then there is no reason why Alexander and I cannot marry?"

"Of course not. Is that what you want?" Sir Robert opened his eyes, looking at her and smiling. "Is that why you came here to find me?"

Dinah hesitated. "In a way," she said slowly. "Oh, Father," she cried, "why didn't you tell us yourself?

Why didn't you tell Alexander when you sent him to find me?"

Sir Robert sighed, closing his eyes again. "I did not, could not, tell Alexander because as far as I knew your mother was still alive. I had hurt her enough, and I didn't know what she might have told you. When I found you knew nothing . . ." His voice trailed off.

"Father?" Worried, Dinah leaned over him.

The man took her hand, squeezing it in his. "Call it pride, selfishness, arrogance—what you will. I was afraid that you, Alexander, Margaret, all of you and especially you, would hate your mother and me for what we had done. I . . . couldn't face your scorn, my children's faces . . ." Again, his voice trailed off. Dinah thought he had fallen asleep until he said in stronger voice than before, "Dinah, what I have just said about myself—pride, selfishness, arrogance, even weakness—is all too true of Alexander. The difference is that I enjoyed business, ships, the challenge, while I am afraid that this bores him. And if he knew he was not my son—Perhaps I have been too impatient, not given him enough of a chance. Well, he has that now, and it is up to him what he makes of himself."

Dinah listened reluctantly, unwilling to admit, Alexander's faults. To take Sir Robert's mind off his son and because she knew he must be tired, she said, "You mentioned a letter?"

"My lawyer has it, along with my will. You, Alexander, and Margaret will all share equally in my property." He leaned back against the pillows. "I have also given a letter to Harrison, which he has witnessed, saying much the same things. In it, I have given my permission for Margaret and James to marry. Sometimes I think I was wrong not to permit it before. You will tell Margaret that, Dinah? I only wanted what was best for her, for Alexander, as," he smiled faintly, "my father wanted what was best for me. I hope it is not too late, that I have not ruined their lives, like your mother's and mine . . ." His voice faded, the effort to talk so much suddenly too much. "I am terribly tired. Go and have some tea, my dear. I'll sleep a while."

Dinah slipped out of the room, leaving the door slightly ajar in case her father awakened and wanted anything. Ian was waiting for her on the small veranda, as he had every day during the time Dinah was with her father. She smiled at him, her expression a mixture of sadness and joy. "How fresh the air seems today," she said.

"It's the altitude," Ian told her, noticing the new maturity in her face. "James has arranged for some horses. He wanted to know whether you would like to go for a ride. I think it's a good idea," he added.

Dinah nodded. "You are coming, too, Ian?"

"If you wish. Unless there are things you want to say to James."

"No. Not right now. I think we should discuss the future, however. There is your ship, Ian, for one thing," Dinah pointed out.

"She's in good hands with Geordie," Ian replied.

"You cannot keep everyone waiting, and my father is not well enough to make the journey even if it were possible to take him by carriage," Dinah added.

James's arrival prevented their saying anything more then. Only when they had gone for a short ride in the country, where James pointed out the shamba and a homestead that had been raided by the Masai, and were on their way back, did the subject come up again.

As Dinah mentioned her father, James glanced at MacKie before saying, "Dinah, it may be a long time until your father is well enough to travel, if ever."

"Surely, he's getting better," Dinah protested.

"It's true that he is more lucid," James agreed, "but the fever has not gone down. There is the color of his skin, too." Sir Robert's ashen pale skin, especially his lips and nails, indicated the severe anemia of advanced malaria.

"I see. Ian," Dinah's voice was firm, "you must leave and return to the *Star of Scotland*. I can stay with the Harrisons, and James is here."

MacKie hesitated. "A few more days won't matter." He glanced at James. "What do you think?"

"A few days," James agreed, returning MacKie's look.

The few days were more than enough. That night, Sir Robert's fever rose, and he relapsed into unconsciousness. Mr. Harrison went for the Army Surgeon, who arrived just as Sir Robert died without regaining consciousness.

As Dinah looked at the silent, white face, the poise and control that she had maintained since the conversation with Lady Janet, that had driven her to seek Lady Jennie's help and then Ian's, broke. Tears welled up in her eyes, running down her cheeks. Pushing everyone aside, she stumbled to her room, closing the door behind her, and threw herself on the narrow cot. Uncontrollable sobs shook her body. Mrs. Harrison brought her a pot of tea and tried to comfort her. Dinah, huddled on the cot, ignored her, and Mrs. Harrison left.

Mrs. Harrison went to the living room, where James and Ian were waiting. She shook her head sadly. "Poor child. I tried to tell her that her father was with God, at peace now. I don't think she heard a word I said. I am afraid she will make herself sick. She has been with him day and night."

James shifted uneasily in his chair. "Ian, you know her better than I do . . ."

Ian, standing at the window, feet apart as on the foredeck of a ship, nodded. "She has been under a terrible strain for months. She needs to cry." He ran a hand over his hair. "I'll go to her and sit with her."

He went into the small room, saddened at the sight of the huddled figure. Sitting beside her, he took her in his arms, holding her like a child and wiping the tears away with his handkerchief. "Love, love," he murmured, "I'm here. It's all right."

Dinah's trembling gradually stopped, and she nestled against the big chest. The beating of his heart on her breast reassured her. "They're together at last, aren't they?" she asked.

328

Ian's lips brushed her forehead. "Together?" he repeated, not sure what she meant.

"My mother. Sir Robert." Dinah lifted her tear-stained face to look into his eyes.

"Yes, Dinah.'" His arms held her tighter.

"Rabbie. Lochleven. How terribly they loved each other," she sighed.

"Have a sleep now, Love." Ian laid her on the bed, drawing the covers over her. "I'll stay with you," he said, as she took his hand, holding it tightly.

The funeral was the next day; a brief service under the burning African sun. Afterwards, Ian summoned Ali bin Juma, telling him to arrange once more for bearers. This time, James was to accompany them with half a dozen soldiers because of Masai raids along the railway line.

Dinah had her first glimpse of the Masai a few days out of Nairobi. The Safari had paused at noon for a rest, and James had sent two soldiers on ahead to check the railroad line. Water for tea was just starting to boil, when Dinah happened to glance toward the rolling grasslands beyond the track. A group of three figures was coming toward them with a long, easy stride that she envied.

"James, look!" she cried.

James got to his feet, raising the pair of binoculars around his neck to his eyes. "Masai!"

Quickly, James deployed the soldiers around the group, telling Ian to stay with Dinah. The bearers, muttering uneasily, clustered close to Ian and Dinah, as Ali spoke sharply to them in Swahili. The soldiers, as well as Ian and Ali, were told to keep their guns ready but not to use them unless James gave the order. His own orders were to do nothing that might excite the warlike Masai into further raids.

As the three warriors approached, fear tightened its knot in Dinah's stomach. No one had warned her of the size of the Masai. The shortest of the men was several inches taller than Alexander's six feet, two inches, while the tallest was close to seven feet. All were slender and wearing wine-red cloths tied over one shoulder. Their ear lobes were immensely enlarged and hung with beaded disks in a geometric design that matched the wide collars around their necks. In their hands were spears almost as long as they were tall, the pointed heads glinting in the sun.

Their long easy stride did not slow, although they had obviously seen the safari. At first, Dinah thought the Masai were going to pass them until the three stopped about 100 yards from the line of soldiers. The ensuing silence was so deep that Dinah was sure everyone could hear her heart beating.

The soldiers and the Masai surveyed one another, as James said, "Hujambo," the Swahili word for "how do you do" or "how are you," although the Masai, who lived inland, rarely understood the coastal Swahili.

The tallest of the men stepped forward, driving his spear into the ground to indicate he did not intend to use it and crossing his arms. James, in his turn, laid down his rifle. The rest of the soldiers and the Masai both kept a wary eye on each other.

"Ali," James said quietly, still facing the Masai, "bring me that box of beads."

Ali went to one of the packs and found the box. Reluctantly, he edged forward to hand it to James. James took it and stepped off half the distance between himself and the leader of the Masai before placing it on the ground and retreating to his former place.

The Masai stepped forward to kneel by the box. He opened it, one hand sifting through the red, white, and blue beads that they prized for making their ornaments. Satisfied, he stood up and nodded, turning his back to the safari to return to the waiting warriors. He picked up his spear and started to walk in the direction in which he had been heading earlier, with the others following.

As the Masai grew smaller in the distance, the members of the safari relaxed, the men once more putting the safety catches on their guns. Dinah turned to the can of water that had been boiling for tea, to find it dry. Her offer to boil more water was rejected unanimously in the desire to put as much distance between the Mombasa-bound party and the Masai.

As they walked, James went to Ian to draw him ahead for a private talk. Even so, Dinah could not help but hear the conversation.

"Ian," James said, "those three were a hunting party. Depending on where they are camped, they could well be back with reinforcements."

"What do we do? What can I do?" Ian asked.

"First, we have to find as good a place to camp as possible. I want you to stay with Dinah. Ali will have to keep an eye on the bearers to make sure they don't disappear the minute darkness falls, and I'll mount a double watch."

Ian nodded. "What do they want?"

James shrugged his shoulders. "They're warriors, and they like a good fight. That's part of it. The other part is that they count wealth partly in the number of slaves they have. I would imagine it's the bearers they want—and the bearers know it."

They made camp early. No tents were set up to draw attention to their location, and no fires were lit. Tinned food provided a silent, uneasy dinner. James, Ian, and Dinah ate in silence, while the bearers muttered nervously to one another under Ali's watchful eyes.

Darkness fell swiftly, a darkness made sinister by the lack of a moon. In the stillness, the coughing roar of a lion sounded ominously close. The bearers' mutterings increased, and the word "simba" was heard again and again. The roar was repeated and then answered by another lion even closer. A bearer wailed a piercing scream, his fear of the lions overpowering that of the Masai.

Ali sidled up to James. "Simba, lion, much too close. You must light a fire. The Masai will not come in darkness, not with the lions."

James didn't hesitate. The bearer's scream had already alerted anyone nearby and given away their position. "Light it, Ali, and you might as well make some tea, too."

The group huddled around the welcome light and warmth of the crackling fire. Dinah, huddled in a blanket, took the hot cup of tea in shaking hands, as the nervous bearers quieted down somewhat.

Hoping the others would not overhear him, James said as softly as possible to Ali, "You're sure it is lions?"

"You mean not Masai, pretending to be lions?" Ali asked. "I do not think so. The cough might be Masai, not the roar." He paused as a series of roars echoed around them. "Captain, I think the lions may help us. The Masai will not move as long as the lions are here."

James nodded. He left briefly to see to the changing of the watch, before coming back to Ian and Dinah to tell them what Ali had said.

"What do we do now?" Ian wanted to know.

"Try to get some sleep."

Dinah had to laugh. "Sleep? Oh, James, with that roaring out there and maybe the Masai, too."

"Try, Dinah," James repeated. "You and I will take turns, Ian. I don't trust those bearers."

The night passed slowly, those who could dozing fitfully. The fear of what morning would bring remained unspoken. Dinah, aroused near dawn by a particularly close roar, drew close to Ian who was on watch. He put his arm around her, sharing the warmth of his body.

"It's all right, Dinah. Dawn isn't far away," he murmured.

"Will we be any safer then, Ian?" An involuntary shiver passed over her body.

"I don't know, my love. If we were at sea . . ." the man shook his head. "Here, I must trust to James. He seems to know what he is doing," he said reassuringly.

Dinah smiled. How honest Ian was. "Are you afraid?"

"Only a fool would not be." His arm tightened, as

his lips brushed her forehead. "Dinah," he went on slowly, "one thing I have learned at sea, and that is that only the foolhardy do not respect and fear the sea. It is bigger and more powerful than any man or any ship. It's that respect and fear, if you will, that makes a good captain, a captain who brings his ship and crew safely home. This land is like the sea, filled with unexpected dangers. We would be fools not to respect and fear it, too."

Dinah nestled against Ian, thinking suddenly of Alexander as she had seen him the first day of the storm on deck. He had not been afraid, she was sure. Had he been in command, he probably would have driven the ship into the storm, not ridden with it as Ian had done. At the time, she had admired that courage. Now, she wasn't sure that he had not been foolhardy. What would he do here, she asked herself? Sadly, she realized that she did not know and could not guess, not after the way he had acted upon learning about their relationship. She recalled his sunken eyes and hollow cheeks. In any case, he would never have admitted to fear the way Ian had.

The sun rose in a spectacular dawn. The safari party stirred and stretched, as Ali built up the fire to make tea. Dinah, along with the others, scanned the horizon, relieved to find it empty except for one acacia. While they ate quickly, James sent two soldiers ahead with orders to fire a rifle if they found any sign of Masai.

In less than an hour, the safari had formed a column with soldiers in the lead and at the end. James, Ian, and Ali took positions at the sides of the column, leaving Dinah to walk alone between the soldiers and the bearers where they thought she would be the safest.

They had gone less than a mile when a bearer's screeching cry of "simba" brought the column to a scrambled halt. Dinah found herself alone, her back to a thornbush.

"Dinah, for God's sake, don't move," James shouted.

Dinah froze, terrified eyes flickering wildly in front of her until she spotted the lion crouched in the grass a few yards in front of her. As she pressed back against the thornbush, unaware of the inch-long thorns scratching through her clothing, she saw a second lion crouched near the first. The first was a male, obviously at the full strength of its power from the color and size of its black-tipped amber mane and massive tawny shoulders. The other was a female, lithe and golden in the sun and nearly the size of her companion. Dinah stared into the yellow eyes, unblinkingly watching her. The lions could have been statues except for the twitching of the tawny-tipped tails.

The sound of a rifle shot made Dinah tear her eyes from the lions to look at the horizon where about twenty Masai were lined in a row. This was no hunting party, for they had adorned themselves with the skins of lions and leopards in addition to their beards. Knowing they had been seen, they began a slow chanting, shaking their spears in time with the beat and slowly stamping and swaying.

Strange thoughts flitted through Dinah's mind. She thought of Alexander reading the letter that Sir Robert had left with the lawyer, of Margaret who would never know that Sir Robert had given permission for her and James to marry, of Lady Janet who would now see to it that Alexander married Mary—if he had not done so already—and of Lady Jennie who might regret having so generously helped Dinah. And Molly and Geordie! How long would it take for the news that the safari had been assassinated to reach them?

Her eyes dropped to the two lions, who represented the greater danger to her. The lioness's head was cocked to one side, ears laid back. The muzzle opened in a grumbling yawn, revealing sharp white teeth.

The chanting and stamping grew louder as the line of Masai moved forward. The air seemed to vibrate with their undulations and the ground to tremble. The men were caught between two dilemmas: the lions and the furious Masai. James, who had seen the two lions, knew he could shoot only one because of the way they were crouching, leaving the other free to attack, and had sent a soldier to move to the other side to shoot the second lion on a signal. Now, the situation was changed. At the sound of the shots, the Masai were bound to rush the soldiers. On the other hand, if they remained still, the Masai might be satisfied with their rituals and throw their spears into the ground, as a warning to the safari and future safaris and soldiers. Either way, it was not an easy decision that James had to make.

Ian, fully aware of the dual danger, felt helpless despite the resolve in his own mind. Whatever happened he would protect Dinah. At the first sign of the lion's charge, he would have to shoot them. Were the Masai to attack, he would still have to shoot the lions, hoping to be able to get both while the soldiers were occupied with the native warriors.

The lions stirred restlessly, heads raising majestically and turning to sniff the air and locate the source of the disturbance. The male rose to its feet, yellow eyes staring into Dinah's amber ones. It shook it mane and gave one tremendous roar. Terror froze Dinah's veins. Ian and James tightened their grip on their rifles.

A sudden silence fell. The Masai, spears raised, seemed like statues. In that instant, the lions forsook Dinah, as if no longer interested in the stranger in the midst, their primeval instincts awakened by a more ancient enemy. The Masai, caught off balance by the unsuspected lions, scattered at the sight of the two beasts charging them. The lions, however, were taking no chance. Outlined against the horizon, they paused long enough to give only one more roar before loping away.

By the time the lions charged, the Masai were vanishing. Ali chuckled. "Safe now. They no come back because we are under the lion's protection."

The rest of the journey was accomplished swiftly and without incident. As the safari descended into the coast lowlands, Dinah and MacKie became increasingly eager. The *Star of Scotland* seemed more than ever to represent comfort and home. Molly and Geordie's welcome was accompanied by tears of joy, despite the sad news of Sir Robert's death.

The major question in Dinah's mind was how soon they could sail for England. To Dinah's relief, Geordie had been busy arranging for a mixed cargo of coffee and tea from the plantations farther north in the Malindi area and of spices from Madagascar, all of which had already been loaded. Captain MacKie, therefore, decided to sail as soon as possible after Dinah had had a chance to talk to James and thank him. To their surprise, however, James had been ordered back to London to make a full report to the War Office and was to accompany them, necessitating a day's delay for him to receive the dispatches that he was to take.

The morning after James had come aboard, Dinah was awakened at dawn by the rattling of chains as the anchors were raised. She smiled, recalling the morning the ship had sailed for Scotland and how she had gone on deck for her last sight of New York. As she had that morning, she rose and dressed quickly in the dark so as not to disturb Molly.

The ship was headed east into the rising sun. Astern lay the coast of Africa, a dark shadow on the horizon. Dinah went to the rail for her last glimpse of Africa. She thought of Sir Robert, her father, lying in the grave under the small white cross in soil so far from the heather and moors of his native Scotland, so far, too, from the woman whom he had loved who lay under a similar white cross in yet another alien land. She wondered at that love between them and the shared secret that each had almost taken to the grave, the secret of their unhappiness. But now she knew and soon Alexander would know, too.

Thinking of Alexander, Dinah smiled again. Now, they could be married. Their love could grow and blossom, as Sir Robert and her mother's never could. Or could it? A cold hand gripped Dinah's heart. With Dinah gone, Lady Janet could easily have pushed

Mary's cause. Her happiness at seeing Alexander again, the delightful warmth of his arms around her, his mouth hot on her lips, his body enveloping her in ecstasy of passion faded before the specter of Alexander and Mary's marriage. Why, in fact, should he not marry her, if he had not already done so? After all, as far as he knew, Dinah and he were half-sister and brother. Dinah shivered in the warm, humid air.

She had not been aware of MacKie's approach until he said anxiously, "Surely you are not cold, Dinah. Dear God," a thought had crossed his mind, "you are not ill?"

"No, Ian." Dinah sheltered in the arm he put around her shoulders. "I was thinking of Sir Robert and my mother."

"I understand." He moved his arm enough to turn her around to face him. "Of Alexander, too?"

Dawn at the equator was all to short. The faint pink burst into brilliant red as the sun rose above the horizon, tearing away the curtain of darkness protecting Dinah from the man's scrutiny. "Yes," Dinah admitted sadly. She laid her cheek against Ian's. "How kind you have been, Ian. I can never forget what you have done for me, how you have stood by me."

Ian's arm tightened. "I would do it again—and more. Surely, you realize that there is nothing I would not do for you, Dinah." He lowered his head, kissing her cheek.

"Ian . . ." Dinah knew she should draw away, but his arms felt too good around her, his kiss reminding her that she was young and a woman. The passions that she had pushed out of her mind under the weight of Lady Janet's words, stirred, desire warming her loins, desire for Ian and for Ian's body. She took a deep breath, trying to still the beating of her heart.

"My dear, what you told me that night doesn't matter. It never did, except in your mind. You were young, alone," he spoke slowly, choosing his words, "suddenly transported into a world you could only have dreamed of. You have nothing to be ashamed of. It was no—"

"No sin?" Dinah finished, when he paused. Saying the words made them real to her. "Perhaps not, Ian, but I let myself get carried away."

"And now you are free," he said firmly, "free to marry and live the life you want."

"Oh, Ian, how sweet, how wonderful you are!" Dinah nestled against his body, enjoying the feeling of his taut chest against her breasts. She imagined holding this man naked in her arms. She could almost feel the warmth of his tanned skin and the teasing coarseness of the sun bleached hair on his chest and arms. She pictured also the firm, burning flesh of his manhood—not with the tingling eagerness of Alexander's movements, but with the exhilaration of Ian's extraordinary control and restraint. The image made her throb between her legs, and she had a sudden, urgent impulse to touch herself which made her blush deeply. Ian saw her color change and drew in his breath.

"I love you, Dinah. Will you now consider my proposal?"

Dinah drew back. A part of her wanted to say "yes." With Ian, she would have a good life. It would not have the same excitement and the luxury of the life she had known in Edinburgh and London, but it would be a life of comfort. And, then, she would soon have her money, too, not that that mattered too much to her, any more than it did to Ian. He had loved her when he did not know she was an heiress, and money would not change that love. Yes, it would be a good life, with other voyages, voyages to China, Australia. . . . She let her mind wander, imagining life with Ian.

The picture had one shadow. Much as she cared for Ian, she was not sure she loved him, at least not in the way she loved Alexander. Besides, despite being almost convinced that Alexander had married Mary, she had to be completely certain. Until she was, until she had spoken to Alexander and given him his father's letter with the story of his birth, she could make no plans for her own life. Then, there was Molly's marriage to Geordie, a marriage that she would not let be postponed any longer, and there were James and Margaret, too, for Margaret had to be told about Sir Robert's permission for them to marry.

"Dinah?" Ian's voice was soft, questioning her and yet not pressing her for an answer.

Dinah took his hands, raising them to her lips and kissing them. "How I wish I could say 'yes,' Ian, but I cannot—not yet," she added carefully. "I have so much to do. First, I must tell Alexander that he is not Sir Robert's son. I must speak to Margaret, too—and Lady Janet." She added the last name grimly. "Above all, I, we, must see to Molly and Geordie's marriage, Ian. They have waited too long," she pointed out.

The man smiled at her, his blue eyes tender. "Of course, my dear. I am not asking you for an answer now, only to consider my proposal once you have taken care of the other matters."

"Then, yes, Ian, I will consider the proposal." She kissed his cheek, once again wishing she could say "yes" freely, and at once.

Chapter 25

🌹 🌹 🌹

THE *Star of Scotland* arrived in London on Guy Fawkes Day, reaching Greenwich on the early morning tide. As soon as the ship had docked, MacKie sent a message to Sloane Square to determine whether Margaret and the Anguses were still there. If not, he suggested they go to the Connaught Hotel until they could arrange passage to Edinburgh. James, in the meantime, prepared to leave for Whitehall. From there, he could find out where Dinah was and meet her later in the day, either at Sloane Square or the hotel.

After James left, Dinah and Molly finished their packing as they waited for the messenger to return. Both shivered in the November 5th cold, not at all used to the weather after their time in the tropics.

"What are you going to say if they are here?" Molly inquired.

"I don't know. I've thought about it so many times, and I guess it depends on Lady Janet and Margaret," Dinah sighed.

"And Alexander?"

"Yes, him above all! If only I can see him first. If only," Dinah said, knowing it was wishful thinking, "he would come here to meet us, and we could talk alone."

At the same time, she knew she was quite afraid of seeing Alexander. Lady Janet and Margaret were women, and if they cried or went into hysterics Dinah felt capable of handling the situation. She did not know what to expect from Alexander, especially if he were married to Mary. The knowledge that Dinah was Margaret's half-sister would not actually affect Margaret, moreover, but she was uncertain as to how Alexander would react to the fact that he was not really Sir Robert's son. A deeper sigh crossed her lips. "All I can do is take each thing as it comes."

"And then," Molly asked hesitantly, "What about *you?*" What will you do?"

"See to your and Geordie's marriage!" Dinah said firmly. "I won't let you use me as an excuse any longer. As soon as we are ready to leave London, we will go to Edinburgh—and you shall have the finest wedding Edinburgh has seen!"

"Dinah . . ." Molly started to say.

"No! Do not say a word unless it it to agree with me. You have stayed with me quite long enough." She laughed, teasing, "If I can manage in darkest Africa without you, I can manage here."

The two women looked up from their packing at a knock on the door. When Molly opened it, Captain MacKie was on the threshold. "Are you almost finished? The messenger has returned . . ."

"Yes?" Dinah interrupted eagerly.

"Margaret and Lady Janet are at Sloane Square." Dinah studied his sober face for a moment before asking, "And Alexander? Is he there, too?"

"The messenger did not say. I have sent for a carriage. The trunks can be sent later," he explained.

"Thank you, Ian." Dinah picked up her cloak. "What about you?"

"I wish I could accompany you. You will have a difficult time, but I am needed here, Dinah." He took her cloak from her and put it around her shoulders.

"I know. I should not ask you to go with me. You have done quite enough. What I meant was what will you do?" she asked.

"The London cargo will be unloaded tomorrow. The second half is for Edinburgh, and we shall sail within the week." He picked up her small traveling case.

"Then, it's goodbye for now, Ian?" She had not expected him to be leaving quite so quickly, and the news made her sadder than she had thought possible. "Oh, Ian!" She kissed him impulsively.

"Only for a little while. You will be back in Edinburgh soon. I intend to stay several months, in order for the ship to be fitted with new sails. If you need me, you have only to telegraph and I will be on the first train, Dinah. You know that," he said soothingly.

"I know that. But I shall miss you, Ian." She kissed him again. "Shall we go on deck?" she asked as Geordie entered the cabin, wanting to give Geordie and Molly a few moments alone.

Even though the carriage arrived shortly afterwards, dusk was starting to fall as they left the dockyards. Throughout London, bonfires were being lit in honor of Guy Fawkes, lending an eerie aura to their entrance into the city. The leaping, dancing figures around the fires and the acrid smell of the smoke sent a shiver down Dinah's spine. Much as she dreaded the interviews that lay ahead, she was relieved when the carriage pulled up in front of the house.

At her knock, Jamison opened the door immediately. He greeted her and Molly warmly.

"Where are Lady Janet and Miss Margaret?" Dinah asked.

"In their rooms, dressing for dinner, Miss Dinah. Your room is ready for you," Jamison told her.

"I will have a tray later." Dinah did not want to wait to tell her news. "Will you tell them, and Miss Mary and Sir Angus, too, that I am waiting for them in the library?"

Dinah went into the library, after telling Molly to go to the kitchen. Molly left her reluctantly, wanting to lend Dinah her moral support. Dinah refused as gently as possible, wishing Molly could stay, but knowing the others would neither like nor understand a servant's being present at such a time.

A fire was burning brightly in the library, and Dinah went to it eagerly, thoroughly chilled from the ride. By the time she had warmed herself up and taken off her cloak, the others entered the room.

Dinah felt more alone than she ever had in her life, as her eyes went from Margaret's face to Lady Janet's and then to Mary's and Sir Malcolm's. Only Sir Malcolm greeted her warmly, without the slightest self-consciousness in his eagerness to hear about Africa.

"I say!" Sir Malcolm clapped a hand to his head. "I'm being a bloody fool, m'dear. Where is Sir Robert? Is he coming later?"

Dinah shook her head, suddenly wishing that James would arrive. "No, Sir Malcolm. He is dead, I am afraid, but not before I had a chance to talk with him." She looked at Lady Janet who refused to meet her eyes. "Where is Alexander? What I have to say pertains mostly to him."

Lady Janet glanced at Margaret uneasily. "Margaret . . ."

Margaret was equally uncomfortable. "He . . . is in Edinburgh, we think."

"Think?" The sense of foreboding that the fires had lit in Dinah grew. "Don't you know?"

"He is in Edinburgh," Lady Janet said firmly.

"Very well," Dinah sighed, making up her mind to go to Edinburgh as soon as possible, perhaps even sailing with MacKie.

"You said that Sir Robert is dead," Sir Malcolm said.

Dinah, still hoping that James would come soon, told them about arriving in Mombasa to find Sir Robert in Nairobi and how she and MacKie had set out to find him. She was about to tell them about his illness, when James arrived.

After he had greeted his parents and Margaret, he turned to Dinah. "Have you told them?"

"Only about arriving in Nairobi."

He left his family and went to Dinah's side. "Tell them the rest, Dinah," he said quietly.

Dinah tried to tell the rest of the story as briefly as possible.

Margaret's shock at the revelation of Alexander and Dinah's parentage was too obvious not to be genuine. Whatever had happened in her absence, why Alexander had fled London, Lady Janet had held to her story. Lady Janet, on the other hand, had listened in stony silence.

"I don't believe it. It's not true," Lady Janet insisted when Dinah had finished. "Why are you lying . . ."

"Mother," James laid a hand on Dinah's shoulder, "Dinah is not lying. You forget, I was there. Sir Robert gave me a letter before Dinah arrived. He dictated it to me."

"It is still a lie." Lady Janet poured herself a sherry with a shaking hand. "His wife was my best friend. She would have told me if Alexander were not her son."

"Lady Janet," Dinah squeezed James's hand in gratitude, "Sir Robert told me that he had told you before you left, that you were to tell Alexander . . . and me . . . in case he did not return." She added, "His lawyers have a letter . . ."

James looked at his mother. "You may have thought that you were doing the right thing in not telling all of the truth. But at least now . . ."

343

Lady Janet covered her face with her hands. "I knew. I always knew, even before Sir Robert told me. It was because of Mary." She turned her eyes to appeal to her daughter. "Don't you see? You and Alexander . . ."

Mary refused to meet her mother's eyes. Instead, she looked at her hands lying in her lap. Her face was pale, and her lips were trembling.

"Malcolm . . ." Lady Janet appealed to her husband.

Sir Malcolm was little help. "To think all these years I've known the man, went huntin' with him, with Alexander, and never a word. I never even guessed. And you," he shook his head in confusion, "you knew all the time, m'dear. How . . ."

"I knew about Alexander, not Dinah." Lady Janet brushed the tears from her eyes. "Sir Robert's wife told me. We were friends, as I said. She almost died with . . . with Alexander. When she was carrying Margaret against the doctors' advice, she was afraid that she might not live. And she told me, in case. She wanted Sir Robert to know, for him to adopt Alexander. She was afraid of the wetnurse, the midwife—"

"And you've known all these years?" Dinah was incredulous. "With that knowledge, with what Sir Robert told you, you let Alexander, us, think we were . . ." She saw Margaret's shock. "Margaret, too?"

"Mary!" Once again, Lady Janet appealed to her daughter, "You can understand, can't you? It was because of you . . ."

Mary looked at her mother for the first time. "No, Mother, I cannot. That you might remain quiet, I can understand. To lie . . ." She burst into tears. "You have ruined Alexander!"

"Ruined Alexander!" Dinah leaped to her feet, running to Margaret. "You said he was in Edinburgh."

"He is." Margaret tried to look at James past Dinah's shoulder. "James!" She called.

James stood his ground. "Margaret, before your father died, he gave up permission to marry with his blessing. He even offered me a position with his firm. He felt Africa had changed me. Maybe it did."

"What do you mean?" Margaret cried.

"At this moment, much as I love you, I am not sure I want to marry you. I am ashamed of all of you. You let Dinah go to Africa alone, not," he added with a faint smile, "that I think you could have stopped her. But you let her go without a word, and now you are still thinking of yourself, after what she had been through."

Margaret started to cry, and Dinah put her arms around her. "Oh, Margaret, it will be all right. James loves you, just as I . . ." The thought of Ian made her pause. "Don't you see?" she begged.

"Alexander started drinking heavily, gambling," started Margaret. "The directors suggested he return to Edinburgh."

"And he did?" pressed Dinah.

"I—we—think so. He said he was going there, but we haven't had any answers to our letters. He hasn't been to the offices there." Tears were running down Margaret's face.

Dinah let her go. "James, go to her," she said quietly. She felt terribly tired. She wanted to sleep, and she needed time to think about what to do next. It had never occurred to her that Alexander might not be in London; at his club, or just out. Now, she had still another journey in front of her.

The young woman started to leave the room. Sir Malcolm stopped her. To Dinah, the man had always simply been there, enjoying his food, his wine, a cigar after dinner. When it came to any decisions, whether it was to go to a party or see a caller or even to dress for dinner, he had always deferred to his wife. Now, despite his shock, he seemed to find himself and make his own decisions.

"M'dear, I know all this has been as much a shock to you as to us, more so, in fact. I am afraid that none of us had acted with, well, the courtesy we should have. If there is anything I can do, I am your servant." He patted her clumsily on the shoulder.

"Thank you, Sir Malcolm." Dinah smiled gratefully at the man. "Perhaps we can talk tomorrow. I am terribly tired."

"Of course. Of course. Naturally you are, m'dear." He patted her again and opened the library door for her.

Dinah went to her room. Molly had a hot tub waiting for her. The young maid eyed Dinah sympathetically, not asking any questions as she helped Dinah undress.

Dinah sank back in the tub gratefully, letting the hot water exert its relaxing powers as she studied her body. For once, she took no pleasure in the sight of her firm breasts and nipples, her slender waist, and long, shapely legs. Her pale ivory skin seemed to be reflected ghost-like in the water, her whole lovely body seemed to make a mockery of passion. She hadn't realized how much she had wanted to see Alexander, how very much she had wanted him to take her in his arms and to caress and fondle her in appreciation—not appreciation for what she had done but appreciation for her body, for her being Dinah.

How tired she was! Never before, not even during the long trek when her legs had screamed at taking another step, had she been so totally exhausted. Her life seemed to have drained from her, the life that she had looked forward to Alexander reviving in her.

She sat up, trying to summon the energy to get out of the tub. Molly hurried to help her, and Dinah half stumbled as she stepped over the high edge, to stand submissively as Molly wrapped her in a towel. After she was dry, she raised her arms like a child to let Molly put on her nightgown. She was even too tired to eat the supper that Jamison brought up on a tray.

When she was finally in bed, Molly sat beside her, stroking her hair. Worriedly, Molly asked, "What now, Dinah? You need a long sleep."

Dinah put her arm over her eyes. "I must find Alexander, go to him, Molly. He has to know . . ."

"I'll go with you. We will find him, and he will be all right, you will see," Molly promised.

"I hope so." Dinah sighed, opening her eyes. "Oh, dear. Oh, Molly, your wedding. You and Geordie . . ."

"We can wait." Molly avoided Dinah's eyes. "We've waited this long. We can wait longer."

"No. I promised. You two have waited long enough because of me," Dinah said firmly.

"Well," Molly stroked the other girl's hair, "you can't do anything tonight, and we can't be married tomorrow. So, get some sleep, and we'll talk about it."

Dinah closed her eyes. Molly blew out the candles, sitting down to wait until Dinah was asleep. Now that she was in bed, she was wide awake and she finally pretended sleep to let Molly get to her own bed.

She had come this far, from New York to Scotland, from England to Africa and back. She was disappointed, that was all. She would not give up now. Determination flooded her, and with it came the warmth of desire. She ran her hands lightly down her body, taking pleasure in its shapeliness. How she longed for fulfillment, to feel her body arousing with the special excitement she had known with Alexander, had almost known with Ian. Well, it would not be long now. Once she had arranged Molly's marriage . . .

Lucky Molly, she thought. Even though that marriage had been delayed, neither Molly nor Geordie had had any doubts. Their lives were their own, and they would not have to wait any longer, Dinah promised herself as she fell into a deep slumber.

In the morning, Dinah set about helping to put Sir Robert's estate in order. At breakfast, she asked Sir Malcolm's help. He was only too eager to do everything he could, and he suggested that he see Sir Robert's London lawyers as soon as possible. "This morning, in fact," he added cheerfully.

Dinah gave him the will and the other papers pertaining to his estate and the business that Sir Robert had entrusted to her. The only papers she withheld were those pertaining to her and Alexander's paternity.

"I do not think, Sir Malcolm, that this is the time to speak to lawyers about that matter, do you?" she asked.

"That is up to you, m'dear. Sir Robert has made it clear that you are to inherit along with his children as his ward and the daughter of a cherished childhood friend," the man pointed out.

"Then I think for Sir Robert and my mother's sake, it is better to leave matters as they are," Dinah said.

"I agree, at least for the moment." Sir Malcolm fingered the papers. "Is there anything else?"

Dinah hesitated. "Do you think, Sir Malcolm, should I telegraph . . . try to reach Alexander? You say he has ignored your messages." She smiled, adding, "I ask your advice as a man."

Sir Malcolm patted her hand. "Thank you, m'dear. I think you should try. He may not answer, but you can try."

Dinah nodded. Before Sir Malcolm left, she drafted a message to be signed with her name, asking him to come to London. Sir Malcolm took it with him to send off on his way to the lawyer's.

After he left, Dinah poured herself another cup of coffee and sat down again at the table. Next, she would have to speak to Molly. Before she could decide what to say, Margaret entered the room.

Margaret smiled timidly at Dinah. "Good morning. I was hoping you would be alone. I wanted to talk to you, to apologize."

Dinah smiled, wondering what to say. In a way, now that she knew the truth, she could not blame Margaret for her resentment at the interloper suddenly in the midst of the family. Then she recalled Lochleven and the trick that had been played on her. "Yes, Margaret?" she said, deciding to let the other girl at least make an attempt at apology.

Margaret sat down, playing with a knife in front of her. "I was jealous, I guess, of Father's attention. I couldn't understand it. For so long, it had been Alexander and me—and then you were there, and both Father and Alexander seemed to adore you. Or, so it seemed to me. But, Dinah," she raised her eyes, appealing to Dinah with the tears that had risen in them, "I didn't even guess. Father should have told us. You, too, for that matter."

"I know. I think he intended to," Dinah said slowly. "I don't think he knew how. He was a proud man."

"At least we know now. Dinah, I am sorry for the past. I am not asking you to forgive me entirely, but perhaps we can start fresh, try again, if that is not too much to ask." Margaret put down her knife. "When I think of your going to Africa, like that. I could never have done that. You are very brave."

"Thank you, Margaret, but I had to know, not only for my sake, but for Alexander's, too. We loved each other." The words were wrenched from Dinah, although she didn't realize she had used the past tense.

"I know." Margaret stood up and went to Dinah's side, kissing her on the cheek. "I know, and he will listen to you, I am sure, although he will listen to no one else now."

"He has to," Dinah said firmly. "Somehow, I must find a way to make him listen."

"You are going to Edinburgh, then?"

Dinah nodded, "As soon as I can." She then told Margaret about Sir Malcolm and the lawyers and the telegraph message. "I am hoping that Alexander will come here," she added.

"He won't. I know him too well," Margaret conceded sadly. "He is proud, as proud as Father. His pride has been hurt because Father did not tell him the truth, because he had to learn what he thought was the truth from Lady Janet. And now, he is ashamed, too, Dinah."

"Then, I must go to him," Dinah decided.

"I will go with you, if you want." Margaret smiled sadly. "What help I will be, I don't know, but I will do all I can."

"Thank you, Margaret. Let us see what happens."

349

Dinah was genuinely touched by Margaret's offer. "Now, let us talk about you and James."

"He has changed." Margaret's tone was somber. "I am not sure I know him any more."

"He had to make decisions, Margaret, to act quickly." Dinah told her briefly about the two encounters with the Masai, adding, "Do you still love him, want to marry him?"

Margaret nodded. "I think so. First, we have decided to get to know each other again."

Dinah agreed with her, and then quietly left to write some notes, first of all to Lady Jennie. For the moment, she put Alexander out of her mind. Only when she was finished, did she let her mind turn to him. How simple it had sounded to tell Margaret she was going to Edinburgh—and how she wished she could leave on the next day. Yet, the decision was not that simple, not with the will to be settled.

She left her chair, going to the window. The day was foggy, with the mist swirling and obscuring even the houses across the street, reminding Dinah of her arrival in Edinburgh. Life had seemed so simple then, had seemed so simple, even predestined, from the moment Alexander had arrived in the house on Washington Square. She had realized her life would change. Yet, in her wildest dreams, she had never imagined that the future would hold what it had. If she had known, she wondered, would she have set off so lightheartedly? Yes, she thought, answering her own question, even knowing that tragedy lay ahead she would have gone, thinking she could change it. What would Mrs. Bradley think if she knew all that had happened? Dinah smiled. She would have to write Mrs. Bradley. At least she would have good news, too, as far as Molly was concerned.

Dinah sat down at the desk again, starting to pull a piece of fresh paper toward her. She was interrupted by Molly, a Molly who was more excited than Dinah had seen her in a long while. The young maid thrust a note into Dinah's hands.

"Dinah, Dinah, read it," Molly exclaimed. "You will never guess."

Dinah's first thought was that it was from Alexander, that he was in London. "Alexander?" she asked, taking the note with trembling hands.

"No. Read it, just read it! Molly cried, her face wreathed in smiles.

"Mrs. Bradley! I was just thinking of her!" Dinah had recognized the handwriting, and she read it quickly, the words slowly penetrating that Mrs. Bradley was in London. The final words puzzled her, "The recent news distressed me so much that I felt I had to come to London myself and see what I could do. After all, it is all partly my fault."

Dinah put the note down, looking at Molly. "Her fault? What does she mean? And how could she know . . ."

"Please! Don't be angry, Dinah." Molly kneeled in front of her friend, taking her hands. "I wrote her before we left about you and Alexander. I was so worried, I didn't know what to do, and I wrote her to ask for her advice."

"Oh, Molly, you should not have done that!" Dinah protested.

"I know, but I didn't know who else to turn to," Molly admitted.

"Well," Dinah smiled, "at least she will be here for your wedding." The young woman rose, thinking quickly. Mrs. Bradley was at the Connaught. She must talk to Margaret and arrange for Mrs. Bradley to come here. In the meantime, she would go to the Connaught to see her.

"Oh, Molly," she sighed. "It will be so good to see Mrs. Bradley again. You should not have written and worried her, but since you did, we must put her mind at ease as soon as possible."

Chapter 26

🌹 🌹 🌹

MARGARET AGREED IMMEDIATELY that Mrs. Bradley must stay with them at Sloane Square. She told Dinah to go to the Connaught while she spoke to Mrs. Jamison about preparing a room.

Before Dinah could leave, however, she said, "Dinah, one thing more. What about Lady Janet? I am sure it is painful for you to have her here. I did not say anything earlier, because it would not be appropriate for us to be here alone with the servants."

Dinah hesitated. As far as she was concerned, she never wanted to see Lady Janet again. Yet, there was Sir Malcolm to consider. She could not ask one to leave and not the other. "Have you spoken to her and to Mary?" she asked cautiously.

"They are confused. Lady Janet was hysterical after you left. It was all James and Sir Malcolm could do to calm her. Mary wanted to leave," Margaret said quietly, adding, "I did, too."

"Do you still want to leave?"

"No. I feel as if I have to help, to make up for the past. There is James, too, who will be in London for a while."

Dinah began to feel that the whole world was on her shoulders. Every time one decision was made, another arose. Actually, with Mrs. Bradley in the house, she did not care whether Lady Janet was there or not. As a result, she told Margaret, "It is up to you and Lady Janet, of course. To Sir Malcolm, too," she added. "Why don't you talk to him?"

"That's a good idea," Margaret agreed, observing.

"We will need him, won't we, especially with Alexander . . ."

Dinah nodded. "Unless Alexander returns, we can certainly use his help as a friend of the family."

Margaret forced a smile. "It is amazing what women can do when they have to, isn't it? I am only learning, I admit. It will not be easy, but I will speak to Lady Janet. And now, go to your friend, while I take care of things here."

Dinah left immediately, taking Molly with her. At the Connaught, she had the desk send word to Mrs. Bradley, saying they were there. As she expected, they were immediately ushered to the suite where Mrs. Bradley was staying.

The woman was still in her dressing gown. Although she had risen early, she had delayed dressing while she took care of other matters. Despite the dressing gown, however, she opened the door herself, embracing both Dinah and Molly.

"Let me look at you," she cried. "My, how grown up you are! Especially you, Dinah. You have become a beautiful young woman, no longer the little girl I knew."

"Oh, Mrs. Bradley, how good it is to see you!" Dinah impulsively hugged the woman. "And how good it was of you to come."

"When I received Molly's letter, what else could I do? If only your mother had told me the whole truth, Dinah," the older woman mourned.

"If only Sir Robert had told us! But they had their own reasons," Dinah pointed out.

"And you and Alexander are . . ."

Dinah shook her head. After having told the story first to Molly and then to the others, the words came easily to her tongue, not that the pain was any less. Mrs. Bradley listened quietly, with only a tightening of her lips at the revelations of Alexander's birth and the love affair between Sir Robert and Dinah's mother, as well as at Lady Janet's duplicity. Dinah concluded by saying, "Now you are here, Mrs. Bradley, you shall come and stay with us at Sloane Square."

Mrs. Bradley did not hesitate as Dinah had expected. "I certainly shall, especially with that woman in the house. I cannot understand how you can permit her to remain, except, of course, if Sir Malcolm is helpful in getting these matters straightened out. There are times when a man can be much more effective than a woman, not," she added, "that a woman cannot do all that a man can, if she is as determined as you."

"And Molly, don't forget," Dinah reminded her, as the young maid flushed. "She has insisted on accompanying me as much as possible."

"This Geordie," Mrs. Bradley said with a smile, "tell me about him."

As Molly talked, her eyes bright and her cheeks flushed, an idea began to form in Dinah's mind. Mrs. Bradley's presence made any objection of Molly's to marrying Geordie as soon as possible obsolete. Regardless of Molly's preference for marrying in Edinburgh, London now seemed appropriate, depending on Captain MacKie. Geordie, she knew, could easily remain behind as it was not necessary for him to be aboard during the short run of the *Star of Scotland* from Greenwich to Leith. On the other hand, she knew that Geordie wanted MacKie to be his best man as much as MacKie would want to perform that service. Thus, she must persuade MacKie either to remain in London or to return with Geordie's sister once he had the work on the ship underway. Then, with Mrs. Bradley undertaking the arrangements for Molly's wedding and looking after Dinah's interests in London, Dinah would be free to go to Edinburgh to talk to Alexander.

First, she must get word to MacKie. She would have to talk to Geordie alone when he came to London to see Molly before sailing for Scotland. She would also arrange with Sir Malcolm to have Sir Robert's agents get word to MacKie that Dinah wanted to see him. Unlike Alexander, she thought sadly, he would come immediately.

She was so lost in her thoughts that she didn't hear

Mrs. Bradley speaking to her at first. Quickly, she apologized, saying, "I'm sorry, Mrs. Bradley, I'm afraid I was rather lost in my own thoughts."

Mrs. Bradley smiled indulgently. "I can well understand that, Dinah. Molly has been telling me about this Captain MacKie. He has been a real friend to you, I understand."

"Yes. You would like him, Mrs. Bradley," Dinah replied warmly. "I don't know what I would have done these past few months without him."

The older woman regarded the younger one thoughtfully. "It is a pity that Alexander does not have some of his qualities."

Dinah flushed, telling Mrs. Bradley all she needed to know. "It is," she whispered. She stood up. "Mrs. Bradley, you are to come to Sloane Square as soon as possible. I must go now, but Molly will stay to help you and I will send someone for your trunks."

"If there is anything I can do . . ." Mrs. Bradley embraced Dinah warmly, knowing it was useless to argue with the girl right now.

"There is." Dinah's eyes twinkled. "Talk to Molly about her marriage. Now you are here, I think she and Geordie should marry as soon as possible, here in London. Why wait until Edinburgh, when we don't know for sure how long we must stay here?" Dinah slipped into her cloak and went to the door, saying in farewell, "You know that is true, Molly."

A hired cab took her from the hotel to Sloane Square. She told Jamison to send the carriage to the Connaught Hotel for Mrs. Bradley and Molly and to arrange to pick up the trunks later. Before she could go upstairs, Sir Malcolm arrived and the two went into the library.

Sir Malcolm had had a busy day with the lawyers. They had not questioned the will, despite being surprised about the inclusion of Dinah. He had then told them the story that he and Dinah had discussed. The will would be filed as soon as possible, although there would be no settlement until the lawyers had had an opportunity to draw up a list of Sir Robert's property and investments as well as any loans or debts.

Dinah listened carefully, the need to see Alexander growing more imperative. When Sir Malcolm had finished, she thanked him, adding, "I know you will do all you can to make sure things are in order, Sir Malcolm. I would like you to stay here, with Lady Janet. And there is James. I know Margaret and he both feel they need a little time."

"M'dear, you are most kind. I would have thought you would want us to leave. If you wish us to stay, I will keep Lady Janet out of your way," he added grimly.

"Thank you. I have one more favor to ask." She told him about Mrs. Bradley's arrival and Molly, concluding, "I know Captain MacKie planned to return to Edinburgh within the week, but I must see him before he leaves. I will speak to Geordie, of course, although I would also like to get word to him through the agents."

"I will take care of that first thing in the morning."

Mrs. Bradley settled easily into the routine of the house. Margaret liked her immediately, and Lady Janet was only too willing to relinquish the reins of the household. To Dinah's surprise, Molly's marriage became a matter of concern to everyone, with Margaret even offering to take Molly to her own dressmaker. On the other hand, Dinah thought, perhaps she shouldn't be surprised. It was far easier for everyone to think about Molly than it was to think about Sir Robert and the past, or about Alexander. She was increasingly restless about going to Edinburgh and to see MacKie.

MacKie arrived with Geordie on the day after he received the message from the agents. Dinah welcomed him in the library, introducing him to Mrs. Bradley, both of whom liked each other at once.

After Mrs. Bradley had left them alone, MacKie kissed Dinah. "I am glad to see you looking so well.

I have been thinking about you, and your message worried me."

"Dear Ian," Dinah smiled, "I did not mean to worry you, but I am afraid I need your help again." At the expression of worry on his face, she added, "Not for me, for Molly."

With that she told him about her plans for Molly's wedding. "I know, of course, that Geordie wants you at his wedding. It was my thought that you might stay here, have the ship repaired here."

"I cannot, Dinah. I have that cargo for Edinburgh. Geordie could stay, however, and I can return in time for the wedding," he added.

Dinah frowned. "Perhaps then, Ian, it would be just as well for him to go with you. Molly will be busy, and there is a lot to do even with Mrs. Bradley and Margaret to help. I want it to be a beautiful wedding. Molly has been a sister to me." Another idea was forming in her mind. "When are you sailing?"

"The day after tomorrow."

"Then I shall sail with you to Leith!" she decided.

"What?" Ian shook his head in amazement. "No matter how long I know you, Dinah, you always have a surprise in store."

The young woman laughed. "I must go to Edinburgh, Ian," she said more soberly. "We have had no word from Alexander. He is destroying himself, and I cannot let it go on."

"The train would be faster," he pointed out.

"I know, but then Molly will insist on going with me. If I go with you and Geordie, she cannot object. I am not sure that Mrs. Bradley will be quite so in favor of that, but . . ."

"But you are determined," Ian finished. "Very well, Dinah, I shall be happy to have you aboard once again, as long as you can get to the ship tomorrow evening. I would come for you, except I must return this evening."

"Geordie is remaining in London overnight. I will go with him," Dinah declared. "Thank you, Ian. Once more, I am in your debt."

"No, Dinah. for will I not have the pleasure of your company?" His blue eyes embraced her, saying more than words could.

Dinah rose from the chair in which she was sitting to go to him. She put her arms around him, resting her cheek against his. "How good you are to me," she whispered, as his arms enclosed her and his lips brushed her cheek in a gentle kiss.

The kiss sent a warmth through her body, a spreading fire through her loins that grew hotter as he stroked her back with one hand. The other hand turned her face to his, and their lips met. "Ian, Ian," she murmured.

"Oh, Dinah, my darling, don't you know how I love you, how I want you?" He withdrew from her, clenching his fists. "Happy as I was for you, I cannot say that I was happy to learn Alexander was not your brother."

The words jarred Dinah. She had not been fair to Ian. She had known that Ian loved her, and she had used that love for her own purposes. Even now, she had gone to him seeking the warmth of his desire to satisfy her own urges.

Ian picked up his cap, preparing to leave. "Dinah, I have taken you this far, myself and the *Star of Scotland,* and now we will see you to Scotland once more."

"Ian . . ."

"There is nothing to say, Dinah. I love you. I will not let you make this trip alone, but do not ask too much of me. Remember, I am a man, too. What happened in the past does not matter. Yet, I want you only if you can come to me freely, with no ghosts, no one's face over my shoulder."

Dinah's heart cried out to him, knowing what it was costing him to say what he was saying.

"Let me finish. I will take you to Alexander, because that is something you must do. After that, it is up to you. I can do no more," he finished.

The naked love on his face, in the blue eyes that never flinched from her eyes, sent a new wave of passion through Dinah, an unexpected yearning to hold him and kiss the laughter into his eyes once more. Yet, she dared not. She could not go to him again, unless she could go freely.

"I will see you tomorrow, Ian," she said humbly.

He nodded, opening the door and closing it behind him. The loneliness that she had felt facing Margaret and Lady Janet that night had been nothing to the loneliness she felt now. Her choice was clear: It was either Alexander or Ian. She could not have both, even though in her own way she loved both for different reasons.

Dinah went to the window, staring out into the street, her thoughts now turning to Alexander. She was not aware that Mrs. Bradley had knocked or entered the room, until the woman spoke.

"Why, Dinah, has the captain left? He was here such a short time."

"He . . . He had to get back to the ship. They are sailing the day after tomorrow. I am going with them," Dinah said, turning to face Mrs. Bradley, her determination showing in her face.

"I see." Mrs. Bradley took a seat on the settee by the fire. "Come, sit here and talk to me, Dinah. From what Molly says, you have been through a great deal."

"Yes, I guess I have." Dinah joined the older woman.

"I like your Captain MacKie. He must care for you quite a bit to come here because you asked him." Mrs. Bradley spoke carefully.

"I am afraid he does, Mrs. Bradley, more than I realized. No, that isn't true. I knew, but I didn't want to know," Dinah admitted.

"Now you are being honest, Dinah. No man would have done what Molly tells me he has done for you unless he loved you a great deal. He would be a good husband. I would like to see you happy, as happy as Molly. Oh, my dear, how I wish it were your wedding I shall be attending," Mrs. Bradley sighed.

"Oh, Mrs. Bradley," Dinah sank on her knees in front of the older woman, placing her head in the comforting lap, "so do I. Perhaps you will when I come back," she half promised.

"But to whom?" Mrs. Bradley wondered. "Sometimes I wish I had not urged your mother to let me write that letter."

'Oh no!" Dinah cried. "I am so happy that you did."

"Are you sure? I would feel much better if I knew you were glad of that, regardless of what has happened, of the unhappiness and the torture you have been through."

Dinah thought of the young, innocent girl who had sailed from New York. If she was no longer innocent, she was still young. She recalled, too, the genteel poverty in which she had lived with her mother, the slim expectations of life as a governess or companion with little prospect of anything except working the rest of her life, even if she were to marry. She could not have done anything except go with Alexander when he appeared in her life. Of course in contrast, a life of luxury and wealth was not all she had thought it would be. There was more to life than fine clothes and parties, and the rich, even royalty, had problems. Yet, she had found a strength within herself, a knowledge that regardless of what happened tomorrow or next week or next year she could and would survive. In looking back, she realized to her surprise that she had enjoyed the challenges she had met, in spite of the problems she had been forced to meet.

Dinah raised her head from Mrs. Bradley's lap, her amber eyes shining as she met the older woman's eyes. "I cannot help admitting there are things that I wish I could change, but I would make the same decision, even knowing what I know now."

"And I cannot change your mind about embarking on this new voyage?" Mrs. Bradley petted the girl's red hair.

"No." The words, "In my end is my Beginning," were suddenly engraved before her eyes. The decision to make this trip had been made for her on the day she was born. "No," she repeated, "I must go. As I could not do otherwise than to go to Scotland, now I cannot do otherwise than to go to him." Her voice was firm, and her eyes were clear.

Chapter 27

THE MEMORY OF her conversation with Mrs. Bradley, and the new knowledge she had of herself, reassured Dinah as she boarded the *Star of Scotland* at Greenwich. Her only regret was the fear that it might be the last time she would set foot on the deck, and she looked around the now familiar ship with fresh eyes. The sails, once as white as the clouds on a summer's day, were gray. Patches here and there were the scars of the storms through which the mettle of the ship and its captain had been tested, just as the lines—far too deeply engraved for a man of his age—at the corners of MacKie's eyes were a symbol of his skill and courage. The decks beneath her feet had been holystoned until the grain of the oak had given way to a soft patina. Yet, how sturdy the ship was, how safely and surely it had carried her under Ian's firm hand, from New York to Edinburgh, from London to Africa and back, and now to Leith once again. Surely, it could not be for the last time, she thought sadly.

The sadness persisted in spite of the morning's exhilaration as the sailors cast off the lines and the ship, under only the necessary sail, moved gracefully down the Thames toward the choppy waters of the North Sea. Dinah savored the wind in her face, the salty freshness of the air, and the sun sparkling on the waves. Her spirits rose, only to sink as she realized that this love of the sea was yet another bond between

Ian and herself. The voyage took on a new meaning, a new significance.

She stored up in her mind every detail, from the way the sails cracked as they were unfurled and caught the wind to the creak of the planks as the ship drove through the waves. Time and time again, her eyes sought out Ian, his stance and his voice as he gave orders to the crew. He was at home here, with the decks under his feet, his love for the sea even greater than his love for her. He had said that he would do anything for her, but that was not quite true: for he would never give up the sea. He was married to it, tied to it with a stronger knot than he would ever be tied to a marriage with a woman. The woman he married, however great his love for her, would always have to share him with the sea, his first love.

The two-day voyage passed all too quickly. She was rarely alone with Ian. He did not avoid or ignore her. In fact, she often looked up to find his blue eyes watching her with a troubled expression. She was not sure whether he was remembering the last time they had been alone together or he was worried about her and Alexander. His words, "Remember, I am a man, too," rang in her ears. Whatever he was thinking, she knew he wanted her and that was one reason why he made sure they were not alone together.

Only when they entered the Firth of Forth on the early morning tide of the third day did he draw her aside. Leith was already in sight, as he said, "Dinah, I hope that this is what you want, that this journey of yours finally ends here."

The words confused her. Her certainty that once Alexander knew the truth then everything would be settled, was shaken. She should have learned by now that life was never that clear cut, that one decision, one journey, only led to another. "Do you, Ian? So do I, but isn't there always another journey? Another voyage?" she asked.

"For me, yes. For you, I hope not," he said deliberately.

She was not sure that he had understood her meaning. "If it is, I will always remember the *Star of Scotland,* the sea we have shared," she managed to say.

"As will I." His eyes lingered on her face, trying to engrave her in his mind. "Dinah, Dinah," he cried, his impassiveness giving way to his desire. He embraced her.

His arms held her close to him, so close that she could feel the beating of his heart beneath his jacket. His mouth crushed her lips, and one hand stroked her hair. Dinah clung to him, her own heart pounding with the burst of desire that sent flames through her body. Her hands caressed him, sending a trembling through her limbs. Yes, he was a man—one she would never forget. She would always wonder what it would be like to lie with him, to be with him, both of them naked and pulsating with the urgency of their longing, his manhood strong and vibrant quenching the fire between her legs.

A sailor's shout forced them apart. Oblivious to their surroundings, they had not realized that they had almost reached the dock. Ian left her to see to the landing. Dinah waited by the rail, eager now to reach Edinburgh. She scanned the shore, looking for the Douglas carriage that Sir Malcolm had cabled the Edinburgh office to have meet her. It was there, just beyond the dock, the coachman standing idly by the empty coach. Alexander had not come to meet her.

As soon as the gangplank was lowered, Ian came to her side again. He accompanied her silently to the coach, a sailor carrying the few traveling bags that Dinah had brought with her, behind them. At the door of the coach, Ian hesitated.

Dinah tried to smile at him. "I will let you know," she said softly.

He nodded, helping her into the carriage. As he closed the door, he smiled. "I will be waiting, Dinah." Before she could reply, he ordered the driver to go.

Dinah leaned out the window, watching him until the coach turned on to the Edinburgh road and he was out of sight. When would she see him again, she wondered, her mind turning to thoughts of what lay ahead.

363

Now she was once more in Scotland, and so near the end of her journey.

Even before the coach drew up to the house on Princes Street, Dinah had her hand on the door. It no sooner stopped than she had the door open and one foot on the step.

The servant couple who had been left behind to care for the house met her. From their uneasy expressions, she knew Alexander was not there. At the news that he had gone to Lochleven, she leaned against the door. Her journey was not yet over. Well, she had come too far to be stopped now. Quickly, she gave orders to the servants to prepare a cold meal for herself and the coachman and to tell the coachman not to unharness the horses: They would be leaving as soon as possible, in the hopes of reaching Stirling by nightfall.

While she ate, Dinah prepared a message to be sent to Sloane Square, telling Margaret and the others where she was going. Then, she was on her way again. By the time that the coach reached Stirling, Dinah was expecting the worst. If it were possible, she would have continued on that night, despite the prospect of the dark, lonely roads, but the horses needed a rest. She ordered the driver, therefore, to go to the inn where she had stayed before.

The innkeeper recognized her immediately, giving her the same room she had shared with Margaret and Mary. Dinner was sent up to her on a tray. Dinah forced herself to eat, trying to put out of her mind the memories of that other night and to ignore the foreboding the room brought back, the foreboding that even the name Lochleven summoned up.

What a hold the place had on her life—and on Alexander's life, too. Lochleven, where he had been born, where the lie that had almost destroyed them had been conceived, where her mother and father had found the love that had given her life. And now, Alexander had sought shelter at Lochleven, but what kind of a shelter had he found on the wintry moors with that grim castle in view? Who was there to care for him? No servant had stayed after the house was locked up. He would be alone. Dinah shivered beneath the feather coverlet. Why could he not have stayed in Edinburgh? Why had he gone to Lochleven?

Dinah slept fitfully, unable to escape the grim thoughts of the tragedy that hung over Lochleven like a cloud, a tragedy that had begun more than three hundred years ago when Mary was its unhappy prisoner. Only after she tried to pretend she was aboard the *Star of Scotland,* safe in the cradle of the ocean, did sleep eventually come. So deep was that sleep that when the maid knocked on her door, she was not sure where she was.

Once the coach started on its way again, she was glad that she had stopped at Stirling. A steady rain had begun falling during the night, making the muddy roads difficult to travel and the journey twice as long as before. Despite the lightness of the carriage with its lone passenger, the coachman was forced to use his whip on the horses as they pulled in the shafts up the hills. Dinah's foreboding increased once they reached the crest of the hills where the road to the house turned to one side.

The loch was shrouded in a fog. There was no sign of the house. Only the square tower of the castle floated above the swirling mists. As the coach began the descent, Dinah began to wish that she had let Molly come with her. Fear rose that she would not find Alexander here either, that she would search forever for him in the fog. The thought that he had no place else to go was little reassurance.

Ahead loomed a dark shadow that could only be the house. Her eyes strained to see a sign, any sign, that someone was there. Once she thought she saw a light flicker, but when she looked again it was gone. She sighed. It made no difference whether Alexander was here or not. In any case, she could go no farther. The horses were blowing heavily with fatigue.

In the dusk, the light appeared again, burning more steadily this time. It was in the back of the house. This meant someone had to be in the kitchen. The coachman had evidently seen the light, too, she realized, since he reined the horses to the left and not toward the main entrance.

The light grew brighter as someone, hearing the coach, flung open a door and held a lamp high to look out into the darkness. Dinah's heart pounded, her eyes trying to peer into the shadows behind the lamp. All she could determine was a figure, the face obscured. Then the coach drew to a halt.

"Who's there?" a man's voice shouted. "What yer want?"

Dinah drew her breath in. Whoever it was, it was not Alexander.

"It's Miss Murray, from Edinburgh," the coachman shouted.

The lamp wavered, and Dinah was sure that the person holding it was about to blow it out, until another voice called, "Boys! Yer damn idiots, help the lady."

At the sound of the voice, Dinah sighed with relief. It was Ol' Tom who had spoken. Yet, what was he doing here with Tom Jr. and Bob? Oh, God, Alexander, she thought, something must have happened to him!

Bob, muscles rippling against the fabric of her skirt, picked her up and put her effortlessly on the ground, just as he had picked her up in the boat. She told him to see to the coachman and the horses and turned toward the doorway.

Tom, his white beard and hair gleaming yellow in the lamplight, ushered her into the kitchen. The curtains had been drawn, and a fire was burning brightly on the hearth, where a pot was bubbling and giving off delicious odors. He looked at her uneasily.

Dinah faced him, clasping her cold hands to keep them from shaking. "I am looking for Mr. Alexander. He is here . . ." The half question trailed into silence.

"Aye. Yer'd best have a seat." He pulled a chair out from the table for her.

"Where is he?" Dinah turned as if to leave.

"Miss Murray, yer'd best have a seat. I'll send the boys after him soon enough."

The tone in his voice frightened Dinah. Her legs began to tremble, and she sank onto the chair. "Is he all right?"

"Aye." Tom picked up a kettle that was boiling on the hob to pour water into a waiting teapot. Deliberately, he set out a cup and saucer and cut a slice of bread from a loaf on the table. After he had poured the tea for her, he sat opposite her. "He ain't, well, himself. That's why the boys and me are here," he explained.

Dinah shook her head. "I don't understand. Is he sick?"

"In a way." Tom picked up a bit of wood that he had been whittling. "He's been drinking, Ma'am. That's why he ain't himself."

"Oh, God!" Dinah started to get up. "I must go to him."

"Wait a bit, Ma'am. He's asleep now. He'll be better able to talk to yer, if he has a rest." Tom put the carving to one side.

Dinah sank back in the chair. "And you, what are you doing here?"

"We found him, yer might say." Tom's eyes surveyed her. "He rode into town. On the way back, the horse threw him, I'd guess."

Dinah knew it was a lie, although she didn't blame the old man for trying to be kind. Alexander was far too good a rider to be thrown. He had been drunk, she guessed, and had fallen from the horse. "Thank you, then, for taking care of him," she managed to say.

"Miss Murray," Tom's eyes shifted uneasily to the table again, "I'm not that sure he'll want to see yer. He's been saying strange things, not," he added hastily, "that he knows what he's a-sayin' all the time."

"That is why I came here. He had a terrible shock," Dinah explained. "What he thinks . . . it was a lie. I must tell him the truth. Do you understand?" Dinah begged. She stood up. "I must go to him, Tom. I will sit beside him, while he sleeps . . ."

"Aye. That may be best. I'll get Tom to take yer to his room." The old man stood up and left the kitchen.

Dinah waited for him to return. Now she was at Lochleven, she could not think. Her heart was in command, and her heart was telling her to get to Alexander. When Tom returned with Tom Jr., she followed the young man to the library. A small bed had been set up near the fire, and she went to it, motioning Tom Jr. to leave her alone.

Her heart cried out to the young man lying there, still in his clothes, a blanket thrown over him. His face was drawn and pale with an unhealthy flush on his cheeks. Several days growth of beard gave him a sinister look. Dinah knelt on the floor beside him, resting her head against his shoulder as tears welled in her eyes.

Time lost meaning as she waited, listening to the rasping of his breath. The room was filled with the odor of stale whiskey, recalling the dingy pub in Lochleven. To take her mind off the smell, she summoned up the memory of the sea, of the salty freshness of the air and Ian. Her limbs grew stiff, but still she did not move. Only when Alexander groaned and stirred did she move. The room was growing cold, and she went to the fire to prod it into life again. As the flames flared brightly, Alexander threw an arm across his eyes. Dinah returned to his side, kneeling once more with the firelight on her face.

"Alexander," she whispered, "Alexander, my love."

The figure stirred again, the lids flickered open, and dark eyes peered at her from underneath the arm. "Mary," he murmured in a hoarse whisper, "Mary, why are you here?"

Dinah stared at him. After all she had been through, he thought she was Mary Angus! "No, Alexander, I am not Mary . . ."

He laughed, the laughter a mockery of any laughter she had ever heard before. "Why do you lie to me? It's . . . it's not fair. You are Mary, Mary Queen of Scots, and I am George Douglas, come to rescue you."

"You are Alexander," Dinah told him, trying to rouse him from the depths of his dream, "and I am Dinah . . ."

"That hair, those eyes, your beautiful neck . . ." His hand traced the features, lingering on her breasts.

The young woman clasped his hand to her. His fingers found her nipples through the fabric of her clothes, she leaned forward to kiss his lips. His glazed eyes struggled to focus on her face.

When he finally recognized her, he groaned and closed his eyes, snatching his hand back. "Get out!" he shouted. "Get out and leave me alone. Haven't you tempted me enough?"

The words struck Dinah with as much force as if he had hit her, even though she knew the torture that forced him to hurt her. When he struggled to stand, she dug her nails into the palms of her hands to keep herself from helping him, from touching him again. Finally he managed to get to his feet, and he swayed over her with his hand raised, fury distorting his features.

For a moment, Dinah was paralyzed with fear. She rose to her knees, starting to get to her feet, as his clenched fist swung at her. He missed her, but the force behind his blow made him fall sprawling onto the bed.

Dinah sat down beside him, her hands pushing against his shoulders to keep him from getting up again. Her pity turned to anger at him, anger at his refusal even to listen to her. "You will listen to me, Alexander. You will open your eyes and look at me, see I am telling you the truth," she told him firmly. "I did not come all this way to be bullied. Now, will you listen quietly or shall I summon Tom to hold you down, to make you be quiet?"

Alexander laughed, the sound hollow. "Take your hands off me."

"Only if you will be quiet," Dinah threatened. At

his nod of assent, she put her hands in her lap. In a calm voice, she told him about his parentage and about her mother. "So you see, Alexander, we are not even related."

Alexander sat up. "I wish you would not lie to me, Dinah. I am neither drunk enough nor fool enough to believe such a story. Whatever your purpose is, I cannot imagine. Do you want the money?" he said cruelly.

"My only purpose is to bring you to your senses. If you do not believe me, I have a letter from your father, in his own handwriting, telling you the same story. James was there, too. He has no reason to lie." Dinah stood up. "I will have Tom bring you some tea and something to eat, and I will get the letter. Meanwhile," she glanced at the room and the bottles strewn around, "I will have Tom Jr. wait with you, to make sure you do not have another drink."

Dinah swept from the room, her head held high. Ordering Tom into the room, she made sure he was standing over Alexander before going to the kitchen where she gave orders for a big pot of strong tea and a meal to be sent to Alexander. Her bags were by the door where the coachman had left them before going to the stable with the carriage. She selected the handbag with Sir Robert's letter, wondering what she would do next. She had given no thought as to where she would stay once she arrived. Well, she would consider that after she had seen to Alexander, she decided, returning to the library.

Alexander was sitting at a table, the tray in front of him and Ol' Tom standing by to see that he ate. Candles had been lit, and one of the boys had removed the bottles, although the room still smelled rank. Dinah wrinkled her nose and went to a window, opening it for a few minutes to let the winter wind blowing off the lake air the room. The fog had cleared with the night, revealing a full moon casting its light on Lochleven castle.

Dinah closed the window with a shiver. Back at the table, she sat down opposite Alexander who was wolfing down the last morsels of food. She refilled his cup and poured a cup of tea for herself, telling Tom to boil water for a tub for Alexander.

After the old man left, she said to Alexander, "Do you feel better now?" At his nod, she handed him the letter. "I told you that the letter was in your father's handwriting, which is not quite true. Your father started it when he became ill, but he could not finish it himself and had to dictate part of it to James. Both the missionary and his wife who cared for him signed it, however, attesting to the truth." She handed him the latter.

Alexander read the letter slowly, pausing several times to drink the tea. When he had finished, he put the letter down. "Why did he not tell us, Dinah?"

"I have no answer to that, Alexander, any more than I have any answer as to why my mother did not tell me the truth. That is one secret they both carried to their grave. As far as Lady Janet goes," Dinah forced a smile, "I am afraid she thought, with me out of the way, you would marry Mary."

"I never had any intention of marrying Mary, even before I met you. Dinah, I have been a fool and a weak one at that." He rubbed his face. "You find me drunk and unshaven—you should have walked out and left me."

"I could not do that." Dinah rose and went to his side, leaning over to kiss his forehead. "Have a bath now and a good sleep. We will talk in the morning." She sighed. "Suddenly, I am very tired, Alexander."

After Dinah left, she realized she still could not go to bed. First, she must find a room in the closed-up house. For that, she would have to depend on Ol' Tom. The old man, however, had already taken care of that. He had fixed up one of the maid's rooms, saying she would be more comfortable there for the night until he could get a woman from the village to ready her own room, which he said he would do in the morning if she were planning to stay. Dinah told him she would decide in the morning.

Dinah was too tired to do more than wash with

the hot water she found on the nightstand, and take off her traveling clothes. Still in her underclothes, she slipped under the covers, smiling with gratitude at the thoughtfulness of the old man who had put a hot brick wrapped in flannel at the foot. For the first time in weeks, she was asleep as soon as her head hit the pillow.

Her first thought on awakening was of Alexander. Hurriedly she dressed in the same clothes as the day before, half dreading the condition she might find him in. To her relief, he was sitting in the kitchen while Tom cooked breakfast. The smell of the hearty sausages and bacon frying reminded her she had had little to eat the day before. To Tom's pleasure, she cleaned up the plate he set in front of her as eagerly as Alexander had devoured the simple supper.

Afterwards, she went with Alexander into the library to talk. The room had been clumsily cleaned up, and the curtains pulled back to let in the weak winter sunlight. Dinah walked to the window that looked out on the castle, unsure of what to do or say now. Waiting for Alexander to speak, she thought of what Ian had said about her journey being over, of her answer that there was always another journey, another voyage. How right she had been. One journey had ended last night once Alexander had accepted the truth. Now another was to begin, one in which she was no longer sure what the destination would be—or what she wanted it to be. Despite the night's deep sleep, her limbs were heavy with fatigue, her mind numb.

"Dinah," Alexander's arm went around her shoulders. When she resisted his attempt to turn her face him, he asked, "Oh, Dinah, can't you even look at me any more after last night?"

Dinah stopped resisting, turning slowly to face him. His face was still haggard, but the unhealthy red flush had faded and his dark eyes were sunken in their sockets. It would take weeks, if not months, for him to recover from the way he had abused himself the past few months. Could he do it himself? Dinah wondered. Would even Margaret's help be enough? She was not sure, any more than she was now sure she had the strength left herself to help him.

"I am so tired, Alexander." She rested her head against his shoulder, and his arms tightened around her. His lips brushed her forehead, her temple, the kisses forcing her to raise her mouth to meet his.

Warmth flowed through Dinah's veins, bathing her in its glow. She felt the familiar tingling. It would be so easy to yield herself to him. Her body ached to be caressed, her breasts trembled for the touch of his mouth and hands on their nipples and the inside of her thighs yearned for the touch of his tongue.

"Dinah, darling Dinah," Alexander murmured, "now there is no reason for us not to marry as soon as possible."

Dinah's passion cooled, and she broke from the circle of his arms.

"Isn't that why you came here? To tell me the truth, so we could marry?" Alexander was bewildered. "We can marry here, at Lochleven, where," he added, a grim tone in his voice, "it all began."

The tone dismayed Dinah. The heaviness returned, and she sank in a chair looking up at him.

"Or is it," he asked, "that you no longer love me, now I am the son of a wetnurse?"

"Alexander," her voice was soft, shaking with the slap implied in his words, "if you could love me, thinking me the daughter of a poor relative, I can love you with the knowledge you are not a born Douglas. I loved you as a man." She could not go on.

"Loved, Dinah?" He sank on his knees in front of her.

"Loved, love, I don't know." She sighed. "What I do know is that you must go to Edinburgh as soon as possible. There is your father's estate to be settled, his business to be tended to."

"And you?" he asked.

"I must go to London. Mrs. Bradley has come from New York." She explained, adding, "Molly is to be married in a month's time."

"Then you will go direct to London?"

This question brought on a new wave of fatigue. The young woman leaned back in her chair, and she closed her eyes.

"Dinah?" Alexander pressed her for an answer. "Will you go to London?"

Dinah opened her eyes, looking past Alexander to the window and the outline of Lochleven castle on the horizon. As she looked at it, the tiredness vanished and she smiled.

"Dinah?" Alexander asked again, puzzled at the change in her.

"I think I will stay here for a while, Alexander. Tom can get a woman from the village to come here, and I am sure that he and his sons will look after me."

"But you cannot stay here alone," the young man protested.

Dinah laughed. "Why not? I went from Mombasa to Nairobi and back alone, except . . . except for Ian. Surely I can stay here alone for a few weeks with a woman and Tom and the boys."

"I don't like it. I think I should stay."

"No," she said firmly. "I want to be alone, Alexander—I need to be alone, to think." She took his hands. "Do you remember the picture, the words in gold, 'In my end is my Beginning'?"

"Yes, but I don't see . . ."

"My beginning was here, not only with my mother and Sir Robert," she could not speak of him as her father to Alexander, "but longer ago with Mary. In some way, she left a legacy that I carry in my blood, in my heart that sometimes rules my head. I do not want to be imperious, but I have her blood in my veins."

"I would not have you otherwise," Alexander told her with amusement. "What does that have to do with my love for you—or your love for me?"

"I know," Dinah smiled, "it was all so long ago. Still it is important to me, and I must straighten things out in my mind."

"Then, you are determined to stay?"

"Yes, I am. I must think." Dinah was firm.

"Very well." Alexander gave in, and asked her more about the will.

"First," Dinah said, "let me talk to Tom about a woman from village."

Tom knew of a woman, a widow, whom he was sure would come. He sent Tom Jr. off to talk to her, telling him to bring the woman back with him. Dinah refused his offer to open up the rest of the house. It was ridiculous to open the whole house for one person, and the maid's room would do. To an extent, the room was a beginning and an end, too. After all, it was no smaller than the room over the carriage house that she had shared with her mother during the years she was growing up.

When she told Alexander, however, he was not happy about her decision. But again, he was forced to give in.

They went for a walk in the afternoon, through the brown garden to the waters of the loch with the waves rippling against the pebbles of the beach. A hawk cried, wheeling in the sky in its search for prey. The night she had spent in the castle with Alexander seemed years, not six months, ago. With what abandon, she had given herself up to the ecstasy of his arms, his hands, his eager mouth, the ultimate joy of the life of him driving inside her. She wondered whether she would ever feel the same way again, in Alexander's arms or another man's.

On the way back to the house, a bit of color under a hedgerow caught his eye. It was a rose, a small, perfect, red rose, the last rose of the year that had somehow survived the winter frosts. He plucked it, handing it to the young woman.

"For you, Dinah." He tucked it in her cloak, kissing her on a cheek. "Like you, it is a survivor."

Dinah smiled, tucking it into her dress for the early, simple supper. The village woman had arrived while they were out and had immediately set to work, commanding Ol' Tom and the boys around until they had put the kitchen in order to her liking. Alexander had no excuse not to leave in the morning. He would return as he had arrived, by horseback, leaving the carriage and the coachman for Dinah.

"I wish you would return with me, Dinah," Alexander urged. "I don't like leaving you here, and it is not too late to change your mind."

"No, Alexander. I need to be alone for a while, to think. This is the place for that, not Edinburgh or London."

"You will stop in Edinburgh on your way to London?"

"Of course." Dinah smiled. "You will go to Molly's wedding, too, won't you? Captain MacKie will be there, too, and Geordie's sis . . ."

"Ian," Alexander looked at her thoughtfully. "You said you went to Nairobi with him. I had almost forgotten that."

"He has been a good friend," Dinah protested.

"Aye, and he was there when you needed him, while I wasn't. My father always liked him, you know. He respected him. That's why he gave him the ship. I think he always intended to take him into the line at the right time."

"Yes," Dinah lowered her eyes, "I think he would have done that."

Alexander reached across the table to take her hand. "You have told me all I need to know, my dear. I would be a fool or worse not to have noticed the expression on his face whenever he looked at you."

"Please, Alexander." Her hand tightened in his.

"I love you, Dinah. I never knew how much until I thought I had lost you forever. I cannot promise to change, but I will try—and I will always love you." His sunken eyes shone with the promise.

"Then, you *will* go to Edinburgh and take care of your father's business there?" Dinah asked gently, knowing he had to go and go alone for his own sake.

"I'll try, my dear, but I'm not sure that I can do all you expect of me alone right now." He rubbed his free hand across his eyes. "I'm afraid." The next words were said so quietly that Dinah was not sure she had heard them, "I have always been afraid I couldn't do what was expected of me."

"You must, Alexander. You must try," she urged. "You can do anything you want, if you want it badly enough. Look at me!" She tried to laugh. "I made that trip to Africa, and I am only a woman!"

"Ah, but you have the blood of a Scottish queen in your veins."

Dinah laughed again, genuinely this time. "That was so long ago that I am sure the blood has become much diluted. Try, Alexander. I will see you in Edinburgh, and we can all go to London together." She rose to her feet. "Now, it's time for bed. You must be up early if you're going to ride to Edinburgh in the morning."

They kissed goodnight. Dinah went to the spare white room at the rear of the house, leaving Alexander to lie on the cot in the library. The young woman took the rose from her dress, setting it on the night table, and disrobed slowly. Before putting on the high-necked, longsleeved nightgown, she studied her body. Her young breasts were still firm and high with rosy-tipped nipples, her waist small, her hips narrow, and her legs were long and shapely. She touched her breasts, her hips, and thighs, igniting a tingle of longing; faces swam before her closed eyes. Hurriedly, she pulled on her nightgown and slipped into the narrow bed.

After she blew out the candle, she lay in the darkness waiting for the sleep that would not come. She was glad in a way that Alexander was leaving in the morning. It was difficult to think with his eyes watching her, with his haggard face in front of her. She yearned to help him, but that was not the way to help him now. Like her, he needed to be alone to do what had to be done and to give himself the self-confidence he would have to have. The last would take time.

She sighed, thinking of Alexander, of how everything she had done since meeting him had been to please him, to win his approval and love. Did she love him? She was not sure whether she loved the man he was or the man she thought he was. Until she was sure, she could not go to Edinburgh where Ian was also waiting.

Ian, dear Ian. How she had taken him for granted! How she had fled into his comforting presence and arms whenever she had needed help. He was so steady, so unfailing in his loyalty—his love—helping her unquestioningly. Her thoughts turned lingeringly to Africa, to the evenings by the campfire under the stars, to their mutual wonder at the sights they had seen, the dangers they had shared—and the passion he had stirred in her. She could not imagine a life without him around. Oh, of course, he would go to sea, and months would pass without seeing him. Yet, a life totally without him was unimaginable. If they were married, he could take her on his voyages. She smiled, dreaming of nights at sea in his arms, of the sights to be seen in foreign lands.

The two lives she could live flickered in front of her eyes: A life of luxury with Alexander, the big house in Edinburgh, summers here at Lochleven, the season in London, the parties and ball gowns; the far simpler life with Ian, a house in Edinburgh, although smaller than the mansion on Princes Street, the months of love interspersed by loneliness, the sea, and those foreign lands. With Alexander, regardless of how much he might be able to change, life would be gay. With Ian, it would be quiet, though she was sure she would not have to give up her relationship with the Douglases where she would always be welcome. In either case, she would have her own money once the estate was settled. She would be rich in her own right.

Dinah smiled, thinking of the money. The money itself meant little to her. She had been poor, and she had been rich. Money itself could not buy happiness. In that respect, her new change in fortune would mean as little to Ian as to Alexander.

Her thoughts drifted to Molly and Molly's wedding

and to Mrs. Bradley who had said that she wished it would be Dinah's wedding she was helping plan. A faint smile touched her lips. That could still happen. Her mind went back over the moments she had shared with Alexander and with Ian. She remembered how willingly Alexander had given in to her that time in her cabin aboard ship and the terrible groan that escaped Ian's lips the time he pushed her from him. In her heart, she knew that Alexander, without her, would marry Mary who would drive him to success as she, Dinah, could not. Dinah's nature was to help him, and that help could destroy Alexander in the end. Ian was different. He would care for her in his way and she would care for him in her way, and they would help each other. But did she love Ian?

She closed her eyes, seeing Ian's face, the blueness of his eyes and the lines engraved at the corners, the mouth that could be so stern and yet so tender. She saw the broad shoulders and big chest, felt his capable and gentle hands, recalled the desire she had known the last time—perhaps each time—he had taken her in his arms. In a few months time, he would be sailing again . . .

Dinah turned over, nestling her cheek against the pillow as she had nestled it against Ian's shoulder by the African campfires. Alexander would be surprised in the morning to learn that she was accompanying him to Edinburgh, after all. Ol' Tom could be trusted to close up the house. She wanted to hurry to Ian, to let him know. They had already wasted too much time. What a beautiful honeymoon it would be with Ian on the *Star of Scotland*. She wondered where Ian would take her this time. Perhaps, she thought dreamily, drifting off into restful sleep, they would voyage together all the way to China or even Australia. This was one voyage she felt that she would never come to the end of—and one that she was sure she never wanted to.

M